Of PROPHECIES & Pomegranates

A DARK FATES NOVEL

T.C. KRAVEN

DIVERSION
BOOKS

Diversion Books
A division of Diversion Publishing Corp. www.diversionbooks.com

For more information, email info@diversionbooks.com

First Diversion Books Edition: October 2025
Trade Paperback ISBN: 9798895150573
e-ISBN: 9798895150580

Design by Neuwirth & Associates, Inc.
Cover design by T.C. Kraven
Chapter header illustrations by Artywings
Interior cover illustrations by Snow_WI

Printed in the United States of America
1 3 5 7 9 10 8 6 4 2

For all the baddies craving a shadow daddy that embodies Hozier's entire catalog, this one is for you.

The Divine
OF THE DARK FATES

HADES
GOD OF THE UNDERWORLD, BORN OF OLYMPIAN ESSENCE

PERSEPHONE
GODDESS OF SPRING, BORN OF DEMETER + ZEUS

DEMETER
GODDESS OF THE HARVEST, BORN OF OLYMPIAN ESSENCE

HEPHAESTUS
GOD OF THE FORGE, BORN OF HERA, BONDED TO APHRODITE

APHRODITE
GODDESS OF LOVE, BORN OF OLYMPIAN ESSENCE, BONDED TO ARES + HEPHAESTUS

ARES
GOD OF WAR, BORN OF ZEUS, BONDED TO APHRODITE

HERMES
MESSENGER GOD OF THIEVES, BORN OF ZEUS + A MORTAL LOVER

ARTEMIS
GODDESS OF THE HUNT, BORN OF ZEUS + LETO

APOLLO
GOD OF MUSIC, BORN OF ZEUS + LETO

NARCISSUS

GOD OF SELF LOVE,
BORN OF HUMANITY'S
WORSHIP

HELIOS

TITAN OF THE SUN,
BORN OF
HYPERION + THEIA

ZEUS

GOD OF GODS,
BORN OF OLYMPIAN
ESSENCE,
BONDED TO HERA

DIONYSUS

GOD OF WINE,
BORN OF
ZEUS + SEMELE

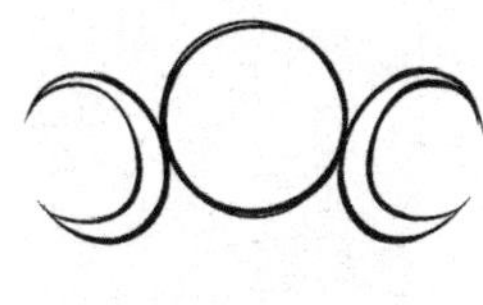

HECATE

GODDESS OF
WITCHCRAFT,
BORN OF
ASTERIA + PERSES

THANATOS

GOD OF DEATH,
BORN OF NYX
+ EREBUS

HERA

GODDESS OF
MARRIAGE + BONDS,
BORN OF OLYMPIAN
ESSENCE,
BONDED TO ZEUS

POSEIDON

GOD OF THE SEA,
BORN OF OLYMPIAN
ESSENCE,
BONDED TO ATHENA

ATHENA

GODDESS OF
WISDOM,
BORN OF ZEUS,
BONDED TO POSEIDON

Playlist

1. Like Real People Do—Hozier
2. Persephone—The Tragic Thrills
3. Sign of the Times—Harry Styles
4. Colour Me In—Damien Rice
5. Delicate—Damien Rice
6. Take Me to Church—Hozier
7. Do I Wanna Know? (Arctic Monkeys cover in the Live Lounge)—Hozier
8. Video Games—Lana Del Rey
9. I Can't Go on Without You—KALEO
10. Work Song—Hozier

Scan the QR code
to access the Spotify playlist:

CONTENT WARNING

Of Prophecies & Pomegranates marks the beginning of our journey into the Dark Fates series. This world of monsters and mythological beings sprung from Ancient Greece. It is important to protect yourselves from any content that may be triggering to you. This novel includes parental alienation and emotionally abusive parental relationships, on-page violence between gods, drugging, coercion, manipulation, suicide, and death. This novel also has explicit sexual content, which includes, but is not limited to, impact play, exhibitionism, praise, bondage (with shadows) and shadowplay (penetration), and degradation (not between the main characters, but witnessed). All acts are consensual.

Of PROPHECIES & Pomegranates

Prologue

Before time wore a name and the stars had thrones, the titans ruled the cosmos. Vast, ancient powers born of Gaia, the Earth, Uranus, and the Sky, they ruled the world not with justice but with weight and silence, their wills scarred into the bones of the earth.

Cronus, the usurper son, rose against his father with a sickle of flint and blood, and from the severed heavens came a curse: His own child, too, would one day cast him down. Fearful of the curse, Cronus feasted on each sliver of his essence that turned into god divinity, those forms who would come to be known as Olympians. He swallowed them whole, god and goddess alike, hoping to hush prophecy within the prison of his flesh.

But Queen Rhea, weary of loss and tyranny, swaddled a stone in place of Zeus and spirited away the last-born to a hidden isle for protection, giving a path for prophecy to become real. Tricked, Cronus devoured the swaddled stone and thought nothing more of it. Zeus returned grown, cloaked in thunder and vengeance, and split Cronus open, tearing the swallowed gods from their prison, raising them for war. With Hades, who would rule the dead; Poseidon, who would shake the seas; Hera the iron-hearted; Demeter of the harvest; and Hestia of the flame, Zeus waged ten years of ruin.

Together, the gods rose against the ancient order, and all the realms shook with the clash of titan and Olympian during what came to be known as the Titanomachy. Mountains burned. Oceans boiled. Titans fell screaming into Tartarus, their chains forged by victory and betrayal. And so the world was broken and remade, not gentler, but crowned with a new tyranny of light.

The Olympians took their thrones in the Upper and Lower Realms, but the sky belonged to Zeus.

The remaining titans who fought against their own were given amnesty but were required to bend the knee and pledge everlasting fealty to Zeus, the God of Gods. Convinced that only absolute submission would prevent the same fate that befell his father and grandfather, Zeus demanded that any marriages between deities required his blessing so that he could control the wells of power these unions produced. For titans, his paranoia knew no end, and he required even stricter constraints: They must bind themselves to a deity of his choosing.

Any deviation or refusal of his command garnered brutal and heinous consequences. As the centuries moved on, there were those who dared to defy his command, and they found the cruelty of the God of Gods endless, often resulting in death and destruction to all involved.

Drunk on power, Zeus became the very dictator he had fought to overthrow, but with his title in place and the magic of the Fates to sustain him, the divine of the three realms had no choice but to obey.

Until now . . .

Persephone

CHAPTER 1

"Again."

Sweat beaded on my brow, exhaustion warred with my mother's demand inside of me, but just as I always had done, I obeyed. I reached deep inside of myself, rooting for the magic, begging for it to heed my call. My fingers trembled beneath the dirt, the disapproving eye of my mother boring into my skull. With a huff, I relented, unable to produce anything more. Defeated, the click of my mother's tongue slumped my shoulders, the breath in my lungs stuttering as tightness constricted my chest like vines.

"I'm sorry," I mumbled, lifting my eyes to the goddess standing above me. Tears stung the corners of my eyes, witnessing my failure, but I willed them to stay, to not make this worse. My mother's hands rested on her hips, disapproval dripping from her gaze as she stared out over the half-bloomed cache.

It didn't matter that I'd been working all day for the last week, ensuring the fullest and most colorful blooms were ready to be displayed for her festival. It only mattered that she'd wanted a full acre brimming with them, and I could barely coax half.

"I just don't understand where I went wrong," she sighed, her golden locks swaying around her chin with the shake of her head.

"I'm just tired is all. I can do more after some rest, I—" My voice cracked, tears spilling at the shame that burned in my cheeks. The Goddess of the Harvest bent down, cupping my face, a small, sad smile on her lips.

"Oh darling, it's fine. We're not all built to get it right the first time . . . or the second. You'll do better tomorrow, won't you?" Her voice was gentle, but the words may have well been swords, stabbing into my gut. I nodded my head as she stroked my cheek, wanting desperately to make her proud.

"Yes, M-mother," I choked, the tears too hot. Her thumb gathered the salty drip, swiping it away.

"Persephone!" Artemis called from across the field as she approached, lips split into a wide smile as she took in all the purple, pink, and yellow blossoms I'd managed to will into being. Mother raised me up, steadying my shaky legs, pulling me into her arms, and for a moment, I let myself believe it was true and genuine. That I was still just a girl, and she was comforting me in my distress because she wanted me to be comforted, not because we had an audience.

Cold air whooshed between us as she pulled back, smoothing the flyaway whisps of my hair behind my ears.

"There, no need to cry. It makes your face red and puffy, and we can't afford for you to not look your best." The tone was gentle, that little bit of honey mixed with venom to seal the wounds.

With a kiss to my cheek, Mother stepped away, waving hello to the Goddess of the Hunt, with that pleasant, shining smile on her face. I watched her back as she strode out toward the estate, feeling so very small in her shadow.

"Hey, oh my Fates, this looks *amazing*. Did you do all this just today?" Artemis asked, slowing her jog to a walk as she neared, but the moment she saw my face, her smile faded, concern replacing it. I swiped at my cheek as another tear broke through. Embarrassed, I turned, sucking in lungfuls of air, praying to the Fates that a gust would come to chase away the flush on my face.

"Persephone . . . ? What's wrong?"

Gentle hands pulled me around, and worry shone in Artemis's silver eyes as she trailed them over my face, the shake of my shoulders. The care there nearly broke me.

"I just, I'm having trouble pulling my power up," I deflected, shrugging it off with a weak smile. Understanding and sympathy flowed from her as her hands rubbed soothing circles up and down my arms. She slid right into comforting, her being one of the only gods aware of my "affliction."

"Okay, look at what all you did. It's really impressive. I've never seen a field so full so fast," she encouraged, gesturing out to the left.

"It's only half done. It looks ridiculous," I countered, looking away. Artemis's head swiveled between my mother's path and my face, a line forming between her eyebrows, questions in her pinning gaze. With a subtle shake of my head, my eyes told her what my mouth couldn't: leave it.

I'd avoided discussing my mother with Artemis outright, but I knew she had suspicions and saw more than she ever let on. I feared for a moment she would finally push, and with so much shame spiraling through me, I wouldn't have it in me to lie.

"Let's go get drunk and watch the boys try to build the pyre," she suggested, bumping her shoulder against mine. As much as I appreciated her attempt at levity, I felt too low to let it sway me. I shook my head, sniffing once before kneeling back down, shaking out my shoulders. With a deep breath, I plunged my fingers back into the soil, closing my eyes in concentration.

"Persephone," Artemis cautioned, but I waved her off. I needed to do this. If I could get it just a little more filled in, it would please her.

Wouldn't it?

I struggled to settle my mind, to focus on birth and life and growth, but the more I reached for the sun on my face, the darker my thoughts became. I felt the spiral beginning, as it sometimes did, a vortex of despair that threatened to swallow me up. It was around me, inside of me, and my mother's voice whispered in my ear, telling me how unnatural it was, how unbecoming of a spring goddess . . .

Something slithered past my fingers, chilling, *electric*, twining and twirling with my frustration. Centuries of criticism wrapped around the magic that reached for me, and I knew I shouldn't grab onto it, that I should run, but I was just too tired, too angry. It was as though the dam in my chest that I kept all those thoughts behind, all the failures, every flaw that I tried so desperately to hide, was cracking up the middle.

In the distance, I could hear Artemis's voice but only barely over the wind ripping around my body. The pressure built and built until I couldn't hold it in for even a moment longer. That dark bolt wrapped around my wrist, and I clasped it. The effect was instant, a buzz of darkness that radiated from my body, and for just one moment, I felt release.

A pulse of power blasted into the ground, and I watched in a mix of wonder and horror as the ground cracked and shook, sprouting thousands of seedlings and vines as black as night, creeping among the onyx blooms. At once, Artemis's hands were on me, dragging me to her, checking over my face and hands.

"Fucking Fates," she cursed, glancing around to make sure no one else had seen. But they would see, the rows and rows of unusual, deformed flora, the evidence of my defective power. I started to shake, panic and fear overtaking me.

"If anyone sees this . . ." I whispered, mortified.

"They won't. They won't," she assured, but the galloping of hooves, thunderous around us, made her a liar. Helios, Titan of the Sun, landed his chariot in the field, his white horses neighing and restless, refusing to step closer to the ichor oozing from the ground. He jumped from his chariot, golden armor shining, eyes bulging in shock as he raced toward us.

"What is thi—" he began, but Artemis halted him.

"Burn it," she demanded, sparing him only a glance as she kept her hands on me, tried to calm my panic. "*Now*, Helios! Burn it before anyone sees."

He didn't hesitate. With his arm outstretched, he started with the blooms closest to us, and sunlight, so intense it burned, radiated from his palm, disintegrating the macabre-looking blooms.

"There's something w-wrong with m-me," I sobbed, unable to regain control of my body. Artemis shook her head then pressed her forehead against mine.

"There is *nothing* wrong with you, Persephone. Nothing," she assured, voice full of fierce conviction, but as she gathered me close and let me cry against her, I could feel the tension in her muscles.

I was the daughter of Demeter and Zeus. My parentage alone should have made me among the most powerful, but I had never coveted being powerful. I was content to just usher in the spring, help the plants grow, but there was something out of sorts with my power. A dark secret Mother insisted we keep close.

Only Artemis knew. And now, Helios.

I looked out over the scorched earth, all traces of the abominations (as my mother had so lovingly referred to the goods produced by my affliction) gone. Beyond the pain and panic and worry, there was a grief, as well, at their loss.

In another world, they could have been beautiful in their differences.

The Titan of the Sun approached us, heat radiating from him nearly too intense to endure.

"What was that?" he asked, his face a battlefield of confusion and concern. He had been kind, if not a flippant deity, and now he knew. He knew that I was wrong. I opened my mouth to speak, to defend myself in some way, but it was Artemis who stepped into his space, her small stature barely bringing eye level to his chest, but her ego and power made her seem as big as him.

"You saw *nothing*. It was *nothing*. Do you understand?" Her words fell from gritted teeth, challenging him, her silver armor pressed right against his. He searched her face, jaw tight, then cut his gaze to me. I wrapped my arms around my waist, feeling too exposed in all of this.

"*Hey*!" she snapped her fingers in front of his face, drawing his attention back down to her. "I asked if you understood me, Helios." I watched as a titan, twice the size of a man, wilted under the scrutiny of a goddess that weighed no more than his leg.

"I understand."

It was so much, too many feelings waging war within my body, the tightness in my chest back in full force. Helios and Artemis exchanged hushed words, but I couldn't focus on what they were saying. I needed out. I needed to *go*.

My feet reacted, and without a word, I bolted toward the forest, to the safety of the trees, where the only thing I had to be was Persephone.

Hades

CHAPTER 2

R*estless sleep, my Lord?*

Charon's voice warbled through my mind, gravely and haunting. I turned to see him guiding his boat silently through the waters of the Styx, gnarled hand gripping his oar to slow his drift.

I dipped my chin, continuing my steps. Hand clasped behind my back we continued in comfortable silence, taking in the Underworld. The skies above waxed and waned with inks of black and blue, the vibrant jeweled glow of the Styx flowing in gentle bends while my mind raced, vexed.

For years and years, I'd felt something was amiss from my realm. I'd crossed the Asphodels, searching every stone, every tributary, the convergences of the great rivers, ensuring every shade remained accounted for. All remained as it should be.

And yet.

Something had ripped me from my dreams, had gotten past the wards put in place by Hecate, Goddess of Witchcraft, to worm into my mind. And so here I was, walking without purpose, alone with my thoughts.

Ahem.

I smiled. Mostly, alone.

Perhaps it's loneliness, my Lord, that has you wandering. A strapping god such as yourself shouldn't lock himself away . . .

I paused, lifting an eyebrow to the ferryman.

"You're one to talk about locking one's self away, old man," I teased. A sharp bark of expelled air rang out from beneath his hood.

Unfortunately, I have a face only a mother could love, Lord Hades. An affliction you don't suffer from.

My sandals sank into the mud of the wet banks, waters seeping over my skin as I walked. I knew better than to try to deny him or make light of what he had endured. Charon had made peace with his solitude long ago, as had I.

"I'm not alone, Charon. I have you, and Cerberus. Occasionally, a visit from Hecate. And the shades, of course," I offered. Charon's robes jostled as he shook his head.

Your dog, your valet, and your subjects hardly count as company, Hades. You need living connection.

"I prefer the dead, thank you very much," I defended. Silence settled between us once more, and I was grateful not to rehash this argument for the hundredth time. My shadows crept out around me, searching, cataloging the Underworld as we walked.

The bend in the Styx that would take Charon to the Upper Realm and I to the cave that housed Cerberus was fast approaching. A small part of me sighed, relieved that I would be once again alone. I had deep love and respect for the ferryman, but he could also be meddlesome, especially when he thought he was right.

The ground around us began to shake, luminescent water sloshed up the dark, wooden sides of Charon's boat, lapping over the banks of the river. A surge of power tore from the very bowels of the Underworld with a groan, and then as quickly as it had come, it was gone again. Charon's boat settled, the rocking steadied as the water receded back into the river.

What was that?

"I don't know," I admitted, a deep sense of unease piercing through my chest. I felt as though I were going mad as the Underworld settled, all evidence from the tremor erased.

Charon's throat cleared.

Hades.

I snapped my head toward him, but he wasn't looking at me. Tracking his gaze, confusion tore through my body as my eyes fell on the tiniest thicket of a shrub; a red orb bloomed before our eyes, growing larger and larger. I knelt closer, and when it stopped swelling, I plucked it from the stem and straightened, examining the curiosity. It had a leathery outer skin, firm and nearly the size of my palm. I pushed my fingers against it, breaking past the barrier. Inside were the most beautiful little seeds, dark and glimmering against the dance of the Styx's glow. Prying the orb open, I found it filled with them, tiny nodes connected against a cradle, the color of bone.

What is that? Charon inquired.

"I don't know, but I intend to find out," I shook my head, gathering one of the seeds between my fingers. Applying pressure caused it to burst, spilling liquid like red wine over my fingers. The smell was lovely, sweet with a hint of bitterness that recoiled on the tongue. Cautiously, I dug for another, but that one I brought to my lips, resting it on my tongue. The deluge of flavor that exploded there shuttered my eyes.

Eons in the Underworld and I had never tasted such a contradiction, a dichotomy of life and decay. I knew every species of flora that grew in the Underworld, few as there were. None of them held a lick of sweetness, of tenderness. Only death and decay survived in the Asphodels.

This tasted like . . . something that had been touched by the sun. I could feel the juices as they slid down my throat, hooking into the very core of my essence, and as I raised my eyes to the sky, to the Upper Realm that rested just above, an urge to *go* overwhelmed me.

"Looks like you're going to get your wish, Charon."

He eyed the fruit in my hand warily but stepped dutifully back, making space for me to board his vessel. Paws and heavy breathing snuck up behind me, the three heads of Cerberus sniffing the air around the fruit. I tossed it to them, and they instantly began to tussle, each fighting for dominance. Large teeth sank into the flesh of the fruit, sending seeds cascading all around the entrance of their cave.

I left them to their devices as I settled onto the wooded bench while Charon ferried us along to the convergence that would take me topside.

What will you call it?

I considered. It had been so long since I'd had to give a name to anything, having only ever needed to provide guidance to those too old to remember their own.

"What do you think of pomegranate?" I asked, rubbing the sticky liquid from the fruit between my fingers absentmindedly.

Well named, my Lord.

Persephone

CHAPTER 3

The forest welcomed me, as it had for centuries. It didn't care about my affliction as I danced along the path, a known daughter of the woods. Life bloomed under my feet without provocation, pulling the vitality from the depths of the earth from contact alone. With a cracked sob, I encouraged it to run rampant across the floor of the forest, to live and thrive and *grow*. I let my soles retrace the roads I had been traveling since I was a child, enjoying a moment without every action falling under the scrutiny of unattainable approval. The sun shone boldly from on high, no longer oppressive through the canopy of trees, and I lifted my face to the sky, relishing in both the relief of the shaded leaves and warmth from the bursts of light dancing along my skin, my sadness and fear momentarily forgotten.

I smiled. It was easy to forget all the pressure of my existence when I was here, among the flowers and trees and earth. The Goddess of Spring finally free in the wilds. I loved the feeling of the earth beneath my sandals, the smell of the trees as the wind carried their scent to me.

Existence felt tedious, an endless loop of day in and day out as an immortal, but I was always surprised that some things felt just as sacred as the time I first happened upon them. Nature was like that for me. Here I could forget that my choices, my life, were not my own. I didn't have to do what was always expected.

A small anthemis flower, bowed and bent, caught my attention as I made my way down to the grove, where I'd taken solace so many times before. I knelt to look closer, moving the long tendrils of my hair behind my shoulder. A frown crept into the corners of my lips as I inspected the patch of flora before me.

These little wildflowers were extremely resilient, yet now they seemed uncharacteristically withered . . . the stems remained unbroken, but limp, sullen as though all life had abandoned them. The white petals appeared almost gray, fraying at the tips and curling into themselves. I ran a finger gently over the fuzzy yellow centers that had dulled in color too, and my scowl deepened when I saw the path of decayed, barren land leading farther into the forest. It looked as though Death himself had visited, pulling the life force from these delicate wildflowers. Beneath them, the ground faded from green moss to the deep brown of dead earth.

I reached my hand out, willing a bit of spark to energize the anthemis. My palm began to glow, and I felt the familiar warmth enveloping my fingertips as the magic danced across my skin. The small flower perked slightly, timidly stretching itself toward my aura, basking in my power.

"You poor thing," I whispered. "You're going to be all right. Stand up for me, I know you can do it," I coaxed, smiling encouragingly. The other wildflowers began to stir, brought from the brink of decay, reaching toward my hand. Soon, the small patch of nearly spent flowers stood tall and proud once more, filled with life. I could only reach so many from the path, however, and the decay seemed to spread much farther through the trees.

I lifted my foot to step off the path before my mother's voice echoed through my thoughts.

Stay on the path in the Fallen Wood. That forest borders the realms of other gods, Persephone. You'll only be granted my protection if you remain on the path. We have enemies; those who would use you to hurt me. You wouldn't want to be the cause of that, would you? Of course not . . .

Her warning, and my deep-rooted desire to never displease her, had always kept my feet firmly planted on the worn earth. I turned to continue but only made it a few steps before my feet hesitated. I'd been struggling for *days* with the lilac fields, but here, it was as though there was suddenly an overabundance of my power, itching to be expelled. It practically oozed from my aura. Should I ignore the chance to use it for good?

I bit my lip nervously, considering the consequences. As Goddess of Spring, flora fell under my domain as crops did hers. How would it look for me to forsake them? The way my power dripped from me, I could clear it up with little fuss, couldn't I? She needn't know. What if the decay and rot were spreading, shouldn't we know the source?

Before I could convince myself to retreat, I exhaled deeply and stepped off the path, urging my feet forward, too afraid that if I gave myself any time to think too hard I would lose my nerve. Willing warmth and light into each step I took, I focused on the affected species in my path. Every corner of my being emanated life, and the fallen flora lapped it up hungrily.

A wild sense of euphoria took over me as I walked deeper into the wood, only slightly aware of how dense the trees were getting. I could hear the bubbling of a river somewhere nearby. The path led on, and I followed, pushing through a small copse of trees and brambles, careful not to break them as I made my way. Movement in the cool blue water caught my eye, and at once I froze. The river had taken on an ethereal glow, unnatural in its beauty, a hue of luminescent I'd never seen before. Warnings rang out clear as bells in my mind, but I couldn't look away from the source of the movement that halted me in the first place.

I felt my breath catch in my chest. In the middle of the river, water roiling around him, stood a man.

No, not a man, a *god*.

Otherworldly beautiful, a faint blue aura pulsed around him, lapping over his skin. He stood naked in the water, and I couldn't help the unfamiliar ache that ripped through my chest as I raked my gaze over the hard, exposed planes of his pale chest. Mother had made sure to keep my interactions with the other deities of the pantheon limited, and there were many I'd only ever seen in passing, but I would have remembered *him*. He was tall, that I could tell from the long torso and arms, his venture into the sun a rare treat if the pallor of his skin were any indication. It was flawless, wrapped around his corded muscles and broad chest, save for what looked like raised sigils, carved into the toned expanse of muscle over his sternum.

His head lifted toward the sky, his strong jaw free of scruff, allowing me a view of the hollow of his throat. His hair was a deep black, tussled and dripping. It was possible that he was the most striking being I'd ever encountered, but there was a melancholy to him that captured my gaze. I'd spent enough time pretending, and it was as though his essence, this total stranger, called out to me. Inexplicably, I wanted to know him.

The god began to wash, a dark smooth river stone clutched in his long slender fingers. Transfixed, I watched as he ran it across the deep valleys of his abdomen, up over his chest and neck. Dark hair hung in messy waves around his face, so deeply black it looked almost midnight blue. I had stared far longer than would be proper, but I couldn't tear my eyes away. In the river, he let out a small moan, head falling back as though smelling something delicious on the air. His nostrils flared and I watched with fascination as he dropped the stone into the river and snaked his hand around himself under the surface, pumping in smooth jerks.

Oh. *Oh*.

An unfamiliar warmth like I'd never known began to flare low in my bones, a deep pressure that had my cheeks flushed as my breath stalled.

It wasn't as though I hadn't seen beautiful men before. I had, of course. Although, none had ever elicited this type of response, and I struggled to snap my mind free of the thoughts suddenly overtaking me. I wanted to know what those hands would feel like roaming over my skin. What color his eyes would be, how soft his bottom lip would feel pressing against mine . . . That uncomfortable warmth twisted into what I could only describe as *want*, pooled between my thighs. A second heartbeat thumped deep inside my core, the sensations overwhelming.

What in the Hells was wrong with me?

Low, masculine grunts fell from his lips, enflaming my chest as I listened and watched like a voyeur. A small dose of shame attempted to wrestle my attention, the voice reminding me what a violation this was. Intrusive, at best and reckless at worst, depending on who that god was. More importantly, I would be mortified if someone watched, unbeknownst to me, while I had an intimate moment. Not that I'd experienced the urge before, but now that I had . . .

The thought sobered me right up, breaking the spell he'd worked over me, allowing some semblance of my self-control to take over. Cautiously, I took a small step back, averting my gaze. A small crack resonated through the clearing as my foot made contact with a bramble under my sandal, but it may well have been a thunderclap. I froze in horror as the god snapped his eyes open, a piercing blue gaze pinning me in place.

Those eyes . . . weren't like anything I had ever seen. Even in the distance, I could feel the blue fire dancing just behind his glare as it raked over my body. He dropped his cock and took a few steps toward the banks, where the water was shallower, unabashedly confident despite his naked and hardened length being on full display. Long legs began to trudge toward the banks, toward *me*, and I knew I should run. There was something feral in his gaze. My rational thoughts were screaming that I was prey, that I should put as much distance between us as possible.

Still, his eyes rooted me.

They were demanding and dangerous, and yet I found my body wasn't reacting with fear. The pull toward him had my nipples hardened, scraping against the fabric of my chiton. His gaze flicked down as though he knew *exactly* how my body was responding. I wrapped my arms across my chest instinctively, embarrassed and confusingly aroused. His feet reached the banks, and as he strode toward me with all the confidence of a dark deity, I felt a pull somewhere around my chest, a piece of myself that called out, almost yearning. I wasn't sure which god he was, but I could feel the power rolling off him, cold and desolate.

Goose bumps painted my skin as he closed the distance between us. The shadows of the wood answered an unspoken command, dark tendrils slithering up around his body, solidifying into an impossibly black himation that left his upper chest exposed to the air. My eyes traced the scarification there, geometric sigils that seemed to whisper around him. Within moments he stood before me, still and quiet, towering over me at nearly twice my height. He didn't seem to be breathing either.

The stranger's eyes were an icy blue with flecks of copper that bore into my own with an intensity that stole my breath. A thin circlet, a crown that looked to be made of bone, rested on his head, adorned with smooth skulls and intricate silver slivers. Plush lips formed into a thin line as he took me in, and I suppressed the urge to reach and touch his furrowed brow.

How I wished he would smile or speak, anything to remove the pained expression he wore. Inches of air separated his skin from mine, his scars in my direct eyeline. He was close, so close I could touch him, so close that I could reach out and trace the whispering white scars adorning his chest if I only had enough courage. My gaze caught on a thin silver amulet that hung around his neck, with a bent crook of what looked to be a fisher's hook. Winter and pine swirled around me, the scents mixing in my nose, pulling me ever closer.

He didn't speak, only studied me as though I were an anomaly of sorts, his gaze a smooth caress roaming my skin. The pressure rose under my skin at his proximity, power and magic begging for release. I pressed my thighs together, nearly moaning at the friction, and I vowed to myself that if I survived this, I would stop holding back on experiencing carnal pleasure. My body leaned closer, ever closer, until I could feel the cold from his body cascading over mine.

Much, too much. Danger.

I broke my eyes away from his and searched for something, anything to focus on while my thoughts unscrambled. My gaze landed on the soft ground around him, my mouth hanging slack at the damage he'd left in his wake. He stood sentry over the path of decay, deep browns having replaced once-green blades of grass and wilted flowers. Anger spiked through me, breaking through my lust and embarrassment, the protective side of my divinity bolstering my resolve. I snapped my eyes back to his, to the infuriatingly handsome smile ghosting his lips, and glared.

"*You* are the one responsible for harming the flora here?" I demanded, knowing my voice commanded all the conviction I possessed.

He curled an eyebrow at me in curiosity, stoic and silent with a growing smile on his lips, as though my anger *amused* him. He may be a god, a powerful one surely, but I was still a goddess, and the flora were *my* domain. I pushed the full weight of my fury against him before shoving my finger into his face.

"Just what makes you think you can throw your weight around so carelessly?" I accused, green eyes blazing with my goddess aura. The pad of my finger jabbed into his exposed chest, against bare skin. A shock resonated from our connection, nearly staggering me back. I faltered only slightly as his blue eyes widened. *Had he felt that too?*

His large hand came up slowly to grip my wrist, giving me plenty of time to move from his space, but I stood my ground, even as sparks skittered over my skin where his fingers held.

"I did not mean to harm your flowers, little goddess," he murmured, thumb tracing my inner wrist. His voice wrapped around me like an embrace, deep and calming. I felt my eyelashes nearly flutter closed, and for a moment, I lost control of my head. Gentle fingers grazed my chin, lifting my gaze into his. Every caress pulled at an invisible string in my chest, tugging me closer until my body pressed willingly against his. The embrace rocked me to the foundation of my divinity. He was cold, but not biting. Strong, but not exacting. He was a stranger, and yet in his arms, I felt an impossible sense of . . . home. His eyes had changed from the raging blue fire to a gentler, somehow more intense, smolder.

"Well, if you didn't mean it then why did you hurt them? They only have a few weeks left before the Fall claims them. They deserve their time in the sun," I scolded, but the smile on his face was so completely distracting, there was no bite to my words.

He chuckled in a deep rumble and simply replied, "I did not mean to offend, Little Flower, but my time here requires a sacrifice." His fingers traced along my forearms, never straying to indecency, the restraint of his body battling the weight of his gaze.

"Who are you?" I breathed, my voice soft between us. His head bent lower, drawing painfully close, so near that our breaths mingled as one.

"I am inevitable," he answered, his smile drooping slightly, as though he were in on a joke that I was not.

"Your name, goddess?" he inquired, stroking his thumb under my jaw. He'd avoided my question with one of his own, but I wanted to bring that smile back.

"Persephone, Goddess of Spring," I whispered. Fates, why did his touch feel like *this*? It gave me the sensation of being underwater, wrapped in the cool of the tide, but not being able to break the surface. "Now that you know my name, the scales are tipped. I need yours, in turn," I pressed.

Time stilled around us, and for just a moment, there were no others in the Fallen Wood, in this realm even. He searched for the answers to unasked questions in my eyes, his pale irises dancing between mine. I had the feeling that he was as guarded as I, but that here, he wanted to reach out a hand in the dark. I wanted to reach back.

The movement against my arms stilled, long dark lashes dusting over pale cheeks as he closed his eyes and spoke:

"Hades, God of the Underworld."

Persephone

CHAPTER 4

Hades's words fanned over my lips, my cheeks, but every inch of my body had gone rigid against him. The icy tendrils of fear trickled along my skin, phantoms of his touch. Wrapped up in the moment, I had lost myself, but as revelations fell from those perfect lips, reality slammed back into my chest.

Hades. God of the Dead. Ruler of the Hells.

The dark god tensed as I tried and failed to suppress a shudder. With a curt nod, his hands fell away, breaking contact, reading my body's reactions with uncanny precision. I nearly whimpered at the air that rushed between us, my body betraying me as it craved more of his attention, even as my mind rallied against the very notion. Hades turned to walk back to the river, and I simply watched him go, both grateful that I'd survived the encounter, but also feeling somewhat hollow.

I had been taught my entire life to fear him, his realm, to never draw the eye of Death, but I couldn't help feeling like he had drawn me to him. Had that trail of cold ground not been a map, a calling that encouraged me to break the rules, to defy my mother? The reactions our bodies had weren't ordinary, of that I was sure. Thousands of mortal men had passed under my gaze, many divine as well, but none of them had ever sent my blood rushing, my power craving as he had. The god retreating to the river was nothing of what I expected, neither withered nor spent nor cruel. He did seem lonely, and that was something I understood all too well.

I was lonely too.

Could I ignore what had passed between us? Bury it and keep it locked in the deepest parts of me, deeper than even the truth of my affliction? Could I live with myself if I did?

"Don't go!" I blurted, my mouth deciding for me. Hades halted immediately, turning back to me with guarded eyes. I gathered my courage, deciding that just for today, I could be brave. I had been so good, all my existence, never taking anything for myself.

"You're scared of me." He said it matter-of-factly, with no hesitation or question. I took a cautious step toward him.

"I am, but now that I see you, I worry that I may be afraid of your reputation, rather than the god behind it." His first step back toward me had my heart beating embarrassingly fast in my chest.

"And what reputation is that, hmm?" he asked, but I couldn't help tracking his steps. I noticed that he made every effort to stay on the already ruined earth. I fought back a smile.

"I'd have to think on that to be sure, but I believe it's the whole, dark, brooding god who eats the shades of children for breakfast and pleasures himself in public waters bit that keeps me wary." Mortification washed over me as his eyes widened in shock. The urge to drown myself in the river was overwhelming.

I was startled by the dark chuckle that passed across his lips.

"Your concern is valid, but also, I think, unwarranted. I'd never eat a child's shade for breakfast, not a very fulfilling way to start the day." His voice rolled off his lips in a deep lilt, gentle but seductive.

"What do your appetites prefer?" The words left my mouth without my permission, and if spoken to any other being would have had me slinking into the floor. However the ravenous look in the God of the Dead's eyes as they raked over my face, my hips, my breasts that wouldn't stop heaving . . .

"I'm developing a penchant for sweeter tastes as of late, it would seem."

My body nearly combusted, jaw slackened at the innuendo.

"There is honeysuckle, if you'd like some," I rambled, feeling too exposed under his perusal. I crossed to the tiny white and yellow flowers that grew untouched on the green vines and plucked two, thanking them for their sacrifice. The rushing river created the only sound between us, as I offered one of them to him on an outstretched palm.

He eyed it apprehensively.

"It's easy, look. You just pinch here," I squeezed the base and felt the gentle snap of the stigma giving way. Gently, I pulled the long spindle through the hollow pith, lifting to show him. Hades bent forward, watching intently as a single bead of nectar slid along the darkened stigma. I parted my lips, shaking the stem gently until the bead fell out onto my tongue. Blue spheres rested on my lips, on the column of my throat as I worked to swallow the sweetness. Hades's gaze was as heavy as a touch, but instead of shying away from it, as I had with any other male who'd ever looked a little too long, I preened beneath it.

"Your turn," I offered, gazing up at him through my lashes. He raised his hands apologetically.

"I'm afraid if I touch it, the bloom will be dead before I can enjoy it's sacrifice."

Brave. I would be brave. I slowly lifted the remaining honeysuckle, snapping off the bottom of the stigma. I stepped right back into his space as I slid the spindle free, another perfect bead of nectar resting and waiting in offering. Slowly, carefully, the Lord of the Underworld's knees bent, and his eyes latched to mine as he sank into the ground, kneeling before me. Even on his knees, he nearly surpassed me but there was enough space for his head to tip back.

Sunlight painted across the silky strands of his hair, danced over his cheeks, illuminating his eyes like sapphires. My fingers grazed over his bottom lip, so soft against my skin, as I lifted the stigma and lowered it past his lips, until the bead of nectar burst against his tongue. A groan ripped from his chest, deep and holy, as his eyes fluttered shut.

"See? Sweetest thing you'll ever taste, Lord Hades," I whispered. His eyes opened slowly, a smile tipping his lips.

"I doubt that," he breathed. A small apprehensive smile tugged at the corner of his mouth as he rose, running his fingers over his lips. The sun dipped lower behind the tree line, nearly orange with the dusk, and as much as I hated to, I knew I needed to return to the estate before Artemis came to find me. Wordlessly, Hades offered me his arm. The connection was calming, as he wrapped his hand around mine. Extraordinarily gentle, as though I was so delicate he feared a strong touch would shatter me.

"I could help you if you didn't want to harm the forest," I offered, with a small smile.

"It's important to you that I don't, isn't it?" he asked, pulling me closer as he spoke, his voice a deep rasp. I dipped my chin in response, gazing up into crystalline eyes.

"Well, yes. This is my domain. If you're going to keep coming here, you have to respect the life that grows." Hades halted our step, turning to me.

"Do you want me to keep visiting you?" he asked, voice laced with a strained vulnerability, as though there were a chance that I could say no.

"I think I want that very much." I motioned to the dead flowers and ground beneath him. "I can't just let this keep happening. So, we will have to find a way for you to walk without hurting them."

"If you wish it, I will make it so," he promised.

Hades stopped just before the edge of the path, an invisible barrier he seemingly could not cross.

"Meet me here, tomorrow?" He tilted his head toward me, almost shyly.

"Yes." I smiled wide, my cheeks straining to maintain my composure, but the one he returned was blinding. By Fates, that smile would be my undoing. Hades lifted my hand to his lips, pressing a kiss into my palm. Cold fire danced along my skin, a promise that resonated like a brand on my shade.

He watched as I made my way back up the road until the path turned, obscuring him from view. Every step I took felt deliberate, purposeful. I was not the same goddess that had stepped off this path earlier. I had chosen and, in return, been rewarded with connection.

In all my years on Earth, I had never taken a lover. For other gods it was commonplace, and I had watched them in sorrow as the mortals grew old or sick or eventually tired of the games of deities and left them, in one form or another. The instability of my powers made pairings with gods dangerous as well, the wrongness inside of me too much a burden for any other to be asked to bear, but Hades was darkness. He was born of the shadows, walked among the different.

Perhaps there was a reason no man had ever stoked the fire in my shade before.

But Hades wasn't a man. He was everything. I knew my resolve for isolation had been undone by his touch. The flames that raged inside of him were cold and passionate, and they called to me like a moth to flame. The power coming from inside his bones wasn't fleeting. Touching him had felt like sticking my hand into a pure cold inferno. Thousands of years, resolute with the life decided for me, so content to be alone, shattered with one touch.

I was ready to burn.

I wanted to be consumed.

Helios

CHAPTER 5

Artemis's glare bore into my back as I made my way over the smoldering earth, crossing the field to answer the summons of Demeter. My sandals dug into the now-scorched earth, and I grimaced at the crunch as I turned over what I'd seen in my mind. There was something . . . *off* about the blooms Persephone had produced, and whatever it was had the young goddess scared. Artemis's reaction had confirmed for me that this was something they were trying to keep quiet, and though I had given my word not to speak of what I had seen, I had other matters to discuss with the Goddess of the Harvest.

I made my way to the ornate linens of brown and burgundies of Demeter's field encampment. I could feel her power seeping into the ground, pushing abundance in such a similar way that Persephone did. Two guards stood sentry at the outer door, young men who were mortal, muscled, and *handsome*. I shot them a stunning smile as I passed, enjoying the way they both faltered, smirks creeping to the largest one's lips as he appraised me just as boldly, his dark hair sitting in thick waves over his brow.

"My Lord," they bowed as I pushed through the fabric. Plush rugs of reds and browns were laid out over the green grass. My golden armor had only just started to cool as I made my way inside, toward the Goddess of the Harvest. Demeter sat, pouring over scrolls, lips moving as she calculated what I assumed were growth charts or seedling almanacs. Her ashy blonde hair sat perfectly styled, but there was a weariness about her that gave me pause. She looked up at my footfalls, her face splitting into the coy smile I knew gods and men buckled for, but it never quite sat right with me.

"Helios, there you are," she sighed, settling back in her chair and gesturing for me to have a seat on the small bench near the side of her tent. "I'll join you in a moment."

With some difficulty due to my armor, I managed to settle back against the cream pillows, and with a groan, I stretched my legs out. It had been brutal work today, the strain of pulling the sun more strenuous than I'd ever cared to admit, and yet that was why I was here. Moments later, Demeter sauntered over, swaying her hips as she passed, and sat opposite me, then poured us both a cup of wine from the table beside her. I gratefully took the golden chalice and savored the drink in my parched throat as she sipped hers. This close, I could see the browns of her eyes were slightly dulled, her golden glow more diminished than this time of year should have warranted. I cleared my throat and blew out a deep breath as she waited patiently for me to begin.

"There's more rot, out on the eastern hills. Swaths of grain, browned early," I announced, watching the goddess carefully as she took in the news. Demeter swore under her breath and stood, crossing back over to her desk.

"Which village?" she asked, irritation heavy in her tone as she leafed through the stacks of parchment.

"Naxos," I answered, rubbing my hand across the back of my neck uneasily. She scooped up the ledger she was looking for, head shaking as her eyes fell shut.

"Demeter, what is causing this? Today it's Naxos, a month ago it was Crete," I prodded, but she only shook her head, squaring back her shoulders.

"It's simply a contamination of the strains I created. Sometimes, experiments go wrong. It's nothing to worry over, I have it handled," she assured, dismissing me with a smile that didn't quite reach her eyes. I stood, considering how wise it would be to push her; Zeus may have ruled Olympus, Poseidon the sea, and Hades the Underworld, but here in the Upper Realm, there was no doubt that Demeter was the most powerful Olympian. Even if she looked beautiful and tender, she could kill a man with less than a blink, leaving his body a hollowed-out husk in her wake.

Still, this was getting out of hand, and I needed answers.

"Respectfully, you don't. There have been too many instances to be merely a crop strain failure. It took me four extra minutes to bring the dawn this morning, Demeter. I feel a strain I've never felt before every time I step into my chariot. Now we have dead fields long before they're due, and you have Persephone pushing herself to her limit to grow tulips in an abandoned field, instead of using the Goddess of Growth to coax out higher yield? Something is happening here, and the time has passed for platitudes. It's time for you to read me in," I demanded, working to keep my voice even despite the piercing glare she had levelled right back at me.

We stood in silence, assessing the other, a titan and a goddess. She was more powerful, but I was older. Her eyes darted around the room, avoiding mine, and for a moment I wondered if I had misread the situation, but then she threw her hands up and slammed them back on the cypress slab beneath her, hanging her head. Her next words sent unease careening through me.

"My power is waning, Helios. It happened little by little over the years, but now it's . . . noticeable," she admitted, her voice shaky. My jaw slackened, shocked at her words, but my mind went straight to Persephone and the decrepit blooms I'd burnt to ash just moments before arriving here.

"Do you know why this is happening?" I asked gently. Demeter's eyes found mine, her mouth set into a tight line.

"There aren't enough of us in the Upper Realm. Most of our kind reside either in Olympus or the Asphodels, and there are too many mortals now. More than there were ever supposed to be. I cannot keep up, and it's just—" Her voice cracked, a moment of vulnerability that I'd never witnessed from the goddess.

"Does Zeus know?" I asked, my head reeling. I had suspected there was *something* more, but I hadn't expected this. At the mention of his name, Demeter's eyes blew wide open as she practically flew out of her chair.

"Do not even *speak* his name here," she hissed, eyes darting around as though she were afraid he would jump out at any moment. "If Olympus gets wind that we're weak, they'll strike, Helios. They want the power we've cultivated here, and I will be damned to the Hells before I give them even an inch of it. It's *mine*," she seethed through gritted teeth, her beautiful face twisted in a snarl.

"What are we going to do?"

I watched as she smoothed down the creamy silks of her chiton and rose to her full height, then circled around to me. I waited as she scooted between my body and the desk, leaning back against the tabletop as she sank her teeth into her bottom lip.

"That depends on if you've reconsidered my offer," she said, eyeing me knowingly. I reared back, creating some distance as I shook my head.

"Your offer for Persephone?" I clarified on a huff. She nodded, waiting. "I have given it no further thought than I did the day you suggested it, and I told you no. She's too young and has no inclination for me, Demeter. Nothing has changed."

Her eyes traced over the exposed skin of my arms, cataloging my body as though appraising me for auction. Though Zeus had the ultimate say on who I married, I knew Demeter held unnatural sway with the God of Gods, and if she pushed for this union, he would sanction it . . .

"Things *have* changed. This progression has altered it irrevocably. We need more deities here to share the burden, or we will lose everything," she said coolly. My palms grew hot at the idea, a deep-seated unease I couldn't shake.

"So have them," I retorted. A dark look flashed across her face, her lips thinning tight as she stared me down.

"I'm afraid that is not an option for me, thanks to Hera. It would seem as though Persephone is all I'll ever get. Plain as she may be, she would make a good, obedient wife to you, Helios."

"Persephone will never go for this," I countered, hating the ire in her voice when she spoke about her daughter, but Demeter only tutted and crossed her arms. I had no desire for subservience in a partner.

"Persephone will do as she is *told*. She understands duty, and besides, she is quite taken with you, Helios."

I reared my head back, nearly toppling over in my haste to back away. "Since when?"

"Since always. Persephone is a shy goddess, Helios." Demeter pressed forward, grasping my hand. "She may not be outright with her affections, but she shows it in other ways. She speaks to you, for one, laughs with you even. When have you seen her interact with others that way, outside of Artemis?" she pressed gently, and I couldn't help but let my mind drift back over our interactions these past years. It was true that Persephone regarded me more warmly than many others. Had I missed the subtle queues of the Goddess of Spring? More importantly, did that truly change anything as far as my feelings went? I swallowed, knowing that my feelings on the matter held little weight.

"You have heard her speak of this?" I asked, standing to pace. Demeter nodded.

"I understand my daughter and am quite adept at reading her affections. She will make you a happy match, Helios. Your children will bolster our power, and we will hold the Upper Realm, provide for those under our sovereignty," She urged, squeezing my hand as she looked up at me. I could feel my insides squirming, rioting against the idea of being tethered to another so completely, even if I had agreed to it when I'd thrown in with Zeus and sided with him during the Titanomachy. I hadn't known then what his rule would encompass, couldn't have fathomed he would have imposed stricter edicts over our pairings than even Cronus. As though she could read my thoughts, Demeter again spoke.

"Persephone is practical, Helios. Once she has children to raise, I am sure that she would not begrudge you your other . . . *appetites*." She stressed the word, letting it fall from her tongue as though she knew all about my string of lovers I'd enjoyed congress with, some of the very soldiers and maids that worked in her own household. I swallowed thickly, my mind at war with my heart. My mind understood the importance of maintaining our tenuous hold on the authority of the Upper Realm, but my heart raged against the cage of marriage.

"She needs you, you know? Persephone isn't immune to this blight either. It's . . . affecting her. She's fragile, Helios, I—" her voice trailed off, the glistening sheen of unshed tears in her eyes as she pleaded with me. All at once, I was back in that field, burning twisted flora while Artemis comforted a panicking Persephone. Demeter's eyes searched mine, before her grip on me lessened.

"You've seen it, haven't you? You know how she suffers."

The knot in my throat held my tongue at bay, so I nodded as best I could.

"Then you know that she needs a protector. And who better than someone who already loves her, in his own way, than a fierce titan? One who has seen war? Who is kind to her? She's delicate, Helios; like a flower, her petals are easy to crush. She wouldn't survive our fall from power, would she? Or to be married off to another of Zeus's choosing, who wouldn't understand her. You gave him the power to choose, at least this way you will be with someone you already care for. Isn't that better than leaving it to his whim, like Athena and Poseidon, Hephaestus and Aphrodite?" she asked tearfully, her voice so soft. I shook my head, knowing that she was right. Zeus had made terrible matches that produced the unhappiest pairings. "That's why I need to make sure she's protected. You'll protect her, won't you, Helios?" she urged, and I felt my head nod of its own volition.

Demeter smiled wide as she released my hand and reached for her wine. My own hand shook as I took mine and lifted it to my lips. I had always known the day would come when I would be forced to fulfill my oath and let Zeus dictate my future, but it had always felt so far away. Now, that leash of perceived freedom felt cut short.

"It's settled then. We accept your proposal, Helios, Titan of the Sun. The two of you will be wed within a fortnight."

We drank her toast down, with snakes twisting in my gut, and then I was dismissed. Satisfied, Demeter went back to her almanacs as though we hadn't just decided the future of Persephone and I, as though this weren't a monumental moment. I stumbled out of the tent and climbed into my chariot in a daze, all sordid thoughts of the handsome guards gone. I took my reins in hand, and when I took to the sky, my mind had worked through the fog that had settled and only one thought mattered.

Persephone needed me to protect her, and I could do that. I could set aside my own tastes and appetites, and I could be the husband she deserved. Demeter would not have pushed this if

Persephone weren't truly interested, and she was beautiful, that was certain. Perhaps I could grow to love her in a way every lover I'd ever taken before had failed to inspire. A fortnight.

I had a fortnight to sow the rest of my wildest oats, to get lost in the bodies of women and men, before resigning myself to just one other for eternity. I mulled it all over as I reached the sun, and with every grunt, every bead of sweat that broke out over my body, I peeled the orb back over the horizon, resolve settling inside of me. My power *was* waning, as was Demeter's and Persephone's, and this was how we fixed it all. I shuddered to think what damage the likes of Zeus, Poseidon, or, Fates forbid, Hades would do with this realm if they sensed weakness.

The air cooled as the last rays of the dying sun peeked over the horizon, but for once, my eyes were on the ground below me. I took in the trees, the earth, the flowers, and grains. Every part of it was under my protection, and I knew that I would do my best to honor my vows.

A glimmer pulled my eye as I flew over a small island, shaded with cypress and olive trees. I pulled the leather reins in my grip, arcing a circle overhead, drawn to the ground by a pull from around my middle. A thousand shimmers echoed back against me, refracting the golds and purples from the sunset in a curious array. My chariot tipped forward, hooves galloping toward the ground, then landing with stunning precision just outside of a copse of trees.

I dropped the reins and pushed forward through the thick brush, a power calling out to me, urging my feet closer. Past the tree line, my breath caught in my chest. Lounging in a circle of reflecting mirrors was the most ethereal creature I'd ever laid eyes on. A long, lithe body with tightly corded muscles peeked through a white himation, his skin beneath free of any blemishes, so smooth and golden in the sunset it stuttered my heart. Delicate, pale lashes dusted over high and sharp cheekbones on each lazy blink, with the most full, kissable lips puckered into a perfect bow, but it was the eyes, those beautiful browns that stared up at me with curiosity and wonder in the reflection that had me moving closer.

He rose up into a sitting position, and across his back I could see his muscles flex and tense. I gazed at the slender slope of his neck as he tilted his chin higher to meet my eyes. A cascade of long, silvery blond hair fell around him, and my chest felt as though I'd been crushed under a boulder at his beauty. An overwhelming urge beat like a war drum in my chest, demanding I move closer, that I covet, that I protect him, unlike anything I'd ever known. His head slowly turned from the mirror to arch over his shoulder, and the full weight of his gaze nearly knocked me flat.

"You are quite beautiful," he observed, his voice melodic and trilling, like the splash of water against my skin on a hot day in the sunshine. I wanted to hear more of it.

"As are you," I offered, my cheeks splitting into a dumbstruck grin in the looking glass.

"I know," he answered, rubbing his fingers over the soft curve of his cheek. My own fingers twitched, desperate to follow that line, itching to touch whatever divinity laid out before me. I watched as he turned fully, rising up on his knees, head lifting to lock eyes with me as I closed the distance between us. He looked so stunning like that, on his knees, gazing up at me with wonder and hunger. My body hummed, responding to the tension building between us.

"Do you have a name?" I asked, reaching out to stroke his cheek. The touch was lightning against my fingertips, and the breathy moan he shuddered had me hardening behind my armor. His eyes fluttered shut, as though overcome from the touch.

"Narcissus," he breathed on a contented sigh, nuzzling his cheek into my palm. He was all softness, delicate and precious against the rough callouses of my palm and fingers. I longed to run my fingers through his hair, and with less than a thought, I ran my hands through the strands.

"So beautiful," I murmured as he preened, skin glowing bright white under the weight of my praise. I could taste his divinity on the air, and I let the weight of it settle against me, allowing mine to do the same to him. There was a curious wonder in his eyes, and it pulled at tethers that I didn't even know my heart had. Gods and titans had voracious appetites, selfish creatures who gave into desire simply because we could. If this were any other day, I would have wasted no time in taking his mouth, letting him take mine. I'd work his body higher and higher, until he was nothing more than a ball of need, desperate for release.

But today was not like any other day. Today, I had promised myself to another, and for better or worse, I was committed to it.

Wasn't I?

"Why does your touch feel so good?" Narcissus moaned, and I felt my resolve flutter. Could I truly give this up? The thrill of the chase, the instant magnetism, the giving in to the most primal urges?

"Because our bodies call to one another," I soothed, rubbing small circles on the thin skin beneath his jaw. His eyes snapped open to mine, holding me captive in his stare.

"I've never enjoyed the touch of another, until this moment," he confessed, filling my chest with possessive pride as I trailed light touches down the column of his throat. "Show me more?"

Fuck. A thrill like I'd never known, calling out to me, tempting and teasing, at war with the weight of responsibility, of duty. Of necessity, a small voice reminded me.

And yet, I could not stop touching him. I considered, I bargained, I pleaded with my conscience to look away as I knelt down, cupping his face in my hands, our breaths mingling as we waited, locked in one another's orbit. Demeter probably hadn't had time to tell Persephone the news yet.

I wasn't engaged until the bride-to-be was made aware, right?

Just one taste.

"I can offer you no more than a taste, beautiful boy. My honor must belong to another," I warned. His brow creased as he thought on my words, and I waited for him to push me away. Instead, the fingers gripping my wrists tightened.

"A taste, then," he agreed, his words caressing against my skin. A slow smile worked over my lips as I gently lifted and turned his chin, exposing the column of his throat to me. I trailed my lips over his jawline, down his neck, teasing the tip of my tongue, relishing every moan I dragged from his lips, before claiming his mouth in a slow, drugging kiss. He opened so beautifully for me, his body arching against mine, eager to take whatever I could give him.

I could give myself this, tonight.

For in the morning, I owed my loyalty to someone else.

Hades

CHAPTER 6

I waited for her at the path's edge all day. We hadn't spoken of a time, and I was terrified that I would miss her. The hem of my robes barely grazed the ground as I floated, suspended slightly above the green grass. She had been upset when I'd accidentally drained the life force from the flora around the banks of the Styx that passed through this Upper Realm, and I wanted to honor her wishes. There was an excitement burning inside my chest, pulling me back to here, to *her*. I'd gone over our encounter a thousand times since yesterday, analyzing every aspect of it, committing her to memory in case she'd changed her mind. I hadn't felt a pull to someone in so long, and even when I'd cared for Minthe, it had never felt as impactful as the few moments I'd shared with Persephone. I didn't believe in love at first sight, and, in truth, I barely believed in love.

I'd seen so many things in my long tenure as the ruler of the Hells, and not much of it gave me hope that something as intangible as love could truly conquer anything. I'd seen it kill, murder, maim, and in most instances, betray. And yet . . . Something in the goddess had brought me to my knees. Before I'd seen her, that intoxicating scent had overtaken me, ensnaring my attention. Rich flowers, earthy and grounding, but also, there was something . . . *familiar*. She'd looked like sunshine, but she had the undercurrent of fruit ripened too long. Still sweet, but just on the verge of death, reminiscent of the pomegranate that had sprouted up all over the Asphodels.

Persephone smelled like the sweetness of the Underworld. At her touch, every nerve in my body felt like a live wire and I needed to find out *why*. I'd never heard of her before, the spring goddess. Not that I took much stock in news or gossip of Olympus. I was suddenly sure that, had I known of her before, I wouldn't have been able to stay away, and that simple knowledge vexed me. *Why her?* She was beautiful, assuredly, but I had met and bedded beautiful women before.

Her golden hair was the color of sunlit grains, but many women held the shine of divinity. When fire had erupted behind those mossy green eyes and she'd stepped toward me, unafraid, unleashing her fury, it took all the willpower I'd possessed not to consume her on the spot. Perhaps it was her challenge that called to me. Perhaps her lack of fear? When she'd pushed toward me, jabbing her finger into my chest, a bolt of energy had pierced through my skin. My power had swelled inside of me, calling to her, *reaching*. I had wanted to touch her, to sink my fingers into her flesh until I was buried beneath her bones, but I'd settled for my fingers wrapping around her delicate wrist.

I'd taken liberties with Persephone, tracing her soft skin, relishing her nearness as I pressed her close to me. The constant pit of despair that usually sat lodged in my chest had dissipated just a fraction in her nearness, and the weightlessness that comfort provided spurned me past propriety. I just couldn't stop touching her. When she'd said she wasn't afraid of me, a rush of hope I'd never experienced coursed through my veins.

"You came." Persephone's soft voice cut a valley through my thoughts. I looked down at her full frame, nearly swallowing my tongue. My gaze raked down that perfect body for only moments before her eyes took me in. Persephone was magnificent, voluptuous, and filled out in ways that mortals could only dream of. Her full thighs peaked out from the slits in her chiton—today a pale shade of yellow that reminded me of the daffodils I'd seen growing on the banks. A flower crown adorned her head, and that face, that mouth, sent a shock of desire straight through me.

I wanted to stare longer, take in the curves of her breasts, the swells of her hips that tapered into her waist, but those green eyes just wouldn't let me go. I floated down on my shadows just a beat closer, careful not to touch a single blade of grass. Persephone's eyes flitted to the negative space beneath my hem and crossed her arms; a growl nearly worked past my lips. I wanted those eyes back on *me*.

"I didn't know you could fly," she teased, a brilliant smile lighting her face. Taming my baser instincts, I couldn't help but return the gesture.

"You promised if I didn't hurt another blade of grass, you'd teach me to control it." I shrugged. She laughed, the sound like windchimes. I wanted to bottle it up tightly so I could revisit it whenever I liked.

"A god of his word, Lord Hades is." She bent low in a curtsey, exposing the golden skin of the top of her breasts, so full and perfect my mouth watered. I averted my gaze reluctantly and cleared my throat. She hadn't come here to be ogled, and my already fraying self-control wasn't faring well being this close to her.

"So, will you teach me, goddess? The view from here isn't as striking as from the ground," I volleyed back, and a beautiful blush painted her apple cheeks. Persephone glanced down to the top of her gown, curling her shoulders in on themselves, some of that fire diminishing. *Hells*. I'd made her uncomfortable.

"Come down, I'll heal the grass once it's done." Her words were quieter now, and I chastised myself. I waved a hand, and my shadows complied, relegating me to the earth. As my sandals grazed the blades of grass, I could feel their life force fade out and feed into mine. My robes floated down with a flourish around me, drawing power, *taking*. I stepped forward, my hand outstretched to take her arm to apologize, but thought better of it.

"I'm sorry if I made you uncomfortable, Persephone. That wasn't my intention," I mumbled, searching for the right words to say. The goddess snapped her eyes back to mine.

"It's fine. It isn't the first time someone has commented on my appearance. I'm the Goddess of Spring, not beauty . . ." Her words were flat, a tiny bit of cold energy emanating from her. They stopped me in my tracks.

"What did you just say?" I asked, bewildered. She lifted a shrug.

"I know that there are those far fairer than I. I care little to be the most beloved or the most beautiful. I can make life grow, a power worthy of respect, and that is enough for me," she answered, meeting my gaze. I closed the gap between us but didn't touch her. There was something practiced in her tone, a mantra she'd clearly repeated to herself as armor against cruel words.

"I meant that being close to you held more appeal than the distant view of your body without your consent. Too much space separates us, it's hard to make out your eyes as you tease me," I explained, face hot. I needed her to understand, and my words tumbled out in a mess. "You are, well, you must know you're radiant. Anyone who'd say otherwise must be blind, and though your beauty is only a fraction of what encompasses you, to hear any man say otherwise would mean to tempt the wrath of the Underworld." Persephone's eyes sparked just a moment, rejuvenated by my praise in a way that shot right to my cock. I kept on, wanting more of that look. "I also want to apologize for my behavior yesterday. I can admit that your presence caught me off guard, and I should not have taken the liberties I did, touching you without your permission." I cast my eyes low before looking back at her beautiful face. Persephone looked confused, cutting glances all around us.

"Thank you for saying that, Lord Hades, but I—" she paused, hesitating, "I liked when you touched me." Her words were soft, and I was rewarded with another flush of heat that colored her cheeks and the tips of her ears. Hells, I wanted to see how far down that blush spread. I shook my head once to clear the fog, to focus on the beauty in front of me, desperate to get myself under control. I was the God of the Dead, for Fate's sake, but this goddess reduced me to a puddle with less than a look. Persephone fiddled with something small and metallic in her hands, and grateful for the distraction, I brought my fingers to hers, sucking in a sharp breath at the current that rumbled between us. She took a small step forward, looking up at me excitedly through her pale lashes.

"I got the idea from this," she whispered, fingertips grazing my sigil that hung around my neck. "The power can be contained, you see. A small bit of my essence should keep the drain away. I would have asked for something of yours already, but I fashioned this one instead. I wanted it to be something to protect the flora, and I could go on and on about the magic behind it, but I don't want to burden you . . ." I brought two fingers to her chin and lifted her face back to mine.

"Burden me." The words were truth, but I felt the tremor that rocked through her body, so damn responsive to me. Her bright eyes turned glassy, as though my curiosity at what she had created was a foreign experience. A hungry need worked through my own body, and I knew I was moments away from losing all control, from dropping to my knees and begging for a taste of her. Instead, I removed my hand from her chin and stepped back out of her space politely, gesturing to the long branch of a felled tree, offering for her to sit. Persephone shook her head with a bemused smile playing on her lips, as though she could see right through me.

Perhaps she could.

"Are you sure?" she asked, and I dipped my chin. "It would be easier to stand, Lord Hades," she said, squaring her body back to mine. I nodded and offered a small tilt of my lips.

"Hades. Just Hades."

Persephone studied me, curiosity sparkling in her deep green eyes.

"Hades." She smiled. The goddess raised her arms in front of her, reminiscent of the priestesses, palms up. The small talisman she had chosen gleamed occasionally in the dancing sunlight that peaked through the canopy of trees above us. Power hummed around her, emanating from the center of her chest and wafting around her like a cocoon. Soft tendrils of her blonde curls danced on the current of power that corded around her frame. My feet moved forward of their own volition, but I knew it was *her will* pulling me close. I could have resisted, instead I complied, transfixed by this show of power in front of me.

She had described herself as a simple Goddess of Spring, but the power pulsing off her spoke to something much *deeper*, more demanding. That sweet taste was back in the air, permeating the small space and threatening to smother me in its perfection. She reached the palm holding the talisman out to me, and I clasped my hand around hers, enveloping the tiny thing in my long fingers. As soon as our skin touched, a scorching heat ripped from somewhere behind my navel and pulled enough power from me to buckle my knees. Eyes wide, I studied Persephone, shocked by what I saw.

The golden glow that had taken up residence around her danced, tinged with something *hungry*. It was as if her power were reacting to mine, bolstered by the vast well of the Underworld. I could see it within her now, deep and resounding as it grew more solid. Though she may be a spring goddess, Persephone harbored a darkness, one she buried deep inside, suffocated under the weight of obedience and expectations. *Such rage.* It tasted delicious and I was salivating for the destruction she could wreak upon me.

I wanted the havoc.

Needed to feel it strip me bare of my divinity. The initial connection had me wary, but the pull was clear to me now: Persephone was a shard of obsidian, broken from the lifeforce of the Asphodels, the personification of darkness encased in light. Her power siphoned more and more as my mind raced, the pull achingly intoxicating. I wanted to offer her everything, show her such lovely darkness . . .

But I couldn't do that. She wasn't of the Underworld, she was of the Upper Realm, no matter her appetites. Fear sliced up my spine, when I thought of what could happen to her below. The withering of her spirit without the light of the sun. I couldn't let myself pull her further into the depths. She was a wildflower, and I wilted delicate things under my touch. My eyes locked on her as she absorbed the power I now offered too freely.

I watched as she morphed the energy around us into a concentrated orb of light that she pressed into the metal between our joined fingers. She drank the darkness from me like a starving woman, pulling in greedy waves that had my body on fire for her. I steadied my stance and pulled the power back slowly, trickling like a sieve instead of a free-flowing waterfall. I stemmed the flow little by little until Persephone settled back into her calm and happy form, all traces of darkness gone, but it was too late. I had seen what she kept buried deep, and Fates did I crave to see more. She let out a breathy laugh as I subtly looked her over, and though she'd imbibed enough dark energy to level a village, she looked . . . unaffected.

"That certainly didn't seem like simple spring magic, Persephone." I kept my tone light as I took in her flushed face, bright eyes. She shot me a shy smile, biting her full bottom lip.

"That's never happened before, actually," she confessed, "But it felt amazing. Here, put this on." Persephone's fingers fumbled with the twisted metal in her palm as she hooked it over the cord around my neck. "It's my power and yours, entwined together. When you walk and seek to pull life from the earth, it will draw on our power in the pendant." She stepped back, satisfied with her work. I sat in the grass, running my fingers through the tall blades. A part of me expected my power to overwhelm hers, to leave the green grass dead and wilted beneath my touch.

It didn't.

Her talisman held strong. Persephone flopped down next to me and laid her body onto the soft grass. I leaned back next to her, both of us staring at the canopy of dark leaves stretching above us. I turned my face to look at hers and was, again, struck by the quiet power I could feel thrumming around her.

"So, tell me, do you like ushering the flowers in?" I asked, desperate to hear her voice again. Persephone turned to face me, a bemused expression on her face.

"Do I . . . do I *like* it?" she asked, confused, and I nodded, brows furrowed. "No one has ever asked me that before. Truth be told, no one is particularly interested in much of what I have to say, except maybe Artemis. She's my best friend. Goddess of the Hunt, I'm sure you've heard of her. She's one of the Big Eleven." Persephone rambled, and I smiled at how animated she was when she spoke of Artemis, or her favorite flowers, or how much she loved the night and the stars. She told me stories of how she used to run through the forest, wild and free, until Artemis suffered a great loss there.

"Tell me about yourself, Hades. My life is tedious. Surely the God of the Underworld has better things to do than to listen to me grouse all afternoon," she teased. I leveled her a look.

"There isn't anywhere in the entire cosmos I'd rather be, Persephone. How about you tell me a secret, something you've kept to only yourself," I requested, and she rolled onto her side, propping her head on her elbow as she studied me, chewing on the inside of her lip, deciding just how trustworthy I was. The goddess let out a deep breath, steadying herself.

"Sometimes, when I try to grow new flora, it comes out as an abomination. Mother says it's because I'm not focusing enough. Their petals are dark and oddly shaped. I think they're beautiful, but Mother insists they're corrupted. They don't feel corrupted to me, just *different*. Sometimes, I think it's my loneliness seeping out from inside of me, evidence of my sadness laid out for all to see." My heart constricted at the quiet pain in her voice.

"Your turn," she whispered.

"For the first time in all of my existence, I don't hate being out of the Underworld," I admitted, and I felt a warmth spread up my palm as Persephone slid her hand in mine. I pulled our entwined fingers up to rest on my chest, just below the amulet she had made for me. We laid there together until the stars peeked through the canopy above us, sharing every secret we'd ever harbored.

Persephone
CHAPTER 7

"It's quite beautiful, the convergence. The great rivers all meet there and serve as lifelines through the Underworld. The Waterfall of Shades is breathtaking." Hades sat on the forest floor, his back to a spruce that lay felled in our meadow, my head in his lap. Above me, his arms flailed animatedly as he described his favorite parts of the Underworld in great detail. I'd learned there weren't many places in his realm he didn't hold dear and could have turned to stone where I lay, listening to his deep voice go on and on.

The Underworld was a mystery to me, something to be feared and respected from the comfortable mortal plane. Mother never had good things to say about Olympus, but she'd never disparaged the Underworld. I'd assumed it was out of fear. Our first few visits to the meadow had introduced me to the quiet, contemplative Hades. He had listened to me talk, eyes and attention on me with rapture as I recounted the most mundane aspects of my everyday life. He'd insisted that none of it was boring to him, and he'd asked thoughtful questions. Every god I knew had a duty and obligation far greater than mine. Artemis had her huntresses, a

Wild Hunt of warrior maidens she cared for. They took shelter with her, and in turn, she taught them how to protect themselves.

Helios, as a titan, bore the sun across the sky each morning and returned it each night. Mother grew the grain and crops, sowing the seeds of agriculture in the land. Even Apollo presided over music, poetry, and prophecy when he could be dragged away from whatever unfortunate mortal he lusted over. He wasn't as bad as Zeus or Poseidon, but he wasn't far off from them either.

They each held title and tenure; they never had time for me, save for Artemis, who did what she could to check in. Of all the gods and titans I lived among, Hades ranked most high, and yet there he sat, listening to me drone on about pranks and marigolds, about the time I settled a dispute between the grains that grew wild across our land. His crystal blue eyes would settle on me, drawing the blood to the surface of my skin at the tiniest provocation. The way he leaned in, cocking his head slightly to me to ensure he caught every word. The sharp cut of his jaw and the way it sat below his prominent cheekbones. It sucked me into his orbit, and I would do anything to stay there. I could have counted every line that graced his brow, every blue vein that shimmered just below his pale skin. When he smiled, warmth spread through me, and when he laughed, it reverberated through my bones.

"I think I'd love to see it for myself, someday," I chimed in during his explanation of the Elysian Fields. Hades dropped his hand to the side of my cheek, caressing it tenderly, his mouth turned down in a sad smile. He did that sometimes, a touch to my cheek or a hand in mine. He never pressed beyond the pale, beyond what would be considered appropriate, though I desperately wanted him to. Hades was an enigma, a puzzle I'd yet to figure out, and though I hadn't had the courage to tell him about the complicated way my stomach knotted whenever he touched me or the heat that built low in my belly while I laid in bed at night and pictured his face, a small part of me hoped he already understood.

"Maybe one day," he whispered, noncommittally. I let out a deep sigh of disappointment and closed my eyes.

"I won't be able to meet tomorrow," I said.

Hades stiffened beneath me, his hand frozen on my face.

"We have the Great Harvest coming. I will have to receive our guests." I scrunched up my nose in distaste. Hades eyed me thoughtfully, his jaw still set. "What will you have to do?" he asked, stroking his thumb along the edge of my cheek. I leaned into his touch slightly before turning back to look at him. Hades was staring off into the forest, so far away from where he'd just been.

"The tributes will arrive with fealty provisions for Mother's altar. We will sit in the courtyard and hear their prayers and grievances. Mother will bestow favor or take it away based on her own criteria, and we will drink and eat while they light the harvest pyre." My voice was bored as I droned on. Hades tipped his head down to look at me.

"You didn't answer my question, Persephone. I asked what *you* do, not what your mother will do."

"I don't *do* much of anything. I'm expected to sit obediently while Mother takes her divinity. They pray to her, and she must abide by them." I stared at him thoughtfully. Hades bent his chin so low it grazed his chest. Both of his icy eyes peered into mine.

"And who prays to you, Little Flower?"

My body seized, stretched taunt. His deep voice rumbled through his chest, shaking through me. I could feel his warmth seeping through my chiton, fire hot where only cool comfort had been before.

"I . . . I don't believe anyone does. Mortals pray for food, not flowers. In many ways, I'm as ornamental as they," I stuttered. Hades clicked his tongue behind his teeth and let out a deep huff of annoyance. His strong hand cupped my jaw gently but firmly, his thumb brushed lightly over my bottom lip. His eyes were transfixed on my lips, and I held my breath, wound too tight to breathe.

"That just won't do," he whispered. His face dropped a fraction closer. Proximity, or the fire at my back, coursed boldness through my veins as I stared up at him.

"Would you pray to me, Hades? Worship at my altar?"

The words were out before I could overthink them, and Hades's eyes blew open wide, blue replaced with inky black that sucked me in so deeply I feared I'd never find my way out. The grip on my jaw tightened, lifting me slowly, carefully toward him. My body ached, willing him to close the distance and steal my first kiss. He was breathing hard, every muscle bent in restraint, and I wanted to break him of it. I needed him to just take that first step, show me that what I felt wasn't one sided, but just as his lips lowered, the bell from the tower tolled, ripping the moment from us. Hades bristled, straightening to open the distance between us once more. My head fell back in thinly veiled frustration, as I suppressed the urge to scream. *Another toll.*

"Hells, I have to go," I mumbled, sitting up. Hades was standing with his arm outstretched before I could even recognize that he'd moved. He took my hand and lifted me with ease, smoothing the strands of grass and moss from my chiton.

"So, no tomorrow, but the morning after?" he asked, eyes hopeful. Warmth washed over me again at how eager he looked, how vulnerable. A man who'd barely touched me but craved my company. It was the opposite of everything I'd observed with others of my kind, and of mortals. I nodded my agreement, and Hades rewarded me with his most genuine smile. He walked me to the path's edge, his hand lingering on mine until the distance broke us apart. I turned to him over my shoulder and shot him a coy look.

"Hades, what do you do in the hours we're apart?" I asked thoughtfully. He stared at me with all the intensity of the Hells blazing in his eyes.

"Pray to you."

Helios

CHAPTER 8

Soft moans echoed off the glass around us, the vision of his body, back flush to my chest, body exposed as he sucked me deeper inside of him, squeezing around my length. Hearing my name fall from his lips, the hours and hours of conversation that followed, the connection that felt somehow bone deep . . .

"Oh, Fates!"

Warm wine sloshed over my chest, the deluge of red staining the white of my himation, pulling me from my memory. I glanced down to see Persephone, startled, fingers desperately clutching a flagon of wine, her green eyes wide.

"I'm so sorry, Helios, let me just—" her small hands fussed over the ruined fabric, fingernails scraping over the ridges of my abdomen, the pads of her fingers cool against my too-warm skin. As though just realizing her bare hand was pressed against my flesh, her green eyes impossibly widened into full orbs, the red of the wine three shades lighter than the stain on her cheeks. She jerked her body back unsteadily. "Oh, I've made a mess, Fates."

With an adorably frustrated sigh, she thanked me sheepishly as I took her wrists gently, righting her before she could fall.

"I am mortified," she confessed, but I couldn't help the laugh that bubbled from my lips.

"It's fine, truly. I think this is more my color," I teased. Persephone scowled, and it struck me that she had been much more open and animated the last few weeks around me, giving more and more credence to Demeter's words. She was more interested in conversation, smiling more, nearly blossoming. It was endearing to see, to watch her flourish after being such a wallflower for so long.

"Don't make fun," she pouted, scowling and crossing her arms beneath her chest. I let my gaze track lower, willing my body to respond to hers. She was actually stunning, and I'd never had an issue finding desire with women, but my body remained wholly unconvinced as the last remnants of my arousal from the memory of Narcissus ebbed away. *Narcissus.*

Fates, my body flushed at the mere thought of his name, a desperate need working its way up from the pits of my desire. Persephone was talking, but I found I could hardly concentrate on her words as want bolted through me. It was a taste, just a taste, for the last few weeks. We had agreed that would be enough, but I found myself at his door nearly every night since that very first time. It was an easy routine of fucking, but also conversating, learning about the god that had sequestered himself to an island, his beauty too intense for mortals to behold. Learning of the safety he felt on the island, the surprise he'd experienced during our first meeting, at feeling desire.

The boost to my ego that it had been *me* to turn his head, to ignite his passion, had me rutting into him every chance I had. From dusk to dawn, I barely slept, the need to be inside of him, next to him, underneath him too great, but it was all coming to an end, and I was free-falling into the Pits of Tartarus over it.

Demeter had informed me earlier tonight that Zeus had formally accepted the proposal, and that she would be telling

Persephone tomorrow morning, which meant I'd spent the last few hours of the Great Harvest convincing myself not to head back to that island. We had both known that carnal pleasure was all we could have. I was lying to myself that I'd been able to keep that line, all the while knowing that the time to back out of this arrangement with Persephone had long passed. I was holding on to the last shreds of my dignity by a thread, but every moment that passed without Narcissus's taste on my tongue frayed that control. Centuries of dalliances that meant little to nothing, but the moment I pledged myself to another, I found something I couldn't live without. Only now, it was too late.

Zeus's edict was law, and if I defied it, it wouldn't just be me to face his wrath; it would be Narcissus too.

"Helios?" Persephone asked, brow furrowed as she leaned closer, concern etched on her face. I shook out my thoughts, aware that I'd been rude and hadn't heard anything she'd said.

"Yes? Sorry, long day," I soothed, shooting her a smile.

"You've got a little something right—" She reached up, swiping her finger over a tender spot on my neck and I blanched as the bruised skin registered in my intended's eyes. I expected to see hurt, or betrayal, but Persephone only smirked.

"You lose a fight with the chariot reigns?" she asked. The tightening in my chest relaxed, as I waved off her teasing.

"It can get a little unruly. Just had to show it who was in control," I countered.

"Just be careful out there, leaving a string of heartbroken lovers in your wake," she warned, voice more serious this time. I softened my gaze and tucked a stray lock of hair behind her ear. She stiffened, but didn't pull away.

"I know what I'm doing, and I'm always up front about what I can offer," I replied kindly, searching her eyes for something, *anything* to flip the lever inside of me, to make me want her in a way that would lessen the ache I held for Narcissus. The corner of her lips tipped up in a returned smile, her hands clasped together in front of her now.

"Knowing something is fleeting doesn't make it feel any less real. You never know what lurks just under those careful facades. Some people are shallow rivers, and some are caverns in the abyss." A sad, haunting look overtook her smile, and I squirmed with guilt. Her words twisted inside of me long after she'd returned to the revelry, but even with them screaming against my resolve, I still found myself dismounting my chariot a few hours later, more than a little drunk on spiced wine and aching with need.

He was there, in that same clearing, moonlight bouncing from the looking glasses, his naked body a vision in silvers. I expected to see him staring at his own reflection, but the God of Self Love knelt in the soft grass, waiting for *me*. The gravity wrenching my body to his pulled me faster to him as I stumbled into the clearing. Clumsily, I unclasped the straps of my armor, caring little when it fell in a heap at my feet, leaving a trail of ornate gold in my wake. Narcissus's gaze raked over my body, savoring, waiting.

He deserved more than this, more than my drunken weakness that sent me crawling back to the comfort of his presence when that was all I could give him. *A taste*. Fleeting moments. I knelt before him, our bodies close, and yet still too far away.

"You came back," he whispered, the relief and hope in his voice nearly undoing my resolve. I cupped his cheeks in my hands, drawing his eyes to mine.

"I can only offer a taste. My loyalty—" I began, but he silenced me with a press of his lips, his body arching to mine, seeking warmth.

"—belongs to another. *I know*."

He tasted so sweet, like nectar against my tongue, and when he pulled back, there was a sad smile on his face. For the hundredth time since my lips first touched his, I considered calling it all off and surrendering to this feeling between us. To openly defy the God of Gods' will and leave the realm, our waning power, and even Persephone to the ruin of Zeus's wrath. But the wheels of Fate were in motion, and it didn't matter if I had found something incredible. The rules were clear; the stakes were too high to let selfish wants cloud my judgment. Millions of mortals counted on us to protect them, to provide for them, and Zeus would kill Narcissus for being the reason I defied him with less than a thought.

The weight of responsibility nearly crushed me, but in this moment, I felt weightless.

I stroked my thumb over the top of his cheek, my other hand cradling him flush to my chest, our hearts dancing in the night, with only the moon to witness our sins. His fingers traced the lines of my chest, over my shoulders and back down my bicep, leaving goose bumps in their wake. Gracefully, Narcissus turned his body around, settling against me, his hand raised teasing the hair at the nape of my neck.

With less than a thought, I summoned fresh warm oil, felt it pool in my hand, drip down my fingers. I kissed against the tender flesh between his shoulder and neck, savoring his moans and whimpers as I spread his cheeks and slid my fingers gently around, teasing and stretching him, devouring the shallow pants that dropped from his lips, the steady acceleration of his heartbeat, and when I lined my cock up to him and pressed in, it stole my breath.

Narcissus's fingers scraped against the skin of the back of my neck as he writhed, working me deeper, greedy hips pressing to claim my full length.

"That's so good for me, relax, let me in," I encouraged, nipping up the side of his throat, coating his body with the remnants of oil as my hands circled his waist, trailing them lower to the full cock hanging low between his legs. "Leaking for me?" I groaned, sucking on his skin the way he'd marked mine, careful not to bruise him.

I could never stand to mar flesh as precious as his.

"More, please, I need, I *n-need—*" he whimpered, the sounds intoxicating. With a grunt, I fed him the last bit of my length, felt the warmth from him envelope me, spellbinding me as he panted, adjusting to the intrusion. I ran a hand over the side of his face, stroking his cock with the other, smearing the moisture leaking from the tip up and down in tandem with my slow strokes.

"Shh, I've got you. Lean back and let me take care of you," I commanded, and with every thrust, he melted against me, until it was only my arms and cock that kept him upright, my chest that supported his head as he let it fall, eyes open, stars reflected in his irises. Connection, deep and terrifying, settled between our bodies, our shades, and when he came, spilling over my fingers with a cry that sounded like music better than anything Apollo had ever created, I nearly wept through my own release.

My hips faltered, his fingers digging into the tufts of hair dusting my thighs as I pulsed inside of him, spilling deep, marking this moment in the only way I could. And when it was over and our bodies were spent, I laid us down, slipping free of his warmth, settling his body against the curve of mine. We were a mess, covered in our release, sweat, and my regret, but the moon was high in the sky and the sun would soon call me to duty.

I tucked his body beneath my chin in the grass as the night hummed around us, my thigh thrown over his hip, anchoring Narcissus's body to mine.

"Tell me something good that happened today," he mumbled, voice heavy with sleep. I stroked his hair and tightened the grip I had around his waist as our heartbeats slowed.

"I don't want to talk about my day, Narcissus." I pressed a kiss to the side of his temple, going against everything in my nature. I did not hold on to lovers past the embrace of release, but perhaps it was because he would be the last before I gave myself over to the weight of responsibility or maybe the cadence of his breathing on the air against my skin gave me courage.

"Tell me about your intended then," he whispered back. I shook my head, not wanting to think about that now, unable to tell him or anyone else the truth about what was on the line.

So instead, I stuck to things I knew to be true.

"She is kind. Beautiful, with hair nearly the color of yours." I lifted a long strand and curled it along my fingers.

"Does she look like me?" he asked curiously, pressing his words into the skin of my bicep. I shook my head.

"No. You're quite different, in that regard. Both lovely. Rest now," I commanded gently. His body burrowed back against mine, and with a contented sigh, his eyes fluttered closed.

"Will you be here, when I wake in the morning . . . ?" His voice trailed off in a sleepy timbre, his breathing slowed to a gentle rise and fall, his chest pressed against mine. I buried my nose in his hair, taking in the smell of nectar, of the moonlight and grass and sex on his skin.

"Would that I could," I whispered sadly, softly, letting myself one more moment of contentment with him in my arms. All night, I watched him sleep, watched the stars dancing across his cheeks, the breeze ruffling the strands of his hair, the salty sweat dry against his skin. I allowed myself this moment of selfishness at this unlikely connection, this stranger, who felt more familiar than my own heart, laying in my arms. I allowed myself to indulge in conversation when he'd rouse to consciousness and enjoyed the sound of his breathing when sleep reclaimed him.

And when the first purples of dawn pulled me from the ground to do my work, I lifted Narcissus and carried him inside the small dwelling he'd fashioned just beyond the trees, laying him in the comfort of his own bed, pressing my lips against his for just another taste.

The last taste.

Hoofbeats underfoot covered the sound of what must have been my heart breaking as I rode off toward my destiny, to bring in a new dawn.

Hades

CHAPTER 9

I returned to the Underworld only briefly, enough to satiate the terms of my reign in the Hells. I couldn't stay top-side for extended periods, but there were loopholes, and I intended to exploit them. I met her that next day and every day after for weeks. We walked through the woods, and I was always shocked when she stepped happily off the path for me. It was dangerous, and she was forfeiting her protection in doing so. Still, I would never let another being harm her. Not my Little Flower.

Persephone and I talked about every subject imaginable in our time together, and I savored every new layer of her she revealed to me. Her mind was sharp, and her intelligence shone through fiercely when she spoke of things dear to her. She had an insatiable curiosity about the Underworld and the River Styx. Her mother, Demeter, had kept her far removed from the den of snakes that was Mt. Olympus, something we shared. I also never returned there unless it was necessary, often finding it a mecca of vanity and petty squabbling.

Persephone's amulet dangled on my neck next to my talisman on an unbreakable chain, protecting the flora of the forest from giving up its life force to me as we moved through it. It pleased her, every time she noticed her power kept my own at bay, and I reveled in her newfound confidence.

Stretched on the forest floor, Persephone rested in my arms as we looked up into the sky together. Her warmth was contagious, my skin craving her contact nearly constantly now. I held her hand between mine, stroking my thumb lazily at the soft flesh of her wrist, tracing the lines of sunlight peeking through the trees as it danced along her skin. She had drifted into a slumber some time ago, and I watched as her full lips pulled up into a content smile, her chest rising and falling in tandem with mine.

Peaks of her tanned skin lay exposed under the soft pink fabric of her gown as it bunched around the thigh she had hiked over my leg, and it was testing every ounce of my control to keep my hands to myself. I allowed my eyes to roam over her resting form, a rare opportunity because, if she was awake, her gaze held mine in an unrelenting stare and I could never bring myself to look away from the swirling greens of her irises. Her long, pale hair fell in curly locks, splayed across the forest floor, and as she rested at my side, I curled a piece between my fingers, so soft and shiny. The golden strands danced in the sunlight breaking through the shade.

Persephone's cheeks were full, the dimple that appeared when she smiled present as she slumbered. Her arm lay flung across my torso, golden bangles tinkling around her wrist whenever she moved even slightly. This was the most contact we had yet shared, and while I longed for her, knowing our worlds could never collide, I relished how easily she let me hold her. It was like caressing a small sun, warm and healing, and I was a god starved by the cold. Persephone was a goddess of growth, and that power pulsed from her in her form.

Her body was bountiful and curved, her stomach soft, her chest supple. I had never seen a more beautiful woman, and I'd risk Aphrodite's wrath to tell her so. Persephone thought she was a lower goddess, but I could never believe that, not after tasting her power. Her lashes dusted her cheeks as she slept, the depth of my attraction for her growing to an unbearable obsession as she pulled closer to me. In the Underworld, she was all I thought about, my night's torment as I counted down the seconds until she could meet me again.

I loved seeing her smile; I loved hearing her run off on tangents about the species of flora and how they interacted, loved her laugh. I just . . . loved *her*. Impossibly, irrevocably, I was setting myself up for a heartache I wasn't sure I could survive because, even though I'd known since the moment I smelled her scent, earth and flora and sweet sunshine, that this was going to be more than just a passing moment, I was realistic enough to know that nothing this beautiful could last in my arms. Curiosity had turned to attraction, attraction to obsession, and now I knew that there was no turning back for me. Long after she'd found someone to love her in the light, I'd be returning to the memory of her in my arms to get me through the still of the night for the rest of my life. That first night on the banks, I had gone back to the palace and lost myself to a fantasy of taking her right there in the meadow, the image of her naked form splayed below me, skin flushed as I pressed inside of her . . . just thinking about it did dark things to me.

Now that I had gotten to know her, seen the brilliant light she harbored inside, I *craved* her. Enough to nearly offer up anything to be with her. Zeus, Poseidon, and I shared power—dividing the mortal realm between us after our defeat of Cronus. I was happy with my spoils of war, had everything I needed there in the Underworld, but I would surrender it if she only asked.

But she wouldn't, and I couldn't leave my people. Unlimited shades to fuel my power and no expectations from the public eye made for peaceful living. My brothers needed worship to fill their cups, but I didn't. The beautiful thing about the inevitability of death was that it came for all mortals whether they liked it or not. They had to believe in it because it just *was*.

I'd watched silently from the Underworld as my "brothers" fornicated and procreated with no regard for what they were putting their children or partners through. Poseidon and Zeus had dozens of children as a result of their various escapades. I had never fathered progeny and had no plans to do so. Not that I hadn't had my fun, I just remained vigilant that a child was never produced. Those days were over, the thought of touching another sent a visceral unease through me. As much as I wanted Persephone, I would settle for whatever she was willing to give me. If that was friendship and companionship only, so be it. As long as she allowed me to love her and be near her, I was more than capable of taking care of my desires privately.

Fates, it was difficult to function with her body pressed against me so intimately. Persephone whimpered, and I gazed down in concern just as the goddess adjusted her leg, locking it around mine, pressing her warm core against my thigh. The heat pooled around me and I felt my cock stir as she began to wind herself slowly on my leg, stars dancing behind my eyes as I sucked in deep breaths. I froze, unsure of what to do as her hands roamed over my abdomen, the folds of my cloak doing little to separate our bodies, desperate for those hands to travel lower. I needed her to wake so we could get some distance before I gave in to my baser desires.

"Persephone," I groaned softly, cupping her cheek. She moaned and leaned farther into me, pressing her body flush. My breath hitched, and the urge to touch her more overwhelmed me, but I held fast. I shouldn't take liberties with this situation, I knew. With a groan, I placed my hand on the soft, exposed skin of her back between the folds of her flowing gown to shake her body, but the moan she let out almost made me come undone.

"Persephone, *please wake up*," I pleaded. Her hands continued to roam over my body, and I gritted my teeth as I hardened beneath her, nearly too far gone to recover.

"Hades, don't stop." She let out a throaty moan, and my heart stopped beating. *My name*. She'd moaned my name. I watched, stunned, as she continued to grind against me, searching for her release. I couldn't help it; she was so needy, so perfect. I slid my thumb across her bottom lip, and she parted them for me, taking me into her mouth as she sucked hard. *By the Hells, I wouldn't survive this*. I was so close, just witnessing what she was doing, that I could have found release at any moment.

"PERSEPHONE!" I hissed, much louder this time. She sprang awake, disoriented, hair wild, and looking extremely sensual. Her breath came in ragged spurts, and I felt guilty for waking her before her climax. She took in the scene before us, her disheveled tunic and my leg still trapped between both of hers. I knew she could feel my length pressed into her abdomen, and her eyes grew wide.

"Hades, I'm so sorry," she choked out, hastily pulling herself to her feet. I hated the sensation of her warmth leaving me. Cold enveloped me once more and I fought the urge to growl out a command for her to lay back down, part of me curious how she would respond. I should be responsible, should end this here, but Persephone's cheeks reddened, flushed with embarrassment, but also with a hint of something *more*. She had said my name. Moaned it. Had she been feeling the same as I? Her body certainly seemed to be mirroring my own desires, and Fates be damned, I needed to know.

For weeks I'd walked with her, tasted her dreams and opinions, as she told me about all the things in this realm she would see changed if she had the power. I'd feasted on her scent, the way she'd showed passion in her convictions. Still, I had not dared to hope that there could ever be something more. That someone so beautiful and radiant could want such a dark, twisted thing. Persephone hastily pulled the folds of her dress down from her hips, covering the swell of her thighs, and my heart constricted, disappointed at the visual loss. The embarrassed blush of her cheeks was so delectable it made me want to devour her. I could feel how hot she was, the heat of lust still circling low around us like a fog.

"You must think I'm horrible," she groaned. I chuckled, casting my eyes low. If only she knew how much I'd wished I could have witnessed that dream firsthand.

"Persephone, it's okay. Do you remember how we met? When you saw me in the river . . ." Heat flooded her cheeks again, and if possible, she turned an even darker shade of crimson. It was so lovely, and my mind wandered to thoughts of how much redder I could make her skin. Would it flush with desire if I touched her again? Kissed her? Fucked her?

"That isn't the same, you thought you were alone," she chided, folding her arms. I sighed, trying to soothe her worries in any way that I could, while shaking away the mental image of her wearing my cum from my mind.

"And you were sleeping, Little Flower," I assured her. Her eyes flitted down to the imprint straining against my himation, the fabric doing nothing to hide the length of my hardened cock from view. Her green eyes shifted back to mine, and a question lingered there in her gaze.

"And that?" she asked, her voice barely a whisper. My throat tightened. There was no need to lie, so I opted for the honesty I had been holding inside.

"You are an incredibly beautiful goddess, Persephone. Intoxicating even. How could I not respond, when you were so close to falling apart on top of me, my name tumbling from your lips in a moan?" The words fell from me, ignoring all manners of propriety. Something in her look had emboldened me, and I wanted to know if I affected her as much as she did me. A dark look crossed her face, as she bit her lip, the power in my chest surging toward her.

"I moaned your name?" she asked curiously. I nodded, as Persephone took a tentative step into my space. "And d-did you like that?" Her voice came out strained, as though she was fighting every instinct within her to flee. I stood instantly, closing the space between us, wrapping my hands around the base of her neck. She felt so good there, so right, the perfect fit. Persephone let out a low moan from the back of her throat that shot right to my cock.

"You cloud every thought in my mind, every second of every day," I whispered as my lips brushed her ear. *This was a very bad idea*, I reminded myself as I pulled her closer to me. Beautiful things did not abide dead things. *Still*. Persephone's arms snaked up my chest, and I felt her fingers clasp the chain there. My knees buckled and took my self-control with them as I ran my nose along her temple, inhaling that addictive scent.

"I have thought about taking you in every way imaginable in this realm. I've spilled myself as I fell apart with visions of you riding me, restrained beneath me, suspended above me, your name a curse upon my lips. I am damned, my flower. You are a divine, pure thing. The most I can have of you is in those thoughts. Watching you, hearing you . . . it was better than I ever could have imagined. You gave me an incredible gift and a curse. I'll never be able to forget what that felt like, looked like, *sounded* like. I will always carry that memory."

The words tumbled from my lips, a dark truth I held inside like the last epic that would ever be recited by the poets. Persephone's eyes bored into mine, glistening. I could feel her heart hammering through our clothing and a second heartbeat, pulsing from deep inside the apex of her thighs, calling to me like a siren song that wrapped around my chest, tethering me to her. I looked for fear or disdain or disgust, certain I would find it in her gaze, but there was nothing but desire, and a look of determination the likes of which I had never seen before.

"So, take me," she whispered. I stared at her in shock and disbelief as she stared right back at me, defiant. Rational thought left my being as I tried to reconcile what she had just said to me.

Sensing my hesitation, Persephone slipped her fingers down my stomach, pushing beneath the fabric of my robes, taking me into her hand. My eyes rolled to the back of my head as she gripped both sides of my cock and gave a long, languid stroke with slightly shaking fingers. I groaned and dropped my head into the crook of her neck, tracing kisses to her shoulder, her inexperience and want of exploration heightening my pleasure.

"You are darkness and adventure, and I want all of you. I don't care if we devour each other; it's our choice," she vowed. Her hands, those delicate, sweet hands picked up the pace, and I knew if she kept this speed I'd be undone. Reluctantly, I grabbed her hands and pulled them up to my chest, pressing kisses to the pads of her fingers. Confused and a little hurt, she tried to pull out of my embrace, sensing rejection. I growled and spun her around, pulling her into my chest, walking her forward as I pressed her front against a large tree. She gasped as I nipped her shoulder before kissing my way down her spine. This could be the only chance we have together, and I couldn't waste it with uncertainty.

"Grab the tree, Little Flower, I need to taste you," I commanded, dropping to my knees. If I was bound to the Hells for eternity, I was going to earn it. I pushed her thighs apart gently, before settling down behind her. Persephone grabbed each side of the bark before looking over her shoulder at me with unbridled lust clouding her gaze. I gathered the fabric of her dress in my hands and pushed it to the side, exposing her bare ass, a low groan leaving my throat as I took her in. It was beautiful, round, sticking high into the air for me as she arched her back. My hands splayed across each cheek just above two small dimples on each side, my fingers digging into her soft flesh.

"Hades," she gasped as I spread her apart and buried my face between them, lapping my tongue against her warm cunt. Persephone let out an earth-shaking moan as I lapped my tongue between her lips, ravenous to taste every part of her, desperate to feast. Her cunt was sweet and hot and dripped with the nectar of the gods, and I groaned against her flesh with each pass of my tongue, each gentle scrape of my teeth.

In all my eons of existence, I had never tasted such divinity.

I pushed inside her as she bucked her hips, moaning my name, clinging desperately to the bark to keep upright while I devoured her. My tongue swirled over her clit, the swollen bundle hard and needy under my lips as I sucked and nibbled around it. I brought my hand up and pulled back as she whimpered in protest, desperately wanting more, but I had to give my body a rest, her taste in my mouth had nearly sent me over. I dragged two fingers around her clit, coating them in her slick before thrusting, lithely, inside of her channel. She arched her head back, panting and biting a bruise onto her lower lip that left me in awe at the vision of her. Persephone's long hair tangled down her back in chaotic curls, tickling her exposed flesh.

She rocked her hips in slow circles as my fingers continued to work inside of her, coaxing her closer to the edge. Her hands dropped to the globes of her ass, and I watched transfixed as she gripped her flesh with command and spread wide for me, putting herself on full display. My tongue flitted across my lips, savoring each taste as hunger burned through me. She had permitted me to devour her, to destroy her.

And so, I would.

I dipped my head back down, burying my face between her cheeks and tracing my tongue higher and higher until I circled the tight ring above her entrance. Persephone let out a broken moan and clamped hard around my fingers as they worked inside of her. My cock wept at the thought of her tight cunt wrapped around my shaft, milking me dry in a vice grip. I kissed her rim, edging my tongue with sure strokes farther inside, driven by the needy whines and pants escaping her body as she writhed above me.

"That's my good girl," I praised, blowing slightly over her exposed core. "Are you ready to come for me, Little Flower?" Persephone's knees buckled with the pleasure my praise lent her, but I lifted her easily and pinned her more securely against the tree. My lips laid slow, dizzying kisses between her cheeks, and she cried out a strangled sound, unable to formulate a proper response. I slowed my fingers and matched their stroke with the speed of my tongue, once again working into her as I summoned my shadows, willing them to grow and harden.

They began flowing from my fingertips, filling her and exploring every crevice until I knew she would be impossibly full. The tremble of her body, the shy, uninhibited way she chased her pleasure, ripped something open inside of me. I knew that I was the first to taste her, the first she trusted to have this part of her, and I would do everything, anything to make sure she never regretted that trust. My shadows curled deep inside, stretching her wide as her body jerked hard, giving me all the permission I needed to pump into her with more fervor. I moved over her relentlessly, allowing a piece of my shadows to grow forth from the tip of my tongue, seeking and searching deep inside of her. Persephone ground her core onto my face harder, frantically riding me, so beautiful as she chased her high. She released her cheeks and wrapped my hair in a death grip, smashing me farther into her sweet flesh, and I loved it, craved her taste, wanted it engraved against my psyche. I groaned, the proof of her pleasure pushing me closer to the edge.

I knew she would be full, with my shadows and fingers and tongue skewering her in place, relentless in the pursuit of her release, but I didn't expect her to be such a magnificent mess.

Persephone shuddered, a lightning bolt shooting up her spine, sending her into convulsive shakes as I coaxed her first orgasm from her. My name tumbled over and over from her lips, breathy and spent before I felt her body weight collapse. Her voice imprinted itself into the marrow of who I was, and I knew that from that moment on I would be forever changed.

Breathing hard and looking at me over her shoulder, her hooded eyes were heavy with satisfaction and lust. I swept my shadows in and slowly, tenderly pulled out of her. She pouted, so much emptier, but I just pulled her dress down, fixing it across the swells of her cheeks. My lips kissed a trail up her back and into her hair as she nuzzled her back against my chest.

"That was *incredible*, Hades," she panted, still attempting to center herself. I wrapped my arms around her soft middle, holding her with everything I had. Her hair was wild, with tree bark peppered through her long curls, and a few bite marks around her thighs sent a prideful smirk to my lips. Her eyes shone with power, and I knew she had been rejuvenated by what we had done, liberated in the exploration of her desire. I let my fingers gently collar her throat, pulling up slightly as I bent forward to kiss her full lips, letting her taste herself on my tongue.

"My Little Flower," I claimed, holding her tightly against me. Her smooth skin slid against mine, still flushed. "You did so well, falling apart for me." Persephone let out a small moan, and I made a note of how much she'd responded to that. Demeter had always been selfish, but her mothering of Persephone seemed to have brought that streak out in the worst of ways. I could work on that, make it good for her, give her the tools she needed to build her confidence and take what she wanted.

With her body resting against me, I swore to myself I would give the Goddess of Spring whatever she needed to thrive.

"More, Hades," she groaned, grinding into me, "I want more." The friction she made caused me to buck my hips into her firm bottom and the last of my resolve crumbled. I would take her in every way she would have me. The temptation to slide her dress to the side and bury my cock in that tight ring of hers drew a guttural moan from deep inside, my self-control nearly snapping as my hand gently tightened around her throat, testing her comfort. Her encouraging moans spurred me on, and I stared at her in awe, wondering where she came from. So prefect, built for me . . .

"There's so much I want to do," I began, before a strong voice cut through the woods, calling out to her.

"PERSEPHONE!" The word was instantly sobering, and I could feel her tense up, the scent of fear radiating from her. A low growl escaped me. What man caused this response in her? Whoever it was had chased all the lust from her eyes and the madness within me threatened to come apart in a tidal wave.

"It's Helios!" she hissed, worry lacing her tone as she pulled away from me, attempting to fix her hair. "He can't see you. If he tells Mother, she will never let me out again." Persephone straightened herself as I scanned the trees. She reached up to place a hot kiss on my lips, commanding and breathless before bounding away. I was left in the clearing alone and sporting a raging hard-on, but also a burning satisfaction that I had just given Persephone her first taste of pleasure. There was no going back, I knew. She would belong to me, and I would spend eternity worshipping her in whatever way she would have me.

Persephone
CHAPTER 10

"SEPH—" Helios's thundering voice boomed up from the path. I ran quickly toward it, pulling twigs from the fabric of my dress, attempting to tame my unruly hair as I made haste. My lips stung with the bite from Hades's kisses, and I could only hope they had not yet started to bruise.

"PERSEP—" Helios bellowed as my feet slapped the familiar dirt path.

"I'M HERE!" I shouted, rounding the corner. Helios's hulking frame took up most of the pathway. I could see the thick vein in his neck strained as his eyes scanned the path. "Helios, quit shouting; I'm right here," I chastised, willing my breathing to return to normal.

"Where were you?" he demanded, stopping me in my tracks as his gaze raked over me, his overprotectiveness catching me off guard. I stared back, anger rising within my chest.

"I fell asleep under the olive trees. I only woke up when I heard you yelling. Lower your voice," I demanded. Helios's eyes instantly softened with what looked like relief, and when he spoke, his tone was much gentler.

"Your mother said you had been gone for too long. She's preparing the ground for the harvest and couldn't come to find you. I was worried when she said you were on the forest path." He rubbed a large hand through the reddish golden strands of his hair, looking down sheepishly.

I felt my anger recede at his concern. Helios was my friend, one of the very few I counted as such, and I knew better than anyone how dramatic my mother could be. I folded my arms across my chest, willing my heartbeat to slow before it gave away what I had been up to.

"Helios, I know you're the God of the Sun, but I need you to keep that hot-headed, impulsive anger in check unless you plan on beating up a tree. Which, I may add, as the Goddess of the Spring, I would never allow." Helios threw his head back and let out a loud bark of a laugh, wrapping an arm around mine, guiding us toward home. A thousand times in as many years he'd done it, but I had to suppress the urge to shrink back from his touch in the wake of what I'd experienced with Hades. Helios's body was hot, too hot, nothing like the cool fire that spread over my skin whenever the God of the Dead touched me.

My mother had always loved Helios and had made many not-so-subtle comments about how good a union he and I would make, but I'd never felt even a passing pull toward the Titan of the Sun. I studied him as we walked, taking in his large body, the towering broad frame more tanned than mine. He was strong, his thick muscles rippling under his golden armor as we walked. His fiery golden-red hair floated on the breeze in short tufts as he moved. The smile on his lips was dazzling, but most importantly, he was kind to me. Slightly quick to anger, but always willing to be chastised for his actions. In all ways that didn't matter to me in the slightest, he was perfect. Just not for me. I knew there was pressure for him to take a goddess consort soon, arrangements made among the gods that I was never allowed to be privy to, but I listened when the others talked, a wallflower barely noticed.

I did all I could to feign interest as my mind wandered, ensnared by a set of striking blue eyes, the vision of his head buried between my thighs, the wicked things his tongue had made me feel . . . Helios made conversation about the weather and harvest while I walked beside him, thighs soaked with the evidence of what Hades and I had just done, and for a moment, I considered confiding in him. Telling someone, anyone, of the hauntingly beautiful face that had become the focus of all my daydreaming lately. Hades had kissed me, made me feel alive. More than that, he had *wanted* me, in every fiber of his being. I could feel his desire when he'd touched me, felt his arousal pressed against my body and I wanted more, Fates I wanted so much more than that stolen moment in the meadow.

For weeks I had been yearning for him, savoring any moment he reached to touch me, willing him to press farther, dreaming about those blue eyes alight with desire, worshipping my very shade. Having had a taste of him, the only thing I was sure of was my need for *more*, I just didn't know how to go about it. Inexperience plagued me, but Helios was a skilled lover, and it was no secret that he enjoyed the freedom of his trysts. I weighed the consequences, the chances that he would tell my mother about what I had done with my need for advice, when his words slammed against me, bursting the bubble of bliss I'd been traveling in.

". . . and when we make the journey to Olympus to receive Zeus's public blessing, I can show you the throne room and the great gardens. You'll love them." My heart stopped as I snapped my attention to the Titan of the Sun, who just rambled on unawares.

"Wait, back that up for me? What blessing?" I asked, confused. Helios's cheeks reddened slightly, as he dragged his hand through his waves.

"Oh. Demeter hasn't spoken with you yet, I see."

Helios pressed on. "We have been set to wed. The approvals have come down from Olympus through the official channels."

I yanked my body away from his, halting us in our tracks, fury and shock flooding my senses.

"Excuse me?" My voice low and deadly. "When exactly was I to be consulted about this?" Rage laced my tone as Helios's eyes widened in shocked confusion, that I wouldn't be happy to be shackled to someone like him.

The hubris had me shaking my head as I blew past him, my feet on a crash course straight to the source. I shouldn't have been shocked, I had feared that, when the time came, something like this would happen. I even resigned myself to it, knowing that my feelings would make no difference in the end for whoever *she* chose as my intended, but that was before. Before Hades. Before he had touched my shade, crashed through my world in a swirl of smoke and darkness, offered me comfort and pleasure I'd never fathomed could exist. I couldn't give him up; I wouldn't.

I wouldn't.

Helios followed as I stormed off the pathway toward our lands, all the while attempting to talk to me. I ignored him as my vision clouded red, thundering through the back fields, past the mortals working to till the grains for harvest.

My mother sat elegantly on her throne behind her altar, wheat and silks stacked high with carafes of deep summer wine spread around the stone table, looking more than pleased with herself.

"Mother," I spat, venom laced in my tone like never before. Her eyes flicked from me to Helios, who to his credit, had the good grace to hang back. I supposed I should thank him for telling me, the faster for me to correct any notion that I would be marrying the titan. Her eyebrow arched as she considered my tone, the anger in it. "I have been informed today that I am to become Helios's wife." My voice shook with anger, but there was a hurt there too, at the lack of consideration for my own choices. My mother studied me carefully, and I felt flayed under the weight of her gaze, of the scrutiny I knew would follow. She was precise with her barbs, somehow always able to see right down to the weakness in me and drag it forward for all to see.

"Helios, I fear that I need to speak with my daughter. The news of your engagement has clearly overwhelmed the goddess, and we seek a moment of privacy." She spoke over my head, as though I were nothing more than a heap of linens between the two of them, her voice soft and demure as if apologizing to him for my outburst.

"Of course. Persephone." He dipped his chin to me, the crease in his brow still prominent as his gaze darted from the serenity of my mother's face to the raging storm on mine. She waited for the large door to close and his footsteps to echo down the hall before her smile fell, her cold stare a brand against me. I knew I should wait for her to speak, but I was too angry, vibrating apart at the seams with my indignation. I balled my hands into fists at my side and sucked in a deep breath.

"I will not be Helios's wife," I vowed, straightening my chin. The fury at my insolence in her eyes reflected in the snarl uncurling her full lip.

"You will. I wouldn't think this was a shock, Persephone. You are the Goddess of Growth. He is the Titan of the Sun. The population is growing, and we need more food to feed these mortals. Your children will help continue the fruitful bounty of this realm, *as is all our duty.* You cannot turn a blind eye from the responsibility of your birthright, Persephone Kore. This union pleases me, as well as your father. Accords have been made, what's done will be done." She spoke with finality, the matter settled in her mind, but I shook my own head.

"You cannot command me to do this," I whispered, hating the plea in my voice. Her slender frame rose from her throne, cocking her head to the side as she searched my face, with each step closing the distance between us.

"Is he not a kind titan?" she asked, and I reluctantly nodded, knowing it to be the truth. "He is handsome and powerful, Persephone. He will make a good husband, and our power will be cemented." Her voice had taken on a lowered tone, and though I knew it was manipulation, I was powerless to stop the pull in my heart, the deeply broken and damaged parts that longed for the adoring look on her face to be real, the concern in her touch to be genuine as a mother comforting a daughter.

"The tulip fields you grew were scorched clear. Helios's work, was it not? He's seen your darkness, Persephone, and he was still willing to take your hand. We may not find another who would be so benevolent, with the shortfalls of your power," she pressed gently, bringing her hand up to cradle my cheek. Embarrassment rushed through me, hot tears stinging the back of my eyes, flushing my cheeks with warmth.

"I do not love him, Mother," I pleaded, one last desperate, pathetic attempt to pull empathy from the woman who gave me life. Tiny lines tightened around the corner of her lips as she studied me, the grip on my face turning just a hair harsher.

"Oh, my girl. I think we should be realistic about expectations. He is the best we are likely to do for you, Persephone. We can't afford to be choosy, no?"

Her words struck against me like slaps. I felt the judgment in her tone, the disappointment in her eyes, as she looked me over. I was not as fair as she, not as lithe or as in control of my power. My mouth opened, then closed, ready to argue my point, but instead of shaking with rage, it was only defeat that flowed through my veins. *And our power will be cemented* . . . Not our power, but *her* power. Her grasp on the realm, power she'd schemed and clawed back from the other Olympians, from Hades. In her desperation to bolster her own position, I knew my mother would not budge for something as comical as my happiness. It was never about what I wanted or needed, only what I could provide. I knew she expected me to submit to her command as I'd always done, and because there was nothing more to say, I fell silent.

"That's my girl," she praised, but the words felt hollow against me, the empty platitudes just more twists of the reality she had created for me. My hands shook as my world caved in on me with stunning clarity. My entire existence I had done as I was told, been the constant, obedient goddess. I brought forth the spring and bloomed the flowers. No matter how harsh the winter was, I was proof that resilience and obligation could spark any growing season. But this was too much. I'd had enough.

Hades's taste was still on my tongue, his handprints still shadows on my body. I would not give that up for any of them, and it was that thought that fueled my last effort, that had me rounding on her, talking back in a way I'd never done before.

"I will not stand for this. If you think I would let you and Father—" I was cut off by a sharp gesture, the mask of the doting, loving mother gone in an instant at my challenge. Demeter's hand dropped from my face as she stood in front of me, power radiating from her in warbling waves. I saw it then, the shift. Her willingness to shackle me to someone whom I did not love, just because it pleased *her*. I was nothing more than property to her, to Zeus. They were not parents to me, not really. We eyed each other, and in hers I saw the reflection of my face, my being. I saw her selfishness disguised as overprotectiveness, her hubris. Yes, somewhere deep down there was love, but it was long buried under resentment. I knew my mother loved me, but I think there was something inside of me that reminded her too much of things she didn't love about herself. She worked endlessly to stamp those parts of me out.

But they were *mine*.

"You don't have a choice. We've let you go unmarried for too long. I should have insisted you marry centuries ago, instead of indulging your immature whims, but enough is enough. The hourglass has run short, my petal. You *will* marry Helios, and you *will* bear his children. There is nothing more to discuss. It's time for you to grow up," she snapped.

I wanted to rage, to cry and scream and yell, but I knew it was no use. Instead, I let the current of anger wash just beneath the surface of my skin, fanning a tiny spark of rebellion, a blue flame that I clung to with everything within me.

Something cold coiled low in my belly, and instantly I recalled the way Hades's hands had roamed over my skin. *He* was the one I wanted, and he wanted me as well. He was of the big three: Zeus, Poseidon, and Hades. If anyone could stop this union, surely it was him? I set my jaw and looked at my mother with distaste.

"When do you plan on trading me off like chattel?"

She barked a laugh. "Such theatrics." I thought of Helios, wondering why he would have agreed to this in the first place. Had I led him on, thinking this was something I'd wanted? I thought back on the years of friendship, and I could find no evidence of it. No, if he wanted this, then he had done what men do, go for something without any regard for consent or remorse, for how their wants would affect others. My mind went instantly to Hades, who'd asked before even touching me, apologized after I'd nearly mauled him, who cared about my comfort, my pleasure. It could be like that, with the right person. Helios was not that person for me. I felt my heart instantly harden against him.

"The audience with Zeus is in three days, but the pact is set," Mother replied coolly. Beyond the window, I observed the mortals toiling in the fields, envious of their freedom to choose. Their lives were short, but the kind of commitment a life together meant for our kind was a shackle around my neck, threatening to drag me into the Pits. There may have been a time I would have accepted this, done my duty as I was told with Helios, but I did not want a life with someone I did not love, who I now could barely tolerate because of this betrayal. I wanted Hades.

And I would have him.

Persephone

CHAPTER 11

I made my way down the grand stairs of our villa, into my garden chambers with a sense of calm settled over me. The soft, mossy floor muffled my steps, the vines decorating the stone walls bursting with flowers and fruits as I took it all in. I called for the servants to bring me water for the large stone basin in my private chambers, and once it was filled with steaming water, I thanked and dismissed my attendants. I needed quiet while I planned.

Carefully, I pinned my hair into large loops on my head before untying the thick golden straps that held my sandals secure. I stepped out of them completely, relishing the feel of the moss beneath my feet. The pink folds of my chiton were still wrapped around me, a few bits of fabric clinging to my skin with the remnants of my arousal from Hades's handiwork. Unclasping the broaches that held the fabric, I shimmied out of the thick folds of delicate fabric, allowing it to pool at my feet before I sank into the hot water.

Dozens of rose petals and lavender bits floated lazily on top of the bath, the heat steaming them and staining the liquid a dark hue. I closed my eyes as a soft hum escaped my lips, the warmth working through my tense muscles. Some of the spots where Hades had touched me were left cooler to the touch, and I relished in the effect the God of the Underworld had on me. I had badly wanted to speak with him, to hear the deep intonations of his voice assure me all would be well.

I should have told him how I felt about him earlier, should have had the courage to pull the billows of his black chlamys away from his body and sink my core onto him. I had seen mortals do it time and time again, never having the urge to try it out myself, but I could figure it out. My fingers danced across swollen lips, still bitten by Hades's kisses. I squeezed my knees together at the pressure building, holding back the whine in my throat. I needed him, and judging from the way his cock had strained against my hand, the way his eyes rolled back when I'd stroked him, he needed me too. The pull I felt for him was too strong; there was nothing left to do but to go to him tomorrow and tell him everything. If the Fates smiled upon me, I would make the God of the Dead mine.

I slept peacefully, dreaming of our time together in the forest, and awoke before the sun stretched out in the sky. Time was short, if I wanted to avoid Helios's gaze as he ushered in the dawn. He would be fixed on me, and even through the thick foliage of the forest, the sun's rays could penetrate. I shuffled out of my bed linens, stretching my naked form to the sky. With a strength of resolve I wasn't sure belonged to me, I strode to my closet and donned my darkest chiton, dyed a deep fuchsia, nearly the color of some of the corrupted flora. I pinned it with gold brooches and set my hair, twisting my curls into loose rings. The chiton gathered seductively around my hips, dipped low against my chest, slightly exposing the swells of my breasts.

I laced up my golden sandals and donned long jewels I never bothered wearing, leaning into the confidence I had been fostering these last weeks. Finally, I was ready for war, my armor intact.

Not a shade detected my movements as I made my way through the shadows, willing them to cloak me and deliver me to their master. I ran swiftly along the path I knew so well and turned to step off at our usual meeting place, the River, with an excited tremor rocking through me.

Hades had explained to me that it was a source of the Styx, and as long as he dipped into it occasionally during our visits, he wouldn't have remained topside too long. The purples of the hours just before dawn illuminated the forest in a blue glow, and as I reached the banks, I willed my galloping heart to calm. I had no idea when he would come, only sure in the knowledge that he *would*. I dropped to my knees, pressing my palms against the ground and prayed to him, willing my plea to burst through the cacophony of wails and lost shades.

And hear me he did.

The surface of the River began to glow, bubbling forth until his mighty form broke the surface. The impossibly blue water glistened as it flowed down his frame, clinging to him in glowing rivulets. The image of him emerging from the depths of Hells for me, his alert stare raking down my body, sent flames down my spine. Dark eyes bore into mine, intensely searching, and I could see the lust as his muscles rippled in response to my appearance. I smirked. He liked the dress.

"Little Flower?" he questioned as he reached me, his clothing instantly drying as he stepped from the depths. My expression must have given me away because he stopped just short of my body and reached for my face. "What has happened?" I gave him a nervous smile, steeling my resolve.

"I have a question for you, and I need you to answer with the fiercest honesty you can muster," I began, feeling scared but determined. Hades tilted his head slowly, taking me in. That gaze, that piercing gaze, would strike me dead if I wasn't careful. He nodded. Staring into his eyes I sucked in a sharp breath, bracing my nerves, and asked him the one question that could shatter my world.

"Am I yours? And are you mine?" Hades stilled his hands inches from my face. His eyes flicked to the hollow in my throat, as though measuring the heartbeats there. This question wasn't a declaration of love—it was a declaration of *intention*, the way our kind proposed an eternity together, the way Helios would have done in front of the gathered of Olympus. I felt the tension build the longer Hades hesitated, and against my will, tears stung the back of my eyes. I wondered if I had completely misread the moments between us. Fates, Hades was the God of the Underworld. He'd had many flings over the eons he had ruled, surely. Of course this was just another tryst for him. How naive could I be? I turned my face down, cursing the tears that fell. Hades looked alarmed and grabbed my shoulders, willing me to look at him.

"What has happened, Persephone?" I flinched at his use of my name, longing for his lips to call me goddess or his Little Flower. I wrenched away from his grip, embarrassed as my mother's words washed over me on a loop. She had been right; I was broken, and unworthy and clung to the first kind hand that touched me. *Fates.*

"Nothing, I misread the situation. My apologies, my Lord," I dipped my head low in a bow, avoiding his gaze, but Hades's firm grip locked around my chin, gently pulling me up to face him.

"Little Flower, if you don't tell me what's happened, I will break my vow and burn this world to ash. Why are you so upset?" Staring into his eyes, all I could see was concern and conviction, and a spark of hope flared in my chest. I hesitated and he clicked his tongue in warning, features steely as he looked me over. Hades was a patient god, but a god nonetheless, and they did not like to be kept waiting. I knew he would do it, would scorch the Earth if I didn't tell him what he needed to know. With his face so close to mine, I could feel his breath fanning my lips as he struggled to control himself.

"Helios has asked for my hand and they have accepted . . . We have an audience on Olympus in three days for the formal blessing. I have no choice." Hades's eyes softened, a sad line crippling his handsome face between his eyebrows. His grip turned gentle, moving to cup my cheek. I leaned into it.

"Helios is a good titan. He could take care of you, walk with you in the sun." I flinched away from him, unable to hear the resignation in his voice. As far as rejections went, he was trying to let me down easily, and I hated him for his gentleness. Anger roiled inside of me, my body exhausted and tuned up from the whiplash of emotions hurtling through me. Hades must have thought me such a fool, throwing myself at him. Even if he did feel for me, why would he bind himself to me after such a short time? My ears burned, bile bubbling in my throat. I needed to get out of here.

"I understand and accept your answer, Lord Hades. Good day," I managed to choke out between breaths, humiliation burning inside my chest. My lungs felt like they were too full, about to burst. Using all the strength I could muster, I broke free from his considerable grip. Shocked, Hades stumbled back but wasted no time reaching for me again before I could clear his hold. Those cool fingers slipped around my waist, burning me with cold flames where his skin touched mine through the straps of my gown. I shivered.

"Little Flower—" he began, but my blood ran hot, boiling over. I rounded to face him, anger rolling off me.

"How dare you?" I demanded, stepping toward him. He stepped back slightly, and emboldened, I pressed in just as I had that first day in this very spot, when I realized what he'd done to the flora. That pendant hung over his heart, and hurt pierced through me when my eyes fell upon it.

"I apologize for my delusions. How asinine must I have been to assume your intentions this past fortnight? I admit that I was taken with you, but now I can see your true motives. What was it that drew you to me, Hades? Looking to go where no mortal or god had ventured before? What was the point of all of this . . . this tension, if you just wanted to take my body? Why waste the time with my words, cracking open my chest and digging out secrets I've shared with no other, if you just wanted to scratch an itch? So easily, you'll allow another to have me? Am I not worthy of even consideration for a life together, or was I merely a passable flesh to sheath your cock? Perhaps I should thank Helios for pressing the issue and showing me that your intentions were nothing more than carnal."

His mood shifted on a breath, the anger building between his shoulders as he tensed, a living force in the air around him. A small part of me recoiled, and somewhere in the back of my brain, a voice reminded me I was addressing one of the three most powerful deities to walk this realm or any other, but I silenced it. I wanted to push him, to hurt him as I was, the flames burning inside of me reaching a fever pitch. My tongue loosened, as I ignored every instinct for self-preservation screaming at me to quiet.

"Perhaps I should call him down from the heavens now, and let him fuck me here for you to watch?"

Hades let out a hiss, and with it, tendrils of shadows billowed from his being, wrapping around me, constricting my body in place. Warning bells screamed at me that I had gone too far, pushed the God of the Dead to fury, but even as the tendrils dragged me back to him, I felt *alive*. Slowly and gently, the shadows lifted me to turn to him. Hades had not moved an inch, but his stare was murderous, his lips twisted in a snarl as his chest heaved. He stepped forward, so close to me I could feel the thrum of power radiating from his barely contained anger.

"Have you truly not been listening to me this last fortnight or are you intent on spearing me with whatever words you think will cut to the bone quickest?" he growled through gritted teeth. I stared in confusion, trying my best to concentrate on his words while my body lit up under his thrall. The tendrils of his power moved freely over my skin, leaving trails of sparks in their wake, so delicate and lovely against my flesh. The feeling was infectious, as though I was lapping up his power, soaking in it. It was intoxicating and made it very hard to focus on more than his body on mine.

"W-what do you mean?" I asked, breathless at the power buzzing through me, arresting my lungs. Hades leaned his head back, retracting some of the shadows surrounding us, lessening the pressure so I could think clearly. My heart was a hammer beating against my chest, and I felt his too, matching mine.

On the banks of the River, I saw the God of the Dead's careful control break as his frustration exploded from somewhere deep inside.

Persephone

CHAPTER 12

Hades let out a terse laugh as his long fingers ran through his hair, exasperated.

"How many different ways must I tell you what you mean to me? How many more ways to show you?" His gaze flicked down my body and I watched as his hunger returned, his need a burning inferno over me. "Centuries I've spent, content with my role and my life. I never needed to come to this realm, sometimes for decades. But now? One word from your lips has me ready to tear my kingdom apart just to stay here with you. I'm not working, and contrary to what you may believe, the Underworld does not run itself, Little Flower. Charon is covering for me as much as possible, but even when I am there, I'm not present. I can't think, can't sleep when I know you're here, too far from my grasp. I listen for your voice in the chaos in the night, desperate for a whisper, a mere whimper, all the while knowing that you are mine, and yet I cannot have you." Hades tugged at the strands of his dark locks, nearly tearing them from the root as he closed the distance between us. "I am bound by curse and duty to remain in the Underworld. I cannot remain topside. And Persephone, nothing grows in the

Hells." He cupped my cheek, all the fight deflating from his voice, his broad shoulders sagging with the weight of his admission, the finality of that simple fact.

"You couldn't survive there. Here, at least Helios could hold you in the sun. He could protect you. And I could be okay hating him and loving you from the depths of the Underworld, as long as I knew you were surviving." A bone-deep melancholy crossed his face, the depths dark and torturous, his resignation blades in his throat. How lonely an existence must he have had, with only the dead for company. My heart fractured as I pictured him alone, quiet and contemplative, watching the world above pass him by. No longer could I bear the distance between us and as I crossed the space, inches felt like leagues between us. Cold wafted from his person, so frigid I could see my breath leaving me in puffs, and when I reached for him, Hades recoiled, shutting himself and his darkness away from me.

He hesitated because he'd thought himself unworthy.

A fierce surge of protectiveness washed through me, forcing my body up on my tiptoes, my lips seeking his, and because he seemed unable to deny me, Hades acquiesced with a ragged breath, letting me taste the sadness as it dripped like honey from his lips.

"All kinds of things can grow in the cold, Hades. And the darkness. As far as my survival, if the God of the Dead falls in love with you, are you truly permitted to die?" I asked gently, savoring the feeling of his body against mine. Hades pressed his lips to my forehead, entwining his arms tightly around me. "Do not leave me to the fate of a loveless marriage, and a broken heart. Do not make me survive losing you because, I assure you, I won't. Every time he comes to me, I will die a little more inside because it would always be your hands I craved touching me, your tongue I wanted tasting me, your length I needed inside of me." I traced my fingers along his jaw, across soft lips, over high cheekbones as I pled my case.

My words were quiet but firm, and I needed him to hear them, to trust and know their sincerity. All my existence, choices had been made for me, and being the ever obedient one, I had never argued. But this was a claim I would not let go of. Hades *belonged* to me, and I to him.

"Please," the word fell from my lips, all my hopes and fears resting on one syllable. War waged behind his eyes, his sense of morality fighting against the most primal wants. We both knew what punishment this could bring down on us, what defying my father's order would mean, but I couldn't bring myself to be scared. I knew Hades could protect us; the power I felt within him was stronger than any I had ever known.

Before Hades could answer, the forest lit up with noise. His eyes shot up, searching the dense tree line behind us, on high alert. I could hear voices as well, calling through the brush.

"Persephone!" My mother's shrill voice speared through the forest, followed by that of Artemis. I had known it was only a matter of time before they realized I was gone, but we needed more time. We had moments left, and judging by the protective tightening of his grip, Hades knew it too. Thundering gallops roared above us as Helios rode his chariot across the sky, eagle eyes searching for me. I could see him swooping closer. Too soon, he would be upon us. I gripped the sides of Hades's face between my fingers and forced him to look at me properly.

"Am I yours? And are you mine?" I repeated for what could only be the final time, so softly, my voice barely a whisper.

"HADES! PERSEPHONE, STEP AWAY—" Helios roared as his chariot crashed angrily to the ground, his white horses marking up the soil around them with their giant hooves, illuminating the clearing with nearly blinding sunlight.

"You are and I am," Hades vowed, pressing his lips to mine. I felt a surge, a Bond stretch between us, lightning hot and overwhelming. I gasped into his kiss and could only vaguely hear the scuffle of Helios dismounting from his chariot, cursing obscenities in my awe. A marriage was one thing, but a Bond? Those were mystical, rare occurrences in our world, but I felt the pull there, entwining our shades together from somewhere deep inside my chest.

"HADES, IF YOU TOUCH HER—" Helios bellowed as he stalked ever closer, drawing his blazing sword. Hades stiffened, drawing up to his full height, and I could feel the power rolling off him. Great shadows burst forth, wrapping Helios in a tight embrace. Hades willed him to submit as the lesser god, but Helios, fueled by rage, fought him. If they reached each other, it would end badly for all of us. There were rules about killing gods of any rank. I grabbed Hades's arm, desperate to pull him toward the River so we could go home. *Home?* The thought struck me. Calling a place I'd never known home felt natural. I wasn't sure what that meant, but Hades's hands were on my body, and I couldn't think with him touching me. The God of the Dead attempted to pull me back behind him, ready to finish the fight, but I grabbed his himation as Helios roared.

"Please, don't kill him. He doesn't understand why I don't love him," I pleaded, and he let his gaze flick to mine, pulling all the aggression from his stare. He nodded curtly, dropping his lips to mine, never breaking Helios's glare as the Titan of the Sun heated the area to that of a supernova with his rage. He broke free of the shadows Hades had trapped him in, rocketing toward us, and I felt Hades tighten his grip. The earth around us cracked apart with a shaky groan, swallowing our bodies whole as we submerged into the soil. Hades kept his arms locked tightly around my body. We floated down and settled onto the Underworld's banks of the River Styx before he let even an inch separate us. My eyes adjusted quickly to the dimness of the Underworld, and even in the darkness, I could make out the shy smile stretched across his face. Hades held out a hand to me as he stepped forward.

"Welcome to the Asphodels, Little Flower. Welcome home."

Persephone
CHAPTER 13

The air smelled different, magical here, and I sucked in a sharp breath, taking it all in.

"Why didn't we just go through the River?" I asked. Hades dusted the soil from my shoulder and gave me a small chuckle.

"You're not a mortal, but the River would still affect you. Even gods can't venture into its waters. Only I can, maybe Thanatos. With anyone else, it would drain your essence, your god power. You'd be mortal after a little while, and then as a mortal, you'd fade, meeting the fate of the lost shades." I frowned as I looked around the great cavern, followed the walls as they stretched above us into total darkness. I made a note not to get too close to the divine, shimmering waters lapping at the banks. Above us, stone etched with ancient sigils glowed blue from the reflection of the Styx. I turned to Hades as he took my hand, guiding me toward the hulking dark palace at the base of the Styx where a waterfall fell in torrents. Hades let out a low whistle into the quietness. In moments, a ferryman appeared in a long black boat.

"Charon." Hades tilted his head in greeting. The ferryman said nothing back, but Hades grinned wide nonetheless. I studied the slight figure, cloaked in worn, brown wool. The hand holding the boat's oar seemed sickly and skeletal, and I wondered if that was why Charon kept his face shrouded by his cloak. Hades held a hand to me as the boat came to rest on the banks, lapping water toward our feet. Frowning, he lifted me bridal-style to make sure the water didn't touch my skin and carried me onto the vessel, though he made no move to remove me from his lap. I glanced nervously at Charon, cheeks pinking, but Hades only let out a small rumble of laughter.

"Charon, she can't hear you. Try speaking out loud," he instructed.

"Apologies, Your Highness," Charon's voice was gravely and haunting, sounding more like a death rattle than a man's voice. "I asked if you would be staying with us long, M'lady," Charon continued, pushing the boat along at a steady pace.

"Forever," I answered quickly, but Hades stiffened uncomfortably beneath me. I turned to look at him, confused. "Is there a time limit I'm not aware of?" I asked, cautiously. Hades lowered his gaze to meet mine, a conflicted look on his face.

"I don't want you to feel stuck here, Persephone. The ebb and flow of time works differently in the Underworld. Time can slow, but it can also move rapidly, of its own accord. What are only hours here could be months in the Upper Realms, should we wish it. You may visit the surface any time you'd like. I would never dream of holding you here against your will. But, please, allow me to escort you. Death is the enemy to many, and as Queen, you will face the same stigma."

Hades brought my hand to his lips and planted a kiss on my palm. *Queen*. I was going to be Queen of the Underworld. The boat lurched forward, forcing me to brace against Hades to stop myself from falling from his lap. He lifted me again as he stood and crossed onto the waiting shore. The god set me down on the banks and turned, pulling a lyra out to pay Charon, giving me a moment to take in the large palace that stood on the precipice of a rocky cliff. The sight moved me. Large and imposing, but stunning in its power, it seemed to be made of some sort of crystalline material, reflecting the glow of the Styx. Three great spires shot off into the dark sky, asymmetrically, the largest nestled in the middle of the palace, a blue, ever-burning flame alight there. A set of stairs lay carved precariously into the cliff face, and I wondered how many shades over the centuries had made that climb. A large cave recessed near the base of the stairs, and I could hear faint breathing coming from inside.

The splash from the waterfall caught my attention, and as I moved farther, I noticed the shapes in the water. *Shades*. I gasped. They were the essence of the glow and fell in great waves gently into the Styx from the palace. Near the waterfall, great thick vines twined over the rock face. Giant red orbs hung there, and I squealed with excitement, rushing forward as my mind worked to process what I was seeing.

Hades said things didn't grow in the Underworld, but here was proof they did. I reached down to the nearest bough and lifted the sphere in my hand. The skin was leathery and reddened, not smooth as an apple would have been. With a gentle tug, I freed it from the brambles and turned to Hades, only to be met with sharp jaws the size of my leg, and three pairs of very unimpressed eyes glaring down at me.

"CERBERUS!" Hades called, rushing from the banks. In front of me stood a giant creature, with three dog heads. Of course, I had heard the legend of the fierce Cerberus, Guardian of the Underworld. I'd just never imagined I'd see him face to face. Hades rushed forward but one of the heads snapped at him, too. He stared in shock. The snapping beast turned to join the other sets of eyes watching me.

Artemis was a great huntress. There was nothing she couldn't catch or tame, and she often relished dragging me along on her hunts. I thought back on what she had taught me. Large animals? Pointy teeth and the possibility of being eaten? Look nonthreatening, but don't show fear. I raised my hands slightly, the strange fruit still clutched tight. Cerberus stood, transfixed by the movement. Hades, too, hadn't moved but instead monitored the scene from where he was.

I offered my hand upward, and Cerberus followed, all three heads fixated on the red object resting there. I watched as they bobbed up and down, occasionally bumping into one another, starting small squabbles. I laughed softly and all eyes turned back to me. An idea struck, and I reared my arm back and threw the fruit as far and high as I could. It sailed past Cerberus and went deep into the cavern behind him. The beast followed, bounding after the fruit, and I took that chance to run to the stairs. Hades still hadn't moved. Instead, he'd stood with his arms crossed and head cocked to the side, studying the situation with stunned interest.

We could hear the growls and scuffles as the heads fought over their prize. Paws dug into the ground in front of the cavern, and the small fruit landed at my feet, a little worse for wear but still intact. I gasped in surprise and Hades let out a laugh. Cerberus kneeled and laid each of his big heads down in front of me like a patient, good boy. I walked slowly to him, palm outstretched, and scratched the closest one behind the ears. He let out a sweet whine, and I laughed again when another of his heads nudged my other hand.

"Head scratches?" I stared at Hades's bewildered expression. He threw his hands up in confusion.

"I saw him eat a man for sneezing once, so I have no idea what's going on." Joy bounded through me, this feeling of acceptance, of bone-deep belonging. Hades crossed to me, wrapping me in his arms.

“Shall we go home?” he murmured, nestling his face in my neck. I smiled, nodding my head, and took his hand in mine, pressing the back of his wrist to my lips.

Persephone
CHAPTER 14

"Hmmm, *home*," I agreed. Smoke and shadows brimmed around us, lifting and dematerializing our bodies. I heard Cerberus let out a whimper when he realized we were leaving, his jaws slack with drool. Hades teleported us to a bedchamber of sorts, and I stared around curiously. This room was his, I assumed. *Ours*, I corrected myself. The bedchamber was vast, rock beams stretching across the ceiling to form beautifully intricate stonework. A roaring fire, blue in flame, danced in the grate of an oversized fireplace, a fluffy rug laid before it. A large chaise sat against the far wall, covered in pillows and soft tufts. It looked so comfortable I had to resist the urge to go over and lay down, the wear of the day heavy on my body and mind. The far wall opened to reveal a vision of the Underworld, the same crystal of the outer palace used as a barrier between them.

The great see-through doors offered very little privacy, and yet I was less bothered by that than I should have been. We were below the highest spire in the tower. None could touch us here. The wall opposite the balcony housed the bed. Four posts studded each corner, and beautiful silk the color of the midnight sky hung a canopy over it. It easily could have slept several people, and a dark thought wormed through my subconsciousness—how many had been in that bed? The dark covers stretched across, taunting me as insecurity raged within. I had never been jealous of anyone before; I was struggling to keep it under control.

The fierce protectiveness I felt for Hades meant I loved him, sure, but I didn't *own* him. He'd had a life before we met. *Lovers. Friends.* I was his future, and he was mine. We'd be the last two to sleep in this bed from here on, and the notion quieted the jealousy rearing high in my gut. Hades moved behind me, wrapping his arms across my abdomen and pulling me flush to his chest, and I made a low sound of contentment at his proximity. He was as touch starved as I, and every moment he could, he took care to connect our bodies. It made me feel desired, *wanted*. He leaned down and kissed my temple, swaying slightly as we looked out over the kingdom. It was beautiful, the way the Styx wound through the landscape, bathing the stone and banks in an effervescent blue glow. The trees were dark and dead, but as I'd seen earlier, some did grow. My mind perked up in curiosity.

"You said nothing grows here, but I could sense that the red orb was fruit. I don't know what kind, which vexes me, but it *did* grow here," I finished.

"Little Flower," he whispered, trailing open-mouthed kisses down my neck. "I have to speak with you about some things. They're important to me. Conditions, if you will." I tensed slightly beneath his touch, but he thumbed circles over the back of my hand in reassurance.

"Like what?" I frowned. Hades walked us over to the chaise and we sank into it together, my body pliant to his touch as he turned me to face him. Hades's nostrils flared, and I could sense his nerves.

"The fruit you picked was called a pomegranate. I've only just decided a few weeks ago. There are seeds inside of it, and yes it technically *does* grow here. Some things only grow in the Underworld, which is why you've never heard of them before. But Little Flower, my beautiful Persephone . . . you can never eat *anything* grown here. I will have stores of food for you, brought down from the surface. But you may never partake in the fruits grown of the cursed land. Do you understand?" he looked at me with his full attention, his voice a low plea. I shook my head.

"Why do I need my own food? Is pomegranate poison? I let Cerberus eat it!" My hand flew to my mouth. What if the pup grew ill? Would that be my fault? "We have to check on him!" I exclaimed, trying to stand from Hades's hold. He grinned but only held me tighter against him.

"Cerberus is fine, Persephone. He's from here." I stared at him, waiting for him to elaborate. Hades brought my hands to his lips, peppering kisses across my knuckles. Every time he touched me, my mind sank further into mush.

"The Underworld is his home. But you . . . you are not of this realm. Eating anything harvested from the lands here binds you to the Underworld. You won't be able to leave freely, of your own volition, not without pain. You must return here or risk madness rotting your mind, like the rest of us." His voice was kind and tinged with a soft sadness.

"You're stuck here. You said so. Are you expecting me to leave?" I asked, my eyes never leaving his. Hades's lips formed a sad smile, his blue eyes dimming.

"Persephone, I don't want you stuck. You will remain free to come and go, to visit the realm of the mortals you love. I never want you to feel trapped here. This is your home, *our* home. But you also have others on the surface. They can't survive here for too long, and sometimes you may want to be there for extended stays. This allows you to always go up. It doesn't make the Underworld any less yours. It is as much yours as I am." I listened to his logic and my heart swelled. He'd wanted me to have it all. My choices, my consent. I nodded my head in agreement, before pressing my lips to his in a chaste kiss.

"I understand. Is that the extent of your conditions?" He glanced at me, a bit more nervously and cleared his throat. "We're to be husband and wife for eternity, Hades. You can tell me," I promised. A childlike grin splashed across his face at the mention of matrimony.

"Well, it's about that." He sucked in a sharp breath. "They will come for us. What we did today was rash and impulsive, and Zeus will not be happy to have been defied. It's in the realm of possibility that we might have just started a war. Your mother cannot come here, but if I remember Demeter, she will not take this quietly. We need to complete the rite of marriage, and . . . the Bond. The less we delay, the better. All of that is to say, Persephone, I love you. I will worship the ground you walk on. I will follow you to the depths of Tartarus. But I do not share well. If you are *my* wife, then I am *your* husband, and I will only allow the two of us into our marital bed. Can you commit to that? I will take you topside right now or at any moment that you ask. But if you stay, if we complete this Bond, I will worship at the altar of your body, today and every day henceforth, but I will require the same devotion." I listened quietly, holding my tongue as he spoke. There was a vulnerability there, a deeper wound from a long time ago.

"Who was she?" I asked, but there was no jealousy in my voice. I felt his hurt, and I just wanted to ease it. To assure him, in any way that I could, that I would never hurt him. Hades regarded me wearily.

"Her name is Minthe. She resides here, in the Underworld, now as the Guardian of the River Cocytus. It was centuries ago, nothing for you to concern yourself with." I couldn't help but marvel at him. Even in a moment like this, showing his scars, he only worried about my comfort.

"She strayed," I clarified. His chin dipped in a small nod, and I felt my nostrils flare. "She did. With Zeus."

"How dare she?" The anger coiled inside of me, cold fury at the audacity of someone to hurt him in that manner.

"It was long ago, and she matters nothing to me now. Hasn't for a long while, but even still . . . if we are Bonded, there will only be us. It is my most steadfast rule."

His deep voice was like poetry, more beautiful than any song I'd heard played on the lyre. He was asking me, one final time, to be his, giving me all the control. The God of the Underworld, kneeling at the shrine of my feet.

Fire blazed in my eyes, igniting the spark that wrested between us. Our budding Bond lit up, and I could feel the rush of desire flowing from him as well. I crawled into his lap, my chiton falling around my hips as I straddled him. The soft swathes of fabric caressed my skin, the chiton rising ever higher. Hades instantly dropped his hands to my lower back, raking a fire across the base of my spine at his touch. I kissed him, letting a moan escape my mouth at his taste. The kiss was simple and sweet at first but quickly I was reminded how hot the fire between us burned.

Hades grabbed my hair at the nape of my neck, arching my head backward to access the flesh of my throat and shoulders. He nipped along my collarbone as the heat pulsated from my core, making my breasts ache. These touches weren't enough; I needed more, need *him*. I rolled my hips against his, desperate for friction, any kind would do. Slipping my hand between us, determined to feel him, I was wanton in my need.

My hand closed around his length, and as I stroked, he let out a strangled sound against my neck. Hades had pleased me before, and now I wanted nothing more than to do the same for him, to take control, own my autonomy. I slid down his frame until I rested between his legs, hands still working him over. Hades let out a harsh breath and leaned his head back against the cushions as I surveyed him laid out before me, a decadent feast of hard planes and strong muscle, but the shaft in my hand was a work of wonder. I had seen many cocks in my life. I wasn't a prude, and Greece was Greece—people were naked.

I'd seen men and women and men and men and women and women have plenty of sex in my existence. I had never, however, seen a god's cock before, and I wondered if they were all this beautiful or if it was just Hades. His was long and thick, warm against my palm as my mouth watered in anticipation, my body responding in a way my mind didn't have to instruct. The smooth skin felt velvety against my touch. The shaft curved slightly upward, a thick vein traveling the length of him, bulging slightly as I traced my fingers along it. Perhaps the biggest difference between Hades and the mortals of my realm were the four strong ridges that ran around his length, inches apart. The rings circled him, and I wondered how they would feel inside of me, became ravenous to know. More heat slicked between my thighs, and I knew that, no matter what we may have wanted, there was no going back to a time when we were not together.

"I've never . . ." My voice trailed off and the heat that rolled off Hades stole my breath.

"I'll show you. Open for me, Little Flower. Taste what belongs to you. You'll be so good for me." He looked down at me through hooded eyes, and I nodded as I licked my lips, the weight of his praise like soft caresses against my skin. Hades raked a hand gently through my hair, curling a fistful into his grip, guiding my head to him. He let out a strangled cry as I took him into my mouth, laving my tongue along his length, savoring the taste of what would be mine evermore.

Hades

CHAPTER 15

Persephone took me into the hot cavern of her mouth, letting out a long, slow moan the deeper she swallowed me down, the move so erotic it curled my toes. The sound that escaped my body was otherworldly. Emboldened, her full lips glided up and down along the ridges of my cock, and as I held her hair to her head, I made sure to not force her deeper, only guide with light pressure, letting her explore. Now and again, she would moan, and the vibrations would do unreal things to my length still lodged in her mouth. I never wanted this to end, never wanted a moment when we weren't ravenous for one another. I'd been with others, but none of them had ever felt like this, had ever paid attention to the sounds and movements of my body the way she did.

"That's my good girl," I breathed, remembering how much she liked praise. "You're taking me so well, so deep—" I sucked in a breath as she bottomed me out, her lips now flush with my base as she encouraged me to take her throat. I wanted whatever she was willing to give me, and though I knew this was her first experience, the way she worked me over owned me. My hips jerked involuntarily, the sounds of her gurgling had me so close to the edge I couldn't think. Hells, I could barely breathe. She was moving at such a rapid pace I was sure it had to hurt her, but she wouldn't relent, and I didn't have it in me to stop her. For a moment I lost myself in pleasure, slamming into her with unrelenting force, pumping my hips in shallow thrusts into her mouth.

Persephone choked, eyes watering as I started to lose control. My darker compulsions slipped closer to the edge, her face blooming a tantalizing shade of red at the loss of air. She sputtered, slamming me out of my haze, but there was nothing but lust and triumph in her green eyes.

"Both hands around my shaft, squeeze. More, Persephone," I demanded, and she obeyed, gripping me with sure strokes. When I tried to pull back, she protested, eager to please, eager to let me use her perfect mouth. She choked again and spit pooled around her lips, working up a frenzy as she bobbed her head up and down with renewed vigor. My head snapped back with such force I knew I was barely hanging on, but I desperately tried to hold out, never wanting it to end.

"Little Flower, if you keep that up, I'm going to spill down your throat," I nearly whimpered. Persephone took my words as a challenge, and I watched, open-mouthed as she twined her fingers with my own, still clutching her hair. Her grip pressed down on top of mine, urging me to thrust harder, faster. My hips buckled, her plump lips swirling firmly around me, choking on my length as I thrust up into her mouth.

The pressure built, almost painfully, as she continued to suck me down. I slammed into her throat with finality, unable to hold back, spilling down the back of her tongue. She took every drop, tears streaming down her beautiful face as she released the tip of my cock from her mouth with a satisfied pop. I watched in awe and wonder as she licked her lips, smiling up at me, clearly pleased with my shaking body. Her eyes shone with mischief, her hair a wild tangle from my hands. I traced my eyes over Persephone's skin as it shimmered, a beautiful blush flushing her chest and cheeks as she stared up at me breathless. Raw power emanated from her, and I watched curiously as tendrils of my darkness lapped at her skin, searching for a way to make purchase inside of her, searching for *home*.

Overcome, she let out a low moan and began trailing her hands over her body, gripping her breasts as the dark glow hovering over her skin traveled across her chest. The Bond between us flexed, and I could feel the ghost of what she was feeling creep through. It would fully form once we were Bonded, but I wasn't sure my control could wait that long to have her. I reached down to cup her face and she leaned her cheek into my palm, gazing up at me with those bright green eyes through her lashes. In all my years, I had never felt something so primal, so guttural, as the need I felt for her. How could something so pure, so full of life, embrace my darkness? I bent low, scooping her into my arms and straightened, carrying her into the smaller chamber adjacent to ours as chills swept through her body.

Water filled the amethyst basin resting in the middle of the floor, large enough to hold several bodies and just as deep. I sat Persephone down in front of it. She looked at me curiously as I quietly began unclasping the ties of her chiton, carefully pulling it from her flushed skin. Once it lay discarded at her feet, I placed my hands on the pins holding her intricate loops and braids together and softly jostled them from their seats. Her hair tumbled down around her, and she shook her head once, letting out a startled laugh that sounded so sweet to my ears.

Persephone stood in front of me, completely bare and beautiful for the first time, stealing the air from the room. I roamed my hands down her neck, over her collarbone, down her curves. She reached a hand up to unclasp my brocade, allowing my robes to fall. Her lips parted in a soft "O" as she took in my naked form. I knew this wasn't the first time she had seen me—the day we first met had bared me to her—but a look of hunger ignited in her eyes, an appraisal of validation that made my blood sing. She moved her hands to touch my chest, but I quickly grabbed her wrists, locking them together and spinning her face away from me. I picked her up easily, ignoring the soft yelp that escaped her lips, and sat down in the amethyst bathing pool with her in my lap. The water was warm, and I felt her instantly relax against me, a hum of contentment reverberating from her chest.

"You did so well for me," I soothed, my lips grazing her ear. Persephone rolled her hips back on top of my length, pressing my cock farther into the cleft of her.

Hells, for a maiden she certainly knew how to work me up. Her hair, darkened from its usual gold to an almost pale-blue sheen, clung to her in wet spirals. I grabbed a cleaning stone from the side wall and began working it carefully over her body, tracing lines across her torso and under her soft belly. She sprawled out against me, stretching her hands to clasp behind my neck. I washed her, dragging the smooth stone over her flesh, comforting her, thanking her for her body, for her trust. My hand snaked down to rest over her thigh, and she moaned as I slid a finger up toward her clit.

"Already wet for me, Little Flower?" I murmured into her neck, suppressing a grin. I loved that her body responded to me, that she wanted me in places she'd never let anyone else go before.

"Yes, when you speak to me, your words . . ." Persephone nodded, writhing as I slipped my hand farther down, pressing through her folds until I had two fingers controlling her pleasure. She moaned when I picked up the pace, cupping her breasts with my free hand as she thrashed against me, seeking her release. Water sloshed around us, as Persephone chased her ecstasy, unapologetic in her lustful daze. It was magnificent.

"You enjoy it when I tell you how well you do for me? How perfect your body is, your shade, the depths of your power?" I whispered the words against the shell of her ear, my fingers slipping lower, circling her entrance, the flesh so wet and warm against the pads of my fingers. I remained trapped between the mounds of her ass, a slave to the friction she created with each thrust of her hips as she writhed against me, riding my hand.

"Tell me, Hades. I want to be good; I want to please you, ah—" Persephone tightened around me, her body bowing, and I felt the pulse rumble from somewhere deep in my spine as she came around my fingers, her sweet moans pulling my own release with her. Her body went limp against mine, still coming down as I pulled my fingers from between her legs, massaging over the swells of her breasts, the tight, pointed peak of her nipples.

"We've made a mess," she trilled, gesturing to the ruined water. Again, I saw a soft glow settle over her as I waved my hand, replacing the spoiled liquid with fresh water.

"Fixed," I said, kissing her neck as she snuggled back into me. "Is there anything else my Queen desires?" Persephone let out a small laugh at that.

"Queen. That will take some getting used to. What if I don't know how to rule?" She twisted her head back to look at me. "I barely manage to run the spring sometimes."

Her voice wavered with hesitation, and I could nearly hear the eons of doubt and criticism Demeter had laid against her echoing in Persephone's mind. I tilted her chin up, water dripping against her skin.

"You are already a Queen, Persephone, but now you will have a crown, and no one will ever be able to control you again," I promised. Her eyes held mine, misting over as she sniffed.

"How do you see me so well, Hades?" she asked, softly. I shook my head, trailing the tip of my tongue over the back of my teeth while my eyes drank her in, so beautifully disheveled.

"Little Flower, you're all I see. I'm afraid it's something of an obsession at this point."

Narcissus

CHAPTER 16

"Helios?"

The crunch of broken glass and furniture sounded underfoot the deeper I went inside, and I steadied myself for the carnage I saw on my approach. The front door was blown wide, nearly ripped off the hinges, the wicks of the sconces burned too low to see well, but everywhere was destruction. Upturned chairs and splintered wood littered the grand foyer of the home of the Titan of the Sun.

I shouldn't be here.

My feet carried me deeper and darker into the bowels of Helios's home, devoid of the warmth and light that normally adorned the halls. I hesitated when I came to the askew door that led to his study, nerves eating at me from the inside. I had not seen or heard from him in days, and while I had known that was coming, I never imagined it would end like *this*. Summoning courage fueled by the ache in my chest, I crossed the threshold. Against the wall, slumped on the floor lay the sprawled-out titan. Pools of wine seeped around him, his armor blemished, the sheen dulled in the darkness. His head hung low, chin to his chest, fingers grasping around a bottle.

"Helios?" I whispered gently, inching forward, careful to avoid the wine. A grunt was his only response, but it was a sign of life. I knelt beside him, reaching gently for the neck of the bottle, but as soon as my fingers closed around it, his big body jerked it out of my reach, nearly knocking me over.

"You can't be here," the gravel in his voice caught me off guard, all kindness leached from his tone.

"Look at me," I demanded. His head rolled back unsupported, his golden-brown eyes glassy and washed out.

"She's gone," he sniffed, the anguish in his voice nearly breaking me.

"I know, come on," I urged, lifting one of his giant arms across my shoulders. With a heave and momentum, I managed to bring him staggering onto his knees.

"He took her. That monster *took* her. She begged him to stop and I f—" He paused to hiccup, and the smell of rancid wine nearly gagged me. "Failed her. Now she's gone and it's my fault. What's to come is because I waited, I hesitated." He made a whistling noise and waggled his fingers off into the darkness. I groaned, using my knees to push his body up the wall, breathing hard from the effort. "Artemis went to the Underworld, with Hecate, to retrieve her, but she's gone. I can feel *here*, she's gone." He pounded his fist over his chest, driving the knife inside of my own deeper at the despair in his voice.

"Yes, I heard. Come now, help me. You smell awful," I panted. With considerable effort, we managed to find our way to his bathing chambers and, through the grace of the Fates, get him inside the large, recessed bath. Helios fell like a sack of stones against the marble, his armor screeching with every slide. The sound tore through the room, assaulting my ears, but I only grimaced and climbed in with him to get the clasps of his armor loose. He was too heavy as I worked to maneuver him free, every moment studiously ignoring his exposed body and the way my own responded to it.

With a snap, the pool began to fill, the water cool and cleansing as it rose up and over his chest. I noticed the smoothing stone on the side of the bath and set to work scrubbing his skin free of the dirt and sweat and wine that had amassed there, careful to avoid going lower than his belly button. Helios's head tipped back, exposing the expanse of his throat, the Adam's apple that bobbed there. He let out a groan as the stone roamed over his arms and chest, down carefully over the sides of his muscled thighs.

Helios cracked an eye open as I took his hand in mine, scraping the dirt from under his fingernails. Beneath the water, my thigh touched his, and even through my himation, I could feel his warmth searing against my flesh.

"You shouldn't be here, Narcissus," he repeated, tone ragged. I swallowed, focusing on his ring finger, avoiding his gaze.

"I know that too."

"So why have you come?" The gentle slosh of water rippled around us, his hand curling against my palm. I closed my eyes as my breath stuttered and reopened them to see a thousand emotions play across his face.

Pain. Regret. Sorrow. Rage. Longing.

Emotions worn for someone else.

"I'm here because the God of War showed up on my doorstep. Any idea how he knew where to find me?" I asked, raising an eyebrow.

"Because I told him how to. I made him promise to protect you, after . . ."

After.

I nodded in understanding, all the while not understanding in the least. I'd awoken two nights past, alone in an empty bed, all traces of him gone, and I had known that it was over. Our time had run out, and he had a goddess to tie himself to, but then today, Ares had arrived and explained the turmoil. The God of War had made me promise that I would come find Helios, and because I am weak, I'd sought the titan out.

"I don't need protection," I countered coolly, my voice far steadier than I felt. His skin on mine was like a drug, cloying and intoxicating.

"I don't care what you think you need," he growled, the possessiveness in his voice sending tingles down my spine. I gathered a breath and steeled myself. Helios didn't belong to me; he belonged to the Goddess of Spring. Jealousy sprung like a waterfall within my chest, even as I tried to tamp it down.

To be taken by the God of the Underworld was not a fate I would have wished on her, but a smaller, darker part of me was glad she was gone. It held out hope that now Helios would see what was so clear between us, how far past simple carnal pleasures it had blossomed.

"Tilt your head back," I commanded, gathering water in my cupped palm and washing it down over his head. My fingernails scraped against his scalp, his eyes fluttering shut as a low groan worked up the column of his throat.

I tried to work diligently, convincing myself I was doing this for a friend, as though I'd ever had a friend to do something like this for. I couldn't let my mind wander to the what-ifs, the what-could-have-beens. I couldn't let the shame of not being able to let him go from my life overwhelm me. I worked quietly, ignoring the way his gaze seared against my skin, refusing to acknowledge how my fingertips lingered over the flesh of his outer thigh, and when I managed to get him free of the bath and tucked into a mostly disheveled bed, I certainly didn't press my lips to his furrowed brow as his eyes sank closed.

No matter how badly I had wanted to.

After tidying up his chambers, I tossed the soiled himation into the closet, next to a golden net that glistened in the low light. My feet carried me across the threshold of his bedchambers until I stood next to his bed, drinking him in for just another moment.

One more taste.

The tips of his fingers grazed against mine, the knot in my chest nearly choking me as he gently stroked the inside of my wrist. I wanted to scream at him to pick me, to choose me and us. His eyes, slivers of sunlight against honey, traced my face, latching onto my gaze and refusing to let me go. A million unsaid words passed between us, but the only words past his lips ripped my heart out as he succumbed to the dream.

"I wish things were different, but she's too important. Without her, there is no hope. She is the hope . . ." His eyes fluttered shut in the darkness, and I watched his breathing even out into a steady rhythm, hating him for choosing the goddess over me, hating her for stealing his love, and hating myself for having ever cared at all.

Hades

CHAPTER 17

A knock at the door signaled the arrival of Persephone's handmaidens.

"Enter," I commanded, and a small troupe of ghostly shades appeared in the chamber. Persephone looked around, alarmed, and draped her hands over the tops of her breasts. I smiled. "My love, these are your ladies' maids. They will help you dress and prepare for the ceremony. I have already summoned the officiant."

"It's lovely to meet you," Persephone said, smiling shyly at the shades, dipping her head. Each of the specters bowed impossibly low and I rose, water dripping in sheets from me. I kissed my Queen on the top of her head as my shadows cloaked my body.

"I shall see you when the bell strikes five. I'll be the one in black." Persephone's lips tipped up, amused, and I swept out of the chamber, smiling at the eruption of laughter and giggles left in my wake.

My love.

My Queen.

She was perfect. All there was left to do was to complete the Bonding ceremony, prevent a war with Olympus, and survive the wrath of Demeter.

A soft bell chimed somewhere in the distance, one only I could hear, signaling someone had passed into my realm. I made my way down the familiar paths of the palace, stepping through the shadows like a portal, and coming out on one of the very secret back entrances into the Asphodels.

Precious few knew of it and even fewer would dare to traverse it. Demeter wouldn't be able to come here, and Zeus wouldn't act so quickly. No, if there was someone on the path, it had to be someone unafraid of the Underworld or its effects. I rounded the corner just as a blazing torch of cold light was thrust in my face, its illumination a small moon set ablaze. I summoned my bident, willing it to materialize and cross blades with the kukri the specter held in her other hand.

"Hecate," I grunted, countering her blow with ease. "Can we talk about this?" I asked, calmly. An arrow shuddered past me, ghostly silver and made of moonlight, striking the stone behind my head and shattering it outright.

"Where is Persephone?" a commanding voice demanded, and I looked to see Artemis, Goddess of the Hunt, notching another arrow.

"I assure you, I have done nothing ill-fitting toward Persephone. And if you'd give me the chance, I can take you to her."

"You kidnapped her!" Artemis accused, rage roiling off her in torrents. She let loose another arrow, one dismissed with a swipe of my bident.

"I did no such thing," I assured her. Hecate stared me down with cool, silvery eyes, and I could see her using her third eye to *see* what she could. Removing the wards I kept locked tight around my mind, I opened to her, boring my gaze into her own, willing her to see the truth. I hadn't kidnapped Persephone, quite the opposite. Seemingly satisfied, the Goddess of Witchcraft and Pathways lowered her kukri just a notch.

"He isn't lying. They plan to Bond," Hecate stated slowly, reaching a hand across to lower Artemis's bow and arrow.

"You asked her to Bond with you?" Artemis snarled, voice deadly low. The Goddess of the Hunt sent a murderous look my way.

"I did not. She asked me. I tried to resist her." I smiled. The way she sent my lips tipping at just the memory was going to make my cheeks hurt. I'd never had the inclination to smile so often in my existence. The goddesses exchanged a weary, confused look, but Hecate sunk into an unnecessary curtsy. Artemis, however, stood her ground. I knew the depth of her resolve from Persephone's recounting their adventures, and I also knew that her trust would never be won. She'd hear it from Persephone or not at all. Stubbornness was a quality of Zeus all of his children seemed to share.

"Where is Persephone?" Artemis repeated, fury laced in every syllable.

"As you command." I swept my arms low, creating another shadow portal and gesturing for them to step through. We rematerialized just outside of our bedchamber, my heart swelling at the sound of laughter tinkling through the hall. The Underworld had only known silence and screams for so long; it was a welcome change to hear joy abounding. That's what Persephone was though, *joy*. She gave life to the world around her, no matter how dark and frigid it may seem.

Hecate eyed me with a sly smirk, noticing mine. We had known each other for many years, and often she was the only living being I encountered. As the Goddess of Witchcraft and Doorways, no paths were closed to her, and over the centuries, she had ventured on these precarious roads on one mission or another many times. Artemis held no such pause for me as she burst through the double doors with a bang, notching an arrow as she moved into the chamber, flagging the shades.

"Persephone?!" she called, eyes sweeping the room past her raised bow. Alarmed, I followed after her, unwilling to let a weapon so near to my future wife. Artemis came to an abrupt halt, causing me to nearly crash into her, a stunned look gracing her strong features. I whipped around to see the vision that had stolen the breath from the room, and my lungs seized in my chest. My capacity to breathe fled from my body in a rush at the sight of the goddess before me, my goddess, my wife. With a slackened jaw, I involuntarily swayed, grabbing Artemis for support.

Persephone stood stunned before us, mossy eyes wide with shock for only a moment, before her face cracked into a smile of such utter happiness it lit the room. Fates, it lit the Hells. Her long locks were half twisted up on her head in intricate swirls while the bottom curls cascaded down her shoulders in thick waves. Golden braids, accentuated by lush flowers, entwined in her hair, blooms that adorned the crown resting on her head. Towers of black amethysts drove hard spikes into the deep fuchsia peonies, and violet sensation ranunculus completed her headpiece.

The flowing chiton she wore hung delicately off her shoulders, the deep pinks splashing across her glowing skin, its soft fabric a stark contrast to the iron bodice cinching her waist. It was made of the same ore my circlet and bident were forged from, though hers seemed to be tempered and stretched to the most delicate sinews and spindles as it crossed her torso, pushing her breasts higher. My eyes roamed to the cinch in her waist, which only served to accentuate the deep swell of her hips. Hourglasses were made in her image, I was certain of it.

A high slit in her chiton revealed her powerful legs, vines securing an athame high on her thigh. I was enraptured, and in the Asphodels, I understood that Persephone was the beginning and the ending of me, of the essence that flowed through my veins, of every star in the cosmos.

Persephone
CHAPTER 18

Artemis burst through the door, startling my lady's maids, and I instinctively flung my arms wide, stepping protectively in front of them. Artemis had her bow notched and ready to let loose, and I knew those arrows of moonbeam were magical, so there was always the chance it could harm them.

She looked at me, shell-shocked, before Hades came rushing in as well, locking eyes with me and nearly knocking Artemis over. He looked incredible, his face all sharp angles and shadows with those deep blue eyes. They stripped me bare and delved into the depths of my very shade. I felt my face break into a huge smile at the prospect that two of my favorite beings were here for me on my wedding, our Bonding. Past them, I could see who I assumed was Lady Hecate standing in the doorway, moon torch still lit, her reputation preceding her. I never had the honor to meet her in the flesh, but tales of her beauty were known far and wide.

Her long hair, black as night, was half twisted up on her head, laced with beautiful braids. Hecate's dark skin shone brilliantly, as though a thousand stars took residence upon her. I strode toward them, dismissing my lady's maids as I approached, and grabbed

Artemis's shoulder. My arms pulled her into a tight embrace while my free hand reached over to Hades, needing to feel his touch. Breaking away from Artemis, Hades gently tugged me flush to his chest, those piercing eyes roaming freely over my form as he drank me in. I could feel lust blooming from him through our burgeoning Bond as he raised my hand sweetly to his lips and pressed a kiss to the palm of my hand. Artemis, shaken loose of her stupor, cleared her throat.

"Can we speak, Persephone?" Her eyes landed briefly on Hades. "*Privately*," she stressed.

"I shall leave you to catch up, Little Flower," he whispered, kissing my cheek as he disentangled from our embrace. I opened my mouth to protest, but Hades's eyes cut to Artemis, who looked on the verge of a breakdown.

"You are such a radiant beauty, my Persephone, that, if I am to even play the part of your consort, I must take the time to prepare myself to be presentable for you," he teased, crossing his hands over his chest.

He leaned in once more to press a kiss to my forehead before sweeping from the chambers in a puff of billowing shadow, leaving the three of us alone. Hecate stepped fully inside, pulling the large doors with her as an intense silence settled over us. I gestured to the small chaise, and we made our way over to sit.

Artemis still hadn't said anything, and I chewed the inside of my cheek anxiously. Had they come to drag me back? Panic worked its way down my spine as we sat, unmoving. Artemis cut her eyes to me, her gaze dancing over my face, my hands, taking note of everything she was seeing.

"That was Hades, then? He's uhm . . . less, you know . . ." —her hands lifted up in an aggressive roaring gesture—"than I expected," she finished lamely. Hecate and I exchanged a smirk as the Goddess of the Hunt struggled to reconcile that the God of the Dead wasn't a morbid, rotting corpse.

"Yeah, he only gets broody when he spends too much time in the Upper Realm," I responded. Hecate broke the remaining tension with a beaming smile.

"Congratulations, Persephone. I've known Hades for a long while, and I'm so happy you found each other. I haven't seen him smile so much probably . . . well, ever."

"That means so much, Hecate, and thank you for bringing Artemis to me, but . . . what are you two doing here?" I asked, eyeing them both.

Artemis sat with her arms folded tightly across her chest, letting out an incredulous snort.

"We came to get you, of course. Helios said he saw Hades take you, and you were pleading with him to stop. We've been traveling here to the Underworld for days." She gestured outward, talking animatedly with her hands, the vein in her temple pulsing slightly as her barely contained self-control faltered. "Did you ask him to *Bond* with you, Persephone?" Artemis blurted, her words laced with distaste, nearly venomous. I recoiled slightly under her gaze, with what felt to be her judgment, for only a moment before something coiled low in my belly, rebelling against the shame. *I* was the one they tried to marry off without my consent. I owed not a single explanation to anyone.

The thoughts broke through my psyche with rage and power, and I stood, pacing away from the two.

"I did, and I would do it again. I don't deserve to have my choices taken from me. This is *my* choice. *I* was the one about to be forced to submit and give Helios children. I do not owe a single one of you any further explanation other than I love Hades, he loves me, and we are doing this. As for Hades and I Bonding, you can support me, or you can leave. He is *mine*, Artemis. My place is with him." My chest rose and fell rapidly as I struggled to unclench my fists. I wasn't sure where that burst of confident power had come from, but I was willing to use it for as long as it would let me. Artemis looked like I had slapped her. Hecate looked amused.

"How did this even come to pass?" Artemis asked in a low voice. I sighed and sat back down next to her.

"We met in the forest, a fortnight ago. He was minding his business, and I noticed decay in all the flora on the forest floor, so I followed the trail to him, intent on having words. When I first saw him . . . Artemis, I felt like I had always known him. My shade called to him." I grasped her hand in mine, her long fingers tightened into fists.

"All those times you slipped away . . . ?" she asked, eyebrow raised. I nodded.

"We spent every day together, talking and sometimes sitting in silence, simply existing near one another. He is so careful with me, Artemis. He tried to warn me off him." She huffed, rolling her eyes.

"*OH*, did he? And once he took your maidenhood? Was he gentle then? Will he be just as gentle when you're stuck here in the cold and dark with him?" she spat, venom thick in her tone once more. Anger thrummed through my body, and I fired back in the most biting tone I could muster.

"He hasn't *taken* anything from me. Hades tried to get me to see reason, to see that the Underworld wasn't a place I could thrive, but he also knows that I deserve to choose for myself. He insisted I don't eat the food from here, so I'm free to come and go, but he does not make my decisions. He supports me in them. I will continue to stand by his side, and just because you don't understand, does not give you the right to attack his character. You have known me best, and I beg you to see me now. See how confident I am in this. Today is a happy day for me, Artemis. I beg you, spend it in joyful celebration with us. I never imagined you could be here, but you are and it's the sweetest gift." I willed her to look at me; could see Artemis's demeanor softening. She had never been able to deny me anything, since childhood.

"What about Helios? You're saying he made it up and you didn't beg Hades not to take you?" I could tell this was the last arrow in her quiver, and she thought the evidence hard to beat. I grimaced, flattening my lips into a tight line.

"He did not make it up. Helios heard me beg Hades no, but it wasn't about taking me to the Underworld. It was me begging him not to kill Helios, who attempted to use deadly force against Hades. I'd never seen him that way, Artemis. He was mad with rage, couldn't be reasoned with. He attempted to take on *Hades* for Olympus's sake. Helios never stopped to consider what I wanted, not in our years of friendship, not when he went to Mother and Father for my hand, despite me showing no interest romantically, ever. He was content to have her force me to marry him and bear his children. Hades was only protecting what belongs to him. And I do, Artemis. *I belong to him*. You have never known me to be impulsive, or disobedient. Please trust me that this is exactly what I want."

A soft bell chimed, and a specter floated through the door, bowing deeply.

"My Queen, m'ladies. It is time to start the Bonding." The specter turned to Hecate, again bowing low. "Lord Hades has requested for me to ask if you would stand to bear witness for him, Lady Hecate." Hecate nodded and stood, straightening her silver gown.

"It would be my honor, Athanasios." Hecate turned toward me, embracing me as we, too, stood. "May the surest of steps guide your path, sweet 'Sephone." She floated gracefully past us, linking her arm with Athanasios's incorporeal green one. Two other shades, Phoebe and Eirene, appeared, holding a shimmering thin veil that stretched as far as I could see. It looked as though someone had captured the heavens and encased them within the material, the way the light reflected the stars.

They placed the veil at the base of my crown, lacing it between the strands. It flowed and lifted of its own volition, light as a feather. Artemis scooped the bouquet that was laid on the stone table, full of contrasting flora, pinks and purples mixed with dark blooms from the Asphodels. She handed it to me, unshed tears glistening in her eyes.

"I just want you to be happy," she murmured. I pressed my forehead against hers, holding her close.

"I know, and I promise, I am. He is what I want. As sure as you knew with Orion, I know now. Escort me? I'm so grateful you're here with me."

Artemis let out a small sniffle at the mention of her former love, all pain and worry as she held my gaze.

"He will not take this rebellion lightly, Persephone. His cruelty at being disobeyed . . . I hope you are truly prepared . . ." Her voice trailed off, eyes glassy, haunted by the horrific events that had surrounded Orion's death, at the part she'd played in it by refusing to marry a son of Poseidon. I shuddered, remembering the day I'd found her in that clearing, red blood of the mortal Orion covering her armor, two of her own arrows protruding from her lover's chest. Even now, I could still hear her wails of anguish in the deepest parts of my mind.

She had defied the will of our father, and he had punished her gravely for it.

"Hades is powerful, Artemis. We will stand together, and we will be ready. As long as we are together, I am not afraid," I assured her, not daring to voice aloud my true thoughts. The more I learned of Hades's power, the sheer strength of it and his realm, the more I wondered if the reason Zeus left Hades in the Underworld was because his dark power rivaled my father's.

With a tight smile, Artemis nodded her head. When she broke apart from me, she summoned her formal garb and instantly was transformed into the Goddess of the Hunt and Moon, her white chiton cut short, cladding her thighs with milky white fabric. Silver-studded armor glinted with unseen moonlight, chest plate and bracers a match with her shin guards and sandals. A silver bow sat low on her back, and an intricate circlet adorned with bits of moonstone rested across her crown with her dark black locks braided into a pleat. She shone with the light of the moon, fierce and cool as she pulled my hand into hers before guiding me to her side. Phoebe and Eirene followed close behind with my veil clutched in their hands.

The bell began to chime again, this time tolling five.

Anticipation shot through my body like a bolt of lightning, the knowledge that I would soon be back in Hades's presence propelling my feet forward. A swirling vortex of shadow awaited us just outside of the chamber door, and I could feel the pull of him through our Bond, urging me forward, calling out the sweetest song.

Persephone

CHAPTER 19

We stepped through the portal and emerged at the back of a small courtyard. My heart felt like it might burst at the sight of it all as we moved through the stone archway. Artemis let out a low whistle, seemingly impressed as we took in the ceremonial space. The courtyard was a stunning stage, illuminated by floating orbs encasing blue flames, the area thick and wild with flowers the size of chariot wheels. An aisle of silk stretched out before me adorned with solo petals as smaller flowers remained suspended in midair around us. The soft pinks floated lazily through the air, defying gravity, just like we defied all odds. A small quartet of spectral shades played softly in the corner near the back, the ghostly strumming wafting around us, filling the air with a hauntingly beautiful melody.

Soft moss coated the ground, and I was so grateful I had opted to go tenderfoot. I could feel the soft rub on the soles of my feet, connecting me to the earth and comforting me in the most primal way. We glided forward, Artemis steadying me as I stepped up onto the aisle, her grip never faltering. I raised my eyes toward the large dais that rose from the hearth at the end of the aisle, struck by the vision waiting for me. Hades stood, tall and strong, facing me, with love in his eyes and need in his heart.

Hells, he was beautiful.

His broad shoulder was draped in black fabric, with small blue runes stitched throughout the hem. Resting on the same shoulder that held the fabric was a pauldron in the shape of a skull with deep sapphires set in the eye sockets. His chest remained exposed on one side, a steel breastplate in the shape of a rib cage covering his torso. A bone circlet lay flat against his smooth black hair, and it was the first time I'd ever seen it tamed and trained back on his scalp, save for the single ringlet in front, breaking rank.

Artemis squeezed my arm, and I realized I hadn't been breathing, too enamored with the god before me. Hades's full lips parted in a dazzling smile, creasing the corners of his blue eyes as he reached a hand out to me. It was all I could do not to break into a sprint to close the distance, and I was grateful Artemis kept her grip firm, guiding us forward at an appropriate speed. After what seemed an eternity, my hand reached for his, and Artemis took her position to my left, opposite Hecate.

The ghoulish quartet lowered their volume as Hades took my hands into his, spinning me to face him. Happiness shone through me, bright and wonderous, welling up like a babbling brook. A soft laugh broke through my nerves, falling past my lips. I could feel my cheeks burn, and Hades narrowed his eyes with hunger before brushing his knuckles softly across my cheek.

I never thought I would be here. The thought of marriage had always repulsed me—I didn't want to be owned, but with Hades, I ached for his bones, craved their nearness to mine when he wasn't touching me. He was often quiet, but attentive, and always listening. When he spoke, he was intelligent and kind. When he did touch me, my dark god dug beneath the layers, reading my body, capturing my shade. Hades thought himself a cruel, cold thing, unworthy of love, but that couldn't have been further from the truth, and I planned to spend every moment of eternity showing him otherwise. Lost in Hades's gaze as I was, the strong *ahem* of someone clearing their throat in front of us startled me so much that I jumped. Glancing sideways, fear struck as the owner of the voice came into focus.

It was a face my mother made sure I knew well, one I could pick out of a crowd, never to be trusted, always to avoid. My stepmother, Hera, stood before us, a disarmingly gentle smile on her lips. I looked between her and Hades frantically, but he quietly calmed me by putting his hands on either side of my face. "Be easy, Little Flower," he soothed, that rumbling tone washing over me in a wave of comfort.

"She is here to help. She will not hurt you. I would never allow *anyone* to hurt you." My breathing steadied as he held my gaze. Hera stayed silent, but the cruelty I expected on her face never appeared. She looked almost . . . saddened. Zeus's infidelity often had Hera exercising her wrath on his conquests and their offspring, including Artemis, her brother Apollo, and me. They were also children of Zeus, and Hera had tormented their mother, Leto, viciously during their birth. I felt Artemis tense near me, and I could understand her uneasiness. The goddess was an enemy.

Mother had kept me far removed from Olympus and its politics, always claiming it was because our duties kept us bound to Earth with no real cause to journey there, but I knew it was her way of giving Hera a wide berth. Hades moved to hold both of my hands in his, and I tried to return to the moment, to trust him over the deeply instilled fear still coursing through my veins. Hades wouldn't have risked her wrath without reason. I kept repeating that in my head as he bade for her to begin.

"We are here to witness the strength of the Bond between two eternal shades, Persephone and Hades. A Bonding is our most primal and sacred of ceremonies, and one that cannot be reversed or broken in this realm or any other. Immortality is a precious gift when one has the right partner to share it with . . ." Hera's voice trailed off, and we all understood the implications.

"The vows you take today are immutable, *unbreakable*. It is a contract of love and devotion, but also honor and respect. If you both agree to these commandments and are willing to honor this commitment, form the physical bridge." Hades shimmied his ore bracer down, exposing the soft, cool flesh of his forearm, and presented it to me. I rested my own much smaller palm on his skin and pressed against him. The muscles in his forearm rippled at my touch, preening, so I gave him a soft smile at the warmth spreading from where we joined.

Hera leaned in with a thin cord of gold coiled loosely in her hands. She wrapped it tightly around our arms, weaving intricate patterns with the string. The loose rope solidified as she tied, forming a gilded cage to join us. I looked up, only to find Hades's eyes on me, still unwavering, blue irises burning with a quiet inferno, his chest falling a little more heavily than normal.

"There's time to change your mind," I whispered, smirking. Hades shot me a dangerous look, possessive and filled with want, as a rumble ripped through his chest.

"It would take all of the forces in all of the cosmos to pull me from you, and even then, my bet would be on me." Hera straightened before us, serving us both an admonishing look.

It was bad form to joke about skipping out on an engagement vow in the Goddess of Marriage's presence. She cleared her throat loudly, and we all feigned a look of shame as she continued, but Hades's jaw tightened as he fought back his laughter.

"The tether will force only truth from your lips. You may now speak your declarations of intention, and then place your hand on the other to complete the Bond. Do you wish to be Bonded?" she asked, and we both nodded our assent. "Hades, you may begin." I watched him slip his free hand around me, splaying his palm on my shoulder blade.

"Persephone," my name fell from his lips like a prayer of old, his deep voice settling in my bones as he spoke. "I have toiled in the darkness alone for a thousand lifetimes. I had never dared to dream, never dared to hope that I would find my equal in this realm or any other. I still haven't succeeded, for you are so much my better that I worry you will realize how lowly I am in comparison to your light. I will never forget that you are my Queen. I will exalt you over all others and smite your enemies at your request. I will worship at the shrine of your kindness and grace, and all the Underworld shall serve at your pleasure, just as I do. You are the most precious to me. I wish nothing more than to be Bonded to you."

Silent tears spilled from my cheeks, and I let in several shallow breaths to fill my lungs. He was the loveliest being, god or otherwise, I had ever known. Hera nodded to me, her eyes just the tiniest bit shiny as well. I lifted my hand, palm forward to rest on the smooth skin above his heart, my fingers splayed wide. Hades had chosen a place of discretion to bear his mark, and I knew it was his way of showing me I was my own person, equal in our Bond, but a possessive part of me wanted my mark on full display, all the time. There would be no mistaking that Hades was *mine*.

"Hades," I began, unsure of what I would say. We'd had very little time to prepare for the Bonding, and I was following poetry. His hand flexed gently, reassuring me in that way of his. I stared into his eyes, and though I felt the words coming from me, I was simply lost in the moment, in the feeling and emotions he invoked within me.

"My life has been a series of events that have happened to me, not by my choice. No one is ever interested in what I want, think, or feel. No one, that is, except you. Never once have you dismissed my thoughts or feelings. You pull my bravery through my skin, dug deep from my bones. You make me demand the autonomy that has been denied. I will rule alongside you. I will stand with you in the darkness, unafraid. You are my Lord in the shadows, and I will follow you into the darkest depths. For all eternity, I will love you. My deepest desire is to be Bonded to you for my whole life."

The golden cage began to heat and shimmer, melting into a molten liquid. It surged up each of our arms, traveling across our chests before pouring into our palms. The gold pooled, and I could feel it, a living thing, as it grew hotter and hotter between our skin. Hera raised her hands high, throwing her head back to the heavens. Her aura pulsated through the room, power radiating from her body in stunning waves.

"In this realm, and every other!" she bellowed, her voice shaking with the timbres of several overlapping octaves. "From this day to your last days!" The vibrations in the gold picked up and began to sting. I let out a low hiss as my shoulder blade was branded, white-hot with the force of her power. Small tufts of smoke lifted from my outstretched hand, as my own brand melted into Hades's skin. Hera smacked her raised hands together, pushing the power she had been building toward us in a rippling arc.

The gust sent flowers and their loose petals flying around us in tiny cyclones, and I felt the last string of our Bond solidify between us. Hades looked triumphant as he pulled me closer, crushing our bodies together and devouring my mouth. He slipped his tongue over mine, slightly tugging my bottom lip between his teeth, as flowers floated around us. Time stood still as he gripped my throat gently, reverently, before bending me backward in his fervor to connect our mouths.

His hands. His taste. He was everywhere, even more so than he usually was, and I felt my knees buckle beneath me at the bolt of desire that ripped through my core. His fingers caressed the spot on my back that now bore his mark, and a moan attempted to fly past my lips at the pleasure that sprang from his touch. Hades groaned as my nails scraped over the raised skin on his chest, and for a moment, there was no one else, only his mouth on mine, his palms as they gripped my thigh hooked over his hip as he pressed into me. I wanted him, right then, at that very minute. I couldn't wait any longer, I needed his—

"Ahem." A very loud throat clearing interrupted what I was certain was about to be the best pleasure of my existence, and Hades pulled back only slightly so we could look at Hera. She stood before us still with an eyebrow cocked, but in our fervor, we had forgotten she was even there. Artemis looked thoroughly embarrassed, and Hecate was barely suppressing her laughter, but Hades only grinned as he gently slid my leg down so I could stand. The Bond between us burned through me, igniting my skin wherever we touched.

For the first time in my existence, I knew I would never again be alone.

Persephone

CHAPTER 20

I glanced down at Hades's Bondmark for the first time, and I couldn't help but let out a gasp. It was beautiful, thin golden line work settled into his skin. The threads wove over his heart, forming a skull with two opened flowers for eyes and a curved half-moon sitting atop two intersecting staves sat in the forehead of the skull.

"The union here cannot be undone, but that does not mean that all is well," Hera warned, looking between the two of us pointedly. "Expect a summons to Olympus. He does not take well to being defied." We nodded our understanding. There would be a fight, we knew, but this laid legitimacy to our claim that could help us stem the tide.

"Thank you, Hera." Hades bowed his head to her. I quickly repeated his words. Hera turned gracefully and began to walk toward the shadowy vortex that would surely carry her back to Olympus, but I hesitated, a question still burning in my throat. Mother had always warned me of Hera's cruelty, but she had done a great kindness today. I wanted to know why.

"Hera!" I called before she had gone too far, extricating myself from Hades with considerable difficulty, as he had no interest in releasing his hold. I stepped toward her as she turned.

"Not that I'm complaining, but I have to ask—why did you help us?" Hera looked me over once, then reached a hand to pick a rogue petal from my braid. I willed myself not to flinch, to present myself as strong. Her mouth quivered into a wicked smile as she flashed her unusually sharp teeth my way.

"To spite your mother. Demeter is furious that you've been taken. She is in constant agony, imploring Zeus to right what she perceives as a kidnapping. She even came to Olympus, demanding an audience. So, when Hades asked, I was happy to oblige. You see, your mother hurt me, long ago. She betrayed me and took what was mine. For all these years, she has lived in fear of my retribution. The constant worry she suffers has been deeply satisfying, but I could not resist this opportunity." A maniacal gleam lit Hera's eyes, and I stared at her in horror. She truly was as cruel as she was beautiful.

"What you've done here is nearly as dangerous as not doing it. You must stay together and keep word of your Bond hidden until you absolutely *must* reveal it. The target you've painted on yourselves will be substantially more dangerous now. I'll see you on Olympus, Little Flower," she winked, before absconding into the waiting shadows.

"What a vile woman," Artemis crowed from behind us. I turned, stepping back into Hades's waiting arms as Hecate walked over, linking her arm with the Goddess of the Hunt's. She pulled out her moon torch, igniting it with a gentle breath.

"We'd better be going. We've been here longer than we should, and we need to report back, or others will follow."

Hades tensed, and I knew the thought of other gods in our realm made him bristle. *Our realm*. How quickly my mind adjusted to the new normal. I nodded and moved to embrace Artemis.

"Promise me we will meet to run under the moon?" she asked, sadness in her eyes. Artemis and I had always been so close, and it felt a little like I was abandoning her.

"Of course." They turned to leave, but I held fast, searching for the right words. "Promise you won't tell them we have Bonded? You heard Hera, there are many who would use the connection to try and harm Hades, and I cannot allow that." Hecate and Artemis exchanged a wary look, but I grabbed both of their hands pleadingly, "Tell them I chose to be here. I'm happy and I love Hades. Just leave Hera and the Bonding out of it." Artemis pursed her lips but eventually nodded in agreement. Hecate looked at Hades for assurance, then smiled and agreed before turning them both on their heels with her moon torch raised high.

Their retreating backs faded into the darkness quickly, and I was suddenly very aware of the silence in the courtyard. Our ghoulish musicians had also dematerialized, only I hadn't noticed until now. I was also suddenly extremely aware that Hades had wrapped his hands around my torso, pressing my back into his chest. His fingers snaked up my stomach, ever higher, over my breasts. The fabric separating us created glorious friction, and I moaned as my back arched against a wall of muscle. His hand finally came to rest around my throat, a delicate pale necklace against my golden skin.

Hades applied just the smallest amount of pressure on the sides of my neck as he guided my face to his, and one look into those eyes speared through me, dominant and controlling, but mirroring the desire I felt. I rocked back into him, ignoring the bite of armor he wore as it pushed into me from my back to my thighs.

"I want—" I began, but Hades silenced me with a slight squeeze. He kissed the side of my neck tenderly before trailing small bites into the crook of my shoulder. I clenched my thighs together, desperate for some relief. Swirls of black shadows engulfed our forms until all light became obscured and the only thing tethering me to reality was the pressure from Hades's hand on my throat, until the shadows obfuscating our view evaporated and we were once more in our bedchambers.

Hades walked us forward, never once allowing even the slightest modicum of distance to separate our bodies, his free hand roaming through the folds of my dress, kneading my flesh with desperate grasps. My skin felt so cold that when he touched me it began to burn, and goose bumps erupted in the wake of his kisses. I was shivering and burning up all at once, so edged out on the pleasure that if he didn't do something to stop the world from spinning, I would very likely combust. My knees reached the bed, buckling against the frame as Hades shifted me quickly to face him. He invaded my space, hand around the back of my head as he guided me down, smooth and gentle as a feather falling.

I arched back, shimming myself toward the headboard to make room for his long frame, aching for the weight of his body pinning me down. The bed dipped as he sank a knee into it, coming to rest between my thighs. His hands untangled from my tresses, tugging with gentle pressure against the root as I whimpered. Eager lips took the opportunity to move down my body, trailing more kisses and nips against me, hard enough to sting but soothed so quickly under the skill of his tongue. He was still in his formal regalia, his circlet glinting in the low light as he settled his face between my legs.

I propped myself up on my elbows, the better to look at his glorious form. Hades slid a hand under my bottom and lifted, positioning a pillow he held clutched in his other hand beneath me, elevating my core. He was moving so slowly, and I was panting with every agonizing stroke of his fingers against my body. *Throbbing*. I was throbbing with anticipation and a needy whine escaped my lips. Hades flicked his eyes to me, that cool gaze alight with a predatory grin.

"Easy, Little Flower," he teased, scraping his fingernails lightly across my inner thighs. His arms hooked underneath my legs, jerking me toward him. I could feel his breath on my exposed core, already glistening with need. "So beautiful, so powerful, when you're dripping for me like this," he purred, flattening his tongue over my lips and dragging up slowly. My hips bucked, jolted by the sensation of his mouth, his wicked tongue against my skin.

Hades swirled his tongue around my clit, applying just enough pressure to spiral me out, the dancing sensations pushing and pulling as his tongue split in two, lapping and sucking my most intimate parts. He uncurled the arm pinning my left thigh down and I shook as his fingers slid slowly through me, inching closer to that place I so desperately needed him to touch.

"More," I released on a broken moan, still grinding my hips onto his face. Hades lifted his head, pausing the strokes of his tongue and I turned down my lips in a pout.

"Patience, my Queen," Hades tsked with a slight hiss, his forked tongue flitting over his bottom lip. Two fingers plunged deep inside of me, and I cried out, fisting my hands in the sheets, riding out the sensations of feeling full while he stretched me. I rocked my hips as he worked his fingers in and out of me slowly, almost lazily. In contrast, his tongue had returned with a vengeance, swirling like a cyclone, causing a sheen of sweat to cover my body. My chest rose and fell rapidly as I threw my head back searching for the heavens, or the abyss, anything to ground me before I disintegrated into nothingness at his touch.

Hades let out a hum of approval, vibrating the bundle of nerves trapped between the wicked forks of his tongue, and I saw the constellations as I hurtled toward my climax, breaking apart among the heavens. I crashed back into this realm, body shaking while Hades continued to stroke me through my orgasm, eyes fixed on me, lips latched over my exposed nipple. His hands slowed gradually, coming to a stop as he unfurled the fingers hooked inside of me. I propped myself back up on shaking elbows, cheeks and breasts flushed pink, still reeling from his ministrations when I saw him, and alarm overtook me. Hades licked his fingertips clean of a slightly glowing substance, completely relaxed. It coated his fingers, remained smeared across his face, stray streams flowing down his chin, marking him.

"It's the Bond, Little Flower," he mused, wrapping that tongue around his long fingers, clearing every drop. "It changes us from the inside out. I'll look the same, spilling inside of you. Or on top of you. Whatever you prefer."

His grin widened, his expression darkening as he looked me over with hungry eyes. The God of the Underworld was bent between my thighs, drunk on the taste of my body, my essence. Need coiled low in my belly, the pang of desire could not be placated much longer. I eyed the bulge protruding from his robes, spreading my legs wider, letting my thighs fall apart in offering.

"I offer myself to you, Hades," I whispered, reaching to pull his body closer, needing to feel his weight, his power commanding me. My husband leaned in, pressing me into the hard planes of his chest, caging me in the safety of his arms as I traced the lines of his bicep up to unclasp the ore cage armor he wore. Hades straightened to shake loose of it before crashing back down on me, his mouth demanding as his tongue slipped past my lips.

I grabbed at his robes, overcome as I pushed them aside so I could feel more of him. My chiton had been ripped in our heated frenzy, but I couldn't bring myself to mourn its destruction as his hips pinned mine beneath him, his gentle thrusts hitting me in just the right spot to make me cry out. His hand pushed between us, stroking his hardened length. A small bead of glowing nectar formed at his tip as I studied how he touched himself, taking note of the strokes he preferred, rough and firm.

The crown of his cock slid up and down my core, mixing our arousal together, slippery and warm, as he placed the thick head lower, dipping the tip in to gently stretch me out. He was bigger, so much more substantial than his fingers had been. The stretch was nearly too much as Hades guided his cock deeper inside of me with his forehead resting on mine, locking my gaze with his.

"I'll be as gentle as you need, Persephone," he promised, and I knew, even as he held back, that his control was close to its breaking point. The knowledge only spurred me on, needing him to break, needing him to claim me from the inside out. "Are you going to be good for me, Little Flower?"

"Don't be gentle," I whined, "break me apart, Hades." I arched beneath him, swirling my hips, pushing and squeezing to try and suck him deeper. He bit back a shocked grunt as he eased in, his restraint legendary. Enraptured, Hades captured my mouth in a deep kiss, swallowed my moans as I struggled to adjust to feeling so full of him. There was very little discomfort as he rocked his hips, inch by delicious inch, and as he began to move in earnest, I was breathless, seeking more. The first hard ring of his cock dragged against my walls, causing my body to shake. I threw my head back in ecstasy as it scraped deliciously against my sensitive flesh, arching my chest higher, my back bowing. Hades's lips caressed under the swell of them, sucking gently, the tines of his tongue cool against my too hot skin.

I could feel myself tightening around him, the ache nearly unbearable as he took his time, sucking over my nipple, winding his hips. My Death God bucked hungrily, driving another inch deeper before stalling and repeating the process over and over, until only one ring remained.

"This pretty cunt opens so beautifully for me. Fates, Persephone, you're gripping me so tightly," he praised, his cock seated well, and it filled me with pride that I'd been good for him, taken his rings and cock in such a way that he was nearly overcome. Hades snapped his hips in soft lulls, pressing drugging kisses against my sternum, between the valley of my breasts, as he went.

"Fates," I moaned, rolling my hips to meet him, "Hells, Hades, right there . . . harder," I begged. Hades obliged, kissing along my jaw, pulling a hand up my chest to wrap possessively around the sides of my throat. My eyes rolled back at the movement, at his control. He stoked the fire inside of me higher, his movements precise and overwhelming.

"That's my perfect girl," he said, raining his praise against the flesh of my neck. "So warm and stunning, look how beautiful you are taking me so deep." A low moan tore from his throat as I tightened, gripping him harder, chasing the pleasure. "I think you can handle more, Little Flower. Do you? There's more to take, but I think you can do it. Will you let me all the way in? Will you spread for me? Take all of what's yours?" he coaxed, and it felt like he was everywhere. Hades's voice was so gentle; it washed over my too hot flesh, my body going limp at his validation. I would have agreed to anything, given him everything, if it meant he kept doing his work. I nodded my head furiously, pupils blown wide as he stared into my eyes, hand around my throat, thumb brushing over my parted lips. Hades snapped his hips harder, giving me the last of himself, stroking deep inside until I could feel his base over my clit, the new angle shooting pleasure down the back of my legs in sharp jolts.

I was once again shaking for him, thrashing as he canted into me. Hades's hand left my throat and gripped the dip of my hip as he rolled my body harder, almost brutally, using me as a vessel for his pleasure. It was intense and shattering, the power welling up inside, threatening to burst from my veins. His strong hand rested on the soft swell of my lower belly, his thrusts growing sloppier, more erratic with every moment that passed. The extra pressure sent me into a state of bliss as it anchored me, tied me to him forever.

Hades panted softly in my ear, moaning his desire, and I *craved* those sounds. I wanted to be everything he needed, drive him just as wild for me as I was for him. The arm he'd used to prop himself up was hooked under my shoulder, palm flat against my Bondmark, adding to the overstimulation. Sparks shot over my skin, and I frantically reached for his chest, completing the circuit. Hades came with a loud groan, spilling into me as he shuddered and shook. It felt thick and warm, and a powerful tremor rammed through my body, rocking me to my core as I shattered underneath him again. His body lit up with a dark glow, the bones of his being shining through his skin, the darkness that lived inside of him, emptying inside of me.

I felt *powerful* as a surge of energy that didn't belong to me settled in my bones. Hades made no move to pull away, instead rolling us over so I was atop him, still sinfully split by his hard cock. He kissed and stroked my hair, running his fingers along my sweat-soaked skin. I was tired, so blissfully exhausted. There had been no time to rest, and emotionally, I was spent. Hades's chest rose and fell in a perfect rhythm as he stroked my hair, grazing his hand over my back, and I let the euphoria lull me into a peaceful slumber.

Hades
CHAPTER 21

She slept for days, my sweet Persephone. *Days*. The morning after our Bonding, I woke to find her draped across my chest, hair wild and chiton barely clinging to her soft skin. Her sweet lips were still swollen from the fervor of our kisses. My mind drifted back to that fateful day in the meadow when everything had changed and my life had begun. She had been splayed across me then as well, only this time it wasn't tormenting to feel her body on mine. I could let my hands wander, let my eyes drink her in with no guilt or shame or pain at the knowledge she would never be mine.

She *was* mine.

Warmth surged through me, my arms tightening around her back, rooting our shades together. I traced my fingers across her Bondmark, and Persephone let out a sweet whimper as she slowly rolled her hips against mine, seeking relief. I glanced down, searching for a sign that she had awakened, but she seemed still content in her slumber. My cock pressed firmly into her stomach, but I willed it to settle. She needed her rest. There would be eons of pleasure, of listening to my name tumble from her lips. We had nothing but time.

That was the difference between me and the other gods parading around. They were quick to anger, quick to strike, and quick to *take*. There had never been a rush for me. My anger was deadlier, vengeance much sweeter, because I could wait. I had found in my extensive lifetimes that death was an inevitability. It came for them all, and in contrast to mortal lives that are pitifully short, the afterlife was endless. Pain or pleasure, depending on where they ended up, stretched before them in an infinite sea.

Yes, I could wait.

The smell of spring enveloped me, rich and succulent as my goddess continued her rest. Once more, I noticed her skin tone slightly changing and took in the knowledge that her golden hair was shifting as well. I twirled it between my fingers, contemplating all it could mean. I had a theory, but I had never tested it and resolved to consult the Fates before worrying Persephone. I had never taken a lover and allowed her any of my essence. I didn't want any progeny walking among the mortals or, worse, touting power on Mt. Olympus.

I had a secret thought that the thrumming glow that lit Persephone as she swallowed me or took me as I came deep within her was more than just my essence. It was my power. I was not yet sure what it meant for her, but I wanted to be sure she would be safe. Persephone's hand ran slowly up my chest, settling over my mark, and any progress I had made getting my cock to settle hurtled out the gates of the Hells. She moved so her hot center pressed directly over my throbbing cock as she slowly sat up, straddling me.

I bit into my lip, a grunt pulling from me as she slid herself against my body while rocking her hips. Soft hands placed against the ridges of my abdomen, trailing greedy kisses as she walked her fingers down, down. I let out a ragged breath as my cock jumped, eager to be inside her, desperate to give her pleasure. Persephone leaned back, reaching between us, sliding her hands through the soft fabric of her chiton and pushing it aside, giving me the most wicked view of her glistening cunt.

Two delicate fingers pushed past the soft tufts of hair over her core and my eyes traced their movement, jealous of the way they got to explore her. A needy moan dropped from her parted lips, sensual and sweet, like nectar on my tongue. What was this woman doing to me? She let free her fingers, now dripping with her essence as she wrapped them around my length, readying it with her arousal. I bucked into her grip, the fire stroking low in my loins as my goddess wasted no time in positioning me before sliding down, eyes locked with mine, taking every inch of my length into her warm cunt.

Her chiton slipped down her shoulder exposing the beautiful swell of her breasts as she rode me, head thrown back in ecstasy. I gripped her hip with one hand as she moved, uninhibited and chasing her pleasure. My other hand slid up her torso, cradling her soft stomach and the curves of her flesh, before I settled my grip just under her rib cage. Persephone moaned as my hips snapped up, driving into her as her jaw slackened. My grip guided her forward as she rolled her body naturally, her walls constricting around me in a vice. I lifted the hand holding her ribs higher to cup her breast, kneading and plucking at the tight peak, desperate for a taste.

"You're magnificent," I groaned, driving my hips upward, sinking into the heavens between her thighs. Persephone bounced above me, eyes rolling with pleasure, as she took every punishing thrust without complaint, with hunger, and it nearly tumbled me.

"Oh Fates, oh hells, oh Hades, *there*." Her words came out strangled, broken, and I grabbed Persephone's neck and bent her to me, still pulsing my hips into her. I devoured her mouth hungrily as she rode out her wave. My gaze was transfixed on the space where our bodies connected, that the curve of her belly that had once made forbidden thoughts race through my mind, of filling her so full that we created new life in the depths of the Hells. I pressed a hand there, pushing down until we could both feel my cock thrusting inside. Persephone's legs shook as she worked over me, riding me, *owning* me.

Her face scrunched up in a frustrated scowl as she tried so desperately to get there. I slowed my thrusts, teasing, just as her lips turned up in a pout.

"What's wrong, Little Flower? You're working so hard. Look, see how I fit inside of you." Her head sagged, chin dropping to her chest as I adjusted, grabbing her hand to place it flat against her lower belly, pinning her hip in my grip as I gave her every glorious inch. Her breathing hitched as she felt my cock, felt her body open for me. "That's it, isn't it?" I asked. She nodded, jaw slack as she rode out my thrusts. "Be a good wife, take every drop," I grunted, desperately hanging on to my composure as her orgasm ripped through her, dragging a mewling cry from her lips as she milked me. "Come on my cock, my love, my flower. I want it all." Persephone's eyes were half open as she shuddered above me. "S'good. So good," she moaned as the second wave of pleasure bolted through her. The white-hot lightning started in the base of my spine, and I knew I was done for.

Her cunt never relented, still squeezing, as I too came hard, slamming into her with finality that stalled my hips. The symphony of moans and wet, slapping skin reverberated as our bodies collided, a crescendo of our union bouncing off our bedchamber walls. Her body stilled above mine, going limp. I lifted her slightly and let my cock slip out of her, grimacing when it smacked into my lower abdomen. I could have flipped her over and driven back inside, but I knew she was spent, so new to her appetites despite the ethereal afterglow that illuminated her. Persephone's body shook slightly as I laid the goddess down on her side and pulled her flush to my chest, ignoring the mess we'd made together. I curled around her body, craving her nearness, seeking that light within, the one that played so well with our combined darkness. Persephone smiled, placing a soft kiss on my forearm as she rested on it. I peppered my own kisses onto her back, over her Bondmark, and as we settled, never in all of my existence had I felt more at peace.

Hades

CHAPTER 22

We followed that pattern over the following days, sleeping and coupling and laughing in each other's arms. By day four, Admentos, my closest advisor, was beside himself over my absence. Persephone lay sprawled out on our bed, naked and tangled between sheets, my limbs entwined with hers as she slumbered. Admentos entered, his spectral glow bouncing lightly off the floor as he paced, head bowed, eyes averted from Persephone. He kept fidgeting with his hands, waiting for me to acknowledge him. I shot him a glare, but true to his nature, he did not cower or relent, instead returning my frown.

I groaned and extricated myself gently from Persephone, untangling the sheets and sliding out of bed. He wouldn't be here if it wasn't important, and that knowledge was currently the only thing keeping me from banishing his shade to Tartarus for interrupting our honeymoon. As I stood, I stretched, twisting my bones and relishing the soft pops of release. I stalked forward, naked, to Admentos.

"What?" I barked, but he knew better than to take the ire seriously.

"I'm sorry to interrupt, my Lord, but you need to return to the throne." Something in his tone caught my attention, and I crossed my arms over my chest, concerned.

"What has happened?"

Admentos cleared his throat nervously, and I softened my tone. The shade had served me for over a thousand years. As a king in his time, he could have ascended to Elysium, but his great love, Phaedra, was destined to stay here. Rather than spend the endless afterlife without her, he'd broken into the throne room, begging to not be separated—threw himself at my feet and *begged*. I took pity on him, the fierceness of his loyalty pulling on long-dead heartstrings. When I'd granted his request, it was on the condition that he served me as an advisor. He'd agreed, and ever since, he had done more than his share to keep the wheels turning in the Underworld. To see him uneasy did not bode well. He dropped his voice and glanced past me to Persephone's sleeping form.

"Could we speak . . . privately?" He jerked his head toward the door. I nodded, gesturing for him to lead the way as I called my shadows to me. The darkness wrapped around my body, clothing me in sweeping black fabric as it solidified. The cut of my chlamys exposed our Bondmark, and a thrill of pride jolted through my chest. Persephone owned me, in every way. That mark was everlasting proof of our commitment.

The joy was short-lived, however, for as soon as I crossed the threshold, a catastrophic weight struck me in the head. There was a cacophony in my mind, screams of anguish and lamenting wails buckled my knees, and I was grateful for Admentos, who had reached to help me stand as my ears adjusted. My bedchambers were spelled to block out the thousands of cries for help or prayers for deliverance thanks to Hecate so I could have a quiet place to rest. Now that I was across the threshold, the wails consumed me. It took moments and several steady breaths to control the volume of them all.

"My Lord, easy now." Admentos didn't look surprised at the onslaught, and suddenly, I felt panic course through me.

"Tell me what is happening," I demanded, still bent over.

"The gates are overwhelmed. Charon has been ferrying boatloads over the threshold. We have thousands stuck on the banks of the Acheron, unable to broker passage to the Underworld because everyone they know is dead and there are none left to place the coins to pay the toll."

"How long has passed in the Upper Realm since we returned?" I demanded, pinching the bridge of my nose as my eyes watered.

"Two months, my Lord." I knit my eyebrows together in confusion. Ares generally warned me when war was coming, as a courtesy.

"War?" I asked, but Admentos shook his head. "Plague?" Again, the answer was no.

"Famine, my Lord." His voice was soft and hesitant. Realization dawned on me instantly.

"Demeter," I growled. The ground underneath us shook with my fury.

"You need to return to the throne. We need you." I nodded my head at once and turned to walk with him when a soft voice caught my attention.

"Hades?" Persephone called, wrapped tightly in sheets as she searched for me. Relief flooded her face when her eyes landed on us. Persephone walked toward me, but her face contorted in anguish as she, too, stepped across the threshold. She fell to her knees, clasping her ears. We rushed to her, and I dropped down, bewildered.

"Little Flower, talk to me. What are you feeling?" I pleaded as she cried out, rocking back and forth on herself.

"Make it stop!" she choked through broken sobs. I ran my hands over her, trying to find any evidence of a wound. Persephone shrieked, and my blood ran cold. She was in so much pain, and

I was beside myself trying to figure out what to do, all the while great bolts of anguish shot through the Bond between us. I could taste her despair, feel her hurt and fear as though it were my own.

". . . so loud . . ." she sobbed, still cradling her head. "So . . . much . . . anguish. They're wailing, Hades, please!" she cried. Admentos stopped short, eyes wide.

"She can hear them, Hades. The shades. *She's hearing their cries.*" Her body slumped as she devolved into a puddle, clinging to my robes and clutching at her ears as I tried and failed to soothe her.

"How is this possible?" I demanded, completely perplexed. "No one else should have been able to hear the wails of the forsaken." That was my burden to bear. *Alone.* Admentos shook his head at me, raising his arms and taking a step back.

"Bring her across the threshold?" he offered. The idea was solid, but if she was going to reign as Queen, she couldn't do it confined to our bedchambers. Breathing hard, I gripped her face and brought it up to my own. Persephone's eyes were bloodshot, lips contorted in unshed screams. I searched her eyes, willing her to see me.

"Persephone, look at me. Concentrate on my voice." Green eyes rolled a few times before settling on mine, still unfocused. Her pupils were blown wide, and I worried I was making the wrong choice. "You're so strong, my love. Focus on pushing them out, settling them behind a door. You're on the other side of it, and they can't get in without you. Look at me, Little Flower. *Breathe,*" I commanded. Persephone's hands shot to mine, her eyes locked on my face. The light that normally shone in her eyes sparked as she fought to claw her way back.

"That's it, my love. Build the door. They don't want to hurt you; they're just in pain. They just want to be heard. *Breathe, breathe,*" I chanted. Persephone's shallow breaths became deeper and more controlled, and after a few moments, she was still slightly shaking but seemed to have locked the wailing out. Admentos stared at me, wearing a mask of fear I'd never seen on him before. I helped her to her feet and guided her back to our chambers, laying her back on the bed.

"You need to rest, Little Flower," I whispered when she tried to protest. "Phaedra will bring you to the throne room when you are refreshed." I nodded toward the door where the shades of both Phaedra and Admentos stood, talking quietly among themselves. Persephone acquiesced after much internal debate, and I was grateful for the lack of fight. I needed to deal with whatever mayhem Demeter had caused, and I couldn't do that with my mind distracted. I needed to know Persephone was safe. I kissed her softly as she snuggled into the covers and then stepped away. When I reached Phaedra and Admentos, I gestured to her.

"Call the Fates, set up a meeting. I need to know what is happening to my wife." Phaedra nodded and settled into the lush chaise against the wall, the better to watch over Persephone. I pulled my shadows to my body and let their power bring me to the unraveling of the Hells.

Hades

CHAPTER 23

I swept into the room, Admentos hard on my heels. We walked to one of the great spires that provided a panoramic view of the Asphodels, and I was stopped immediately by the sight before me.

The Styx overflowed, flooding the banks by over ten feet on each side. The ethereal ghostly glow of the shades of mortals flitted about in the waters aimlessly. Charon floated to port, his boat overburdened with at least fifty shades on a craft fashioned to handle no more than twenty. The weight of their essence dipped the sides of the boat dangerously low, and I feared they would take on water or capsize if the shades underneath got brave enough to tip it. The plains of the Underworld were overrun as well, shades wailing and milling about, directionless. Hordes of them stretched out through the gates. Children cried out, motherless and searching. My hands tightened into fists at my sides as rage flooded every fiber of my being.

"*Petulant fucking goddess,*" I spat, as thoughts of vengeance floated through my mind, urging me to give in to my darker natures.

"There's a messenger, Hades," Admentos said, breaking me from my spiral. "They're waiting." I let him drag me off the balcony where, below, my beloved realm was on the verge of collapse. The throne room remained mercifully empty, save for the shade of a small boy, freshly made and glowing brightly. My throne rose menacingly behind him, elevated and adorned with the bones and skulls of the dead. I crossed the marble floor, my chlamys sweeping in wide arcs as cold fury laced through my body. The boy's dead eyes widened in my presence, and he began to tremble. His shade looked impossibly thin, and I knew if I tried, I would be able to count his bones. The inferno inside me spiked with rage.

That bitch would pay.

Death came for all, yes. One would think that having such an influx of shades would only add to my power and boost it. In a way, it did. But the Underworld, like all ecosystems, was a delicate balance. A balance that if tipped too far in either direction could plunge *all* the realms into chaos. Demeter knew that better than most, and she was playing a dangerous game.

The Underworld, Olympus, and the Upper Realms were to always be in balance, and here, the scale was far too burdened on one end—ours. The rules of the cosmos would begin to bend, and a collapse of this world meant a catastrophic collapse of the Upper Realm, then, by extension, Olympus. Hard to pull power from worship if all the mortals were too dead to build altars and make sacrifices in tribute. How had Zeus allowed this? I fumed as I crossed near the boy, settling onto my throne with a deadly fury. My bident instantly appeared in my outstretched right hand, my most powerful weapon. Admentos took his place near me, expression serious, hands crossed in front of him as he studied the messenger.

"Nikoli, this is Hades, Ruler of the Underworld and your Lord. Speak your message to him, as you did to me." Nikoli's eyes widened into that of a trapped animal, terrified of the monsters hunting it. I sighed.

"Nikoli, do not fear. You are my subject now, and I will never let another harm come to you under my protection. Whatever message you bear will not be taken out on you. Speak your truth, and you shall be rewarded." I kept my voice level and calm. I needed him to trust me, to tell me whatever he knew without the distortion of fear. Nikoli looked back and forth between us, swallowing thickly.

"The goddess Demeter sends her regards to Lord Hades of the Underworld. She hopes that this offering appeases the Lord, and he will accept this ilk in exchange for the return of her daughter, Persephone, Goddess of the Spring. Should your Excellency accept the offering, Demeter will stem the flow of shades crowding into the Asphodels." Nikoli began wringing his small hands, glancing around nervously. His eyes locked with Admentos, who gave him a somber nod. Nikoli cleared his little throat again, looking up at me with his back straight as he spoke.

"Goddess Demeter has also warned that should my Lord *not* accept the sacrifices, then she would . . . she would continue to flood the Underworld until the Asphodels became so heavy it fell into the pits of Tartarus, such is the strength of her resolve," he finished in a soft voice. A thrum of power radiated from my skin, pulsing into the air around me, but before I could move to respond, a deadly voice spoke from the side entrance of the throne room.

"My mother said *what*?" Persephone swept in, her dark purple chiton whirling around her as she strode into the middle of the hall. Something was different about her aura. It pulsed and shifted the air around her, growing darker and more powerful with every step. Her pale hair wound loosely down in spirals, but she looked . . . hauntingly beautiful. Her green irises were alight, and as I rose to walk to her, I felt her fury rolling outward from her power. Her mossy orbs were flecked with dark specs, a deep gray ring encasing them.

"You should be resting, Little Flower." I looked her over, concerned with the sudden change.

"I'm fine, Hades," her voice softened, but I could still feel the rage bubbling beneath the surface.

"She cannot get away with this, all these people. Starved, Hades. She starved them. All because she isn't in control. *She cannot get away with this*. She must be punished. I will strip her bare of all she holds dear for her disrespect of our people." Persephone's voice was cold and detached. I watched, wide-eyed, as shadows slithered around her, caressing her skin, lifting the tendrils of her hair. She looked incredible . . . she looked glorious. My mouth hung agape as I took her in. My Bonded. My Queen.

"How do we stop this?" she asked, focusing her attention on me. Her gaze was again warm, her fury tempered, but no less resolved. She gripped me close, staring into my eyes. My first instinct was to protect *her*, lock her away in our chambers until I sorted this mess her mother had made. Another part of my mind spoke to me, encouraging me to lean on her. We were partners, both monarchs of the Underworld. This realm belonged to her as much as it did to me, and she already showed such protectiveness toward it and its subjects.

"We need to stem the flow at the gate, give the hordes purpose, a meaning. Help with the judgments and expedite the deliverance to Tartarus or Elysium." I sighed, pressing my fingers once more over my nose to stem the headache I could feel building. Persephone's tongue pressed against the inside of her cheek, then I saw that familiar fire rise from behind her eyes.

"Children are guaranteed entry into Elysium, correct?" I nodded. "I could escort the children to Elysium. It's in the Upper Realm, but at the edge, and I can travel freely between without it extracting a toll, unlike you."

I considered her offer. "That would help alleviate the children, but what of the others on the banks?" I asked, curious to see where her mind would take her. Persephone thought for a moment.

"Set the hordes to build a barge, large enough to help Charon ferry those without the ability to pay for passage. If Mother caused a famine, I imagine entire families were wiped out in quick succession. Call forth any shades in the Underworld with sailing experience. Offer them leniency in exchange for ferrying the new shades across for judgment." She turned to address the others. "Phaedra, you and Admentos set up a queue here in the palace. Hades and I will hear out any plea for a pardon. This should take some pressure off Minos, Aeacus, and Rhadamanthus. They are the judges you were telling me about, right? It may alleviate the flow, and once we've gotten to a level of stability, I will deal with my mother." Her voice dropped dangerously at the mention of Demeter, and I stood, transfixed at the incredible blessing the Fates had cast upon me to make Persephone my wife. I turned to find Admentos, Nikoli, and Phaedra sunk low into deep bows of respect at her power.

"Hail to the Queen," they whispered. She looked back at me, wide eyes shocked and confused.

"Hail to the Queen," I murmured, moving to press my lips to the side of her cheek. There was much to be done, but I continued to stare at my wife in awe. I knew there was no task she could set for me that I wouldn't complete, no test of loyalty she could demand that I would not pass. Judging by the way the subjects of our realm were regarding her now, I knew I was not alone in my devotion.

"You have your orders," I commanded, and they moved, Admentos and Phaedra off to carry their tasks to completion. I looked down at Persephone, her eyes glistening.

"I'm so sorry, Hades. This is my fault. She is punishing my defiance. I just could never believe she would go this far as to starve out mortals." Angry tears splashed down her face as I held her close.

"This isn't your fault," I assured, fresh anger spiking toward Demeter. "She will pay. For now, we have a plan. I'll send you with Cerberus; please do not fight me on this." She nodded, wiping her tears as she pulled out of my grasp. I turned to make her look at me. "Persephone, if you get into trouble, call me like you did the day we left. I will come find you, no matter where you are. I will *always* find you," I swore. She dipped her chin before placing a quick peck on my lips and turning toward Nikoli, reaching a delicate hand out to him. He wrapped his thin fingers around hers without hesitation.

"Come, little one. Let us start an adventure." Her voice was soothing and gentle. They walked from the throne room hand in hand, and I set off to find a few sailors. We would make right this mayhem and then I would rip Demeter's fucking heart out.

I couldn't wait.

Persephone
CHAPTER 24

I hated my mother. There would be no peace between our houses after this betrayal. The suffering of the mortals was barbaric, ungodly in every sense. I would make sure the truth came out, and I would make it so she never had a single altar built in her name again.

I made seven trips to Elysium with the children alone. Hecate and Dionysus came to our aid and were traversing the worthy to the Elysian Fields in droves. Hades had secured several of the finest craftsmen the Underworld possessed, and together, they had fashioned a barge so glorious Charon himself joked of trading in his skiff for the "grand vessel." I had caught a glimpse of Hades and the others constructing the mighty barge, and by the Hells, he looked incredible as he helped hammer and lift the large beams into place. Sweat glistened down his pale chest, and I had to remind myself that the impending crisis took precedence over the way the muscles in Hades's broad shoulders rippled with every smash of that maul.

To my defense, we were newly Bonded, and I hadn't had his hands on my body in days. Far too long, in my opinion, but we had a realm to care for, and on the nights he worked long and hard, I had shadows to keep me company, extensions of Hades to pleasure myself with. It was enough to keep me sated while we waged war.

Several other gods and goddesses had come forth in support, assisting in any way they could. Artemis was with Hephaestus, reforging the gates that had been damaged by the onslaught of shades entering our realm. Eros and Eris were even working together, albeit begrudgingly, to try and unite families that perished to be judged together, so they could help make the best choice for themselves. Hermes ran between the realms, collecting the shades of the dead and bringing them to Charon with Thanatos. The palace bustled with activity, queues of shades patiently waiting for an audience with Hades and me. These were the damned, the judged. We gave them one opportunity to plead their cases, an effort to rectify being taken from their mortal coils so soon, unjustly.

This was one of those such judgment days. We had been at it for hours, and it was indeed an exhausting endeavor. Hades was the picture of a caring monarch, but I could tell the day was wearing him thin. Even so, he gave every shade his undivided attention and heard them as they spun their tales and spoke of their hardships and woes. He was just and fair in his sentencing, even though that meant a great deal still made their way to the Pits of Tartarus. Right before he spoke, he would flick his eyes to mine, inviting me to the floor to pass judgment on my own. He never contradicted me, declaring my word as law.

Hades didn't seem bothered by my ruling as an equal. He never sought dominance, and I wondered if it was because he could sense my submission to him privately. Ultimately, I felt he was in charge—his realm, his rules, Lord of the Underworld—but it seemed he never felt the need to show it. His quiet assuredness left me in wonder, invaded my senses, and watching him listen to a poor shade, Crina, tell her story with rapt attention made me want to crawl onto his lap and bury myself in his scent. Hades was so incredibly . . . *kind*. I felt my cheeks flush and squirmed in my seat.

He cut those ice-blue eyes to me, a small smirk dancing at the corner of his mouth. I turned my thoughts back to Crina, the shade almost in tears, and it instantly sobered me up. This was her life, or afterlife rather, and she deserved all our attention.

". . . and then night after night, he climbed into my bed. I let it go on for as long as I could, at least it was me and not my little sister, Sophie. Then I got accepted by the scholars as a cupbearer, and I would have had to move into the Hall of Records." Her voice caught, as my heart broke for her.

"When I tried to take Sophie with me, he slammed me up against the wall, knocking me down. I was badly injured, but he advanced on Sophie, mumbling about her being 'ripe,' and I just . . . My Lord and Lady, I just lost it. I screamed and ran at him, tackling him into the wall . . . He went down hard, and I rolled away from him, but he wrapped his hands around my throat, squeezing the life from me. I saw stars and blackness. I thought I would perish. Then pressure from my neck loosened and I saw his shocked expression . . . an athame fell to the floor as he rolled sideways, blood pooling around him. Sophie's hand was soaked in blood, and I knew she had stabbed him. She was shaking and crying. We hid the body, and we carried that secret with us to the grave.

"King Minos decided that, since he committed violence against me first, there was no fault in attacking him." She took another ragged breath, turning to me pleadingly. "He didn't attack Sophie, and with the sudden influx, the King had no choice but to sentence her to Tartarus. So, I am here to beg you—allow her to swap places with me. Let her spend her afterlife in Elysium, and I will bear her punishment in the Pit. I understand the debt must be paid, but I beg of you, mercy, my Lord and Lady. I am more than ready to pay that toll," Crina sobbed.

Hades leaned forward, forearms resting on his knees, attention rapt as he considered. His long fingers resting steepled under his chin, and my heart broke for Crina over and over as I raged at the injustice she'd endured. The laws were harsh, and this would be a far bend of even his authority. He locked eyes with mine, urging me to speak. I could not let these girls, *these children*, toil away in Tartarus. Even just one of them. Their guardian was raping her. Artemis would never forgive me for allowing her to be tortured as well, even in someone else's stead at her request.

"The laws of balance are strict, and swapping your shade for hers would create a very dangerous precedent." I watched anguish wash across Crina's face and held my hand aloft before she could protest. "You are destined for a paradise, for heroes and those who lived their life for good. Sophie is bound for the darkness and pain that would haunt her for eternity in the Pits. May I offer that you meet in the middle? Remain here, in our realm together. Neither eternal pain nor eternal bliss. But you would be safe, untouchable by any predator ever again. I shall take you as my Ladies, and you can serve the palace, should you choose." I glanced at Hades, who was still looking at Crina, judging her expression. There was no tension in his jaw. *He agreed with my proposal*. Crina burst into sobs, great wracks of relief clanging off the walls of the chamber.

"Thank you, we accept!" she cried with no hesitation, tripping over herself in her attempt to bow. Admentos came forward, gently escorting her from the hall with her arm tucked into the crook of his own. A small smile played on his lips as well. It mattered to me that I did a good job ruling. I needed to earn their trust, to deserve their respect.

"Admentos," Hades called to his retreating form. "That will be all of the audiences we take for today." Admentos dipped his head in a small bow still carrying the weeping Crina with him.

The hall was suddenly very, very quiet. Shadows inked out, dragging closed the large double doors and obscuring them in obscene darkness. Hades slinked from his throne, eliminating the short distance between us. The throne that he had crafted for me after our Bonding was beautiful, overly opulent. Made of the same ore smithed in the Underworld, with skulls and bones to match his, but Hades had ensured living vines and flowers from the Hells adorned it as well. Plush dark fuchsia cushions kept me comfortable during the long sessions we sat through, soft and comforting against my skin.

Hades's shadows spilled from him, slithering toward me as he approached. They twined around my frame, circling my neck and arms with the sweetest caresses, gently restraining me.

My forearms were laid carefully on each armrest, my head smoothly guided to the plush backrest. The shadows twisted and tightened, inch by inch, until I was bound to an immovable fortress. Hades strode up, towering above me standing between my knees, and my breathing ticked up with anticipation. He was close, so close I could smell that wintry campfire smoldering on his skin. He dipped his face low and placed a soft kiss on my lips before straightening. I pouted and tugged against my restraints, needing more, but they tightened slightly with my movement. Hades bent low again, pressing another kiss to the soft flesh just under my ear. I shivered.

"What an incredible Queen you've become," he praised. My back arched, scraping the fabric of my dress against my nipples, hardened at his words. Lifting his hand to cup my jaw, Hades drew my gaze to his.

"I wonder just how good you can be?" he teased. His words shot straight to my core. My tongue flicked across my bottom lip, and Hades traced his thumb across the wetness there. A deep rumble resonated from his chest, and I clamped my knees together, rolling my hips, begging for relief.

Hades lowered himself, prying my knees apart, kneeling between them. I strained against the restraints holding me, enjoying the way they rubbed against my skin. The God of the Dead slid both hands, palms up, under my bottom and lifted, dragging me to the edge of my throne. The shadows moved me with him, and I slumped, spread wide and exposed at his whim.

"These walls are not like our bedchamber, Persephone." Hades ran his lips from my knee down to my thigh. His hot breath left a smattering of goose bumps on my skin as he got closer to my core. "I'm going to feast on your cunt, and I am going to take my time doing it, should my Queen wish for it." He lifted a long fingernail, sharpened to a wicked point, and slit the ties binding my chiton down the middle, leaving me a bound, needy mess before him.

"I will it. Do not keep your Queen waiting," I whispered, but the confidence I tried to portray was not quite convincing as my voice cracked with need. Hades flashed me a coy smile before moving the shredded chiton down the sides of my body, exposing me, leaving me bare. Shadows coiled around my torso in intricate patterns, thick ropes that caged my breasts in neat angles, circling but not obstructing my sensitive areas.

"Look at this. So pretty for me, Persephone." His praises sent me throbbing and I writhed, wanting. The pressure from the shadow ropes created a delicious tension, but it wasn't enough. I groaned.

"Ah, ah," Hades admonished, swatting my swollen clit quickly. I let out a sharp hiss, and he immediately rubbed his palm against it to soothe the sting.

"I told you. This room isn't our bedchamber. There are no enchantments to keep listening ears at bay, and currently, we have many guests in the palace." He dragged a finger slowly through my slick core stopping just short of my entrance, before dragging it back up again and pressing on my clit. I understood. He wanted to see how high he could take me before I alerted everyone in the realm of what their King was doing to their Queen.

"And if I'm good?" I asked, struggling to keep back the needy whine building in my throat.

"If you're good, I'll do anything you want to do. Any desire, any fantasy, as long as it doesn't involve sharing." That caught my attention, and I fixed my gaze on him. There were things I wanted to try.

"And if you win, and I'm not able to keep quiet?"

Hades flashed his signature wicked grin as he lowered his head between my thighs, keeping eye contact while he lifted both of my legs over his broad shoulders.

"If I win, same terms. Anything I want." I considered for less than a second. His offer gave me pleasure either way.

"However, if at any point you start to lose yourself, or you want out of the bet, you'll say . . ." He thought for a moment. ". . . petal. If you say 'petal,' we'll stop, and it will be perfectly okay. Say it for me now, Persephone. Petal." He looked so serious. I nodded my head in understanding and obliged him.

"Petal. I agree to your terms, Lord Hades." He grinned, dropping his eyes to take in the sight of my exposed core. Quick as a cobra strike, Hades spat, spattering me with his warmth before he dove in, flicking his tongue over my flesh. His tongue split, the opposing forks stretching me wide as he worked the pads of his fingers in a tight circle. I was shaking beneath him, lost to his touch, and he'd only just begun.

It had been too long since he'd been inside of me, and this was an explosion of sensation my body struggled to process. I locked my ankles around his head, crushing him tighter into me, concentrating on not making a sound, as his tongue and fingers reduced me to a dripping mess. Hades slid out of me, rising for air. My chest heaved with exertion, nipples painfully hard as they moved against the shadows. Still, not a sound escaped my lips. His eyes narrowed, and he did the one thing he knew could break my resolve. *He talked to me.* The whispers carried softly up through the shadows as he pressed two fingers back inside, curling toward himself while his thumb worked me over.

"So pretty, look at you," he teased in his deep timbre. "So spread for me. What a good fucking girl, *my* good fucking girl. Such a beautiful, messy girl. You want to come on my fingers, Little Flower?" My spine arched and the softest cry broke rank as he slid in and out, extending the pleasure. The sound of him plunging his fingers into me felt obscene and delicious, and I didn't doubt that every shade in the palace knew exactly what he was doing to me, but I mustered up all the resolve I could. It felt incredible, the way he consumed me, but I wanted to win so badly. I was so close to my climax I knew I would only have to hold out a minute longer.

"Come now, my Little Flower. Don't you want me to win? You love what I do to you, how deep inside of you I can go." His words were undoing me, and for a moment, I contemplated simply letting go and screaming my pleasure for the entire Underworld. Hades, sensing that I was close, slowed the steady pump of his fingers to an agonizing pace, drawing it out.

Cheater.

I bucked my hips and tried to rip the orgasm from myself, but he plunged his fingers in and out rapidly again like he was trying to punish me into cracking and screaming his name. He pulled out a dripping finger and slid it down over my tight ring, and a forbidden jolt rocketed through my core.

My entire body tensed, taut as a tightwire. Hades pressed the pad of his soaked finger against the rigid muscles that were flexing into his touch, craving more. I held my breath as he eased back in, sliding either side of his tongue around my mound. Without warning, he pushed his finger inside, knuckle deep. I felt so full, and an electric bolt shot down my legs, curling my toes. His finger felt so much more substantial than the shadows I'd been playing with. The time apart while we'd worked on our realm had left me wanting, needing to explore the new sensations of sexual desires. Each time we were together, Hades toyed with that forbidden space, but he never pushed for more. *I wanted him to*. I wanted him to own me in every way. Pressure built ever higher, and with a final crook of his finger my world cracked apart.

I shattered beneath him.

Silent screams wracked my body, tears running down my face, but I made no sound as I rode the lightning of my orgasm. Hades stared at me like I was the most insanely beautiful creature he'd ever seen.

"That's my girl," he praised, sliding his finger gently from my behind and rubbing slow circles over my oversensitive flesh as I came down, shaking, under the weight of sweet release. The shadows lessened, gently sliding me into his arms as Hades soothed my heavy breathing, caressing my face. Strong arms held me tightly, kissing away the tears of pleasure leaking down my cheeks.

"Speak to me, Persephone. I need your words now, Little Flower." His voice was very serious, and I didn't like it.

"I won." I grinned, and he let out a relieved sigh before kissing my forehead.

"Did I push too far, my love? You didn't say the word, but I should have paid more attention to your body." His voice still had that worried tremble, and I suddenly became aware of the tension his aura was filled with. I looked up into his worried face, reaching a finger to massage the crease on his forehead.

"Hades, what are you talking about? I'm perfectly fine. More than fine. I'm . . . exhilarated. *Exhausted*, but satisfied. If I'd wanted to say the word, I would have. I promise you." The tension in his muscles disappeared as he lifted me, cradled in his arms. He stalked through a portal of shadows, landing us in our bedchamber, carrying us straight past the bed and into the bathing chamber. I tested the strength of my arms only to find them still weak from the strain.

Hades sat behind me and washed my hair, kneading his knuckles into my tight muscles. He took extra care when he washed between my thighs and over my breasts, and in every touch was a promise. He would bring me intense feelings of pleasure, bordering on pain, but he would always take care of me after. There was nothing sexual about what he was doing, it was . . . intimate, *gentle*. After the water ran cold and was refilled twice, Hades lifted me from the basin and wrapped me in a large towel before carrying me to our bed and settling me onto his side, still bundled.

For centuries, I'd watched the mortals love and kill and betray one another. I had never understood what would possess them to endure all the pain that went with love, until I'd met Hades. I would endure a thousand years of torture in the Pits to know only a single day with his love. Hades stroked his hands through my hair until he fell into a deep slumber, his soft snores filling our dark paradise.

Hades

CHAPTER 25

Sweat beaded over my brow in the heat of Hephaestus's forge, deep within the bowels of the Underworld. Blow after blow from mallets and hammers fell around us, the smell of soot and iron filling the air as he tempered steel to his will. We'd been working for days on the barges to ferry shades to the newest plains of the Underworld, and Hephaestus hadn't hesitated to work on them every waking moment. Part of me suspected it had something to do with Aphrodite and Ares, but I felt no inclination to pry. He had always been so private, and if he needed comfort or advice, a small part of me hoped he knew he need only ask.

Hephaestus's harsh grunts punctuated each strike, bashing the metal, shaping it to his whim. His blond hair was slicked back on his head, iron dust matted to his corded muscles that glistened in the reflections of the flames dancing off the sweat on his chest. I turned back to my own work—the wooden beams felled from the Asphodel Forest I'd refashioned into ship planks for the cause. A wave of pain overtook me, and I grimaced. For weeks, the sounds of the Damned had assaulted my ears, even seeping in beneath the wards of Hecate in our private chambers.

There were simply too many to contain. There was no room for the barrage of shades demanding retribution for their lost mortality. Demeter had killed them with no remorse or impunity, thinking I would buckle under the onslaught. She hadn't anticipated my resolve or the depth of my love for Persephone. I steadied my breathing and lifted the beam to settle it into its rightful home.

A gust of wind blew around us, the smell of slightly soured grapes and sweet nectar overtaking the metal in the air. Dionysus stood before us, his dark crimson chlamys whirling around him in a flurry. He stopped, sparkling eyes and ruddy cheeks upturned in a mischievous expression. The God of Wine was the embodiment of a good time, the perpetual party. His fiery curls bounced under his wreathed headband, adorned with Grapes of the Everlasting. He was lithe, with a strong jaw and tanned skin. Golden bangles adorned his arms, accentuated by the gold breastplate he wore. The God of Wine had come to us when he'd heard about the influx of the dead and, as a Guardian of Elysium, had firmly placed himself on the side opposite Demeter. He cleared his throat.

"Hades, Hephaestus." He nodded to us in greeting, his normal jovial lilt missing. My heart softened a bit—this toll was wearing on him more than most.

"Dionysus. What's going on? Did something else happen?" I asked, suddenly urgent. He was to work with Persephone today, and if she was hurt . . . Dionysus held up a hand dismissively.

"Everything is fine. Well, as fine as could be with a war going on, mortals dying in droves, and Zeus summoning me every day." He spat the name with disgust. I grimaced. I'd never meant to pit anyone against another. We hadn't started this war, but I felt responsible, nonetheless. Dionysus shook the bitter tone and brought his gaze to mine, forcing mirth back on his face.

"It's my Name Day today. I know we've had enough going on, but we need an excuse to let loose, even for just an evening. I expect that you'll all be there?" His eyebrows arched, and I gave him a tight smile.

"That depends. I need to speak with Persephone. Also, Dionysus, the tribute aspect . . ." My words trailed off and Hephaestus stopped his assault on a piece of tempered metal. It clanged off his anvil, falling to the ground unceremoniously.

"You can't be serious? You want to throw a party?" Hephaestus's usual calm demeanor was gone, annoyance clear in his tone. Dionysus straightened slightly, schooling his features.

"The atmosphere down here is draining life from us all. A night of revelry is exactly what we need. *I need it*. There is a famine happening up top, in case you had forgotten. There are no celebrations of life, no joy. It's . . . affecting my power. As it is, Ares and Thanatos are having to pick up my burden when I fall short." The mask of mirth slipped from Dionysus's face, replaced with worry and shame. Hephaestus deflated, apologetic.

"I hadn't realized. I'm sorry, Dionysus. Of course, I'll be there," Hephaestus said, stepping forward with his hand outstretched. Dionysus waved him off with a small chuckle.

"It's been difficult for us all, Hephaestus. You're not the only one struggling," he whispered, not unkindly. The God of the Forge stiffened, a warning clear in his stance. I took a steadying breath, willing for Dionysus to drop it.

He didn't.

"If you three could just talk to each other, then maybe you could come to some sort—" he began, but Hephaestus cut him off with a yell. Impossibly fast, Hephaestus hurled the hammer in his hand right at Dionysus, who disappeared almost too late, reappearing a few feet away with wide eyes. The hammer lodged itself in the stone wall, embedded a finger deep. The stone groaned from the pressure. I rounded on Hephaestus, alarmed.

"Hephaestus!" I barked, shocked at his outburst. "Get it under control." Command was clear in my voice, and I watched the God of the Forge's chest rise and fall with barely controlled rage. I jerked my head to Dionysus, a clear signal for him to make himself scarce. He looked at Hephaestus with sad eyes and nodded reluctantly before being swept away on the crest of the breeze. Hephaestus huffed past me to retrieve his fractured hammer from the stone.

"Hephaestus," I called, but he continued to show me his back. The Hells loop he'd been stuck in with Aphrodite and Ares was a special level of torture that even I couldn't comprehend. He'd walked in on his betrothed, Aphrodite, and her former lover, Ares, together in his bed before they were Bonded. When Aphrodite had confessed that Ares and she were Bonded already, Hephaestus had demanded to be released from his marriage contract, but his mother had refused and had forced their marriage under Zeus's command. The warring Bonds corrupted and what followed was two centuries of a completely avoidable love triangle. I often wondered what offense Aphrodite had hurled at Hera to incur her wrath, but it wouldn't have surprised me in the least to discover Zeus had been the intended target. Aphrodite had been his favorite, after all.

"Don't. Just . . . don't push it right now." Hephaestus's shoulders slumped as he laid his head against the wall.

"I'm not going to push you. I can't imagine what's going through your mind. One Bond is difficult enough to navigate, and two just seems . . . an insurmountable task. I would hope you know that if you *did* need to talk, you'd know you aren't alone." Hephaestus turned to face me, amber eyes shining a little too brightly.

"She loves me. I *know* she does. But she loves him, too. And I don't know how to not hate him," he confessed.

"Maybe you don't focus on not hating him. Just focus on loving her?" I offered and he rolled his eyes.

"He's a part of her, Hades. I don't know if I'll be enough to keep her happy. As grateful as I am for Ares's help here, a selfish part of me wishes he'd sided with Demeter. If he'd fought alongside her, then it would solidify that he isn't *good*, isn't worthy. I could justify to myself that I was the better god. Even now, he sticks to the fields, hasn't tried to contact her once. Even though she insists he isn't what she wants, I know she's lying. It hurts her and I can't do anything about it," he answered miserably. I crossed my arms over my chest and rested them over the beam.

"Do you wish you could break your Bond?" I asked and his eyes went wide in alarm.

"No," he answered. "When I went to Hera, it was for Aphrodite. She was already Bonded, and though it hadn't quite taken, I wanted her to only Bond with me if she wanted it. An arranged marriage was one thing, but a Bond? It should never be unwanted. The night before, she told me she wanted to go through with it. That she was done with Ares, that after I'd caught them together it made her realize that she'd loved me. But our Bond didn't erase theirs, and now we're all stuck. But I love her, Hades. I would just as soon walk into the Styx and pour my divinity into it rather than sever my connection to her. Does that make me a monster?" he asked, sadness leaking from him. I shook my head.

"Why would that make you a monster?" I asked. Hephaestus looked away, avoiding my gaze.

"Because it hurts her. It rips her apart," he answered flatly.

"It hurts you, too, Hephaestus." I brought my hand down on his shoulder. "Come, enough for today. Let's get cleaned up for our wives." I willed a portal to open in the shadows, and we stepped through it, landing in the palace throne room. We needed to prepare for whatever carnival of debauchery awaited us deep in the forest.

•

"We can leave the moment the tribute starts," I reassured Persephone as we walked through the clearing to the sounds of music and laughter. I'd explained the tribute to Dionysus meant that, at some point, ritual magic settled over the air and an orgy typically took place.

"Not a fan of having an audience?" she teased. My pulse quickened, and she stepped into me, pressing the swells of her breasts against my chest. I shot her a feral grin.

"Would you like that, Little Flower? Does the thought of me taking you right there, in front of everyone we know, turn you on?" I slipped my hand between the slit of her chiton and palmed her hot center, stroking her wet core. I let out a sharp breath. *She was dripping.*

"Oh, it *does*." I thrust upward in slow, shallow strokes. Persephone's grip tightened on my robes, her breath stalling as I continued my ministrations.

"You wouldn't," she dared, eyes wide with defiance. She was taunting me, and I rewarded her with a third finger, buried to the hilt inside of her. Persephone's knees buckled, and I circled my arm around her waist, holding her up.

"Oh, I absolutely *would*. I'd spread you wide and worship you on the steps of Mt. Olympus for all to see, such is my love for you." Persephone whimpered. "You'd take it for me, my needy Little Flower. Remember that I own you, as you own me. You're a brand on my shade, on the very marrow in my bones, and I will demand your pleasure when it pleases me. You will lap at the power I give you until it consumes us both." I slowed my strokes, savoring the way Persephone trembled under my touch. Her chest was flushed as she ground out her pleasure on my hand.

"Beg me for it, Little Flower. Beg me to fill you to the brim with my cock, my power. Let me hear it come from that beautiful mouth." Persephone's lips hung open, jilted from my touch.

I crashed my lips into hers, unable to take the distance between us, swallowing her moans as I pushed her higher, stroking faster.

"Hells, you two couldn't wait until the tribute?" An amused voice sounded from over my shoulder, and my fingers stilled as Artemis passed us, smirking as she walked along the path that led to the party. A frustrated grumble rose from inside of Persephone, who breathed hard against my chest, furious about her interrupted climax. I straightened, pulling my fingers from deep inside of my wife. She looked at me with murder in her eyes.

"Don't you dare," she warned, but I just shot her a sly grin, straightened her crown and smoothed out her chiton before bringing my glistening fingers to my lips and licking them clean of her sweet taste. She let out a frustrated yell and turned to storm off, but my hand shot out to wrap around her throat, loving the defiant side of her. I squeezed, yanking her body back to mine in a searing kiss. Persephone melted, lush lips parting to take in my tongue and taste herself. I pulled back slightly and angled her head up to look at me. Her eyes were full of lust as I brushed my lips along her jaw, fingers still flexing over her throat.

My mouth watered with want for her, with the aftertaste of her. I spit it directly into Persephone's mouth, and she grinned, bright green eyes alight with anticipation.

"Taste yourself, Little Flower. Later, I'll stuff you full and my taste can join yours." I released her neck gently and backed away, gesturing for her to continue down the path with the promise of what was to come clear in my eyes. Persephone took my outstretched hand and led us into the grove, still dripping for me, the edge of our restraint excruciatingly delectable torture. That knowledge sat between us like a precious secret.

Dionysus had outdone himself, and Persephone's eyes shone as she looked around in excitement. Orbs of light floated in the air, and forest nymphs flitted through the crowd with flagons of mead and wine. Many of our friends were already on the dance floor, entranced by the flutes of Pan as he wove a tune around us. Persephone turned to me, eyes bright, and led us through the gathering. We spun, bodies flying together around the statue of Dionysus in the middle of the dance floor. The air cackled with revelry and the look of pure joy on her face lit a fire within me. This was how our life *should* have been. Happy. Free. I pulled Persephone into my arms, kissing her hard, wanting her to enjoy every second of this reprieve.

A bottle crashed on the other side of the clearing, and the music stopped as everyone searched for the cause of the commotion. The crowd parted and my stomach sank—*Minthe.* My former lover sauntered into the middle of the dance floor near us, long black hair wild, her dress half hanging off her shoulders. Unsurprisingly, a bottle of Dionysus's wine was clutched in her hand as she stared at Persephone with a smug expression. My grip on my wife tightened defensively.

"Is this it, Aidoneus?" she slurred, gesturing to me with the hand holding the bottle. The liquid inside sloshed around and spilled unceremoniously onto the ground. Dionysus rushed forward as anger flared from Persephone's chest. I could feel the possessiveness rolling off her in waves. Minthe had called me by my ancient name in some show of power, as proof that our history was deep and meaningful, but that couldn't have been further from the truth. I'd told Persephone of how Minthe and I had been together, how I'd discovered her unfaithfulness with Zeus. Persephone moved to stalk forward, but I steadied my grip and held her to me.

"She's drunk and unwell, love." I pressed a kiss to Persephone's temple and Minthe let out a sound of disgust.

"He loved *me* first!" she cackled, drunkenly dancing out of Dionysus's reach. "He loved me first—above all others. You're just a placeholder. He will tire of you, Virgin Spring Queen. When he can't stand to fuck a plain goddess, he will return to me." Her words were malicious as she stared down Persephone with unwarranted condescension. The rage building within me paled in comparison to the anger coming from my wife. Minthe was belligerent and sloshing wine everywhere as the others tried to corral her. I held Persephone calmly, willing her to feel how insignificant Minthe was, grounding her in our steadfastness. I felt the shift as cold fury settle over the Goddess of Spring.

"Minthe, there's no need for all of this. You should go sleep off the drink." Persephone's tone was light, singsong. She stepped forward out of my grasp as she spoke, peppering in just the right amount of pity in her tone, enough to provoke Minthe. The nymph's unfocused eyes bulged from her face as she rounded on Persephone, marching forward. I moved to step in, but Persephone raised a hand to halt me.

"You are nothing compared to me. My beauty is known throughout the realms. You're just an uppity minor goddess with a dry cunt," Minthe spat, the spittle landing inches from the hem of Persephone's chiton. Anger ripped through me, but a small smile played on my wife's lips.

"Hades keeps my cunt quite flooded. In fact, I'm full of him now, and later this evening, he'll fill me up again. If you're having issues of your own, I'm sure someone could help you out. Maybe try Thebes? Their standards are low." Persephone clicked her tongue. "You don't have to hold on to this much bitterness, Minthe. Whatever you had with my husband died the day he found you sleeping around." She shrugged and Minthe lunged at Persephone with a shriek in drunken rage. Dionysus, Hermes, and I rushed forward, but before she could get close enough to make contact, Persephone snapped her fingers and watched with satisfaction as a plume of smoke enveloped the nymph's body.

The entire gathering went silent. The smoke cleared and the ground where Minthe had stood moments before held a small, green-leafed plant. Hermes stared at Persephone, wide-eyed, as she bent forward curiously and broke off a stem.

"Is she dead?" Hermes asked, bending forward to whisper to us. Persephone scoffed and straightened, twirling the twig in her hand. It smelled sweet but also slightly bitter.

"She'll be fine. It'll wear off in a bit . . . I think. Nobody, you know, step on her until then. She'll have a headache, but I'd wager that it's a result of drinking too much of your wine, Dionysus." Persephone motioned at the area around Minthe. I was as stunned as the rest of them at this new growth in her power, but Persephone seemed unfazed. My hands wrapped around her again, pulling her body to mine in a heated kiss. That display had me fully lengthened and needy to be inside of her, to show her the depth of my devotion. Our bodies wrapped each other as I pulled us toward the earth, Persephone underneath mine, uncaring that we were in a clearing full of our friends.

"I need you *now*," I panted open-mouthed between kisses. Somewhere my subconscious recognized that the others were doing the same thing, that our lust had ignited the kindling of the tribute. All I cared about was burying myself inside of my wife. She was still thrumming with power, as I slid my body down until I was settled between her thighs. My tongue split as it caressed over her, licking deep until my nose nuzzled against her core.

Persephone arched in pleasure, arousal flooding her channel, as I reached my hand up to release the straps of her chiton. My fingers trailed over her torso to cup each breast, teasing and tweaking her pointed peeks as I devoured her core, groaning against her in approval of her responsiveness. Shadows seeped out from me, roaming her body and wrapping around her most exposed parts. I didn't care that we were in front of everyone, though many were too busy chasing their own pleasure to pay us much attention, but I could not leave the possibility that they'd see what was *mine*.

I slipped farther down, spearing my tongue into her cunt, drunk on her taste, but I needed more. Both of Persephone's thighs clamped around my ears as I lifted us with ease and turned our bodies over. Persephone let out a squeal and flailed to stop herself from falling forward into the grass, but my shadows caught her and kept her suspended above me. I pulled her down, settling my meal over my mouth. At this angle, I could dig in deeper.

"Little Flower," I growled in between mouthfuls of her succulent cunt. Her arousal ran down my chin. and I lapped it up with my tongue before delving back inside. Another gush of liquid showed me her appreciation, and I groaned in satisfaction, lavishing in the baptism of her.

"Ride me, Little Flower. Drown me in the divinity that lives between your thighs," I commanded, and Persephone managed to sit herself up, knees locked around my head while she worked her body against my lips. My tongue stroked in and separated to hit as deeply as possible, savoring every drop she had left. Shadows wound up and down her torso, stimulating and covering her breasts while she rode out her pleasure.

I reached my hands up to take hers, clasping her fingers around mine until she shook apart from above me. More than once, she glanced over at the plant that was Minthe, smug determination in her eyes. When I flipped her over and finally drove my cock inside of her, Persephone's tiny fingers wrapped around my throat from below with a possessive strength that had me melting from the inside out. She squeezed and my cock pulsed.

I drove into her harder.

"Mine," she growled, green eyes darkened. I nodded, lost to the bliss of her possession, snapping into her with unrestrained power.

"Yours," I promised, spilling deep.

Helios

CHAPTER 26

The smell of burning dead choked me, the air too thick and heavy with the smoke and flesh and bone. In the fields of Greece, crops wilted, withered and rotten from the root to the tip of the stalks. The moans of the starving assaulted my ears with each step, ghastly frail hands reaching into the darkness, searching for sustenance.

The cold of winter bit at my bones, the suffering around me unimaginable as my eyes fell on bodies, emaciated and discarded. Entire families starved and punished. I pushed through the dirty linens of Demeter's field camp with no resistance, no guards or servants. Even in the household of the Goddess of the Harvest, famine claimed what it was owed. The goddess herself was hunched in a chair, staring out as snow drifted down from the dark clouds above.

"Demeter, you have to stop this," I pleaded, kneeling next to her seat. Her body vibrated with a barely controlled rage as pulses of her power rolled from her, seeping into the ground in an ichor that felt necrotic, even against my own divinity.

"He'll give her back this way. This is the only way," she seethed, cutting her eyes to me.

"This isn't right. Hecate and Artemis saw her; they said she chose to go. You have to reign this in. All these people, Demeter . . ."

She turned, regarding me with a trembling lip.

"Do you think I would do this if there were any choice? He has *bewitched* her. He can do that, you know. Hypnos resides in the Underworld, as does Morpheus. They could have her blissed out, living the lie they have made reality to her," she cried.

"Artemis—" I shook my head, but Demeter stood, trembling from head to toe as she towered over me. I rose to meet her gaze, but she only shook harder, as wrecked as I'd ever seen her.

"*I know my child*. She was worried about her duties at first, but after our talk, she was happy. Excited, to be your consort, and on that same day, Hades steals her to the Underworld? No, this manipulation is a power play against me. He has shown his hand, taking Persephone. If he wants power, let's see how he handles an overflow. Let the gates of the Asphodels rattle with my fury. This is the only way."

I raked my fingers through my hair, the chilling air a sting on my skin as I searched for words that would make her see reason. I understood her fear for Persephone, and the goddesses' behavior that last afternoon had been . . . off, but Artemis had been clear that Persephone was in the Underworld of her own volition.

All the while, the number of dead rose higher every day.

"There will be no one left to worship any of us, if you continue down this path," I tried to reason, but Demeter's resolve was set as she turned her piercing eyes to me.

"Good. He wants to take my power from me? Disrespect me in my domain? If I fall, so does *everyone* else."

The hatred in her tone sent another chill down my spine that had little to do with the cold. The Goddess of the Harvest showed me her back in a clear dismissal. I hesitated, conflicted by Artemis's account and Demeter's insistence of Hades's ability to manipulate Persephone's mind. When it was clear I would be making no progress here, I set out back across the ground and mounted my chariot.

There was one who would know for sure the extent of the God of the Underworld's powers, and it was time he and I had a conversation.

"Hiyah!" I ordered, snapping the reigns. We rose higher and higher into the bleak sky, path set for Mt. Olympus.

I kept my eyes on the sky, unable to bring myself to look down and take in the scope of the devastation below. The Golden City rose into view as I pierced the clouds, the air bright and clean, free of the stench of death, so high above it all. I wasted no time, heading straight to the High Hall, praying to the Fates Zeus would be in residence.

I knew it was a risk coming here, spilling everything, and it could cost me the tentative power I still held in the Upper Realm, but it had to be done. Demeter had completely lost sight of the reason we were even in power there, so intent on protecting her daughter and her own interests, but what about the mortals? Were we not supposed to stand for them?

My soles echoed over the pristine marble floors as I pushed through the large double doors to find Zeus lounging on his throne, chin tucked to his chest as he watched his cock disappear into the mouth of a black-haired woman. She knelt between his spread legs, knees pressed against the hard dais, the sound of wet slurping bouncing off the marble.

I cleared my throat, drawing the God of Gods' blue eyes to me as I shuffled awkwardly, waiting for his acknowledgment. The mess of black tangles lifted, the intake of air loud in the silence, but Zeus's eyes narrowed as a meaty palm dug into her tresses and forced her back down over his length.

"Helios, to what do I owe the pleasure?" he asked as she resumed bobbing up and down over his shaft. His fingers tightened as he guided her movements, and though I couldn't make out her face, she felt familiar in some way, the subtle power barely there in the might of Olympus Mons. When it became clear Zeus had no intention of pausing his pleasure, I swallowed and focused on the task at hand, shocked at his causal display of infidelity. His transgressions were legendary, but to be so brazen in the home of the Queen Mother caught me off guard.

"Can Hades alter mind and memory?" I asked, cutting straight to the point. The woman stilled, shoulders tight with tension, but the God of Gods merely shrugged.

"He can. There are many resources at his disposal in the Asphodels." His nonchalant tone sent a shockwave through my body as dread settled deep in my gut.

Demeter had been right.

"The taking of Persephone must be accounted for, Zeus. If he stole her, has her under some sort of thrall, we need to get her back," I demanded. His lips split into a knowing smile as he studied me, keen eyes dissecting me. With a tut of his lips, the woman resumed her work, the pace he set nearly punishing as she gagged and sputtered obscenely over him.

"I see. You are feeling slighted because you were denied a bride?" He grunted, canting his hips up, holding her head tight to his lap. Her fingers dug into his thighs as a sob broke past her lips. Anger burned in me, as he clocked my reaction, mirth dancing in his eyes.

"Helios, are you worried for this nymph?" he smirked, pushing his cock impossibly deep, his eyes rolling. "She's so tight like this, but she loves it. Loves being used, don't you?" He pulled her off him by her hair, tilting her chin to meet his eyes as she drew in ragged breaths. "You like being fucked like a whore, don't you?" he mocked, and she nodded frantically before dropping back down on her own accord and taking him deep.

I glanced over my shoulder, worried of being caught in the crossfire of Hera's wrath if she walked in on this.

"Helios, Persephone is in the Asphodels. That domain belongs to Hades, and it sets a dangerous precedent for me to intercede here." He waved his free hand dismissively, but I couldn't understand his nonchalance. The God of Gods had been swift and exacting against the few others who had dared deny his order, harsh far past the point of cruelty, but at this he hesitated? At his own daughter's abduction? His lack of action made no sense. "We had a contract, and I understand that you demand satisfaction, but I have already made arrangements for you to take a new bride."

My blood froze, eyes sharp as panic rolled through me.

"Iris, Goddess of Rainbows, will make a suitable match," he concluded, hissing as his eyes dropped back down to the nymph whimpering around his length.

"But Persephone—" I began, stuttering as my head spun. I knew Persephone, cared for her. If she was stuck in the Underworld against her will, being coerced, we needed to retrieve her. Iris? The goddess preferred the company of women; she could not have been happy to learn of this either. I opened my mouth to protest but was stopped cold at his next words. "I am looking into the situation, as Demeter has petitioned, but you do not know all of the workings of my will. You will be matched, one way or another."

"I do not wish to marry Iris," I blurted, causing Zeus to freeze. "If I am not to be matched with Persephone, I would ask that you allow me a reprieve to focus on my work," I added hastily. Keen eyes narrowed on me as my lungs constricted, pieced by his gaze.

"Your hesitation to take a bride would have nothing to do with a dalliance with a certain young god, would it?" he asked. My mouth went dry at the current of anger that simmered beneath his tone.

"I do not catch your meaning, Zeus. I have explored many pleasures of the flesh, no one more than any other." I hoped he couldn't hear the stress in my voice, but that hope was snuffed out when a smirk appeared on his lips.

"I was under the impression you had found consolation in the God of Self Love. Is that not accurate?" he sighed, and I flinched, teeth grinding just hearing Narcissus's title fall from another's lips.

"I don't know what you're talking about," I responded coolly, but Zeus's patronizing grin was enough to let me know he'd struck his mark. I cursed myself for not being careful, for not being strong enough to stay away from Narcissus. Everyone thought Zeus ruled with brute strength, but I had seen his mind in action, the shrewdness in which he collected information, squirreling it away as leverage to use later. If he knew how deeply I coveted Narcissus, it would put him in danger.

Zeus's eyes flashed dangerously.

"My mistake. I have heard he is quite stunning, Narcissus. Unparalleled in his beauty, so they say. I had designs to introduce myself before he fled Mykonos, but now that he seems to have resurfaced, perhaps I'll call upon him. See for myself what all the fuss is about, if you truly have no claim. Perhaps he would enjoy what I could show him. You know how naive this new crop of gods being born of mortal worship can be. It has been a while since I've tasted someone so lovely . . ."

Rage burned within me, but also a deep-seated fear. It stunned me, clawing at my insides as panic ripped down my spine. It was no secret the way Zeus treated his lovers, the way he broke them . . . especially if the intention was to make another pay. I had come here to protect Persephone and instead had put Narcissus in more danger. The God of Gods was goading me, and to prove his strength, he would take Narcissus if he thought it would hurt me.

I shrugged, the scrape of my armor heavy against my chest as I changed tactics.

"You'll have to let me know once you meet him. Now Persephone—she was to be my wife, Zeus. We went through all the proper channels, and Hades took her. I witnessed the abduction, and she begged him to stop. If he can come into the Upper Realm and take a goddess with no repercussions, what message does that send? That the God of the Underworld respects no boundaries and no rule of law. As the God of Gods, *you* are the rule of law. This isn't just an attack on us, but a challenge to your power as well." I finished, resting my hands on my hips.

Zeus mulled over my words, his eyes glazed as he watched the nymph service him. I tried to maintain a cool demeanor, to appear reasonable when everything inside of me screamed in trepidation. The silence stretched too long between us, and I worried I hadn't been convincing enough. With snakes twisting in my gut, I laid my last card on the table.

"Demeter is beside herself, Zeus."

"This tantrum will pass. She is just strong willed, and besides, the prayers have been more powerful than they've ever been," he waved me off, content with the bolster of power he got from their worship, the altars built to try and garner favor.

"No. Not this time. She has committed to an endless winter, and with Persephone gone, there is no spring in sight to temper her nature. The stores are rotten, the soil tainted. This isn't going to be a growing season lost, or even a small culling. She's prepared to take this all the way, and when she does, those prayers will turn to ire. They will assume you've turned your back on them, and they will curse not only those of us in the Upper Realm, but you as well. How long can Olympus sustain without their worship, Zeus?"

The muscle in his jaw ticked as his body tightened, as he came with a grunt, jerking and stalling until the face of the poor nymph in his lap was completely flush to him.

"She will come around," he repeated on an exhale, but I shook my head.

"She won't. I've never seen her this way."

Breathing hard, he pulled the nymph off him and swiped a finger over her chin.

"Go make yourself ready for me. On your knees, ass presented, hole stretched," he instructed as she stood on shaking legs and turned, stepping away from him to hurry from the hall. His hand smacked against the swell of her ass as she went, the dark curtain of her hair hiding her face from view. The God of Gods tucked his cock back under his white himation, and with a snap of his fingers, a golden chalice appeared in his hands.

"You truly think she will extend the winter?" he asked before taking a sip. It felt like betraying Demeter even being here, but what good was a ruler with no kingdom to rule, and if this got Persephone home and safe without the complete annihilation of the mortals of the Upper Realm, the goddess would just have to find a way to cope.

"I do."

Zeus sighed, running his fingers thoughtfully through his golden beard.

"Hades is complicated. We will need to go about this carefully, do it publicly. I'll call an emergency summons, and we will get to the bottom of this one way or another. In the meantime, you will tell Demeter that she is to cease this nonsense with the famine. Make her believe that it is in her best interests to obey me, Helios." The last felt like more of a threat than instruction, but the message was clear.

"Hermes!" Zeus boomed, his voice rattling the halls. In seconds, the God of Messengers appeared, golden hair the same as his father's, windswept, as he skidded to a stop before us. Zeus snapped his fingers and a scroll appeared, hovering in front of

Hermes. The Messenger God snatched it with breakneck speed, the golden seal of Olympus glimmering in the light.

"Go to the Asphodels and deliver my summons to Hades and Persephone. They are both to appear here for a formal tribunal. A ceasefire between the realms will commence, by order of Olympus. They will be in these halls in a day's time."

Hermes cut his eyes to me, his expression impassive as he sank into a bow in front of his father.

"As you will it." In a blink, he was gone, the fluttering wings of his sandals carrying him off to the Underworld. Zeus stood, stepping down from the raised platform. He was a tall, broad god, with muscles that bulked his large frame, standing nearly an inch taller than even myself as he stepped into my space. Uncertainty burned in my chest, and I had to ask, once more, just to be sure.

"Do you think Hades is capable of doing this? Of taking a woman and dragging her to the Hells, altering her memory so she thinks she's there of her own choice?" I asked. Zeus stared down at me, jaw set.

"Are you asking me to condemn my brother?" he asked, raising an eyebrow. "Poseidon, Demeter, Hades, Hera, and I are connected by our essence, siblings not born of blood the way others of our kind are. We are family in our own way, forged and connected by nothing more than a sliver of Cronus's power. Hades has always been unnatural, never quite belonging, even among us, because in him lies the worst of our creator. There is a reason he rules the Hells, Helios. I think it would be easier to ask if a beautiful, vibrant goddess with the match of her dreams would choose death and decay over the domain she'd always known? Would she leave her friends and family behind, give up growing and creating to rot in the darkness of the Asphodels? I think he wants so badly for someone to love him, that he'd sink to any level to make that fantasy real."

It was as much an admission as I would get. Zeus sauntered off in the direction the nymph had gone, and for the second time in as many hours, I was dismissed.

My head reeled, my body too heavy, and I was so lost inside my own mind that I was already halfway to Narcissus's island before I caught myself. I pulled the reigns up sharply, changing course. He would be expecting me, open and willing and ready to receive my body, both of us lying to ourselves that it would be the last time, that it meant nothing more to either of us than the hours of pleasure we'd stolen together.

Zeus had changed that. The hunger that had shone in his eyes when he'd spoken of Narcissus set me on fire with fear and fury. I had placed him on the radar of the God of Gods, and if I hoped to keep Narcissus off the board as a pawn to be played with, I would need to destroy his piece altogether by severing our connection. Keeping him on that island, away from the mess of Olympus and the petty squabbles of the gods, was the only way to ensure he wasn't taken advantage of. New deities appeared every day, and most of them became sport for the gods of old. Bright and intelligent as Narcissus might be, he was too consumed with himself to see when someone had ill designs on him, especially if they showered him with praise and comfort.

I would have to give him up, in all ways, make him hate me to keep him safe. Hot tears, thick and wet, splashed over my wrists, cheeks, and armor as I flew aimlessly through the sky, breaking my own heart to keep him safe.

To keep them all safe.

Hades

CHAPTER 27

When the Fates finally arrived, weeks after my request, Persephone was not pleased.

"We have real work to do, Hades, this is a complete overreaction," she snapped as I dragged her to the throne room.

"You're changing, Little Flower, shifting into something *more*. We need to make sure we know what that is, what's causing it and if you're at any risk," I reasoned, pulling our entwined fingers to my mouth to press a kiss to the back of her hand. She stopped us short, a flash of hurt in her eyes.

"You don't like who I am now?"

"Persephone. I. Love. You. I love *everything* about you, even the very, very stubborn bits. But you are not of this realm, and you are developing abilities unheard of to someone not of here. You can control shadows more and more every day. You command the hordes of the Hells with more authority than I do. You are beloved, and all the Underworld is grateful to have your love and light. I just need to make sure the new power you're wielding isn't going to hurt you. That's all." I enveloped her hands in mine, holding them to my chest as I stared down, giving my sincerest eyes.

"It's just a precaution, my love. I promise." Persephone sighed, seemingly satisfied with my response, and gestured for me to lead the way. Her fingers tightened in my grip as we approached, and I knew she, too, was nervous about her sudden abilities, even if she was reluctant to admit it. A lifetime of bitter disappointment from Demeter had given her a complex, and I could tell she worried now about her power being wrong. The doors opened as we approached, Admentos and Phaedra bowing low as we entered. They fell into step behind us until we took our seats.

The Fates stood in the middle of the hall, swirling masses of black fabric and energy, the greatest enigma of us all. Clotho stood front and center, her sisters Lachesis and Atropos swaying slightly behind her. The Fates bowed impossibly low to the floor, offering their respect and I returned it in kind. They righted themselves, quickly, and dropped their hoods in unison. Wild tendrils of white, black, and fire red floated around their respective owners, while the black hollows of their empty eye sockets stared through us, a truly harrowing sight. Persephone squeezed my hand but otherwise showed no other shock or discomfort.

"Hail the Moirai, the Destiny Goddesses: Spinner, Allotter, and the Unturnable. The Asphodels welcome and thank you for your journey," I greeted, thinking a formal heralding would be best. The Fates were notoriously fickle creatures, easily offended.

"Hades," their voices trilled, three different octaves overlapping as they spoke in unison, "God of the Underworld, Lord of the Dead. Persephone, Goddess of Spring, Lady of the Dead."

Silence fell, then Clotho spoke, independently of the three. "You have a question about your consort, Lord Hades," she said. A statement.

"I do. *We* do. My wife has begun a metamorphosis, of sorts. She is wielding power born of deities of the Underworld. What does this mean for a spring goddess, and is she in danger?" I was concise with my question, thousands of years of practice guiding me to understand their unspoken rules. The Fates demanded clear communication, though they often spoke in riddles themselves. To my surprise it was Atropos who answered, a small giggle trailing from her ghastly lips.

"A metamorphosis? You speak of her imbibing of your seed, Lord Hades?"

Beside me, Persephone choked on air.

Lachesis's silky tenor wafted over her sister's. "The Goddess of Growth is given a seed, as the lily grows tall and proud, so shall she."

I let out the breath trapped in my lungs, my suspicions confirmed. "Is this dangerous?" I inquired, the only true question that mattered to me.

Clotho barked a laugh. "Dangerous to the goddess? No. The power will grow, and she will thrive in a beautiful midnight bloom. For you? A word of caution, Lord Hades. That power that grows within her may very well dwarf your own soon, and others. It will not go unnoticed, and *that* is enough to make it dangerous."

"Your time is up, Death God. Consider our boon repaid," Atropos's singsong voice floated through the air, and with their business concluded, they were dispersed back to the mysterious realm they called home, billowing shadows in their wake.

Persephone stared at me, mortified.

"Did you understand any of that?" she whispered, a panicked look on her face.

"I think I do. Let us retire to our chambers, and I'll explain," I reassured her. She looked rattled, and I didn't want an audience as I tried to get her to understand.

"Did you know what could have been causing this all along?" she accused, anger flashing. I sighed, resigned.

"I had . . . suspicions, but no confirmation."

With a huff, Persephone flung herself onto an overstuffed chaise. "Out with it, then. Spill," she demanded. I chuckled at her chosen phrase, earning myself a death glare.

"Well, that's just it, my love. I *do* spill. Into your mouth, deep inside of you, even on your back or on those perfect, beautiful breasts. My essence . . . my seed, as they put it, is powerful. I have always been stingy with it, careful not to let a drop spill into another. That is, until you. You're the Goddess of Growth, Persephone. You make things bloom and flourish around you. Just look at this place!" I gestured around, eyes pointedly falling on the new species of flora that had cropped up around the Underworld. "You are an incredible goddess, rooted in duality. You are now life and death."

She stared at me nervously. "And the last part? About me becoming more powerful than you if I continue to imbibe? It was not my intention to surpass your power or usurp it."

I tucked my tongue behind my teeth, tutting as I moved to stand in front of her, resting my hand to cradle her face.

"Persephone, your growing power doesn't scare me. It excites me. Every day, you become more and more the formidable Queen you are meant to be." I said gently, searching her green eyes. There was still so much hesitation, so much damage her mother had done to her self-worth. I could feel her folding in on herself, hiding behind those walls she'd spent a lifetime constructing. I tempered the frustration rising in my chest and focused on her, on what she needed.

Praise. She needed something to latch onto. I stroked my thumb over her lips, so warm and soft and delicate under my touch.

"I will feed you this cock every day, in every way, anytime you want it. You'll take it because you're my good girl, won't you?" I lowered my tone, coaxing her back out to me. A tender moan slipped past Persephone's lips, pupils blown black with the sudden rush of her desire. Those eyes flicked to my cock, causing an ache to pulse behind my hip bones. "You'll grow more powerful, and I will worship you. Are you hungry now?"

Persephone's tongue swiped over her lips, moistening them as her eyes lifted to meet mine once more. I reached for my hardening length, fisting it roughly, bringing it to her ready and willing mouth. The spark had returned to her eye, excitement as she grinned, swirling her tongue around the soft flesh of the tip before hollowing her cheeks and sucking me past her lips. She was such a quick learner, and my cock had rapidly become her favorite subject. I fisted her hair in my hands and let her drag me forward, nipping and sucking along my shaft, teasing and tasting at her pace. She moved those sweet hands along my base, down my seam, back again, driving me wild. My stance widened, hips canting to her, and in a motion that paid me back for our throne room escapades, she coated a finger until it dripped with her spit. Slowly, she slipped it over my hip, parting me, stealing my breath as she dipped inside of me. I cried out her name as she wiggled that finger, the movement kissing so deep it toppled my control, tearing an orgasm through my body.

My hand flew out to steady myself, ripping a chunk of stone from the wall as it collided with my fist, raining pieces of shale over the ground. Hot, thick ropes of cum spilled down her throat as Persephone moaned, drinking me down, every drop. I pulled my cock from her mouth slowly, the glowing seed dribbling down the corner of her lips, transfixed by the goddess on her knees. I swiped the trail up with my fingers as Persephone opened her mouth, sucking the spend from my skin.

"Such a powerful goddess, owning me from her knees," I whispered, leaning down to capture her lips in a kiss. I could taste her, my release, the thrum of darkness with every lash of my tongue and the previously satiated need inside of me roared back to life with a vengeance.

She could become more powerful than me or Zeus, or any god for all I cared.

There was no demand she could make that I would not freely give.

Hades
CHAPTER 28

The sound of a throat clearing startled us both, causing me to hastily slip my cock back beneath my robes before pulling Persephone to her feet. We turned to see Hermes leaning up against the doorway, a golden scroll clutched in his hand, a sly grin plastered across his face.

"Interrupting, am I? Please don't stop on my account," he chuckled. I shot him a glare, but he held his hands up in mock surrender, his eyes darting to the scroll he held aloft.

All the air deflated from my chest. "You always knew this day was coming, lovebirds," he said on a gentle sigh as he handed me the scroll. "I've also been told to inform you there is a ceasefire by order of Zeus, God of Gods. You have been summoned, and you *will* heed the invitation. I'll see you on Olympus." With a blur, Hermes was gone.

The scroll felt like an anvil in my hands, crushing me under its weight. Persephone twisted in my arms, wrapping me close, nuzzling into my chest. Tomorrow was suddenly the greatest adversary we had yet to face.

"You don't think they could separate us?" she said, her whisper muffled against my chest. I hugged her to me just as fiercely and kissed the crown of her hair.

"They can certainly fucking try, but I wouldn't advise it. I'll reduce their realms to shadows without a second thought," I vowed on a growl, determined to soothe her worry, as she fell quiet.

We spent the night entwined together, drifting in and out of sleep, holding on to every moment with the utmost reverence. I committed every inch of Persephone to memory, every freckle, every curve of her hips as I battled the quiet rage building beneath my bones. My indignation rose with every errant thought, at the audacity of the Olympians to think they could command me, command *us*? It seemed a reminder about who held the true power was in order.

When the morning came, I nearly locked the gates and refused to go, but it would only stoke the inferno. For the first time in months, new shades weren't pouring past the gates, thanks to the ceasefire. I folded my arms behind my head and watched my wife as she dressed, memorized how she wore her hair. Persephone looked radiant in her black gown, newly made. It lifted and wafted around her frame, a beautiful backdrop against the stunning armor she wore—a match to my own. Thin spindles of Underworld-forged ore wrapped her torso, a skeleton cage mimicking her ribs, protecting her heart. Her pale hair fell behind her in soft curls, crown high and conspicuous on her head.

Terrifying in her beauty, it took three attempts to get us out of the door of our chambers. Neither of us spoke of it, but every moment felt precious, the last kiss, the last touch. I was insatiable for her moans, the tiny gasps that dropped from her painted lips. Persephone fixed her crown as she studied her reflection in the mirrored glass of the throne room, frowning at her flushed cheeks and tousled hair, but I'd never thought her more beautiful than how she looked now, wild and freshly fucked.

"Can we stop and see Cerberus before we go? I need to hug him."

Her voice was small, as if she had retreated in on herself, and it broke my heart. I could deny her nothing, this day, or any day, and though we were already behind, I summoned a portal to take us to the banks of the Styx. "Of course, my love. We'd better go now then."

She rose, gliding to me, stepping into my embrace, fitting so perfectly against my body. The familiar grip of shadows overtook us, teleporting us to the Guardian of the Underworld, the fierce creature my wife reduced to a lap dog with merely her presence. True to form, as soon as he smelled her scent, he came barreling out like a lost pup, nipping and whining for her attention. Persephone's smile was sad as she snuggled him close, so I walked to the new flora growing high on the banks of the Styx to pick her something. When I returned to them both, small spiky flowers in hand, Persephone was laughing as Cerberus demolished his pomegranate "ball."

Seeds flew everywhere, staining his muzzle and sharp teeth, yet he didn't seem to care as his other two heads fought for possession of the fruit. Persephone bent low, straightening the folds of her chiton with shaking fingers. When she righted herself, I pressed the small bundle of flowers into her hand.

"Did you pick these?" she narrowed her eyes.

"I did, but I asked permission first," I replied holding up a hand in honesty. "They were happy to die in the service of their Queen. Just ask them." She shot me a disbelieving look, but the corners of her lips pulled up into a smile. Cerberus flicked his destroyed pomegranate once more, sending seeds sailing through the air, a few landing on her dress. I stooped quickly, picking them off before they could touch her skin.

She frowned.

"They aren't going to kill me," she sighed, rolling her eyes.

"Eating or imbibing food from this realm will tie you here permanently. Even if it's an accident," I responded, swiping my finger lovingly across her cheek.

"Nothing in the Underworld will hurt me, Hades." I knew she was right, but that was the one freedom I could ensure she had—the ability to leave. She stepped into my arms, clutching her new flowers. "Let us get on with this foolishness so we can return home."

Persephone pulled back the fabric covering our Bondmark and pressed her lips to my chest in a gentle caress as I reluctantly conjured a portal, willing it to bring us to my least favorite place in the entire cosmos —Olympus Mons.

Persephone

CHAPTER 29

I had never seen Hades as out of sorts as I did while we'd prepared to leave for Olympus. To anyone else, he looked calculated and calm, but I could see the subtle pulse of the vein in his neck, the tension corded in his shoulders. He hadn't let me move farther than an arm's reach from him since getting the summons, and when we'd arrived in the Golden City, his grip was so firm on my hand that if I hadn't been strengthened by his power I would have been crushed. We'd arrived just outside of the gates, the picture of a united front, as Hermes greeted us, his usual roguish grin replaced with a strained grimace.

"Hades, Persephone," he welcomed formally, as though he hadn't just seen us yesterday. Hades had warned me that there were eyes everywhere here. I worked to unclench my jaw as he and Hades clasped forearms. Stepping back, the Messenger God let out a low whistle as he took us both in. I felt emboldened—we had dressed to impress. Hades's dark tunic and himation swept low, the color of brimstone, same as my chiton. We both wore new armor made of Acheron ore in the shape of bone cages across our torsos. His himation was tied over his shoulder, displaying the pauldron adorned with a skull and jewels and my new flora. Hades's bident stayed gripped in his hand, clinking against ore bracers inscribed with the runes of the Hells.

He looked beautiful, a destroyer of realms, the dark deity of my dreams. Hades had a new crown fashioned for me, adorned with gilded skulls and flowers, with pearls harvested from the Dead Sea. He'd also presented me with a necklace made of those same pearls that draped over my collarbone and molded down my chest.

"You look like the ultimate power couple," Hermes offered, and I grinned at him. "No, I mean it. The power is *oozing* off you two. What's happening here?" He quirked an eyebrow, wagging his finger between us. Hades cracked his first smile since we'd left the Underworld.

"Thank you, old friend. Tell me, how bad is it? What are we walking into?"

Hermes's smile faltered—a bad omen—as he ran his fingers hastily through his rose gold locks, upsetting his golden circlet fashioned with small wings. His blue eyes dimmed, but he looked at us both squarely.

"I'm unsure. They know I aided you both in the catastrophe that was Demeter's doing, so they've kept a tight lid on whatever the details are, at least from me. The tone overall is messy. Demeter is a colossal pain in my ass, and Zeus is pissed that she caused a famine. And then, there's Helios . . . Persephone, I don't know what you ever saw in him, but he's acting like a child." My eyebrows shot up in surprise.

"What do you mean 'what you ever saw'? I never saw *anything*, which is why I was so upset when he asked for my hand without asking me." I didn't understand what Helios had to do with any of this. Hermes looked at me amused, clearing his throat from a stifled laugh.

"To hear Demeter tell it, you were both deeply in love. He watched Hades steal you, fought bravely to retrieve you, and almost succeeded." Hades let out a snort of distaste, rolling his eyes.

"Was that before or after I knocked him on his ass? Persephone had a better chance of disarming me than that sun stain." Hermes chuckled in response.

"In the official recount, it was an epic battle. He only held back because you were holding Persephone hostage, and he was afraid of letting loose the power of the sun and hurting her."

None of this made any sense. There was no universe in the cosmos in which Helios stood a chance against Hades, and the air of dramatics seemed out of character for the titan I had come to know all these years.

"I'm not sure what he's talking about, but I assure you, that was not what happened," I answered.

Hermes opened his mouth to respond, but a bell tolled high above us. The Messenger God's jaw tightened as he clasped the large gate, heaving a push.

"It's time. Welcome to Olympus, Golden City of the Gods."

The opened gates revealed, at first, a truly breathtaking visage. I myself, had never had the privilege to visit in person. To a mortal, the palace of Olympus Mons would have been too grandiose to take in. Massive golden pillars rose high into a nearly oppressively blue sky, a stunning backdrop to the carved golden tableau of the eleven original Gods and Goddesses of Olympus. Even Hades was depicted in his dark chariot. He stiffened beside me as we passed. This place caused him great anxiety, something I could understand, seeing it up close. Everything here was meant to overwhelm the senses with bright beauty and opulence.

But underneath that golden glow, I could feel something sinister. A seedy undercurrent of treachery and deceit that speckled goose bumps along my skin, unlike the Asphodels where things were as they seemed, comfortable in the true darkness. Hades swiped his thumb over my wrist reassuringly, sensing my uneasiness, doing his best to hide his own nerves. I entwined our fingers, squeezing tightly. Whatever happened today would not find us separated. He would fight for me and I for him. Hells help anyone who thought themselves brave enough to test the wrath of the Underworld.

"Deep breaths," Hermes cautioned before swinging wide the opulent golden double doors that led to what must have been the High Hall. I let out a small gasp at the crowded room behind him. Countless pairs of eyes turned toward us as a hush settled over the previously buzzing gathering. Hermes strode in, chest raised, back straight as his voice rang clear in the silence.

"Lord Hades, God of the Underworld, and Lady Persephone, Goddess of the Spring, Queen of the Underworld." Hades held my arm aloft as he escorted me into the High Hall, all eyes on us as we made our way. Audible gasps could be heard as we came into view. I had to suppress a small smile and school my features to indifference at the unfamiliar weight of divine attention.

The room was circular, with a high-raised platform running along the walls. Various thrones sat occupied around that circle, a bird's-eye view of whatever proceeding took place. Hades guided me to the only unoccupied throne—his. We ascended the stairs, and Hades planted me firmly in the seat, moving to stand behind me with his hand resting on my shoulder. I reached up, searching for the comfort of his touch before staring around at the shocked expressions of the others. Zeus, God of Gods, who fancied himself as my loving father, sat directly opposite us, slouched back with an amused expression on his face. My mother sat a few seats down from him on his left, a murderous glare etched into her features, opposite of the Goddess Mother Hera.

Hera shot me a small smirk at the secret we shared, and I felt a surge of warmth to her. Her reputation of rage and ruin was legendary, but Hades trusted her, and she had done a great service to us in facilitating our Bond. It endeared her to me. Hermes, Dionysus, Artemis, and Hephaestus sent us encouraging nods from their own thrones. Poseidon sat next to Athena, whose back was ramrod straight, the Goddess of Wisdom pointedly ignoring the God of the Sea any time he tried to make conversation. Poseidon looked sullen and moody, his attempts falling on deaf ears. Artemis's brother, Apollo, sat next to her, fidgeting with his nails, his golden glow unnaturally dulled. Aphrodite and Hephaestus were close, but her eyes traveled often to Ares, and the God of War's to hers. The remaining lower gods and goddesses were gathered on a small dais in the middle of the floor, shooting looks of shock toward Hades and the throne he'd placed me in. It was a safe guess that no one thought he would put me in such a place of honor, a lowly spring goddess as I was. I smirked. They didn't know my husband.

My eyes searched the throng, landing on Helios. He looked enraged and spoiled, so unlike the titan I'd known him to be. I wanted to pummel his face at his arrogance, at the sheer audacity. The fact that he'd thought he had some barbaric claim to me dissipated any warm feelings of friendship I'd once harbored for him. He was one of *them*, and I would treat him as such. Zeus stood, silence once again falling among the gathered. His deep voice boomed, ricocheting off the golden ceilings and marble floors.

"It is not every day that a meeting of the gods is called together. It does my heart good to see us all here, under the same roof." My mother made a distasteful noise as he shot her a warning look. "Unfortunately, this gathering comes at the bequest of our search for the truth. Heavy accusations have been leveled against a member of our ranks, causing a great calamity on the mortals of the Upper Realm. We must investigate and be sure that there is a satisfactory ending, so we may all know peace." Rage flooded through me at the notion there could be peace after all we'd endured, the hordes of children, the innocents. Peace was pointless in the face of the dead.

"Demeter has claimed that Hades has stolen Persephone and refuses to return her to the Upper Realm. She has withheld the harvest, causing a food shortage. Many of you have heard the pleas and prayers. Demeter, you may lay your claim." Zeus sat, gesturing for her to speak. My mother stood, staring daggers at Hades above me, avoiding my gaze altogether. I leveled a stony look at her as she placed two hands on her throne to steady herself, looking shaken but resolved.

"My daughter is my greatest love. She is a Goddess of the Spring, and she cannot survive in a wasteland like the Asphodels and would never do so willingly. I have begged Hades to return her to me, sent offerings and emissaries. All attempts have gone unanswered." Her voice shook over the sighs of sympathy ripping through the crowd. I glanced at Hades, so collected and stoic. Unshakable, in the face of her outright lies. "Helios witnessed the abduction. She screamed at Hades to stop as he clutched her, then ripped her into the Earth, absconding into the Underworld." Her voice broke on a sob as I bit back the bile in my throat. This was vile. Many were staring up at Hades with disgust etched onto their faces, but an overprotective urge surged inside of me at their condemnation. I wanted to peel the flesh from their bones for daring to even look at him. Demeter continued on, lamenting the loss of the good, happy girl I once was, singing praises I'd never heard with my own ears. My hands shook as the taste of copper filled my mouth, the lip trapped between my teeth split and bleeding with the effort it took to stall my wrath.

My mother always could spin a story, but I had to wonder *why*? Was it just the lack of control over what I was doing? I knew Hecate and Artemis had told her that I'd chosen this. The look of disdain they both wore was evidence enough. I truly couldn't see the point of what she was trying to accomplish . . .

"Her power is essential to the hierarchy of the Upper Realm. Without a Bearer of Spring, we are crippled in our efforts, the waning power a sieve . . ."

Ah. There it was. *Power*. My power was a reflection of *her*, as she'd so graciously reminded me every day of my life. There must have been a reason she chose Helios, was desperate to tie me to him. Hades gently squeezed, offering me his strength as I seethed, the pieces finally falling into place.

"And what say you, Hades?" Every eye in the room fixated on us at Zeus's introduction. It was clear many had never been in the presence of Hades, much less heard him speak. He had always been a private god, conducting his business in the Asphodels, staying far from Olympus. Hades addressed Zeus directly, ignoring my mother altogether.

"I did not kidnap Persephone. She is not a prisoner of the Underworld. She can leave at any moment she desires. I do not control her. Your accusations have no basis," he finished coolly, succinctly, as the power of his voice echoed throughout the crowd with an authority others could only dream of possessing. I beamed up at him, unsure if I was even allowed to speak in this hall but needing to show my support for my husband. Helios broke through the crowd, presenting himself in front of Hades and me.

"THAT IS A LIE!" he bellowed, pointing a shaking finger at the God of the Dead. "I saw you. She begged you." Hades's grip bit into my shoulder, but I made sure to show nothing as I speared Helios with a glare that would have frozen the Asphodels.

"The only thing I begged him to do was spare *you*, despite your repeatedly feeble attempts to attack us. I begged him to take me *home*." My words were biting, laced with venom, and Helios practically stumbled backward at my outburst, confusion and hurt warring in his eyes. I watched as he looked me over, saw his gaze catch on the crown I wore, the proud and resolute lift of my chin.

"He has bewitched her!" my mother wailed, throwing herself onto her throne, dissolving into a flood of tears. She played her part well, garnering support and playing on the sympathies of the gathered.

"Mother!" I hissed, "I am not bewitched. I *chose* Hades." My voice started to rise, but I didn't care, I'd had enough of this. "Hades encouraged me not to choose him. To spend an unfulfilled life in the sun, with Helios. And he learned that day, as I should have had the courage to show you eons ago, that I will not be made to do anything that I do not want to do, ever again." I declared, and my mother's face blanched. A cool satisfaction raced through my veins as power welled at her shock. She had never heard me address her with such disrespect, but the dam, once opened, couldn't stop the tirade from flowing freely all over the marble floor.

"I am no longer the obedient goddess, content to sit modestly, to grow the flowers, to chase the frost. I have a partner. I have a kingdom to protect, and vows to fulfill. You cannot order me home like a child. I am finished."

Persephone

CHAPTER 30

I stood, edging dangerously close to the drop-off of the platform, power dripping from me as I flexed my aura. Those nearest to me, including Helios, backed up slightly. The Titan of the Sun's eyes darted from Demeter to me, his confidence clearly shaken, but my mother regained her composure, the measure of my defiance igniting her anger.

"You aren't the same daughter I raised. That just doesn't change. This—" she gestured up and down my body, "doesn't just change. He has altered you. We cannot trust anything you say because it cannot be known that it isn't corruption." She stood firm, arms crossed over her chest. Hades moved forward, wrapping me against him, guiding me back to his throne. He placed a kiss on my crown, the picture of strength.

"What power do you think I possess that could tame a goddess?" he asked, regarding her coldly. Her lip lifted in a sneer as she met his gaze.

"There are all manner of foul tricks at your disposal," she spat.

"Am I to understand that you are unwilling to hear testimony recounting how happy Persephone is in the Underworld, Demeter?

That no character witnesses attesting that she *chose* to be with me could convince you, such as the recounting that both Artemis and Hecate delivered to you when this all began?"

"The decrepit things you get up to in the Asphodels aren't proper to repeat in polite company, Hades. Admit that you took her, that you came to the Upper Realm and stole a goddess because you have always coveted our power and strength."

"Which is it, Demeter? Am I so powerful that I could alter the memory and oppress the will of not one goddess, but several others that have seen her interacting in the Asphodels, or am I a weak, wickedly jealous god who aims to steal your power?" he countered, his tone bored.

Demeter's eyes briefly cut to the low murmurs of the crowd, before she lifted her head high. "They don't know her as I do. They cannot say for sure that she wasn't coerced," she replied, choosing to ignore Hades's second point altogether. A small smile played at the corner of my husband's lips as he turned to Zeus.

"I would call to witness, Hera, Goddess of Marriage and Unions," he said calmly. My mother balked, her gaze bouncing between us and the sister she betrayed. I smiled as Hera stood, wondering if it made me evil that I took satisfaction in the Goddess of Marriage's revenge. A small part of me felt bad for my mother, knowing that this vengeance was heavy and cruel, but then I thought of the thousands of shades she had reaped before their time over power and entitlement, and that pity disappeared just as quickly. For too long, I'd made excuses for who the Goddess of the Harvest was, desperately wanting to be enough for her, to be enough to make her proud of me, but as I searched her face, I could find no grace to give. She had caused so much death and destruction over wounded pride, and now I was going to enjoy watching her being taken down, smiling sweetly at her panic-stricken face.

This gathering was not going in the direction she had planned. In this High Hall, she couldn't manipulate from the shadows with whispers.

Hera glided forward with effortless grace, commanding the room, ignoring Zeus's bewildered expression. Hades dipped his head in a small bow of respect to his sister. The two held a silent conversation in front of us all, and then Hades cleared his throat, slicing through the tension in the room.

"Lady Hera. You are the Goddess of Unions, is that correct?"

"Indeed, I am." Hera nodded.

"And as such, you are the only being able to perform a Bonding, is that, also, correct?"

Again, Hera nodded.

Hades pressed on. "When you are performing that particular ceremony, you ask the participants if they truly want the Bond, as it is a commitment that stretches across the ages and cannot be broken. That golden thread that binds the hands also forces truths, is that not also correct?" Hera's eyes glinted maliciously as my mother's face paled, the tumblers clearly falling into place in her mind.

"That is correct. They may still perform the Bonding under duress, but the question will be answered honestly. If they are being forced, they will express that they do not want to go through with it. The thread drags the truth from them," she responded. Hades looked back at me, a brief question in his eyes. Bonds were sacred, private ties that could create more power, but also created vulnerability. Two halves of a whole meant that losing one piece was catastrophic for the other. That knowledge, loose in the cosmos, was dangerous, but it was time and possibly the only thing that could put an end to this.

Hades turned back to address Hera.

"And when you asked Persephone, my *wife*, if she wanted the Bonding during our ceremony, what was her response?" he prompted. The room went deadly silent, all eyes focused on Hera, including my mother's. Hera shifted her gaze and flashed a brilliant, viscous smile.

"She spoke of never knowing a love as deep as hers for you, and yours for her. She then bound herself to you in words and body, tying your shades together for eternity. But you know this Lord Hades, as she rules beside you as not only the Goddess of Spring and Consort, but as the Goddess of the Underworld."

"*You lie*," Demeter choked.

Grief, anger, disbelief, and a thousand emotions I could never name washed over my mother's face as Hades shifted the cloth of his himation, exposing our glowing Bondmark, the proof irrefutable. Helios roared, thrashing forward, attempting to draw his sword to Hades, who made no move to defend himself. Several other gods reached for the titan, restraining him. Narcissus, the God of Self Love, rushed forward, placing a hand on either side of Helios's face, his touch familiar and intimate. It was curious, the way their bodies bowed to one another, almost seeking.

"Do not destroy yourself over the spurns of a lowly goddess. She is not worthy of your heart, your love." Narcissus sneered, the venom and ire in his words slapping against me. I didn't know him, and yet there was a hatred spilling from him that set me on edge.

"Don't fucking touch me!" Helios ordered, ripping himself from Narcissus's grip. The handsome god flinched back, as the titan stormed from the hall. The crowd around Narcissus thinned as they backed away, frightened at the disrespect he'd leveled toward me, at the rage in Hades's eyes. My husband tensed, that slight roll of his shoulders his only tell, but I could feel it brewing, that storm inside of him. Narcissus stared around at the others, lip quivering with shame and embarrassment. I watched as he swallowed, his eyes landing on me just as his face contorted in a punishing snarl. Recognition tugged at the edges of my mind, a sneaking suspicion of who the lesser god was to Helios, the jealousy that poured from him tangible in the room.

"I don't understand what this whole mess is about. Thousands dead, over a lowly goddess, clawing up the ladder for more power. It's embarrassing, but what do I know? Maybe she does have a golden cunt, otherwise I—" Narcissus's words were cut short by Hades, before the shock of his insults could land with the gathered. The God of the Dead dematerialized from our platform in a cloud of shadows, reappearing on the floor, hurling his bident toward the God of Self Love. Two prongs speared Narcissus on either side of his neck, pinning him against the hard marble pillar he had been thrown into. I was too stunned to focus on what had happened, but the power that swelled around Hades as he stalked toward Narcissus snapped me out of my thoughts. The killing of gods broke rules, with consequences even Hades would have to answer for. My eyes cut to Narcissus, frantically clutching the prongs of the bident, desperate to free himself, and a rush of pity surged from my chest.

The air around Hades darkened, creating a barrier between the two of them and the surrounding crowd. I moved to stand but a light hand on my shoulder cautioned me down. I turned to see Hermes had zoomed to me, quick as lightning, a calculating look on his face.

"Narcissus," Hades growled, voice low. "You seem to be misinformed, so allow me to enlighten you. Persephone is no 'lowly goddess,' and the mere fact that you compare yourself to her status in any way is more than laughable; it's inconceivable. She is not just my Consort or my wife. She is my *Queen*, and she commands the hordes of Hell with ease. Should she wish it, they would reduce this realm or any realm to ash. Not because they fear *me*, but because they adore *her*. The next time you feel an inkling to speak to my wife in that manner, consider that I have no issue severing your tongue from that pretty face." Hades grabbed the handle of his bident, pulling it from the pillar with ease, sending Narcissus dropping unceremoniously to the ground along with shards of marble and dust. He coughed, sputtering with a heaving chest. Trembling hands dabbed at each side of his neck. Two long slices adorned either side where the bident had made purchase in his skin, small streams of golden liquid trickling slowly from each of them.

"That will scar," Hades cautioned before turning his back on the god and addressing the room at large. "This meeting is over. The only place my wife will be going is *home*. She can leave anytime she desires, and should she wish it, she will return to the Upper Realm but make no mistake; her hand will not be forced, by my control or any other." His eyes found mine as emotion welled up inside of my chest. He was everything I could never have hoped for, my greatest champion, and I couldn't help but love him more. Hades shot me a wink, a promise that our energy would be exercised later, devastatingly handsome in his assertive power.

Demeter laughed, a broken maniacal sound that sent goose bumps down my spine. That careful mask she wore so elegantly slipped, showing the barren cold beneath, the one that had starved children, starved families, who'd only ever worshipped her. Who'd locked me away when my power, when my very presence, displeased her.

"I'll starve them, Zeus. Test me if you wish. Torture me, kill me, the result is the same. She is *my* child. I don't care if they're Bonded. Break it. You're the God of Gods, are you not?" she goaded, challenging him. The blue sky overhead darkened, storm clouds as black as the Underworld darkening the High Hall, but the streaks of golden lightning that crackled throughout it could only have come from one god, and he was vibrating with fury. I wondered for a moment if my mother had truly gone mad. One did not speak to Zeus in that manner; it was a challenge he could never allow to go unchecked. Zeus looked thunderous as the storm swelled, the lightning in the air raising the hair on my arms.

My mother and Zeus were locked in a battle of wills, but she didn't back down for one second. I opened my mouth to intervene, to halt all of this before catastrophe could strike, but it was Athena, the Goddess of Wisdom, who cleared her throat, attempting diplomacy.

"A Bonding cannot be broken, which is why Bonds are so rarely formed. God of Gods, Goddess of Marriage and Bonds, Fates themselves . . . it matters not. They have no power to remove what is forged by magic. It is immutable, even long after the participants wish it weren't." She grimaced, shooting a side glance at Poseidon who squirmed uncomfortably, shifting his trident.

"I've told you how many times I'm sorry?" he groaned, sitting up and throwing his hands wide. Athena whipped around on him, fury building in her steely eyes.

"Not enough! It will never be enough for what you did. She was my *priestess*, you coward. I told you never to speak to me again, that has not changed. I've considered walking myself into the Styx and becoming mortal just to get out of this Bond with you. Cross me again and I'll throw you instead. See if your power can survive," Athena snapped, shooting Poseidon a poisonous look as she did so. He sat back, sheepishly.

Undeterred, Demeter pointed between Ares and Aphrodite.

"You've done it before! They're Bonded, and you ripped them apart to appease Hera," she accused, hands landing on her hips. Ares locked his jaw, looking pointedly away, but I had seen the way his eyes had found the God of the Forge and the Goddess of Love's joined hands, nearly felt the longing pouring from him. Aphrodite's eyes fell, a deep shame clouding the Goddess of Love. Hephaestus's eyes touched on both of them before clearing his throat and standing.

"With respect, and not that it is anyone else's business, but neither of our Bonds are broken, and I can assure you, being on the outside of it in your marriage is not a fate I'd wish on any other." He turned, addressing my mother directly, the distaste in his tone plain. "And you; keep my marriage out of your mouth, Demeter. I, and scores of others, have seen Hades and Persephone together, and I know I'm not alone when I stand in testament that there has never been a more devoted pairing in all the realms," Hephaestus added. Murmurs rocked through the crowd at his testimony, but my mother only glared at Zeus.

"I will scorch the Earth before I let another crop grow, Zeus. I mean it. I will not bow if she isn't returned. There's no reason she cannot come home and resume her responsibilities. Who do you think they will blame, God of Gods? Who will worship at your altar if there are none to do so?"

Understanding flooded through me, a hurricane of rage but with a quiet blade of hurt. To secure her amassed power, to solidify her realm, she would starve them slowly, torturously. In one blow, she had lost me, the prospect of adding the Titan of the Sun through marriage, and the legacy of the children we would produce for her, her own selfish desires tunneling her vision. This was *never* about my safety or fear for her daughter. I studied the God of Gods' face, the piercing blue eyes, the hesitation I saw in them, and I wondered why he hadn't struck her down for her insolence.

Besides Hera, I had no doubt that he would have already maimed any of the other gods, but with her, he faltered. Over the years, my mother had gotten her way always, in one manner or another but I had just assumed Zeus had a soft spot for her. His eyes cut to mine, and in them, I saw what looked like an apology, as though he cared very little if I married Hades or Helios. Dread sank through me as he swallowed, seemingly considering how to proceed, but I knew it was no use. She had pressed on a deep wound with the mortals, challenging his power. *This* was the leverage my mother held over him. My father's power, *all his power*, came directly from the worship of the mortals. It would threaten his rule, decimate the reach of Olympus, if she took away the source. The more I learned about the power balances and dynamics of our cosmos as Queen, the more I understood.

The Underworld required nothing more than passive worship because death was inevitable, but the Upper Realm . . . they supplied Olympus's worship, of which the Golden City required copious amounts to maintain. It was a façade, an illusion, and now, she was calling his bluff. Without worship, Olympus would fall. In my revelation, a slight *whoosh* caught my attention. Hermes had at some point raced in and out of the High Hall.

Persephone

CHAPTER 31

"Persephone will return to the Upper Realm until further notice. This union was not blessed, and in fleeing to the Underworld, it broke a contract that was in progress. There must be consequences, and until reparations are made, my hands are tied. Demeter, you will resume your duties—*immediately*," Zeus declared. I felt the floor fall from beneath my feet, taking my hope with it. The triumphant smirk on Demeter's face was sickening, so smug and pleased with herself.

"*No*." Hades snarled, his fury shaking the walls, the ground beneath us. Sensing the challenge, Zeus appeared in front of him, drawing his thunderbolt. They circled each other, power ricocheting between them, visible as Hades twirled his bident, blue flames arcing in its wake. This was going to come to blows, and I was again caught in the crossfire with no recourse. I turned to Hermes, who stood next to me with a serious expression on his face, his fist extended. He turned his hand, palm up, uncurling his long fingers.

In his palm sat six seeds of the pomegranate. Six little seeds that could change the course of our lives. They couldn't separate us if I couldn't survive away from the Underworld, if my very survival was bound to it. This would strip me of the Upper Realm for extended periods, but I had learned to love the darkness, to adapt to it. For Hades, I would not fear. For myself, I would thrive. The clash of power as Hades and Zeus lunged for one another rocked the very halls of the room, but everyone saw it. Hades held his own against the God of Gods in a way none had ever witnessed.

Hermes gave me a tight nod, the time running low. If anyone found out he'd done this, there was a good chance his punishment would be the most severe, but he was taking this chance for me. For Hades and me. To the realms, Hermes was the servant of Zeus, the obedient son, but he had also shown up to help with the Asphodels. He had borne witness, and now, he risked the wrath of the Almighty to give me a choice. Like me, there was more to him than the role he was given, than the lineage that shackled him to service.

"Six won't be enough to keep you there forever, but it's a compromise. One month for every seed, Persephone. Be *sure.*" His words were whispered, full of both good intention and warning.

A brother I never was able to know, in an act of defiance for the sister he wanted to be free.

Around us, all eyes were fixed on Zeus and Hades, trading blows in the middle of the room, too busy to notice what was happening elsewhere. I raised a shaking hand, allowing Hermes to tip the seeds into my palm. As soon as they touched my skin, the power of the Asphodels ignited inside my bones, leaking into the air around us. I was a *Queen.* A monarch with a realm that needed me, a husband who adored me, and subjects who revered me. I would never again just be the Bearer of Spring.

I would never again just be my mother's daughter.

I'd made my choices, and they had all led me here, to *this*. To him, and this version of myself. One unafraid to shine, unafraid to be worthy. I crossed to the edge of the dais. Hades and Zeus were locked in a tight grip, landing punch after punch, shaking the very ground beneath us. I raised my hands in the air in front of me, calling shadows forth, *my shadows*. I could feel the surge of power from the shades of the Underworld exalting me, rushing through my veins like the Styx, the shades of warriors rattling their spears and shields at my call.

"HEAR ME!" I bellowed, my voice vibrating at a timbre laced with righteous fury. I willed the shadows to lift me, to place me in the center of the floor in front of Zeus's throne, and they obliged, responding to my order without hesitation. I could feel the eyes of the others on me, and I demanded they see. Shadows overtook the room, stretching and searching, daring any who felt themselves worthy enough to challenge me.

"I will not be sold or bartered. I am a Queen. I *choose*." I opened my palm, showing the seeds resting there, dark red droplets on my skin. I heard Demeter's shrill voice yelling, heard the bellow of Zeus, but it was Hades's eyes I searched for, his lovely face split with panic, the desperation clear.

"Don't," he pleaded on a whisper, agony lacing his tone.

"I choose you. I choose the Hells." I lifted my palm to my lips, knocking back the seeds, felt them tumble down my throat, bursting, electrifying my insides.

"PERSEPHONE!" he cried, launching Zeus away from him with ease as he reached for me. It was too late, when his hands found my body, the fruit of the Underworld was already doing its work, claiming me for its own, a deathless death for the Goddess of Spring. I could feel the nooks and secrets of the realm open for me, imparting the history and idiosyncrasies of the Asphodels. The knowledge imprinted itself inside of me, a guidebook for the custodians of the realm. Hades's fingers curled around my wrist just as a dark pulse of energy erupted from deep within. It sent him and everyone else flying back, blasting the gathered with shadows and darkness. I felt the chords connecting me to the Underworld latch into place, great hooks that made purchase under my bones, pulling at my skin, dragging me from this filth into the comfort of the Underworld. Instantly, I understood why Hades hated it here, in this Golden City. The very air grated my skin, choked me. It was a bone-deep reckoning as I tied my life force to the Lower Realm, to every shade and monster residing there. Whispers erupted into shouts around the room, and I turned to face Zeus, still righting himself from the blast. His hair, the same as mine, was blown askew, his himation tangled from the blast that had shaken through the High Hall.

Silence reigned, as I flexed my fingers and toes, testing the full weight of acceptance within me.

"What have you done?" Demeter demanded.

I found my voice clear and strong as a sense of assured calm lifted my shoulders, high and proud. "I will be returning to the Underworld. It is no longer a discussion. As for Demeter and the fate of the mortals, I offer you this—I will return to start the spring and chase the winter. I will not stay, as I cannot without the madness taking me, but I will help."

Zeus gave me a curt nod.

"I am your mother—" she began in that same sharp tone that had lashed me countless times, but it could no longer reach to cut me. Not anymore. I silenced her with an open palm.

"You have proven, time and again, that title means nothing more than control. When affection is used as manipulation, it is not love."

I regarded her, the goddess who always seemed indestructible, who assured me I was a burden, now exposed and vulnerable for all to see. I thought of all I endured, the cruelty, the countless lashes to my mind, the cold, shallow embraces that only came in the presence of company. Her eyes danced around, taking in the judgment of the gathered. I could taste her anger, her rage for my insubordination stayed on her tongue. Predictably she began to cry, fat tears streaming down her cheeks, body bowed, ever the picture of the grieving mother.

The perpetual victim. First with Hera, now Hades and me.

I wanted nothing more than to leave her there to rot on the floor in her misery, but Zeus had shown he couldn't control her, leaving us without a force to hold her to any edicts handed down. Though it pained me, I knew that the only way to ensure her compliance was to offer her something that saved face, casting her in a better light. The damage done to her reputation today was harsh, but not insurmountable, with the right posturing.

"Scores of dead have passed through the gates of the Asphodels, gathered on the shores to find eternal rest before their time. You *will* pay for your crimes, even if this is the only way I can ensure it. You will work diligently to produce an overabundance of crops, until there is no more hunger in the Upper Realm. You will do this without complaint, without resistance, expeditiously." Her brown eyes were hard stones, the challenge in them clear.

"You claim this has all been for the love of your daughter. If that is true, then consider the seeds a blessing, as I have agreed to continue my work, placing me in your realm. But if you do not hold fast to these terms, or you choose to continue your vengeance, for every harvest you withhold I will refrain from any contact with you. Even when I am in the Upper Realm. You will know nothing of me, and every god, mortal, and creature will deny you even a morsel of that comfort. Do you understand?"

She regarded me then took a sweep of the room, a beat longer.

"Yes," she mumbled. Her surrender shocked me, having never witnessed it before.

Hades's body loomed over mine, the broad expanse of him crowding into my space as his hands took stock of my body, my face, subtly checking for any maladies or marks. Controlled anger radiated down our Bond, but I had no regrets. They could never again separate us and that was worth his ire. When he was satisfied I wasn't wounded, he held his hand out, which I gratefully accepted.

"We are leaving. Do not summon us again," Hades snapped over his shoulder. The God of the Dead's carefully crafted mask was back, showing only a united front as we left, showing he would always support and stand by me publicly. I wasn't scared of his anger, temper, or ego. Though I knew serious words would be exchanged later, a zap of anticipation coiled low inside my core at the thought of the aftermath, when tempers cooled and there was nothing but adrenaline and lust to burn between us. When we got back to the Underworld, I had no doubt I would be punished in the most delicious of ways.

Hades

CHAPTER 32

Anger wasn't the right word to describe the thrum of emotion radiating through my bones. What she had done was reckless and impulsive, and even though I knew it was what had saved us, the lick of panic that battered through my Bondmark when she'd eaten those cursed seeds was a visceral reminder of what I could lose. Teleporting home, our feet barely touched the ground when I turned on her.

"How could you?" I accused, betrayal clear in my voice. My hands fisted by my sides, too afraid to reach out and touch her, not with the darkness spilling from me. This feeling was foreign, knocking me off kilter. "You're stuck here now, you understand? Cursed to this land, to me, for eternity." The words flew from my lips, harsh condemnations.

Persephone's shoulders fell, and I hated how I sounded, hated the thunder in my voice as she shrank in on herself. I tried to calm myself, to temper the rush of blood in my head before I irrevocably damaged her trust. There would be consequences for my fight with Zeus, but I didn't care. I would have killed them all if they'd tried to take her, realms be damned. My shadows flared around, agitated and restless, but so did *hers*. Persephone twisted her hands together, clearly torn in her own emotions, but those eyes pierced me with a glare that rivaled my own.

"I did it for us," she shouted, advancing unafraid into my space. "I did it for *me*." Our eyes locked, her body vibrating with power as she smacked her chest. It took a moment to realize my body shook too, though it wasn't from the steady thrum of power being pulled from the Underworld. It was . . . fear. I was scared of losing her, terrified of failing to protect her, and now, with her mind anchored here and our Bonding openly known, there were so many ways she could be harmed, so many that would covet the power inside of her.

"I can't lose you." I dropped my chin, the weight of that statement heavier than any burdens the Asphodels had ever laid on my shoulders.

Persephone sighed, the fight leaving her. She looked at me pleadingly, needing me to hear her. "I was once again being left out of the conversation that concerned my fate. You and Zeus were fighting like barbarians, and my mother refuses to see sense . . . This was the only way that didn't end in bloodshed and ruin."

I lifted a hand to her face, felt her soft cheek under my knuckles.

"But you don't have a choice now. You are bound here."

Persephone let out a soft laugh.

"Hades, I was always going to be bound here in one way or another. This is my *home*. These are our people, and you were so concerned about me having a choice to leave that you took away my choice to stay." Her words cut me deeply as they resonated. I had only wanted her freedom, but she was right—I had taken her choices. I was no better than the others. Gentle fingers cupped my face, pulling my gaze down to meet hers.

"Don't. Don't do that. Don't blame yourself for something that's done. We won. It's us, and they can't take what we've built. I won't let them, and neither will you. Today we showed what can happen when they test us. Be here with me. Don't retreat into yourself, Hades." Persephone lifted up on her tiptoes, winding her arms around my neck, reaching for me as my emotions stormed and raged.

"Still . . . it was dangerous, what I did. That wasn't very good of me . . ." Her voice trailed off, a slight tease to it that had my body thrumming. The adrenaline from our argument faded, giving way to a very different need. I could feel her desire through the Bond, strong and intoxicating, and all I wanted was to give her what she needed now, tomorrow, every day we had left in the cosmos. I leaned down, closing the distance between us to plant a kiss on her nose, showing just a little more tenderness, giving my own mind time to slip into a healthier headspace before taking charge of her care and desire.

Persephone hummed, pressing her body into mine, soft and pliant, needy and wanton. We had only been gone for hours by our standards, but it was far too long to go without hearing her moans, the little whimpers that fell from her lips when she surrendered to me. I needed her. Craved her.

We smelled like the sickly sweet ambrosia the Olympians loved so much, and I was desperate to put the scent of flora and clove back onto Persephone's skin, to see her bathed in the Asphodels, but first . . . I walked over to the bed and sat on the edge, unclasping my armor. It fell to the floor with a thud as I patted my knee. Persephone smirked as she approached, lilting her hip, swaying seductively. That black chiton certainly did something to me. I inhaled deeply, suppressing a groan, fighting to hold myself back from ripping it from her body. The pinks and purples she normally wore looked beautiful of course, but the darkness suited her as it lovingly painted her skin. Sensing my motives, she stopped short and began removing her armor before shimmying her gown off her shoulders.

"I like this one far too much for you to destroy," she quipped with a knowing smirk. All anxiety and turmoil drained from my being as I trailed my eyes over her smooth shoulders, the dip of her hips, the curves of her breasts. The realms fell away while Persephone removed her crown, before coming to a stop in front of me. Stripped completely bare, save for the pearl necklace adorning her throat and a thin sheen of shadows that caressed over her skin, she presented herself to me in offering. A dark, avenging goddess was born today, one that had been long dormant in her bones, a fierce force of nature that commanded all in her path but gave her everything to me.

"I understand why you did what you did, but you cannot deny that it was dangerous. We are very lucky there weren't more side effects." I sighed, lifting one of her fingers to my mouth, sucking it in deeply and withdrawing slowly. Her breath stalled with every lash of my tongue, the air thick with the scent of her arousal. "You broke your promise to me, to not imbibe the food of the Underworld, but you did, didn't you? Promises broken must have consequences, Little Flower. Goddesses that break their word get punished." I guided her body over my knee savoring the way she laid her stomach gracefully on top of my thighs, hair falling all around her. Every inch of her body was punishing, and after being so worked up, this would be a crucible of restraint. I palmed the globes of her flesh, desperate to feel her beneath my fingers. She let out a small whimper and widened her legs, already so beautifully on edge. I smiled. She would enjoy this as much as I.

"You disobeyed me," I repeated softly, swatting her cheek sharply, watching the marks bloom a succulent shade of crimson. Persephone bucked as I ran my palm over her skin, soothing the fire. "You could have gotten hurt, Little Flower. Are you going to do something like that again?" My hand ran circles over that same cheek, and when she hesitated to answer, I smacked it again, applying just the tiniest bit of force. Her body bucked against my thighs, an encouraging moan escaping her lips as I soothed the sting, so responsive it nearly rolled my eyes into the back of my head. Persephone squirmed, searching for pressure, and I knew without looking that she'd be soaked.

"Such a pretty little mess for me," I praised, stroking a line up her spine with the pad of my finger. Persephone's thighs trembled as I leaned forward to check her face, count her breaths. Her eyes were wide and glossy, beautiful as she panted, squeezing her thighs together to build more tension between her legs. The Bond pulsed between us, her pleasure feeding into mine, and like that it went, nine lashes peppered between soft praises and needy whines. All in the service of my goddess.

"Hades, by the Hells, if you don't do something to relieve this pressure, I will surely perish," she whined as my hand crashed down a final time.

"Poor Little Flower, shaking for me, *dripping*. The ache must be unbearable," I teased, savoring the little whimpers that fell from her lips. When she neared her limit, I took mercy. "Give me your hands, Persephone," I commanded, pleased when she brought them up beside her thighs. "Grab your cheeks, spread them wide for me." Her compliance had my cock hard and leaking beneath her as she did as she was told. I blew a gentle breath over her reddened skin, then over the tight hole she presented to me so exquisitely. Her body wounded me in its perfection, punishing, and because I had far less restraint than I thought, I rewarded us both by pressing one finger, then another inside of her tight core. She let out a cry as I pumped them leisurely, curling and twisting my fingers inside, warm walls clenching, trying to hold me in place. I bent to press a kiss to her spine, skate my lips up her back as she rolled her hips, hanging on by a thread as her orgasm built. Right at the edge, I pulled them gently from her cunt, earning a grumble of rage that threatened to tear me apart.

"*Hades*," she pleaded, turning to face me, "I'll be good. I promise, I'll be good," she mewled, seeing her edged and desperate the highest form of validation. I smirked, running a wet finger up to her tight little hole, swirling her arousal around, testing the waters of her pleasure. Persephone groaned, canting her hips to push the pad of my finger deeper inside, seeking more. She was devilishly tight and warm, the urge to sink my cock into this part of her overwhelmed me. I let my hips wind, seeking friction on my cock that lay trapped between her body and mine.

"Do you like that, My Lord?" she teased, pushing herself deeper on my finger, sucking me knuckle deep. I grunted, focusing on keeping control, but I was nearly overcome. I wanted to be inside of her, but she needed to prepare, and no matter how long that took, I wouldn't risk hurting Persephone. She must have felt my hesitation because she turned that pretty, proper mouth on me and the salacious taunts falling from her lips stole my breath.

"You want to fuck my ass, Hades? Want to sink inside, stretch me out with those rings? Fill me until I'm leaking with you?"

If we weren't already in the Asphodels, my heart would have stopped.

Persephone didn't talk that way. I had never heard her say the word "ass" before, and rarely did she say the word "fuck."

But she was right.

I *did* want to fuck her tight ass, and I *did* want to stretch it out over my cock until she was so full of me it leaked from her. I grabbed her jaw with my free hand, shifting her to look at me.

"Where did that pretty mouth learn to talk like that?" I asked, my face inches from hers.

"From you, My Lord. You're always gentle with me, but I know you want to be rough. It's your nature and you fight against it. Don't. I want it. I want to feel every bite, every sting. I-I've been practicing with the shadows . . . I think I can take you." A beautiful blush crept up her neck, her cheeks. A wounded noise dropped from the back of my throat, my muscles stretched taut as her words thundered through me. Everything she was saying was true. I *did* hold back because I didn't want to hurt her. Those desires ran dark and deep, and I couldn't take the chance they would turn me into a monster in her eyes. I was happy with how we fucked. Ecstatic, even. I could wait for her to handle more, to *want* more.

Persephone had noticed. She had seen and paid attention to my body, clocked its subtle betrayals as I'd tried to be good for her. She not only accepted it, encouraged it, but she'd worked for it.

The shadows? *Fates*.

My mind exploded, picturing her on our bed as she used our power to stretch herself open wide.

"Hades?" Her voice was low, seductive, captivating every ounce of me, this beautiful, powerful goddess, unafraid of my darkness. My chest heaved in anticipation of the pleasure. The bite of pain, to make it all feel more real.

"What do you say if you want to stop?" I growled, summoning warm oil to my palm. Persephone shot me a wicked grin.

"Petal."

Hades
CHAPTER 33

I pulled her body close, crushing my mouth to hers as she cried out at the loss of my fingers. Persephone's hands tangled through my hair, clawing, yanking at the root, desperate to bring us together. I stood, flipping her onto the bed so her chest pressed against the headboard. She rolled her hips back against mine, teasing and seeking, while I pinned her arms above her against the headboard. Fevered, I kissed her down her neck, bit bruises over her shoulder, sucked mouthfuls of her flesh between my lips until she cried out.

Rough. Nearly feral.

Shadows crept over our skin, binding her wrists, holding the top of her body straight as I trailed my fingers over her abdomen, one hand cupping her breast, the other traveling farther south to delve inside of her. I was grateful for the differences in our stature, loved that I could take her this way and still curl over her body, watching her face as she chased nirvana. Persephone's head tilted up, offering herself to me. I devoured her lips, swallowed her moans, salivating at the wetness leaking between her thighs. She whimpered when I untangled my fingers, sliding over her clit, her perfect ass pressing into me. I reminded myself to be easier, be gentler, but those thoughts fell away at the sensation of her body sucking my cock between the swells of her flesh, my essence spilling in thick drops, smearing between her cheeks. It was too much, and I pulled away, allowing some air between us, trying to regain some semblance of my composure.

I pulled my fingers free of her cunt, dripping with her slick, and slid them over my cock, before pouring some of the oil I'd summoned over my length, giving us both every chance for comfort. Kissing a trail down her back, I took special care to trace my lips over her Bondmark, to spreading her wide, teasing her. I licked from my goddess's dripping core up to her ass, splitting my tongue, pushing inside her rim. Persephone bucked and let out a cry, shaking with sensation, and the sounds, those perfect fucking whimpers, were too tempting. I straightened, notching the tip of my cock at her core, letting a dribble of spit fall from my lips to coat my head. Stars erupted behind my eyes as I pushed my crown inside, wrapping my arm around Persephone's torso to control the angle and speed.

Her body relaxed, pliant against mine, head and eyes rolling back as I fucked up into her, deepening each thrust until I was fully encased, her walls pulsing with an iron grip. With a groan, I pulled out slowly, teasingly, moving the tip from her warm cunt to her hole. I waited for her to tense, but she only let out a whine and pushed back, both of us feeling incredible, as I sank into her body, losing myself.

"You are my altar, Little Flower," I groaned, her body sucking me deep inside, pulling a prayer from my lips. "I give you my body, my mind, my shade. I am a vessel for your worship, your pleasure, your desire." I panted against her temple, the pleasure so intense it bordered on pain. Persephone's breathing hitched as she opened for me, accepting the sacrifice of my body for her use. I recalled my shadows, and her hands fell to brace against mine, every soft curve of her body pressed against the sharp planes of mine as I pushed past the first impossibly tight ring. Persephone made a noise of ecstasy that imprinted itself onto my shade, and I stilled, waiting for her to adjust to the intrusion, trying to not lose myself in the inferno consuming us both. Sharp nails dug into my forearms, marking me as she flexed and tightened considerably around my shaft. Whimpers ripped from my lips, whines like nothing I'd ever heard my own body make, fell into the crown of her hair, my body shuddering in the wake of her divinity.

Persephone pulled away, turning to shoot me a wicked look over her shoulder. On a sharp exhale, she began to thrust back, pushing past my second ridge. I sent shadows down her body, caressing and pulling at her nipples, farther south to slip through her folds, stimulating her nerves. Her body started to shake in my arms, as much of a mess as I was, the power between us shifting.

"More?" I asked, stroking her back, admiring the length already inside of her. A frustrated cry fell from her lips. I stilled instantly, concerned.

"Persephone, do you need to stop? What's wrong? Is it too much?" I grabbed her chin, lifting it to look her in the eyes.

"Y-you promised," she pouted. "You promised you'd feed me your cock every day, in every way, whenever I wanted. You're stalling now." I grinned. Her sweat-slicked skin trembled beneath me, our bodies fire and ice, hurtling through the darkness together, tempering each other.

"Do you need me to feed you this cock, Little Flower? Are you hungry, my Queen?" She closed her eyes, nodding through a shiver as I snapped my hips, pushing past the final two rings until I was fully seated. "*FUCK!*" I cried, the fit too tight, too warm, too overwhelming.

There were no words to describe what it felt like to be so deep inside of the one made for me. My cock twitched and jerked as she flexed, adjusting to the fullness. My lips kissed over the tops of her cheeks as she cried out her pleasure, her body arched and bowed into my chest. I let her rest until she began to squirm, until she rocked her own hips, chasing her need, instead of running from the shadows and me. I savored the way her body worked, our shadows caressing her skin, soothingly as I rolled her hips, working her ass over my cock. Breathless, her words fell between us, moans of my name as small tears formed at the edges of her eyes.

"Claim what's yours, Hades," she rasped, falling forward to grip the headboard, bending over for me in the ultimate act of submission. The darkness in my veins took control of my body, of the offering her flesh provided. Each stroke was punishingly exquisite, the way her body received me a divine miracle.

"How does it feel?" I asked, checking in as I pounded into her.

"So full," she whimpered, lost to the sensations.

"*Mine.*" I grunted, sinking my teeth into the tender flesh of her neck, canting my hips. Time ceased to exist, the moment between us stretching to eternity as I worshipped her body, coaxing her pleasure, drinking in every moan selfishly. She had chosen me, my darkness, my feral power.

"Yours," she panted, losing herself as she shattered. And when that word of surrender fell from her lips, I was nearly at my limit, ridden hard and wrung dry, as our bodies fell to the sheets and she curled against my chest, her fingers tangled in my nape. We laid together, just as we had done in the meadow in those early days, delving into the deepest parts of our shades, exposing all the darkest bits for the other to see. I committed her to memory in ways that would haunt me every moment she spent in the Upper Realm.

Persephone never asked me to open for her, never waited to get to know me; she sunk her fingers into the earth and pulled me from the dirt, relishing in my abyss, exposing her own.

Narcissus

CHAPTER 34

Don't fucking touch me.

Tremors rocked through my body, my legs unsteady against the steps of the High Hall. Inside, I could hear a cacophony of sound, shouting and arguments, but all I could focus on was the slippery golden blood that coated my hands, dripped down the sides of my throat. The sting of the God of the Underworld's bident throbbed as tears blurred my vision.

That will scar.

Olympus spun around me, the ache in my throat unbearable as I fought for air. The bident had done its work, slicing me, maiming my unblemished skin, *ruining me*, but all I could hear were his words, all I could see was the look of disgust and disdain, as he stared straight through me, to the goddess seated in a throne in the High Hall.

Don't fucking touch me.

My heart bled onto the steps, the cruelty in his touch breaking me. I had fallen for the titan, let him touch me, given him my time and affection, and yet he could see nothing past the Goddess of Spring. I heaved, my lungs seizing, the weight of the air too much to endure as I sobbed harder. My body was trembling as I tried to stand, to make my way to the portal that would take me home, but each step was agony. and I practically tumbled through, thinking of my island.

My loyalty belongs to another.

Helios's face arrested my thoughts as my body slammed into soft grass, the portal closing behind me, sealing me off from Olympus. I inhaled a ragged breath, pushing up on my palms in the middle of my meadow, looking glasses reflecting the light of the sun around me. Even here, he was everywhere. The sun. The light.

I screamed, lurching forward to grasp the gilded edge of the nearest looking glass. With a heave, I sent it crashing to the ground in a cascade of broken shards. Another yell, more shoving, until the ground lay littered with them, but even destroyed, the slivers refracted the light, a thousand rainbows dancing against my skin, the trees. My face stung, streaked raw from my tears, as exhaustion pushed the adrenaline from my body. I couldn't stand one more moment in the sun, under the weight of him.

Turning, I sniffed, letting my feet carry me along a dark path, the thick overhang obscuring the trail in darkness. Pieces of glass lodged in my heels, ripping a whimper from my lips, but I could only faintly register the trail of gold blood in my wake. I walked and walked, following nothing but the path and my desire to burrow deeper into the earth. The path gave way to a rushing river, deep with an ominous glow, nearly purple in hue. I teetered on the edge of the banks miserably.

This is all I can offer.

Darkness threaded throughout my vision as I swayed, standing in a pool of my blood, the bottoms of my feet shredded. The roil of the water was soothing, beckoning me closer, and as the water rose up to meet me, I heard his voice whispering my name, carrying me beyond.

•

Soft linens scratched against my skin as light peaked through the slits of my eyelids. Gentle light filled my vision, low and ambient. Pressure against the bottom of my feet snapped my head down, and I gasped, pushing myself up into a sitting position against the headboard. My heart thundered through my chest as I tucked my knees up defensively. At the foot of the bed sat a dark-haired water nymph, a cloth in her hand, the salve she had been applying to the bottom of my feet streaked all across her linens.

"What's happening?" I croaked, my throat raw. Dark eyes, the color of the night sky looked me over, smiling gently.

"You're alright. No harm will come to you here," she assured. I searched the room, looking for an exit, struggling to control my breathing.

"Where am I?"

"The River Cocytus. I found you, two days ago, washed up on the banks. Your feet were badly bleeding, so I brought you here to help you," she explained, gesturing to the feet I had tucked tight. Memory flooded my mind: the High Hall, the bident, *"Don't fucking touch me,"* the looking glasses. "You need one more treatment, and then you'll feel no more pain. See?"

Cautiously, I lifted the bottom of my foot, turning my ankle to examine the skin. Pink, shiny lashes painted the pale skin like a canvas, and I flinched, repressing the urge to be sick. I was ruined, destroyed. An anvil of despair dropped through my chest.

"You pulled me from the water and healed me?" I asked, and she nodded, hiccupping slightly. The small dwelling smelled faintly of wine, the bookshelves filled with large tomes covered with sigils I didn't understand. "Who are you?"

"I'm the Guardian of the River Cocytus. Minthe, but my friends call me Min. Or they would, if I still had them . . ." Her blue eyes fell, a deep melancholy etched into the few lines on her face. She was quite beautiful, even in her sadness. My mind warned me about the dangers of letting anyone close to me, of what they could try to take from me, but this Guardian had fetched me from her river, healed my feet. My hand flew to the side of my neck on instinct, passing over a freshly raised scar. Tears welled up in my eyes. I swallowed the lump lodged in my throat, the tip of my nose stinging.

"What's your name?" Minthe pressed, the tiniest inkling of hope in her tone.

"Narcissus. And I don't have other friends either," I confessed, surprised by how wrenching acknowledging that fact out loud was. I had never needed anyone but myself, only ever seen the worst part of others . . . until him. The nymph tilted her head, studying me in a way that would have had me running out the door if it were anyone else, but I didn't get the feeling I would be in danger with her.

"I find it hard to believe you have no friends, Narcissus." She lifted a hand up, drawing invisible shapes in the air in my direction. Her eyes flicked back and forth, as though reading something. "God of Self Love, hmm?"

"Yes, wait; how did you do that?" I asked in wonder. She smiled, extending her hand out over the bookshelves packed tight.

"Magic. Don't tell anyone though. It's forbidden for me to know officially, but I have my ways," she whispered, conspiratorially. I felt the corner of my lips tug up just a touch.

"Who am I going to tell?" I shrugged. A soft laugh broke past her lips, the sound contagious, and in moments, I was grinning just as hard, momentarily saved from my constant loneliness by the company of my first friend.

Persephone

CHAPTER 35

"I'm not going to make it," Hades whined into my neck, his large fingers splayed around my hips, pulling me closer. It was time I returned to the Upper Realm, and while my new powers meant I could travel by the Styx, Hades insisted on escorting me. The earth above us cracked open, and we rose, settling in the bright cold of the biting winter. He kissed me softly, but I returned it with fire, already missing him, our home, our life. His hands began to roam, but a sharp intake of breath reluctantly broke us apart. Demeter stood near us on the frozen ground, a small olive wreath in her hand.

A peace offering.

I resisted the urge to roll my eyes and instead kissed Hades softly on the cheek, reluctantly disentangling from him. He eyed Demeter with cold regard, and I saw her bristle, the urge to chastise me for keeping her waiting warring with the "I've changed" act.

"I can be here in a moment's notice," he grumbled, shooting daggers at her. A muscle in her jaw jumped, but he simply lifted an eyebrow, daring her to retort. I watched with a heavy heart as Hades stepped back into the cracked earth. With a longing gaze that matched my own, he descended to the Underworld, taking my heart with him.

Demeter came to meet me, hand outstretched. I took the wreath and begrudgingly allowed her to embrace me.

"You look pale," she quipped, stepping back to appraise my body with her ever-critical eye. I sucked in a deep breath, sliding down my mental armor at the jab. There was a time, not long ago, that her words would have wrecked me, but as we walked along the fields and she spoke of the intended work, I found that her well-placed needles and barbs held little power over me anymore. "You'll need to start in the East fields, it will be so nice to have fresh flowers around the estate again. You know how dreary it can be without them."

"Actually, I'll start in the North, the ground is coldest there, and it will require more energy to break the frost," I corrected. It took a few moments for me to realize she'd stopped walking. I turned to see her head cocked to the side, nostrils flaring. Her eyes pierced through me, that same gaze I'd withered under a thousand times before. I stood tall, now.

"So what? You think you'll just come in here and set the rules now. Is that it?" Her mocking tone bristled, but I didn't give her the satisfaction. "I'm still in charge here; this is *my* realm."

I couldn't help the smirk that lifted the corner of my lips, or the delight that flooded through me at the anger it caused her. "Yes, Mother, it is your realm and look at the mess you've made of it."

"The mess *I* made?" she asked, incredulous. "Dear girl, if you hadn't run off like a spoiled brat, circumventing your responsibilities, none of this would have happened!" She was surgical with her cuts, but when I didn't react, she dug deeper. "I gave up everything for you. Everything I've done, *everything* I've worked and sacrificed for, even when your magic wavered, and you throw it back in my face? Embarrass me in front of the whole of Olympus, whore yourself out to that monster—"

The fortress inside my mind fractured at the mention of Hades. Thousands of years of resentment churned in my gut. I wanted to avoid this, told myself I could grin and bear it, but it turned out my patience had a limit. There would be no more bearing it, not when it came to her.

"Watch your mouth," I warned, anger rising. Her head reared back, the pleased smile on her face evidence that she knew exactly what she was doing.

"What's wrong? Can't handle the truth? That after how hard we worked to find you a respectable match, despite your abysmal control over your powers, you jumped into the bed of the first god to look your way? There is a *reason* he went after you, Persephone. He's sought a foothold in the Upper Realm for centuries. You, my petal, were nothing more than low hanging fruit. Why else would he have bothered when there are other eligible goddesses who are surely more suitable to his tastes . . ." Her eyes raked over my body pointedly, a pitiful sigh falling from her lips as though she hated to be the one to tell me such horrible things about myself. I waited for the shame. I waited for the self-loathing.

It never came.

I laughed, the noise unexpected, but undeniable.

"I am never going to be enough for you, am I, Mother? Not as fair as Aphrodite or as resourceful as Artemis, right? You've reminded me a thousand times of my shortcomings, made sure that any moment when I felt good about myself, even a morsel, was snuffed out. You think Hades chose me because he wants your realm? He wouldn't take it if you *gave* it to him. You think you have power here? You don't know what true power is, Mother." I shook my head as another laugh broke through my chest, the revelations of my confessions freeing. "You think there is no world in which he chose me for my mind, for my shade and all the parts of me that aren't quite perfect, because *you* never loved me for those things. I used to crave even just one kind word from your lips. I was starved for it, but no more. I don't need your approval or your love because I love who I am. I am excited for my future and what is to come, and you know what? Your bitter heart can't take that away from me. You can't fathom a love as real as ours because the ugliness in your heart has never known what real love is, only stolen lust, and for that, I feel sorry for you."

The Goddess of the Harvest's composure snapped, my words striking deep at old wounds. She stalked toward me, hand raised to strike, rage rolling in waves off her body. With less than a thought, shadows ripped around us as my hand came up, arresting her swing. Flurries of dusted snow kicked up on the wind, tossing the silks of our clothing around with wild abandon. Her eyes widened as my chest swelled, and with great satisfaction, I advanced, forcing her retreat. Every step sent a shockwave of power through the air, battering against her until Demeter's shoulders bowed. I towered over her, my skin rippling with darkness, glowing with righteous fury.

"You will *never* raise a hand to me again. You will hold your tongue, if you can't control your cruelty. I am no longer your puppet, your trophy, or your whipping girl, Demeter. I am the Queen of the Underworld, and you will respect me, or I will drag you through Tartarus and toss you into the Pits."

Her eyes widened, and in them I saw something I never expected to see from her: *fear*. Her arm trembled in my grasp and, only when I let it go and stepped back, did she make her way to her feet. We stared at one another. Seconds turned to minutes, a stretch of eternity as large as the emotional chasm between us.

"Do you understand me?" I repeated, my voice soft on the dying whirlwind.

"Yes," she conceded. A moment passed between us, and if I didn't know better, I would cautiously wager that, for the first time in my life, my mother regarded me as something akin to an equal. It was a step, the first, I hoped, of many. For the moment, I was content to leave her there, in the bed of thorns she made me sleep in. The sooner I got the work done, the sooner I could return to the Asphodels. A small shadow danced around my wrist, purring and comforting me on the walk toward the villa, a fiercely proud preen on display as it wiggled. From the very depths of its darkness I swore I could hear Hades's chuckle whispering through it.

Now was the time for new beginnings: A spring awakening.

Persephone
CHAPTER 36

I had nearly forgotten how much energy ushering the spring in demanded, but I was grateful for the concentration it required and the exhaustion that came with it. It helped the days pass, and in the nights, I had less time to miss Hades before I drifted to sleep. We'd started in the North, as I had suggested, and worked, pulling and willing the first bulbs of life to crack through the dead earth. We never spoke of the altercation that took place the day of my arrival, but in moments where the work required both of us, Demeter minded her tone. It was a monumental step for her, and I could see that she was heeding my words, whether from personal growth or from fear of me making good on my threat to throw her in Tartarus, only the Fates knew.

In other ways, she was wholly the same, never missing a chance to tout her own accolades.

"They were able to pull in almost double the yield with less farm hands. I helped, of course, but they need not know that," she preened.

They need not know it was because she caused a famine that killed thousands for nothing more than ego.

I couldn't help the intrusive thoughts that filtered through my mind, but I worked hard not to let them slip from my lips. I wondered how much of her essence she'd sacrificed for the higher return on crops. It wouldn't be enough to cover her debts, but I was glad that she was paying at least some penance. The thousands of extra shades in my realm demanded it.

All around us, beings both mortal and divine pitched in to help the world heal in the aftermath of the famine. Every day, word reached us about new inventions the mortals were coming up with, inspired by the Muses to better harvest crops.

We worked side by side over the following weeks, bringing forth spring. When it came time to plant, Mother stayed with the farmers to help with the crops, and Artemis and I took to the woods to deter the resurgence of cold that had cropped up.

I was a hot, sweating mess with my fingers plunged deep into the soil, but magic radiated from my touch at the slightest provocation. Artemis sat perched up high in a tree, kicked back, lazily watching me work. Through the hardpacked brown earth, thousands of tiny sprigs of green burst, and I grinned as I sat back on my haunches, watching it spread over the ground, pleased with the progress.

"Missed a spot," Artemis teased around the bite of an apple, pointing to a small patch of soil still stubbornly barren. I shot her a raised eyebrow.

"Oh? Is that your professional opinion, Huntress? Did you become an expert on growth patterns while I was away? You can come down here and help, you know," I quipped, wiping the sweat from my brow. The Goddess of the Hunt shrugged her shoulders apologetically.

"No can do, I'm afraid. I've been tasked with serious business, providing game for tonight's revel; got to stay sharp."

"Ah, yes, and a fine job of hunting you're doing up there. Tell me, are you waiting for the game to climb your tree and present itself to you, or are you hoping the scent of the apple will lure them to your thrall?" I snarked, gazing up at her. With one last bite of her apple, Artemis rose gracefully from her perch on the branch, reaching for the silver arrows bundled in the quiver on her back, pulling four free.

Her body stood perfectly balanced on the branch as she nocked them, her silvery eyes on me as she raised her bow and let loose the arrows into a copse of trees. Four sharp cries rang out, and the distinct crash of beasts colliding with the ground reverberated through the clearing. Artemis shot me a wink and matching cocky smile.

"Show off," I grumbled, dusting off my hands as she jumped from her branch and landed swiftly and steadily on her feet, extending her hand to me. I clasped it, letting her haul me up, my arms and legs covered in soil as she collected her spoils, tossing them over her shoulder. We began our journey back to the estate to make ready for the Feast of the Bounty, a ritual to bless the newly planted crops, but that patch of dirt vexed me, and I couldn't let it go. I rounded on it, kneeling down to really dig my hands in, determined to make this ground whole.

"Persephone, it's just one patch. There's no need to overexert. You've been working yourself too hard," Artemis warned, concern creasing the corners of her eyes. I shook my head, digging deep, searching for the spark in the ground, willing it to come to me. It felt as though it were avoiding me, running even. I trapped my tongue between my teeth, focusing harder than I ever had before, demanding its bloom.

My power rooted deep, encasing the frozen roots, infusing them with a burst of energy I couldn't fathom having let loose. The kickback smacked into my chest, knocking the air from my lungs, but the power release was so intense it rippled not just over the patch of dirt, but the entire field . . .

"PERSEPHONE!" Artemis exclaimed, kneeling instantly to help me up, but her eyes moved past my head, to the earth around us.

"What in the Fates?" she asked, wonder laced in her tone. Around us, the grass didn't just bloom it *flourished*. Waves of wildflowers ripped from the earth, a dazzling array of colors it was too soon in the year to produce. The wildflowers stretched tall, stalks thick and proud, supercharged with my divinity.

"It's beautiful." The Goddess of the Hunt flung her arm over my shoulder as we looked out over the miles and miles of rolling fields now packed full of precious blooms.

"I don't know what happened." I shook my head, perplexed. Artemis's eyes cut to mine.

"Your power seems . . . stronger. It's in everything you do, your aura, the way you carry yourself. It's noticeable."

I bit down on the inside of my cheek, wondering if I should tell her what the Fates had disclosed. Her eyes were steel, piercing through me like a moonlight arrow, and I softened. Artemis had kept my council, held my secrets close, and shared my burdens. I'd kept Hades from her and then promised not to leave her in the dark again. I decided to tell her, and as she listened intently and asked many, many questions, I knew I had done the right thing by confiding in her.

"No one else knows?" she clarified, glancing around to ensure we were still alone. I nodded. "Good. Persephone, power like this, it's rare. I've never heard of a well like that, and if the others find out . . . it won't be safe for you. Hades was right to make you keep this quiet." She tucked me close, squeezing my shoulder as she guided us back through the flowers, then through the darkening forest.

"Have you spoken with Helios?" Artemis asked. I shook my head.

"Not yet, and I'm not even sure what there would be to say." She pulled us up short, her arm resting under my elbow.

"She convinced him that you loved him. That Hades had enthralled you, altered your mind. He'd said he went to more than one source, and they all claimed Hades *could* do it. I think there's more to it, but he's not talking much about it. Something is broken in him, Persephone." The worry in her tone made me anxious. I had already surmised as much, my mother's influence almost too easy to spot now that I was outside of it.

"Perhaps I'll see him tonight, clear the air," I offered, still unsure if that was something I even *wanted* to do. Helios had been a good friend to me for many years, but now there was a bitterness that tainted those memories, a pain lanced through them.

"He won't be there tonight. He doesn't come around, barely smiles. I think he tried to protect you, and he blames himself for the death of the mortals." Artemis pulled a stray blade of glass from my hair and blew it off her fingers. "Listen, I'm not saying you should forgive him. I stand beside you with whatever you choose," she promised, and I appreciated her for it more than she would ever know.

I missed Hades, of course, but I missed moments like this too, with Artemis. I longed for a world where the two parts of my life may one day exist together, where we could have it all. I touched the pearls that sat nestled in the hollow of my throat. I hadn't taken them off since that day on Olympus. Something about the weight of them was a comfort in Hades's absence, and as I washed and prepared for the Feast, I let myself get lost in the memory of his eyes. The feel of his fingers, how he held me with so much reverence it made me feel precious.

It was those memories that carried me through the small talk and ceremonies of the evening. Offerings crowded the altar of Demeter, and even through that, the memories of Hades soothed me. I danced, reveled, and drank my fill of wine, but none of it soothed the ache of him.

"I need a rest!" I panted, pulling from Artemis's grip. Another body took the place of mine, and they twirled, their forms a blur in the firelight. I was startled by something from the edge of my vision, and when I turned fully, I was sure I'd seen it. There, in the dancing light, a shadow wavered, out of place. I waited, just to make sure, but there was no denying the unnatural way it moved, teasing me. Tempting. The music rolled over the gathering, seducing hearts and spirits with such absolution that none even noticed when I slipped out into the darkness, heart racing, chasing the rogue shadow. It flitted over the grass, wrapping around my ankles occasionally just to make sure I kept up, and when it darted between a large crevice in stone, I slowed my steps, willing my breath to calm.

Moonlight danced over my skin, blessing my passage into the abyss. My steps never faltered, and when I passed through, my body hummed in anticipation. His scent was everywhere, the feel of his body hard and possessive against mine as Hades wrapped me in his arms, burying his face in my neck.

"This is a risk, Little Flower," Hades cautioned between kisses, his hands urgent as they pulled my body impossibly close. His teeth scraped over my throat, and I let out a breathy moan, loud and resounding in the small cave.

"Shhh," he cautioned, slipping his hand over my mouth to muffle my sighs as he lifted my chiton and gently spread my thighs. I was hot all over, burning without him, and when he pushed me up against the cold stone, I relished in the damp bite, the pressure of his hard cock splitting me wide. It had been weeks since I'd left him in the Underworld. We'd sent shadows back and forth, and he'd left me gifts, but today I had needed *him*, and he had come. We were playing a dangerous game, one that threatened to shatter the fragile peace we'd worked so hard to build. But being without Hades felt like a dagger through a butterfly's wing, and I was trapped without him here.

Hades always came for me.

He pressed into me, his body hard against my softness, and I cried out against his hand at the ache building in my core.

"I missed this, *fuck*," he groaned in my ear, the lowered tenor shooting sparks up my spine. The stone bit into my breasts as he thrust in deeper, that glorious cock dragging along every inch inside of me. Hades's hand slipped down from my mouth to clasp my neck, controlling the angle of my head until I was bent backward, arched up for him.

"There, yes, Hades!" I moaned and he kissed me hungrily, swallowing the sounds he pulled from deep inside of me.

"I couldn't stay away, Little Flower. I haven't slept since you've been gone," he confessed, his words and shade wrapping around me. I threw my hips back into his, meeting him thrust for thrust.

"I needed you, Hades. Hells, I needed you. Please don't let me go," I panted, desperate for the release building deep inside of me. In his arms I felt safe. *Loved.*

"Never," he promised, his grip turning possessive as he pulled out of me to flip me around. My back pressed into the wall as he lifted my legs, locking them around his waist. I reached between us, gripping his hard cock, and Hades cursed, pressing his forehead to mine.

"Do you love me?" I asked, slipping his head up and down as his breath quickened.

"I would die for you," he vowed, his eyes fluttering shut with pleasure.

"Then show me. Give me everything that's mine," I commanded, sliding him down. A feral growl rocked through Hades's chest as he thrust, jolting my body under his intrusion. Shadows wrapped around my wrists, bringing them above my head, and his hands followed, pinning me to the wall as he fucked into me with wild abandon.

"Forever," he groaned, all thoughts of silence and discretion gone. "There will never be another, Little Flower. I belong to you, and you will only ever belong to me." His cock swelled inside of me, my body shaking as his length kissed deep inside, my own body weight pulling me down deeper on top of him.

I came with a cry, his hand back on my throat, and Hades gasped into my lips as he shuddered against me. Warmth bloomed, heavy and comforting as he spilled inside of me, and a zing of power set my skin on fire. Hades stilled and I slumped when the shadows released me, but my dark god cradled me to his chest and walked us back to the bed he'd conjured.

"Stay with me," he pleaded, as I tried to untangle myself. I placed a kiss to his lips and pulled the strap of my chiton back up my shoulder.

"You know I have to go." I hated saying those words, the space between us too great. Hades sprung up from the bed, grabbing me around the waist and pulling my back against his chest. A peel of laughter pulled out of me as I thrashed to stand upright again, but I made no real effort to break his hold. He pressed his lips to the side of my neck, licked at the line of sweat he'd worked up on me with that wicked tongue.

"I don't know if I'll survive another few months of this," he whined, the sound so unbecoming of the Lord of the Underworld.

"You will. And then I fully expect to not leave our bedchambers for even a moment when I return." I lifted my chin expectantly, as his hand came up to cup my jaw.

"As my Queen wishes."

Moments stolen in the dead of night made for too early of a morning, but even though my body protested, the soreness between my thighs tender and biting, I dragged myself out of bed to heed my calling, knowing that below, Hades was waiting for me to come home to him.

Helios

CHAPTER 37

"Get up," Ares grunted, nudging me with the toe of his sandal. I groaned, my body pressed against the hard floor and my head spinning from the finished bottles of Dionysus's wine that lay discarded around me, soaking the floor and a scroll Hermes had delivered with the golden Olympian seal.

"Now, let's go," the God of War commanded.

"Fuck off." I batted him away, turning my heated cheek against the stone. It felt good, soothing nearly.

"Have it your way," he muttered. My body lurched as Ares bent down and, with a heave, slung me over his shoulder like a sack of grain. I cried out, arms flailing, disoriented as my body bounced against him until I was falling backward, my reactions too slow to catch myself. With a sharp grunt, Ares deposited me in the dirt outside my door, but before I could scramble to my feet and right myself, a crack of thunder overhead heralded a deluge of icy rain that pelted against me.

"Argh, fucking Fates!" I snarled, ripped out of my stupor. The cold water relented, and I swiped at my eyes, clearing the sleep and the drink as Ares stood over me, hands resting on the sword at his hip.

"You smell like shit," he observed, staring down at me over his nose. Stars glinted off his golden armor as his horses neighed near mine, hooves pawing the ground.

"What do you want?" I asked, pressing the backs of my palms into my eyes, hoping to ease the near-constant dull thud that had taken residence there. Ares tilted his head, as though considering the question.

"You missed our meeting."

I reared back incredulously.

"You showed up to my home, tossed me outside in the dirt, and sprayed me with water because I didn't go drinking with you?" Anger lashed through me, and I stood, sucking in a deep breath to try to stop the vertigo that had my head reeling.

"That sounds right, yes," he answered, looking so fucking unbothered. My lips lifted as a thousand insults flew through my mind, searching for one to spear him with, but the General only waited, brown eyes taking me in.

"This is beneath you, Helios. They all think you're self-destructing over Persephone, but it occurred to me that prior to all this, I'd only ever heard you speak of her platonically. Suddenly, you're beating your chest like an animal over a broken betrothal, waging war on the Asphodels, and now what, drinking yourself into oblivion in a manner that makes Dionysus look downright restrained?"

I swore, averting my gaze.

"You're too observant for your own good, you know that?" I groused. Ares's mouth tightened in a brief frown as he shrugged.

"Or maybe you're just a terrible liar."

Nausea ripped through me at his words, a panic that ran bone deep.

"Fates, I hope not."

Ares leaned against the side of my door, waiting. Watching. I contemplated telling him everything, telling somebody the weight of the burden that had been on my shoulders through all this. If anyone could understand a hopeless love and the sacrifice made for it, it was Ares. I pushed my dripping hair from my face and leaned back, tilting my head to the heavens.

"This isn't about Persephone, not completely anyway." Ares pursed his lips, shuffling in his armor, the metal tinkling as he waited, and because I was exhausted from the lie, tired of being on an island all alone with this, I told him. I told him everything, of Demeter and what I'd come to learn was manipulation. I spoke of the waning power, at the role I'd felt duty-bound to play in securing the safety of the Upper Realm. Ares's face remained impassive until, on choked breath, I told him about Narcissus. Shame washed through me as I recounted all the ways I had failed him.

"You let them all believe it was jealousy over Persephone that has wrecked you, so that none suspected your feelings for him," he said. I raked my hand over my face, steepling my fingers beneath my chin.

"Yes. Narcissus isn't like us, Ares. He's delicate, naive in the ways of our world. He'd only ever focused on himself, and I couldn't let Zeus get his hooks in him—"

Ares's head snapped down, affording me his rapt attention.

"Zeus knows the depth of your feelings?"

"I believe he suspects. It's what scared me into pushing him away in the first place. Persephone is his daughter. He wouldn't hurt her, but Narcissus . . ." I trailed off, the implications clear.

"You would be shocked to know the lengths my father would go in order to punish his children," Ares whispered, a far-off look on his face. He pushed off the wall, striding to stand in front of me, arm extended. "I have heard he has already ordered your betrothal to another? Iris, yes?"

"In two weeks' time." I nodded, miserably, knowing he had chosen her because our children would be half of the sky and would serve him. That scroll had felt like a death sentence in my hands, and I had refused his summons.

"You were right to disguise your true intentions. Zeus will wield any weapon he can, not caring who it maims if it means garnering more control. He's been looking for a stronger foothold in the Upper Realm for ages. Just look at what he did to Artemis and Orion, when she tried to marry him against Zeus's wishes, or Apollo and Hyacinthus after Apollo wouldn't bend and marry Cassandra."

I clasped his hand and let him haul me up. Soaked, I pulled the heat of the sun from my bones, until my skin glowed with heat and warmth, evaporating the droplets and trails of water.

"I thought Zephyrus killed Hyacinthus over jealousy?"

Ares nodded.

"He did. But do you think the Wind God would ever act against a child of Zeus without regard for retribution? Nothing is done without his command, Helios. Apollo defied him, and Zeus punished him for it. He always manages to keep his hands clean, but that doesn't mean he doesn't orchestrate and manipulate the conditions. If you deny his command to marry Iris, he'll kill Narcissus to punish you. In case you were considering that path."

Ares walked over to his black chariot, leaning over the edge, the clink of glasses filling the air. When he righted himself, a bottle was clutched in his fist. The God of War blew right past me, inviting himself in my home for the second time tonight.

"You owe me a drink," he called over his shoulder as he disappeared inside. Silence fell around me as I took in the night, watching the stars shoot across the heavens. When I finally followed him inside, I felt a fraction lighter for the first time in months, having shared my burdens but still heavy and sad at his cautionary words.

He was right. I *was* considering begging for forgiveness and telling Narcissus everything. Ares was also correct that it would just get him killed faster.

When we'd drank ourselves into a stupor, the night filled with laughter and camaraderie, and though the crater in my chest still ached for the sweet, delicate face of Narcissus, I comforted myself that I had done the right thing in letting him go.

Narcissus

CHAPTER 38

"I hate that I can't just stop thinking about him. It shouldn't hurt so badly still, r-right?" A wine-induced hiccup worked its way up my throat, catching in my chest. Across from me, Minthe uncorked another bottle, refilling my empty chalice.

"No, of course it does. You loved him. There isn't a time limit on heartache; trust me on that," she mumbled, lifting her glass to toast with mine. The warm liquid washed over my tongue, unleashing my inhibitions, and with it, the humiliation I couldn't help but relive without the reprieve of Minthe's wine.

"I did, but that's not what ruins me." I leaned forward, gesturing two fingers for her to come closer. "I'm embarrassed because how pitiful is it to love a man that tells you outright all he wants is sex? It's so hard to hate him because he told me, over and over" I groaned, draining half my cup in one gulp. Minthe rocked her head from side to side, pursing her lips.

"He was sending you so many mixed signals, no matter what his mouth said. Titans and gods, all the fucking same."

"Right?" I replied, reaching to pop a scoop of ambrosia onto a grape before taking a bite. "Thank you, truly, for being here for me these last few weeks. I've never had someone I could count on, be really vulnerable with before, not without them wanting something from me in exchange." My words caught, emotion mixing with the libations. I had begun to live for these interludes, to lean on the strength and comfort they provided. Even if the wine she brought made me feel fuzzy, it was a welcome oblivion compared to the misery I sat in without her. Minthe smiled sympathetically, reaching her hand across the table to grasp mine.

"Happy to do it, Narcissus. Sometimes I think the convergence brought you down my river as an act of the Fates." Warmth bloomed from my chest to my fingers, as I allowed her words to comfort me.

"You know, I've been wondering something. More and more we talk about Helios, about that feeling of connection when it was only the two of you, but then when she was around, it was as though you didn't exist? I'm curious if that wasn't by design . . ." Minthe trailed off, sipping thoughtfully.

"What do you mean?" I asked, my wine-logged mind working hard to keep up.

"Well, you haven't been around the other gods as much, but did you know that before they Bonded, Hades had another lover?" she whispered, eyes cutting around the room. My jaw dropped.

"What? *No*!" I exclaimed, leaning in. Minthe pursed her lips and leaned back, nodding.

"Oh yeah. He was *obsessed* with her for centuries. There was a misunderstanding, and they were taking some time to work through things, but everyone knew they would end up back together." My eyes blew wide, the onslaught of information sending me reeling. "That was until that spring cunt strutted into the Underworld and moved right into the palace. It was a scandal down here in the Asphodels. When my friend confronted little miss flower princess, that bitch turned her into a fucking *plant*."

"She can do that?" I gasped, shocked. Minthe nodded, gulping down the rest of her wine.

"Apparently. She never could before, but I think she learned how. Persephone had one job for thousands of years: make flowers bloom. And now she's transforming nymphs into herbs. Sounds like witchcraft to me, and we both know it can be taught." She shrugged, reaching for the bottle to refill our glasses. Her disdain for the Goddess of Spring seemed to rival mine, and now that made so much more sense. Minthe cared deeply about those she considered friends. She would have taken that death hard.

"You think she could have done something to Helios?" I asked softly, but even as I said them, the words didn't quite feel right. She poured more wine into my chalice, adding to it the herbs she said gave it a little more kick. I took a long sip and felt more of my body relax.

Minthe pursed her lips, dragging her finger over the rim of her chalice.

"I didn't want to say anything while you were still so torn up over it, but hearing you tell it, yes. I think she probably had her sights set on the titan, but when one of the most powerful gods presented himself to her, she took the opportunity and turned her tricks on Hades." I drank again, and her words made more and more sense. Jealousy curled through the pit of my stomach. I was drunk on the wine and wounded from the ache in my chest, a Helios-shaped hole that never seemed to heal, only scar, still throbbing.

I rubbed my fingers absentmindedly over the raised skin on the side of my neck.

"Could it be broken? The spell?"

Minthe sighed, stretching.

"There are ways to break anything, but something of that caliber would be dangerous, and she's proven to be resourceful. It's late; we should retire." The nymph drained the last of her drink then stood, stumbling over to my bed, snuffing out the dancing flames in my sconces with a wave of her hand. I drained the rest of my glass and followed, collapsing on top of the blanket next to her, grateful she'd imbibed too much to make her way back to the Underworld. My bungalow felt too quiet most days, with just me alone with my thoughts, but Minthe had a way of making me feel heard. She helped me see things as they were, was protective when she spoke of the hurt I was entitled to feel at the injustices that had happened to me in the name of the Olympians. I listened as her breathing slowed, evening out as she drifted into the Dream, but my mind raced.

"Minthe?" I whispered into the darkness.

"Hmm?"

"How would we do it? Break her hold?"

My eyes adjusted to the low light in time to see Minthe prop up on her elbow, facing me. I turned on my side, meeting her gaze. I could see the hesitation in her eyes as she searched mine, but after a few moments, she spoke.

"The only way to break someone in that deep of a thrall is distance and time. Lock her up, throw away the key, and let the magic leech from her victims. I actually—" she stalled, as I leaned closer. "I really shouldn't say."

I pushed up on my own elbow, giving her my full attention, wanting her to trust me, to confide in me. I wanted her to like me and keep being in my life. She was my only confidant.

"*Tell me*," I pleaded.

"It's dangerous, but Hades's former lover had worked out how to do it. Came to me to trade a few things in preparation, but before she could get the last component, boom. Plant." Minthe snapped her fingers together. I settled back down, staring up at the canopy above us. The introspection lasted only a moment.

"What was the last component?" I asked, telling myself it was simple curiosity, that I would do nothing with the knowledge.

"A golden net. Fashioned by the God of the Forge, Hephaestus. It's the only thing strong enough to trap that kind of power, and if we wanted to keep her tucked away, we would have to ensure she couldn't be found or escape." My head snapped sideways, my heart beating so fast I thought I might explode. "Wouldn't that enrage Zeus? We couldn't kill a goddess, much less his daughter."

"We wouldn't be *killing* her. It would be easy enough to bind her in sleep then release her once we were sure the spell was broken. As for Zeus . . ." A glint of mischief passed over Minthe's eyes, her lips curling back into a ferocious grin. "He would never have to know it was us. Mortals are easy enough to manipulate; there's always a pressure point at easy access. Money, power, the promise of immortality. Someone to bear the wrath while we work uninterrupted."

In the darkness, I felt my mind work to imagine it, the wine floating me on Minthe's words. She, too, was a witch, though a hidden one, and she was right about the dangers of bending free will. Hearing of Hades's first love, how many others had to suffer for the aspirations of one goddess? I listened as Minthe recounted the details of her friend's plan with rapt attention as she laid it all out, step by step, mulling it over. They had been close to bringing it to fruition when Persephone had murdered her friend, with the exception of the net. By the time dawn broke over the horizon, Minthe's words had taken root inside my mind, twisting and turning like vines, hooking deep. It was insanity, but there was enough drink in my system to lend me courage, as I spoke into the quiet rays of morning light.

"I know where we can get a net like that," I whispered.

Helios's door opened for me with little resistance, his estate still seemingly devoid of servants as I made my way inside. It had been weeks of wavering, of scheming, of second-guessing, over bottles of wine with Minthe, but the time had come. All the moving parts were primed, and I was eternally grateful for Minthe's guidance, her fierce loyalty, her steadfastness when I had wavered. The plan was a risk, with strings that could unravel, but she had shown up for me, and soon, Helios would be free of the hold Persephone had on him.

I found the Titan of the Sun in his bedroom, a place I'd only ever been in once before, the night Ares bade me come to him. Helios's naked body stretched out, entangled in the sheets, the broad expanse of his chest exposed to the air. He tossed and turned in a restless sleep. A thick beard covered his jaw, his unkempt strawberry-blond hair fanning out over his pillow, and for a moment, I allowed myself to watch him.

I traced my finger over his brow, my touch barely there, but his eyes opened slowly, his body arching, chasing my warmth even half asleep.

"Narcissus?" he mumbled, his voice gruff and gravelly with sleep. "W-what, why are you here?"

I brought my finger down over his mouth, relishing the low moan that exhaled from his parted lips at my touch. Heat burned with the blaze of a thousand suns in his eyes as I slipped my leg over the top of his waist, straddling his wide torso. Warm hands fell to the tops of my thighs as he stared up at me, questions in his eyes, our lips breaths apart.

"Just a taste," I whispered, hovering above him, waiting.

"Just a taste," he repeated.

His lips melted against mine, hungry but tempered, savoring as our tongues danced. I should have come earlier while he was carrying the sun across the sky, but I was weak when it came to Helios. I gave myself permission to be self-indulgent, as my hips rocked over his cock, the thin sheet and fabric of my himation all that separated us. My body roared to life under his touch, the sloppy kisses that turned more urgent as I nipped at his lip, wrapping a fistful of his hair in my grip, tugging him up until he sat flush against my chest. His hands gripped my hips, strong arms banded around me, and I nearly wept at the depth of this position. Staring into his eyes was too much, too intimate.

"Tell me what you need, baby boy," he said, pushing my hair back behind my ear, golden eyes staring into mine.

"Make me hate you," I replied, too raw for his gentleness. A sad smile ghosted over the corners of Helios's lips as he dipped his chin, just once.

"Okay."

He turned urgent in his lust, rough hands on my body, commanding. Hastily, I slid my fingers down past the barriers between us, gripping the massive length underneath with considerable force. Helios hissed, cock hot in my palm, my body buzzing with anticipation, even while my heart raged against the aftermath. His fingernails scraped over my scalp, his hands back in my long tresses as he tugged my head down until I was kneeling between his outstretched legs, my mouth inches from his throbbing head.

"Suck," he commanded, and I instantly stroked him faster, taking him past my lips. Helios groaned, tilting his head back as he snapped his hips into me, fucking my face in harsh thrusts that shot lightning down my spine. He tasted salty, mixed with citrus and sunshine, and Fates how I'd *craved* him. So long without his hands on me, his body and scent and tongue worshipping me, had left me needy and shaking for him. His cock swelled in my mouth, thick and veiny as every brutal push filled my mouth, tickled along the back of my throat. I flattened my tongue against the underside of his length, flicking along a throbbing vein as I stroked him in and out of my hollowed cheeks.

"Look at me," his voice cracked, movements erratic. I snapped my eyes to his as he released in jerky spurts. His seed slid down the back of my throat, a small pool catching on my tongue. He held my face to him as he groaned, using me, a soft hum escaping him as he pulled past my lips. I opened my mouth, exposing the little puddle of his desire waiting for him, just how he liked. The titan smirked, holding out his hand for me to spit into it. I obeyed, and he abruptly pushed me away from his chest, spinning my body, kicking my legs apart with his muscular thighs as he settled behind me. His hands gripped my hips, hauling me up on my hands and knees.

"So ready and willing for me," he whispered, sliding his hand down my spine. Goose bumps erupted in his wake, and I panted, desperate for him, hating myself and lost in the moment all at once. Of course, I had spent the day readying myself for him, inspecting every plane of my body in the mirror until I knew I was perfect, or as close to perfect as I'd ever get again. I nodded, draping my head over my arms, pressing into the bed. He took his time, running his hands over the globes of my ass, tracing up the inside of my thighs as I shivered beneath his touch. I needed him to fuck me hard and fast, to make me bend to his will one last time because every caress pushed me closer to losing my nerve.

Helios leaned over me, whispering praises against my shoulder blade, up over my spine. I took a steadying breath as he coated his cock and my hole with the remnants of his essence and something warmer, oil he'd no doubt conjured to ease the ache. I arched my back, as he pushed inside slowly, calmly. Fucking veneration, his strokes lovely, deep, shade-crushingly gentle. I pressed my head into the bed, swiping the evidence of tears from my eyes as he stretched me wide, splitting me in two. The intimacy of how he held me was the thing that did me in every single time he took me, had me questioning how he truly felt, because the way his body tempered mine was holy work.

I rebuked the emotion surging between us. This would be the last time, on my terms. I wanted him to fuck me roughly. I wanted to hate him, needed him to wound me, if I was ever going to be strong enough to let go. The longer he whispered how beautiful I was, how good it felt inside of me, my name falling from his lips as he fucked me into oblivion, was dangerous for me. I would cave and we would spend eternity in this endless loop of misery and pleasure, just like Minthe had said. The wine I'd drunk earlier gave me strength and courage as he took me faster, harder.

"Helios," I groaned as he worked his hips to hit a spot inside of me that stunted my breath. "Helios, *harder*. I want you to take me. I can handle it. Punish me." I bucked back against him roughly, squeezing my muscles around him as I canted my hips.

"Hit me," I demanded. "Wrap those fucking hands around my throat, *now*." Helios all but stopped thrusting, eyes flashing with warning, but I would have none of it. "If you won't fuck me, I'll find someone who can." I taunted.

A growl rumbled from deep inside of him as Helios gripped my hips with both hands and began the most cosmos-shattering assault on my body I'd ever experienced. His large hand came down in a smack against my sensitive flesh, and I hissed as he smoothed it over with his palm.

"Is this what you want?" he grunted, plowing into me relentlessly. Helios bent my head back to look at him, his large hands splayed around my throat as he devoured my mouth. "You want me to rip you apart, beautiful boy?" He slipped in and out of me as I begged for more, relishing when his palm smacked into my cheek. There was a time when a mark on my face would have devastated me, but my once perfect skin was already in ruin from Hades, and I didn't care if Helios bruised and scarred me for all to see.

I didn't care about anything in this body anymore.

"Yes, harder," I groaned, slumping forward. Helios flipped me to face him, bending my knees as he spread my thighs wide.

"So. Fucking. Tight," he ground out, grabbing my hair as reigns while he drilled into me, my cock bouncing between the two of us. His hands were just as punishing, and *Fates*, I hoped there would be bruises. He would ruin this vessel on the outside like he already had on the inside. Helios leaned forward, his heavy body covering mine as he kissed a trail up my neck. I melted, arching my head backward, letting myself have this. I could feel his tongue move over one of the raised scars from Hades's bident, and I clenched up, constricting the cock buried deep inside of me.

"*Fuck*," Helios swore, straightening to drive his hips into me harder. When his hand wrapped around my cock I exploded, coating his toned torso and parts of his face in my cum. I writhed beneath him as he snapped into me with an almost lazy, circular motion, letting me ride my high. My eyes rolled back, my body buzzing with pleasure and the drink, until all I could see was the full glow of his aura. It had never been like this before, and I lost myself in the pleasure of pain, all plans of resistance momentarily stilled. Helios grabbed my jaw, lowering himself to me while he thrust deeper.

"Who do you belong to?" he demanded, voice gruff. I faltered. He'd never asked that before.

"You, My Lord," I managed to pant while another orgasm ripped through me, this time spattering us both as the thick streams shot between us. Helios pumped into me with wild abandon, opening his mouth, dragging that massive tongue in a circle from his nose to his chin before delivering a punishing kiss, pushing my own desire past my lips. I moaned at the eroticism of it.

"Mine. You're mine, my beautiful boy," he whispered, his tone softer, eyes bright with something I couldn't quite place. My heart stalled at his words, and I chastised myself for letting them affect me. Quiet whispers during sex held no weight. Actions did, and while Persephone had him wrapped up . . . Helios's grip moved lower to my throat, and I felt the pressure he applied as he jerked hard inside of me—once, twice, three times—before he stilled.

He dropped his head into my shoulder, biting the soft flesh, our breathing heavy and erratic as he kissed up the column of my throat, his lips a hot brand against my skin. Helios pulled back, sweeping the hair plastered to my forehead in a sticky mess out of my face before I felt him soften and slip from me, leaving me empty and spasming. His massive cock bounced against his leg as he stood, gently lifting me to my feet. I could feel his seed slipping out of me, seeping slowly down my leg.

The titan pulled me to his chest, our spent bodies far too hot with his radiant heat, but I allowed him to hold me, to care for me, once more. I told myself this would be the last time. After what was to come, there could be no future for us in this vessel. His snores filled the room quickly as he slipped into a peaceful slumber. Too many times had I lain here, thinking things would change. Too many times had I fooled myself. No, if all the players were on the board, we were a tragedy. I could not survive this way. He would never see reason under her thrall, and I couldn't continue to subject myself to this existence, disfigured and scorned.

It wasn't always like this. I had been beautiful, the most beautiful god, some said. Men and women alike lusted after me, coveted me, though I'd never returned their affections. I was sought after, pushed upon, a fixation in their eyes, so I'd left society and built a small paradise for myself, full of looking glasses and mirrors and crystal lakes, the better to see my own beauty and worth. I was alone, and I was happy with that. No one could make me happier than I could. Until *him*.

He had been honest with his intentions, but I had lied about mine, or maybe I truly thought I could handle it, that I could never have loved anyone more than I loved myself.

How wrong I had been. Helios buried himself into my skin, branded my shade. Every time he touched my body felt like heaven, but after, all I felt was shame for myself and hatred for a goddess who had stolen our chance of a future. When Hades and

Persephone ran off together, Helios had been beside himself with worry, but for the first time I'd felt hope.

It was short-lived; he had lost her and, still, hadn't chosen me, her hooks too deep to let him go. Minthe's suspicions had been a revelation for me, and as I slipped from his arms and padded over to the closet, I ran through my part, over and over again, reciting it down to the letter. The golden net lay exactly where it had the last time I'd entered this closet, then to help a pining Helios lick his wounds for another. The embarrassment of how I'd allowed him to debase me, to rip apart my dignity nearly made me retch, but I knew now it wasn't his fault. Minthe had helped me see Persephone's manipulation, had understood my pain and offered a way to help.

I didn't allow myself to look back as I dressed quickly and made my way out into the night, net slung over my shoulder. After the way Hades had disfigured me, I couldn't let the offense slide. He had to pay, and when Persephone was gone, the debt *would* be paid. He took something irreplaceable to me, so I would do the same to him. The punishment for killing another god was desiccation, and I would make sure that he committed that offense publicly.

I was through sipping poison. When the spring goddess was gone, and my body made whole once more, Helios and I would find our way back to one another. When he was free and I was made anew, all would be forgiven, just as Minthe said. I was sure of it because she was my friend.

I could count on her.

Persephone
CHAPTER 39

The warm sun pricked at my skin, the surest sign spring was returning. A few more days of work, and I would return to my beloved Underworld. I longed for Hades, his touch, his kiss, and I hungered to be impaled by that delicious, throbbing co—

A rustling in the trees broke my concentration, and I stiffened, the hair on the back of my arms standing to a point.

"Show yourself!" I commanded, my voice thrumming several octaves at once. The trees shook, and a small woodland hare hopped onto the path. I let out a sigh of relief, working to calm my racing heart. The hare was shaking, twitching even more than usual for a creature of its kind, and I bent down curiously to better examine it.

Pain.

Pain and blackness overtook me as a net cast forward, pinning me to the ground. I felt the earth scrape against my cheek, held down by an immense weight, as though Mt. Olympus itself were pinning me. The rope burned, the metal acrid and *wrong*, tearing a blood-curdling scream past my lips. I tried desperately to call my shadows to me, but they either wouldn't or couldn't come.

I felt void and empty, like a lifeline had been severed.

I screamed for Hades, for my mother, for Artemis. Golden sandals invaded my field of vision, and thundering footfalls congregated around my prone body as I writhed, *burning*. Several large men had burst through the tree line, flooding the path in leathers, an unfamiliar signet on their armor.

"Hades!" I screamed, throat raw and hoarse. I willed my power out as much as I could muster, but my divinity felt weakened, tempered as my shadows dissipated, failing to break me free.

"Hades . . ." I whimpered, his name heavy on my lips before it all went black.

Words whispered in hushed tones in the darkness beat against my throbbing skull as I struggled against the chains weighing me down. Panic lanced through my chest, my wrists bound by chaffing metal.

"Do it quickly."

Light flooded inside the dark space, harsh torchlight that may well have been the sun itself the way it burned against me. I squinted as my eyes attempted to adjust, just as several pairs of hands reached in, grasping the golden net around me, lifting my body. I grappled for control, my body twisting and fighting with every ounce of my waning strength.

Men grunted, *mortal men*, as they worked to force me inside the tight confines of a deep box. My fingernails scraped against harsh wood, a cry wrenching from my lips as the taste of dark magic drifted over me from the sigils carved in its walls.

"Please, please—" I choked as my back hit the hard bottom of the casket. "*HADES! HADES!*" My screams fell on deaf ears while hands stuffed my legs and arms down tight, my vision blurring through tears, the acrid taste of fear clawing up my throat. An invisible power weighed on my limbs as they worked to remove the tangled net from my body. Inside this box, the magic pinned me, draining every ounce of strength from my bones. My fingers wrapped around the nearest captor's wrists, his brown eyes wide as he hesitated.

"Help me," I whimpered. He looked no older than a boy, bare faced and conflicted as his companions tied me down. A large man loomed over me, dressed in fine silks, rings adorning his fingers, a crown on his head.

"Why are you doing this?" I asked, my lungs fighting for air through the hysteria rising within me.

"I'm afraid I am merely a conduit in this transaction, young one. But for my service to the gods, I'll earn distinction, the chance to ascend to the halls of Olympus," the man replied, an air of arrogance to his tone that grated against me. Confusion battered against my mind as the last vestiges of my strength fled my body. A meaty hand traced the pearls tangled around my throat, fumbling with the clasp until their weight left me too. "My wife thanks you for your generosity," he said, straightening. I tried to lift my head, to cry out for Hades once more, but I had nothing left to fight with.

My eyes fluttered, rolling back as the tethers that bound me to the Asphodels strained. *Too long, I'd been gone too long.*

The man placed a small, crystal orb near my head before gesturing with his fingers. Several grunts rang out above me as a large plank of wood was laid over my body, entombing me in total darkness.

Hades

CHAPTER 40

I slouched on my throne, sulking. The passing of time without Persephone was torture, and I could not fathom how I had done it for so long before her. Not that distance didn't have its merits—I thoroughly enjoyed the shadows she sent me, the way they slid up and down my shaft as I did the same for her. We made the distance bearable, in our own way. I was trying to give her the space she needed to do her work, hastening her return in any way I could.

"Hades!" The desperate cry echoed through my head, sending lightning through my spine. I had only ever heard Persephone sound that scared once before, and it was when she'd called to me to take her away. White hot fear bolted through me. In moments, the earth broke apart from where she had called and my shadows teleported me there. The path was barren, without life, but I could smell the stink of fear, see the marks in the dirt where a struggle had taken place.

"PERSEPHONE!" I yelled, spinning to search for her. There was bent flora and upturned dirt everywhere, an impossible pattern to follow with the turmoil. Something small and white glinted out of the corner of my eye, and I bent to retrieve a lone pearl from the dirt. A pearl from the Dead Sea. A pearl that usually adorned Persephone's neck.

"DEMETER!" I roared, pulsing my power into the air. In moments, the Goddess of the Harvest arrived in a whirlwind, shrewd eyes wide in alarm.

"Hades, what are you doing—" She stopped short, taking in the scene and my heaving chest. I couldn't breathe, couldn't think. Fates, I couldn't fucking speak without panic threatening to choke me.

"Where is she?" I demanded, my voice laced with rage.

"Persephone?" she asked, confused. I held up the lone pearl to Demeter's face, advancing on her.

"She called out to me, terrified. There's been a struggle here, and my wife is gone. Where. Is. She."

Demeter's eyes took in the scene as she twirled, calling for her daughter. I felt the fear and panic radiating off her—if she was lying, she was certainly very good at it, but again, that was Demeter's general behavior. My shadows wrapped around her neck, ripping her off the ground, inches from my face. Cold fury radiated from my bones, frost nipping from the tips of my fingers up and around her chin.

"If I find that you have done something to her, or had a hand in any way, I'll drown you in the Styx myself," I growled. My shadows dropped her, coughing and sputtering to the ground, but Demeter was on her feet in an instant, shakily. She shot me a glare reminiscent of her daughter, but I tore off through the path, calling out for my wife.

"We were getting along. We had reconciled," she spat back, rubbing at the skin around her chin as we searched. "Why would I jeopardize that? I get to be in her life again, Hades."

"Spare me the wounded mother act, as if you give a damn of the Hells about being in her life, Demeter. We *both* know this entire calamity was about your power and how terrified you are that everyone is going to find out how pathetically weak you've become," I scoffed. Demeter's shoulders stiffened, her own anger rising.

"How *dare* you speak to me this way." The growl in her voice had zero effect on me, as frustrations and pent-up aggression spilled out around us.

"In what way? In a kinder way than you spoke to Persephone for her entire life? Less cruelly? Like the mercy you failed to show those shades who now take up residence in my realm?" I shook my head as she lifted her chin.

"I did what I had to," she replied, her venomous tone no match for my own disdain. "This is my domain, Hades. You will treat me with the respect I deserve." I rounded on her, my control at my breaking point as I pushed right up into her space.

"Let me be clear; the only reason I haven't let the shadows drag you kicking and screaming into the Pits is because, despite reason, your daughter *does* love you. Fates help you if I find out you're responsible for this. I'll bury you under the Pits. Even now, you're only worried about you, how you're respected. My wife is missing. Help or fucking *move*."

Demeter gnashed her teeth together but relented in her challenge, turning to call out for Persephone once more.

"Where is Helios?" My mind shifted gears, immediately ticking to the next likely suspect.

"I don't know," she answered flatly. "Spread out; see if there is anything left to find," she commanded, and for once, I gave her no friction, instead doing exactly as she instructed. Through the forest, the south fields, the freshly bloomed meadow, we searched and searched but came up wanting. *Nothing*. Whoever had Persephone somehow had her completely blocked from me. Even her shadows were lost, unable to pull to her.

They wailed in my ear, tragic, ultimately brain-shaking in their anguish. I couldn't concentrate, so I sent them back to the

Asphodels before I left Demeter and tracked Helios to the beach. My palms itched with the call to violence, my patience too thin to deal with the titan, but I could think of no other with more motive. And if he *did* take her, Apollo just might inherit another domain.

The dark aura surrounding me announced my presence far before I could speak. Apollo and Helios turned to look at me, clearly alarmed by the darkness that leaked from my body. Hermes stepped forward to intercept me before I could get too close, but I sent a deluge of shadows toward Helios, knocking him prone against the rocks. Apollo stepped back as I stalked over and lifted Helios by the throat.

"Where is she, you fucking maggot?"

Hermes had a grip on my shoulder as he attempted to diffuse the situation.

"ANSWER ME!" I roared, spit flying in the titan's face.

". . . don't know . . . what . . . talking . . . who?" he sputtered, and I loosened my grip on his windpipe by a fraction.

"Persephone is *missing*. Now tell me where she is, or I'll test the consequences of killing gods." I could feel the unnatural heat of his pulse searing my fingers and sent back biting cold in response. Hermes tried to reason with me, again.

"When did this happen?" the Messenger God asked.

"Just now, she called for me," I grit out. Hermes gestured toward Helios and Apollo.

"We've been here all day, Hades. Since sunup. I swear to you, I would never cover up something like this. You know I care for her, too." Hermes spoke reason, but something inside of me, a darker something, urged me to snap Helios's neck and drag him to the Styx, to drain his power and let him rot for everything he'd done, the part in it he'd played.

I gnashed my teeth together, flexing my fingers once before dropping him. To my surprise, he jumped up immediately, but not to fight. Worry etched into the creases of his face.

"What do you know? What do you need? Have you informed Zeus?" He fired questions at me rapidly, but I could only shake my head because I had no answers. She was simply . . . gone.

"Demeter is informing Zeus. We are the only others who know." Hermes gripped my shoulder, as anguish washed over me.

"I must get her back, Hermes. She has to be safe."

Apollo cleared his throat loudly.

"I'll need to inform Artemis. She will want to hunt." A bright light flashed, taking Apollo with it as it dimmed, but Hermes looked from me to Helios.

"I'll do a lap around the realm, see what I can find. Don't kill each other while I'm gone." With that, he leapt out of sight in a blur, leaving me standing on the sand with the bane of my existence, crushing helplessness shredding me apart inside. Helios grabbed his armor and gear from the sand at his feet.

"Where should we search first?" he asked. I leveled him a look, still not trusting him.

"Everywhere."

Hades

CHAPTER 41

Weeks passed like grains of sand in the hourglass, every moment drifting me farther from hope. Twenty-six days had passed without her laugh, her touch, and I was falling apart. I'd searched all realms, even Tartarus, leaving no stone unturned in my pursuit. Demeter had devolved in a manner I'd never seen, throwing herself full force into finding Persephone. Most of the Greek pantheon were living in my palace, the ones who could survive the Underworld, anyway.

Artemis called upon the Wild Hunt to search and came up empty in the skies. Dionysus himself combed through the Elysian Fields and was sober while he did it. Hermes laid tracks around the world, the cosmos, crossing into the territories of other deities to do so, each round building his frustration as he returned with empty hands. Athena even made Poseidon search the sea . . . My feet traced every trail in the Asphodels, the hordes of the Hells on patrol as every shade sought out their beloved Queen.

Nothing.

The darkness within me grew, and I couldn't even pretend to try and keep it at bay. I lashed out at everyone, slipping, deteriorating into madness. Every day I saw the glint of hope fading from the eyes of our companions, as her absence normalized for them, their duties and responsibilities outweighing the hope they couldn't cling to.

Eventually only myself, Artemis, Hermes, Demeter, Hecate, and, as much as I hated to admit it, Helios, refused to give up the cause.

There was a bitter nag of distrust toward the titan, but he was looking almost as frequently as I was, his golden sheen dulled, and I couldn't believe he was that skilled at subterfuge. There were no clues, no trail, and we were all fighting despair.

We'd gathered in the throne room, which had become our makeshift base. Admentos had a large table installed, and we stood, chasing down our tenth useless oracle prediction, none of us willing to turn down any lead, no matter how farfetched. News of Persephone's abduction had spread far and wide, but the promised reward for any information that led to her recovery had us up to our chest plates in false claims.

Hecate was quick to determine who the real seers were over the charlatans. I groaned, dropping my head into my hands as she shook her head and, with a tight smile, dismissed the elderly woman who'd been summoned for her "vision" to the Asphodels.

"We already searched those islands. Leto and Artemis made three rounds, unless they both managed to miss something." Helios sighed as I stood, frustration bubbling over. Artemis made a snide comment to Helios, the stress causing the two to bicker. I was tired. I was in pain and out of my mind with worry.

I snapped.

"ENOUGH!" I swiped my fist across the table, sending scraps of parchment flying, maps upturned, floating to the floor. A stunned silence settled over us, and I hung my head, chest heaving. Out, I needed everyone out of my home, my realm. I just needed *her*. I looked up at them, ready to tell them all to clear out, when a small voice sounded from the doorway, breaking the tension.

"I'm sorry to interrupt, My Lord, but I think I may know where Queen Persephone is." All eyes snapped to the frail body of the ragged girl standing barefoot, shuffling forward with bright eyes. Confusion creased my brow, but it was Artemis that spoke.

"Cassandra?" She stood, coming around the table to embrace the girl, who seemed painfully relieved to see a friendly face. She looked half-starved, thin as some of the shades that haunted these halls.

"How did you get to the Asphodels?" Artemis asked, smoothing the girl's frazzled red hair.

"I took the Black Steps, near the falls. I know Hecate uses it sometimes. I got as far as the gates, but I couldn't get in so I just . . . pounded on them until someone came to get me." The young girl's voice was steady, but she looked depleted.

"It was me, My Lord." Nikoli stepped around her, the young shade glowing green. "Sometimes I . . . when my chores are done, I wander, searching for Queen Persephone. I heard yelling from the gates, so I let her in and led her here. I'm sorry if I overstepped." He cast his eyes low, the bite of hope in his voice encouraging. He missed her as much as any of us.

"Be well, Nikoli. You did the right thing," I assured him. Cassandra wasted no time peering around Artemis, who fussed over her.

"I think she may be on an island, and I think she may be buried. In my dreams, I had a vision of a pearl necklace. Beautiful and ornate, with dark pearls, the color of burnished brass. I don't know how, but I feel as though they belong to the goddess. I tried to retain as much as I could, but there was so much pain wrapped around the vision. I heard a name, whispered from the deep. *Titus*. Do you know it?"

"I do. He's a mortal, rules the kingdom of Pompeii." Hermes frowned, his body vibrating with energy.

"And you're sure?" I asked Cassandra, something akin to hope sparking in my chest for the first time since all this had begun.

"Cassandra is never wrong. She is the greatest oracle of our time. If she says Persephone is there, she is. Or at least, Titus knows where she is," Artemis answered without hesitation.

"Greatest of all time? I've never heard of her," Helios mumbled. Artemis shot him with a venomous look.

"That would be because my cockhead brother cursed her. She could have the most accurate visions of any oracle, but mortals would never believe her." Artemis and Helios volleyed back and forth, but I could hardly hear them over the raging inferno that had erupted inside me. If this was the truth, then it was the first lead we'd uncovered, and I didn't intend to waste any more time discussing it. I stood, summoning my helm and bident to me.

"Let's have a chat with Titus, shall we?"

Hades

CHAPTER 42

We ascended to the throne room of King Titus, Ruler of Pompeii, without restraint to our divinity, in an overwhelming show of might. No other mortal had seen a gathering of the gods so vast, and as he stood in the middle of the great hall, pillars holding nothing up but sky, I let the full pressure of my rage seep onto the marble floors.

I landed, cracking the marble below my feet as the mortal Titus recoiled, holding tightly to a woman I could only assume was his wife. She clung to him, shaking with eyes wide at the array of divine power radiating around her. A soft trill from her tremors drew my eyes to her neck, as both relief and wrath clashed within me at the sight of those pearls. Persephone's necklace. He began to babble, spouting apologies, all but confirming his guilt. Rage ripped through my chest as I advanced, snapping my fingers once.

"That does not belong to you," I snarled. Titus's eyes went wide with terror as he gripped his wife, watching in stunned horror as the mortal woman fell apart into millions of salt chips, cascading through his panicked fingertips. Titus let out a wail of anguish, as salt dusted over his skin, the floor, falling from his robes. Persephone's necklace hit the mound of salt with a soft thud, thunderous in its damnation. Titus backed up, his eyes wandering, searching for a way out.

"MY WIFE," I yelled, shaking the tower around us. "Where is my wife?" The Asphodels shuddered as I took and took, my power a direct line from them, the rage of the realm wrapping me tight. Titus shook his head, begging for leniency, for mercy, my own rage mirrored in his agony.

"I would have given her back! They promised me immortality, and once I got it, I would have returned her!" An agonizing wail tore from his lips as he stared, transfixed, at the wife that was. "But now, you have taken everything, and there is no place I could go that you would not find." Tears streaked his face, as a pinprick of power jostled my senses.

Whispers, soft whispers. Titus passed a gilded tray, catching his reflection as he backed up.

"Yes . . . it is my fault. My greed. Yes . . . true agony . . . yes."

An infernal ringing pounded against the drum of my ear, drowning out the rambles of a soon to be dead man. I concentrated, cutting through the buzz of magic, Hermes's ear cocked as he, too, listened. It was barely there, murmurs built to a crescendo, and then we heard them, whispers, so soft and soothing.

"*Jump . . .*" they said. "*Just jump.*" I searched the room with my eyes, looking for the source, but the distraction cost me. Without fanfare, King Titus opened his arms wide and tumbled off the side of the balcony. A chorus rang out around us, but we had all been too late to notice his intention, too focused on finding the source of the magic. Hermes took off, winged sandals fluttering, but it was as though Titus's body were hooked by a thread of Fate as it careened to the earth at incredible speed. Royal robes and a mortal body made impact with the ground with a sickening crunch, the force of his velocity cratering the stone beneath him. I raced to the balcony, hurtling myself over the edge, dropping gracefully next to the red pool oozing from beneath shattered bones. I flipped him over, ready to extract his shade, determined to get my answers. Titus didn't need to be alive for me to do it. I placed my hand between the gore and bones protruding from his chest, rooting inside for that tiny spark. Nothing. *Nothing*? How could there be nothing?

"No," I whispered, digging the pads of my fingers through viscera and blood, searching desperately as the small ember of hope I'd allowed to fester was snuffed out. Gone. It was gone. "FUCK!" I shouted, wracking my mind. How would a mortal king know how to destroy a shade? That was the darkest of magics, forbidden by Hecate, by the very laws of the Underworld, and Titus's shade was marked for death, already inscribed in Thanatos's book. Mortal shades existed in the Asphodels or the Upper Realm; there was no in between, and yet, the proof of the gore under my fingernails said otherwise.

I sank to my knees, throwing my head back. Hermes's hand came down on my shoulder, giving it a squeeze.

"Leave him for the birds, Hades. Let's see if there's anything we can work with at the top of the tower." I knew I was in pain, that I should have been able to feel it, but I only felt numb. In a stupor, I allowed Hermes and Helios to haul me to my feet, to lead me back up the tall tower.

We didn't bother teleporting—there was no longer any rush. Stair after stair, my body moved, but my mind was still at the bottom, bleeding into the earth with the last shred of resolve I possessed. I ran through Titus's last words, my mind forming connections through the shock. Who could make a mortal a god? Had Zeus betrayed me? Had Poseidon? We couldn't just freely make a mortal immortal. There were rules, processes. Even those born demi-gods had trials. Who did this, and why? My only suspects were currently just as grief stricken as I.

Helios supported Demeter on our return, the goddess's tear-streaked face gaunt and hollow. At the top of the tower,

Artemis's feet hit the landing first, followed by Helios who stopped in his tracks.

"Narcissus?" he asked, confused. "What are you doing here?" We rounded the threshold to see the God of Self Love sitting on Titus's throne, legs draped over the sides.

"Looking for this, Lord Hades?" he goaded, raising his hand high enough for me to see. My breath caught in my throat, and I tensed to spring. In his left hand, he held a small sphere of glass, the size of a plum and swirling with bright, white light.

"What is that?" Hermes asked.

"Titus's shade," I answered out of the side of my mouth. *A shade*. Somehow, he'd managed to capture the king's shade, to trap the spirit with dark magic. Tension swelled within the room as Helios shook his head, staring at the young god, a mask of confusion and hurt on the titan's face. My shoulders flexed as I coiled to spring. Narcissus caught the movement.

"Ah, ah, ah. Not so fast, Hades. Or I'll crush this between my fingers, and you'll never find her." I stopped cold. Hermes's eyes flashed, and I knew he was weighing his odds, deciding what the risk would be if he took off now. He was fast, but Narcissus knew that, and I didn't mean to underestimate him again. He had prepared for Hermes's speed, ensuring the Messenger God wouldn't be fast enough to stop the King's descent.

"I hold the power, so I am going to talk. And you," he glanced between Helios and I, "are going to listen. There will be no interruptions, or I will reduce this to nothingness in my grip. And before you get any ideas, I don't know where she is, Hades. Precaution in case you think taking me in a rush will improve your chances."

I nodded, slowly lifting my hands up, palms out. After the meeting on Olympus, I'd taken the time to learn about Narcissus. The God of Self Love, borne of the worship of mortals, ones who had grown strong in their autonomy, but he was new to the cosmos, and if he had somehow found a way to dabble in dark magics, there was no telling what other tricks he had up his sleeve. *Feed his ego. He is ego*, my shadows whispered, advising me.

"You're in charge here, Narcissus. The floor is yours."

He stared back at me with a bemused smile on his face.

"Flattery now, is it? If only you had used your words instead of your weapon on Olympus." He gestured to the symmetrical scars on either side of his neck. "Perhaps we would be having a much different conversation."

I wracked my brain. He took Persephone over scars? No, this felt deeper, more unhinged. There was pain here, in his eyes, in the way he carried himself. Deep wounds buried beneath ego and bravado. Pain was good; I could exploit pain. My shadows swirled, sizing up the situation, tasting the air as they searched the grounds, looking for their Queen. Helios was still as stone and rigid, save for the eyes he had locked on Narcissus.

"Why?" he gasped, the single word rife with confusion and guilt, and . . . *Fates*.

"Because she never loved you!" Narcissus hissed, leaning forward suddenly. "She chose *nothing* over you, then she chose *him*. She scorned you, bewitched you, and she's got her hooks in you so deeply that, even now, you remain at her call." Several shocked murmurs ran through the gathering, with Hermes's jaw nearly on the floor.

"*What?*" Helios asked, confused.

I, however, was beginning to understand. More times than I could count, a scorned lover had stood in front of me, pleading their case. The Hells were overflowing with them, with their bitter indignation, the pain that twisted good people into something ugly and withered. Helios wore his heartbreak plainly now, for all to see, but the God of Self Love was too far gone, glassy eyed, potentially drunk as he swayed. I wanted to demand answers, but one thing was clear above all.

This cry for attention was for Helios, and Helios *only*. I may have had a small part with his scarification, but all of this was an effort to make his lover see the pain that ate him up.

"I never wanted to hurt you. I thought you always understood. I had obligations; there was no spell, Narcissus. You took an innocent, a goddess. You have to tell us where she is." Helios's plea fell on a hardened, scared heart, his words a spark of flame on slick oil.

"Even now you defend her."

"It's not what you thin—" But Narcissus interrupted him.

"You can't see it because you're so deeply blinded by what she has done to you. Both of you threw away love for her." Narcissus shook his head in disbelief. "You *destroyed* me, Helios. Tell me, that what you felt when your body was pressed to mine was just carnal."

"It wasn't," Helios admitted, inching forward. "It wasn't. I'm so sorry, just let me explain—"

"No, I don't think I will. You'll say anything right now to get your precious spring goddess home." Narcissus twisted the orb in his fingers, before shooting a dark look to me. "Then, God of the Cocks, over there, you ruined me. Stole my beauty."

Helios balked.

"Narcissus, you are still the most beautiful. You are unmatched and those marks show nothing less than your bravery." Frustration shook the titan's armor, and we all stilled as Narcissus reached into his himation and pulled a small bottle from it. He uncorked it with his teeth, downing the swirling blue liquid in one gulp. The air shifted, pressurizing like a coming storm. Whatever his plan was, we were coming to the crux of it, but Helios kept his eyes on Narcissus while Hermes made slow progress toward the God of Self Love. A bleak resignation sunk Helios's shoulders, as he made one last desperate attempt to talk Narcissus off the ledge.

"I do love you, Narcissus. If you want us to give it a real shot, I'm willing to do that for you, my beautiful god, Zeus be damned. Just give us the sphere, let us end this and we can be together."

Narcissus looked at Helios with dull eyes, and I knew that, even though Helios was saying all the things he wanted to hear, Narcissus didn't believe him. We were running out of time. Silent tears streaked down Narcissus's cheeks, his eyes full of misery and longing as he swayed on unsteady feet.

"Even now, you're protecting her. And the worst part? I'm protecting you. Without her, you can be free of this."

Hermes's eyes locked with mine. Our time was up, we could wait no longer if we had any hope of retrieving that orb. I hurled my shadows at the blond god at the same time Hermes shot off like a bolt. My shadows tore through Narcissus, slicing his chest up, ripping the arm holding the sphere clean off. Hermes scooped it up as Helios roared, diving across the distance to catch Narcissus as his body crumpled. Shock welled up on Helios's face, splashed with red blood, but I could only focus on the shade cradled in Hermes's fist. I opened the little clasps with shaking hands. The shade inside writhed, squirming away from my touch as I gripped it tight.

Too late, I recognized the feminine energy pulsing through it was not of King Titus—it belonged to his wife. Hermes grabbed my arm, worried as the room filled up with my shadows, obscuring the light from above.

"Hades, I-I think he's dead." The Messenger God's voice shook.

"Of course he's not. He's a god; he'll heal. I didn't put nearly enough power behind . . ." *Red blood.* It'd flown over Narcissus's face when I'd grabbed the sphere from Hermes, now covering Helios's face and neck, mixing with his tears. *Red blood.* Not golden. *Hells.*

"Not anymore," Narcissus sputtered, reaching a shaking hand into his himation, retrieving something tight in his fist, a bright glow peaking from between his fingers. "Don't!" I screamed, but the soft smattering of shattered glass filled the space like a sonic boom, somehow the loudest noise I had ever heard, as the shade inside crumbled into nothingness, releasing the energy in a wave of particles and stars. Helios clutched Narcissus in his arms, sobbing, bargaining with the Fates, but there was nothing more to be done. Narcissus's eyes faltered until he found mine, his lips peeling back in a bloody grin.

"Now," he choked, tongue slipping over his own blood, "She is lost to you forever. There are no others left to tell the tale."

He closed his eyes as the gurgling in his throat ground to a halt, and I knew at once that he was gone. There would be no retrieving his shade, as he had surely made arrangements to keep his own out of my hands, just as he had done with Titus and his wife. I bent low, scooping the bottle he had downed between my fingers, bringing it to my nose as traces of the substance dripped around the edge. *Styx*.

He had drunk from the River. Become mortal so he could die and take the knowledge of what he did with Persephone with him.

"Hades," Hermes whispered gently, but there was nothing to be done. I smashed the bottle against a pillar and stalked back and forth, grinding the marble down beneath my feet. My chest tightened as my very heart disintegrated behind my ribs. She was gone—there would be no more clues to find. Narcissus had proven to be cunning, and he would leave no spark of hope, no reprieve in this final act of selfishness.

I clawed at my face, fingers tugged my hair from the root, breathing in ragged drags.

I screamed. It came from deep within the darkest parts of my essence, a frenzied rampage that only Persephone could tame. Glass shattered, and a cyclone of air rocked the shores of this palace. My sorrow consumed me, overwhelmed me, feasted on the corpse of what was left without her. These fucking mortals and petulant gods. They were all responsible, in some way, even me. I had lost my temper. I had cut him. Her abduction was just as much my fault as theirs, and I hated myself for it.

I screamed again, pulling the elegant pillars down around me, vibrating the plates of earth below the island. Large cracks split the marble, split the streets, as screams rose up from the citizens of this cursed kingdom. I wanted it gone.

I tasted ash on my tongue, and I relished it, let it burn through me. Dropping to my knees, I threw my head back one final time as I let the darkness I kept corked inside loose, let the chaos run wild in destruction and decay. I grabbed ahold of the tether that linked me to the Asphodels and wrenched with all my might, willing the Underworld to come to me, to comfort me, to bury this fucking place beneath the Pits. A volcano to our west rumbled at my plea and erupted, spilling down its slate walls, covering the island in a blaze of righteous vengeance. Fires raged, and ash rained down. For an entire day, I knelt and screamed.

I could taste the fear in the air, the desolation that reflected my own, and I clung to it like a blanket, letting it wash over me. I would bury this place and the memory of what I'd lost here with it. I would let it take me, too, if it had the strength.

Helios

CHAPTER 43

I couldn't stop the tremble of my hands, the sharp, shallow breaths that threatened to seize up my lungs as the weight of his lifeless body sagged in my arms. The dulled skin, flecked with blood and purple bruising from the slice of Hades's shadows . . . I'd taken every part of him I could, brought him back to his island home.

There would be none to mourn Narcissus, none to grieve with me or prepare his body. His shade may have never made it to the Underworld, but I would build his pyre, surrender the divinity of his vessel to the Fates and the cosmos.

I would mourn him.

My fingers shook as I bathed his skin, carefully, reverently, each pass of the stone and water revealing the softness below. My own tears flowed from my cheeks to his as I washed his hair, used the heat of my hands to dry it out, the silken, silver-blond strands so delicate against my palms.

It struck me that I would never hear his voice again or see his eyes, deep and wild, glisten as he laughed.

I'd never gotten to tell him how much I loved him.

Wrapped in the softest linens in his wardrobe, I laid him on the pyre, stroking my hands over his jaw, the frame of his brow. I placed a coin on his tongue, parting chapped lips to slip it inside, then pressed my own softly to the corner of his mouth. The deep, cataclysmic void in my chest cracked wide on a sob, pouring all of me out as I hauled my body up onto the expanse of stacked wood next to him. Kindling scraped against my flesh as I slid as close as I could manage, as my arms wrapped around his middle. I buried my face in the crook of his hair, inhaling that sweet scent of his washing oils for the very last time.

The pyre ignited, flames licking up the wood, smoke and heat engulfing the tinder with gusto until there was no sky above us, no Pits beneath us. There was only Narcissus in my arms, and my heart burning beside him. Heat brushed over my skin with flame, catching his linens, and I held him closer, so tight that it felt like my bones might break.

History would villainize him, call him a monster for what he'd done to Persephone, but I knew better. This was *my* fault, for not having the backbone to stand up to Zeus, for not protecting him that day on Olympus, from incurring Hades's wrath . . .

We burned together, until the logs beneath us cracked and broke, until he was ash beneath my fingers, and I wished, fucking Fates how I wished, I could follow him.

I wanted so badly to follow him into the darkness.

We burned through the night until there was nothing left but the smoldering remnants of kindling and my body on the ground. When the stars fell, the pull of duty hooking beneath my bones in protest, I resisted.

No sun rose in the sky that morning. I didn't care if it ever rose again.

I heard the beating of hooves, the whinnying of war horses, before I saw Ares's chariot, and when his sandals stepped into my limited field of vision, I let my eyes flutter shut, not ready for him to pull me up. I wanted to rot. I deserved to suffer.

"Helios?" His gruff voice was tender as he bent down through the tendrils of smoke and ruin and grasped my shoulder, shaking me.

"Let me die in peace," I croaked, my throat raw from tears, heat, and the inhalation of smoke. Ares clicked his tongue behind his teeth, and I cracked an eyelid to see the stars behind him, dull and hazy through the heat rising in the air.

"You know that I cannot," he responded gently, and I groaned as his fingers hooked under my armpits, lifting me up. Anger seared through me as the spot where Narcissus's ashes lay grew farther from my body. I thrashed, grunting as I kicked and swung against the God of War. He took every hit but never relented in his goal of pulling me away, and I hated him, hated Hades and Zeus and every fucking god that did this. Screams, there were screams so agonizing the leaves shook on the trees, and it wasn't until I was kneeling in the dirt, Ares's arms around me, my fists clinging to his armor that I realized they were coming from me. Anguished.

Despair.

He was gone, and I wanted to go with him.

"I want to go, let me go with him," I pleaded, begging for the True Death from the only person I thought would give it to me. "I want to g-go." I choked on my words, on my tears, on the fucking ache inside of me. Ares pressed me closer to him, whispering "I know" and "I know, but you must live," over and over against my hair. We sat together in the darkness until there was nothing left inside of me to cry, my hands and fingers and toes numb as, for the first time in all of my existence, I felt frozen from the inside out.

It was Ares who carried me inside Narcissus's bungalow, who sat me at the same table we had shared meals over. I avoided looking at his bed and was grateful that Ares called a himation to him from somewhere to cover my body as he poured drinks from an uncorked cask of wine among the clutter of the table. He sat the chalice in front of me, the metal cold against my fingertips.

Neither of us spoke, and I avoided his steady gaze, my eyes darting around the small space. What I saw broke me all over again, seeing his meticulous home in such chaos. He'd always been so careful that everything be in its proper place, and it was as though the sadness and turmoil that had driven Narcissus to madness was reflected in the mess around us.

"Tell me about him," Ares instructed, catching me off guard. I dragged my eyes back to his as he regarded me, fingers tapping the base of his chalice.

"What?" I asked, confused.

"Narcissus. Tell me about him, Helios."

I shook my head as tears misted my eyes, my throat constricting. What could I say? That I had failed him? That I had driven him to this destruction with my love and weakness? Anger spiked through my grief as a tear fell down my cheek, but Ares simply waited, relaxing back in the chair opposite me.

"He hated being around people," I finally whispered, shaking my head. Ares's eyebrows lifted as he pursed his lips appreciatively.

"I can respect that," he offered. "What else?" I swallowed past the lump of my throat, dragging in a shaking breath that still smelled like smoke.

"Why are you here, Ares? To drag me back to work?" I groaned, too destroyed to accept any kindness. With as much force as I could manage, I threw my chair back, standing, needing to get out of this fucking house, away from being surrounded by the smell and memory of *him*.

"Sit. Down," Ares barked, the command in his tone heavy enough to buckle my knees. I fumed as I let my body sink back into the chair unceremoniously. "I'm not here to drag you back to anything. I'm here because you just lost someone precious, and you shouldn't have to be alone with this. No one should. So, sit the fuck back down so we can honor his memory."

Ares lifted his chalice to me, eyeing mine expectantly. My chest heaved, the weight of his comfort nearly too much, but I lifted my own. The metal resounded in the small bungalow.

"To Narcissus," he announced.

"To Narcissus." I nearly choked around his name, my tongue too big for my mouth. I lifted the glass to my lips, felt the liquid wash bitterly over my singed taste buds, the wine spoiled from being left out perhaps, but I felt it, the loosening of my tight muscles as it washed through me, doing its work.

I took another drink. Then another, ignoring the bitter burn until I felt lighter.

The sound of liquid spilling against the ground drew my attention, and I glanced up to see Ares's mouthful of wine splashed deep burgundy against the floor, shoulders tense as he brought his cup to his nose. I watched him sniff at the liquid, then stand, swiping the bottle and swirling it once before taking a swig, and spitting that too, onto the ground.

"Ares, wh—" I began, but my words slurred slightly.

"It's dosed. *Henbane*," Ares barked, drawing his sword swiftly as he looked around, readying for a fight. My own magic worked inside of me, and I felt the haze lift as the alcohol burned out of my system. I shook out the daze and stood, more alert.

"Henbane?" I asked, but Ares was already moving, searching the few rooms of the bungalow. When he was satisfied there were no threats, he returned, sheathing his blade.

"I've seen it used before, on mortals. Makes them more susceptible to suggestion. Clouds their judgment. When it's made correctly, it's strong enough to affect Olympians . . ." He crossed the room to the pile of casks near the door and swiped one, bringing it to his nose before quickly jerking it back.

"*Fates*, if he ingested all of this, he couldn't have been in his right mind. Helios . . ."

Anger ricocheted through me as I took in the tousled bed, the way the table had held glasses for two, the mess . . .

"He wasn't alone. Someone did this *to* him, Ares. Someone is going to burn for this. Who do you know has access to this Henbane?" I demanded, vengeance igniting like a beacon inside of me. Ares's lips thinned into a grimace as he stepped forward, using his hand to lower my balled fists, sparking with sunlight in my fury.

"*You know,*" he whispered, eyeing me pointedly. It took me mere moments to catch up to his meaning, and when I did, another wave of grief and despair washed over me because we both knew I could do nothing to make him pay.

The God of Gods was indestructible.

I made a move to the door, determined to get my pound of flesh or die trying, but Ares grabbed me, shoving me back into the house.

"You can't do this. It will solve nothing, and you'll be dead," Ares warned, and I nearly laughed.

"I don't care," I grunted, pushing back against him, but with a huff, he sent me sailing back, hands fisted in my himation.

"But *he* did. Narcissus would care if you died over this, you know he would. He stood in front of you on Olympus and put himself in the line of Hades's fury to protect you. Don't sully his memory this way. If you die, there will be no one to remember him as you do. No one to honor his shade. And we don't know what happens next, Helios. He may not be wherever we go when we die. You still wouldn't be together," he reasoned, and I hated him for it, hated the thought of there never being a part of Narcissus left in this realm.

The roar that ripped from my chest shook the house around us, and I swiped up a bottle and hurled it against the wall, glass shards and wine cascading to the floor. I tore through the place, destroying everything in my path, taking out every ounce of my rage and heartache on the remnants of this house.

He had soiled this place, manipulated my love, and then he'd led him like a lamb to the slaughter. We'd never find Persephone, and it would be Narcissus's name that always bore that blame and shame, but the worst part?

We'd never prove it.

Ares left me to my grief as I tore the bungalow down to beams and bones while night stretched on nearly endlessly, and once there was nothing but destruction, I sat in the rubble and waited.

It wasn't long before the god himself appeared, shiny and golden as his sandals crunched over splinters of wood.

"You've made quite a mess here, Helios," Zeus noted, and I shook with rage, but I held myself back, clinging to Ares's words.

"Did you do it? Did you put him up to this?" I asked through gritted teeth. Zeus cocked his head, frowning as he looked around.

"I am sure that I have no idea what you're implying," he answered, but there was a smugness to him that told me *everything* I needed to know. "Surely you would have some shred of proof before making such a baseless accusation to your Lord, Helios? *Surely.*" His eyes narrowed, and I ground my teeth together, working to keep my temper in check.

We stared each other down, the God of Gods completely unbothered at the death and destruction he'd caused.

"You have a bride waiting for you, and I've been generous, allowing you time to process your loss, but you have a job to do," he chastised, voice stern and disapproving as he glanced up at the perpetual night sky.

I barked out a laugh and shook my head, stunned by his callousness.

"I'm not marrying anyone. And I'm not pulling the sun up any longer. I can't prove your hand in this, but I can assure you that you'll never use me for your gains again."

Zeus's jaw ticked as he stepped forward, lightning crackling around his fingertips.

"You *will* do as you are commanded! You swore an oath!" he seethed, thunder booming around us in his anger.

"So did you! When I pledged my sword and fealty to you, you *swore* that you would be a better ruler than your father," I snapped, disgusted. "*You're worse*. And you'll be just fine with that, unless you want me to tell Hera of your little interlude with the nymph on Olympus. We know how passionate the Queen Mother gets when provoked. And Hades . . . you're scared of him, aren't you? That's why you were hesitant to order Persephone back . . ."

"I wouldn't harm my own daughter. The actions of a heart-broken god do not lay at my feet. The blood of them both is on your hands, Helios." His words pelted against me, the truth in them earth-shattering, but I could feel in my bones that I was right. That he was somehow involved in this.

"I guess we will find out, when Hades starts to dig."

Zeus's blue eyes darkened to chips of black, his lip curling, but he made no move to stop me or kill me for my insolence. There was no relief at my survival, no righteousness because he was correct that I had no proof, and baseless claims would only serve to cost more lives. "Such a disappointment," he muttered.

"As are you," I spat back, but he was gone on a bolt of lightning, leaving me alone in the destruction I'd caused. Around me, I couldn't bear to look at the debris even a moment more, and though my power felt drained, it still responded when I called upon it to clear this place of the rubble until all that remained was the outlined ashes of the funeral pyre I'd burnt Narcissus's body on.

I knelt, digging my fingers in the dirt, exhausted and spent. When the light painted over the sky, I felt another string of my divinity snap and fade, felt the moment Apollo picked up the reigns to chase the sun, no doubt at his father's command. Warmth bathed over me, casting golds and oranges of the breaking dawn all around the isle, and because my fingers were already in the dirt, I reached deep in that way I'd seen Persephone do, crying out as my power pulsed and rippled into the soil.

I thought of my friend, of the Spring Goddess lost to us. I thought of Hades, and the loneliness he and I would share like a phantom wound. I thought of Narcissus, of his laughter and beauty, of his stolen kindness, and screamed as I wept at the memory of him. When I opened my eyes, the island was filled with the gentlest of blooms, a twined, white flower with pointed petals and a belled center, stretching toward the sun. A sob racked through my chest, and I smiled as my fingers traced over the delicate flower, knowing that a piece of him would bloom in this realm, forever.

Narcissus.

Hades
CHAPTER 44

"Hades, you must come." Thanatos's voice trilled softly as his wings beat heavy thrums against the air of the throne room.

"Later, Thanatos, I'm not in the mood."

His feet landed right in front of my throne as he tucked away his great, white wings. The God of Death snapped his fingers in front of my face, earning himself a scowl.

"*Now*, Hades."

A bite of trepidation laced his whispered words. I forced my body to stand as he turned on his heel, flinging a portal of swirling shadows open. I followed him through, my feet landing on the banks of the Styx. The portal closed with a sharp snap, but Thanatos didn't hesitate as he set a brisk pace, stopping just short of something long and lithe in the disturbed black sand. I took two steps forward, glancing down, the force of my shock expelling the breath from my lungs.

On the banks of the Styx, deep within the Asphodels, the body of the Goddess of Harvest had washed up, skin tinged a white blue, her bones stiff and rigid, a pomegranate clutched in her hand.

"Demeter." I knelt slowly, pushing back the curly, wet strands of her golden hair, *Persephone's hair*. My heart panged with shade-deep ache at the mere thought of her.

"What happened?" I asked, glancing up at the God of Death. He shook his head.

"I have no idea. I felt a pull, an urgent one, and when I landed here, I saw, Fates—" His face contorted, grimacing as hands tattooed with the runes of the Hells fisted through his dark hair. I looked her over, forcing myself to check for injury, any sign of a struggle, but there were none. Demeter could have been resting, if her pallor weren't so exaggerated.

"Do you think she did it to herself?" I asked. Tos shook his head.

"Surely not . . . right?" he responded, scrubbing his hand over his face. A bell tolled in the distance, and Thanatos and I both snapped our heads toward the gates. That sound only resonated for Zeus or Poseidon . . .

"Fuck," I swore. I pushed Demeter's body flat onto her back. Her fingernails were unbroken, her face nearly . . . peaceful. I felt him before he spoke, heard the sound of his entitled fucking feet in my realm before he cleared his throat, but when I turned, the sight of the God of Gods still ignited a deep hatred inside of me. There had never been love lost between the two of us. Zeus had never toiled in the darkness of Cronus as the rest of us had, and there was an artifice about his very essence that set my teeth on edge, but since Pompeii, the tension had steadily built. I blamed him, nearly as much as I blamed myself. He could have put a stop to it from the beginning, but he didn't. He watched, waiting, playing both sides. His very proximity made my skin crawl.

"Scores of crops have died, where is Demeter—" Zeus stopped short, eyes raking over her body, the look of shock on his face nearly comical. "What have you done?" he asked, his voice low, but his words weren't directed at us. No, they were for the goddess. Above me, Thanatos and Zeus spoke in frantic, hushed tones, but I couldn't bring myself to hear them, couldn't bring myself to feel sorrow or remorse.

Because I was the God of the Dead, I would do my duty, just as I had been forced to do every moment since the day Vesuvius erupted. I dug my fingers under the mud and dirt, lifting her frail body in my arms. Demeter's head swung back, her arms wild, as water sloshed, raining from the soaked fabric of her chiton.

"Where are you taking her?" Zeus demanded, but I ignored him as I carried the Goddess of Harvest to rest in our family crypt, that pomegranate still clutched in her hand.

I felt nothing when I laid her to rest next to our mother. I felt nothing when I crossed her arms and lit an everlasting flame to illuminate her face. I felt nothing when I placed a coin inside her mouth, just in case there was a toll for gods we weren't aware of. The True Death was as much a mystery to us as the Asphodels were to mortals, but just in case, I paid her toll.

And when I rolled the stone back to seal them inside, I felt nothing then, too.

I let the pull of power guide me back to Thanatos and Zeus, who were conversing by the gates. The God of Gods looked perturbed, as though Demeter's suicide was an inconvenience to him in some way.

"And the crop yield. We're already suffering; this will be a critical blow," he huffed. I watched the way he spoke, how he took up space in my realm as though I owed it to him. "Helios has abandoned his post, and you missed another summons to Olympus," he chastised, pointing a finger in my direction.

"I didn't miss it. I chose not to go."

Zeus's eyes flashed dangerously as he pulled himself up to his full height, his bulked muscles flexing as though it mattered to me.

"Watch your tone, Hades. I am still the God of Gods; you would do well to remember that." My eyes narrowed at his challenge, and suddenly I felt it, the only emotion I could produce of late: wrath.

"Or you'll do what? What will you do to me, if I continue to defy you, Zeus?" I mocked, raising my eyebrow in question. Thanatos eyed us both warily, taking a few paces back for good measure, as Zeus came closer.

"This has gone on long enough, Hades. Have you all lost your minds over this? You have responsibilities that require your attention. I've let you wallow here, let you sulk, but enough is enough!" he snapped, just as my shadows coiled around my fingers, entwining us together, handing me full control of the tether to the well of the Asphodel's power.

"You've *let* me wallow?" I clicked my tongue as the air grew impossibly thick, the golden glow of Zeus faltering just a smidge in the Underworld. "You don't *allow* me anything. You want me to come to Olympus, sit in council while you and the others panic over your fading power?"

"This affects us all," he growled as I took a step closer, severing the space between us.

"It actually doesn't affect me, Zeus. Or Thanatos. Or Hypnos. Or Morpheus. The Underworld remains strong while Olympus rots from the inside out, and it's no less than what you deserve. *Get. Out*." I turned, intent to leave Zeus to see himself out, but the buildup of power called my attention back as a meaty hand reared back, lightning striking in blue eyes.

"You ungrateful—"

Power radiated from my body, shadows exploding in a wide arc of cataclysmic fury that swept Zeus up and hurled him past the open gates. The God of Gods landed hard, sprawled out with anger burning though every part of his body, but I couldn't care.

Great billowing clouds of starless night swelled around us, the roar of the shadows deafening as I lifted my arms and with a grunt, pushed the ore gates of the Asphodels closed for the first moment since the dawn of time. We stared at one another behind the iron bars, both breathing hard as the gravity of what I'd done registered.

"Hades—" Thanatos cautioned, but there was no fear to temper me. I had already lost everything, been denied even the mercy of desiccation after Narcissus's death on a technicality that he had relinquished his divinity willingly before the killing blow.

"I am the Lord of the Asphodels, the Endless, *the Reckoning*, and I decree from this day to all other days that only the shades of the dead and divine born of the Asphodels may freely traverse here. The vow and protection of Persephone Kore, Goddess of the Underworld, Bearer of Spring, is theirs and theirs *alone*, and I will uphold it, until such time as she returns to resume her post.

"You fool. She is *dead*, Hades."

Zeus fumed as an invisible pulse of power surged from the gates through the Underworld, binding my will as law. I heard the echo of the other doorways slamming shut.

"Fuck you," I spat,

My work done. I left him at the gates, having said all I needed to say.

Time passed. I woke and ruled and listened to the pleas of the Damned. I walked the fields when Persephone's memory made the palace feel overwhelming. The absence of her laughter haunted the halls, never giving me a moment of peace, until I could bear it no more. To preserve what was left of my sanity, I moved our household to a smaller dwelling on the banks of the Styx, so we could be near if any of our shades required assistance, leaving Admentos as custodian of the palace in my absence.

I had a duty to our subjects, and for her, I tried. None of it made me feel better. None of it made me feel alive.

She was gone and I was alone.

Persephone
EPILOGUE

Total darkness surrounded me as my breath bounced off the confines of this wooden box in shallow pants. I could feel the edges of the wood, commune with the knots, touch the essence of the cypress. Foreign, dark magic radiated from the sigils carved into the outside of the box, the taste of acrid bitterness of hex magic choking me. I could move my fingers and my limbs, so I was unbound, but I could not call my shadows to me.

For an eternity, I shouted in the starless void until my voice was shredded, throat raw. Dirt seeped into the cracks and crevices, and I tried futilely to push my power out. I had no way to track time, and the only sounds I could hear were the ones I made, the echo chamber nearly maddening. I scratched my voice ragged from screaming, broken and bloodied fingernails leaving deep grooves against the cypress as I desperately clawed at my tomb. I thought of Hades, only of him, and when I found myself losing hope, I pictured his eyes—those icy blue eyes, the constellations that danced in them, the way they tracked me as I moved through a room. The way he said my name. I clung to those two things with a vice grip, knowing he would search for me. He would tear this world apart to find me.

I will always find you. A promise he'd whispered against my skin a thousand times, a vow that tethered me to hope. This would not be what separated us; I would hold out for him. I would be strong.

I cried, not knowing when relief would come. I spoke to the darkness as though he were listening, and sometimes I heard a voice whisper back. It was anguished, guilty, full of apology but ever present as I recounted my favorite memories on a loop. When the voices of chaos came, I forced myself to hold steady to the parts of me that I loved. The flowers, the music of the realm, the sun on my face, and the shadows of his touch. One by one, those anchors were stripped from me as chaos overwhelmed my mind, too far from the Asphodels, my fate sealed by the seeds of the pomegranates I had so willingly consumed.

I clung to the visage of Hades's eyes, willing myself to remember his voice. I begged and bargained with the madness to let me keep it. In the end, to save what was left of my broken and fragile mind, I slept.

I slept for years. Decades. Centuries. I could not remember my mother's name or a time without the darkness. There was only chaos and madness and a pair of sapphire blue eyes, calling to me.

"*Little Flower.*"

Acknowledgments

I have to start this by thanking the person responsible for the Dark Fates series and the subsequent books of the KravenVerse, Janessa. Without your loving bullying, I would not have written *Prophecies* for you, and to piss you off, I would have *never* included the cliffy that gets me cussed out to this day. You are an *incredible* soul, light, and friend, and I am so very grateful for your love and for you bullying me into publishing.

I would also like to thank my team for all their love and support. They keep me moving along every single day, and I write these stories for them, *always*.

To Jess, for keeping me sane and focused, for being the entire boss of me.

To my sensitivity readers, Tatiana, Jeremy, Kendall, Ashlee, Brandy, Ethan, Diana, and D'Andre. You have been by my side through so much, keeping me honest and on my toes, and I am forever grateful for your consideration, guidance, and our shared commitment to making sure the diversity of the Dark Fates is represented with careful mindfulness.

To Amy, who believed in me, fought for me, and has been the best damn agent anyone could have asked for.

And lastly, to my dad, who chuckled and asked what I was going to do with a degree in folklore, and when I shrugged because *I also* had no idea, told me to get it anyway.

Now we know:

I'm gonna write a whole lot of smutty little novels about gods getting down.

This journey started three years ago on a dare and has grown into a world of its own, and for that, I am so damn thankful to my readers. It's brought me so much joy to be able to write stories around the community I love, to represent us in media in what I hope are novels that will last a long, long time. Thank you to the team at Diversion for taking a chance on an indie author with an insane backlist, who talks way too much about her hyperfocuses, and eats her weight in Waffle House.

See y'all in the '90s!

The story continues in

Of DEATH & Desires

A DARK FATES NOVEL

Persephone

NEW ORLEANS 1990S

Darkness. I had only known darkness and the maddening screams that tore through my mind for so long. It was impossible to remember a time without them. A cacophony of dreams and lost moments overwhelmed me, ensnared my thoughts. I had slumbered for so long that the screams dulled to mere whispers. Grateful for the quiet, I slept, trapped.

Until now. A soft tremble shook the world around me, the tiniest crack in the darkness. I felt the movement in my finger first, a slight tingle, calling my limbs back to life. I didn't know where I was or how I had come to be there. The air was stale, ripe with the scent of dirt and moisture. It crawled into the crevices of my skin, lingering like a leech as I willed my body to reanimate.

Why was I here? I couldn't remember. I needed to remember.

No, the madness had taken my memories long ago, stolen them, and locked them away. I poked and prodded at the wall of stone encasing them. If my body wouldn't respond, maybe my mind could be coerced. I felt the great crags etched there, blocking me from the answers I sought. Something stilled inside of me, urging me to turn back.

Danger there. It echoed in my head, a warning. *Very well.*

I focused my attention outward again.

My cracked lips let out a small breath of air, propelling my body forward. Something had changed, as the oppressive weight of chains no longer sat upon my chest. I lifted a shaking hand toward the top of my prison and pushed.

Nothing. Solid wood. Willing for someone, *anyone* to come save me, a pair of ice-blue eyes flashed across my mind. I shook my head at the thought, unsure who they may belong to. Desperate, I pushed on my prison once more, and this time, it moved. With renewed hope, I bent my knees slightly and heaved, willing my feeble body to work for me.

It did.

I was rewarded with several pounds of loose dirt cascading into my prison as the wood gave way. Groans escaped my lips as I pushed forth, crawling from the depths until my hand broke the surface. I squeezed my shoulders through the oppressive earth with gusto, until my head and torso joined my hand. I gulped in several mouthfuls of air as thundering sounds of metal and yelling amped up around me. A putrid stench assaulted my nostrils, causing my stomach to roil. The air smelled . . . sour. The taste of metallic residue rested on my tongue, and I resisted the urge to bury my face back into the heady scent of the dirt. The ground still smelled like home, like musk and rainwater in the lower levels I had traversed through.

The sun was harsh against my eyes, and I pulled my hand high to shield my face. No, not the sun. Some sort of conjuration of light, as the world around me sat dark still.

"What the fuck, lady?! Are you okay?!" A crowd of men stood above me, strangely dressed as they yelled at each other in nasally accents that I had never heard. Rough hands hooked under my arms, pulling me from my would-be grave. They settled me gently down as one of the men pushed the hair from my face, clearing the residual dirt from my nose. "I gotcha sweetheart," he soothed, bringing a strange cup to my lips and offering it to me. "Who hurt you? Did someone bury you down there? What's ya name?"

His voice was smooth, and I could sense kindness and concern in his deep brown eyes. He was older, with wrinkles around his mouth and white hair that peeked out haphazardly from under his yellow helm. I wanted to answer him, but my throat croaked when I opened my lips to push air through. He tilted the bottle toward me, and I took it, relishing the cool liquid as it soothed my dry and aching throat. A rancid aftertaste hit, and I gurgled on the clear liquid. Was this poison?

"That's it, ya safe," he encouraged. "What's ya name, sweetheart?"

I glanced around at the small crowd of men who had gathered around and saw many were yelling out orders and murmuring to each other. I looked back at the man kneeling before me, eyes wide.

"M-my name . . ." I managed to choke out, "My name is . . . my name . . ." Confusion flooded me. It was just on the tip of my tongue, dancing at the far edge of my consciousness.

Tears pricked the back of my eyes as I began to panic. My name. What was my name? Who was I? A loud buzzing noise shook through my ears, humming high and obscuring the world around me. A tightness coiled in my chest and constricted my breath. "I don't know my name." I sobbed, clutching my chest. "I don't know . . . I don't know." I rocked back and forth, shaking and light-headed. Darkness crept up into the corners of my eyes, and I felt the sweet relief of unconsciousness take root as I collapsed backward into the disturbed earth.

"Jesus Christ. Mike, call 9-1-1!" the man with the kind eyes yelled, somewhere far in the distance.

It wasn't his eyes I saw last, those dark brown orbs etched with concern. Instead, it was a pair of ice-blue irises with brutal rivers behind them, deep as the currents that pulled me under as I sank into blissful nothingness.